The Scattered Flock

The Scattered Flock

Part Five of
The Marshes of Mount Liang

A New Translation of
the *Shuihu Zhuan* or *Water Margin*
of Shi Nai'an and Luo Guanzhong

By

John and Alex Dent-Young

The Chinese University of Hong Kong Press

The Scattered Flock: Part Five of **The Marshes of Mount Liang** *by Shi Nai'an and Luo Guanzhong*
by John and Alex Dent-Young

ISBN: 978-962-201-990-4

First edition 2002
Second printing 2022

The Chinese University of Hong Kong Press
The Chinese University of Hong Kong
Sha Tin, N. T., Hong Kong
Fax: +852 2603 7355
Email: cup@cuhk.edu.hk
Website: cup.cuhk.edu.hk

Printed in Hong Kong

For

Esther Maria Tao

wife and mother

Contents

Acknowledgements xi
Introduction xiii

Chapter 91 1
Song Jiang leads his army across the Yellow River;
The Unicorn takes a city by trickery on a dark night!

Chapter 92 15
Colonel Hua shows his mastery of the bow;
The Professor's clever plan defeats Gaizhou!

Chapter 93 29
Iron Ox dreams he is fighting the courtiers;
Song Jiang divides his army into two wings!

Chapter 94 41
Scimitar wins over three leaders;
Iron Ox lands them in a mess!

Chapter 95 57
Song Jiang remains loyal to his lord;
Qiao the Wizard wins by magic!

Chapter 96 69
The Wizard takes refuge on Five Dragon Mountain;
Taoist Gongsun besieges the Hundred Valleys!

Chapter 97 79
Commissioner Chen takes over the administration;
Princess Jade Arrowtip becomes a leader of men!

Chapter 98 93
Hotshot meets his destined bride;
The Professor plans to poison the Royal Brother-in-Law!

Chapter 99 113
The Monk is delivered from the well of karma;
White-Water Dragon floods the town of Taiyuan!

Chapter 100 125
Hotshot and Arrowtip work in tandem;
Song Jiang and the Commissioner jointly announce victory!

Chapter 101 137
The theft of a burial plot leads on to rebellion;
A stroll on a fine spring day provokes dalliance!

Chapter 102 149
Wang Qing is punished for his adultery;
Gong Duan takes a fighting instructor!

Chapter 103 161
A warden loses his life because of his brother-in-law;
A prison official removes his cousin's scar!

Chapter 104 173
At the Duans' a bridegroom is welcomed;
The chief on House Mountain fights two opponents!

Chapter 105 185
Song Jiang gives his men a break;
The Wizard sends the fire right back!

Chapter 106 197
A scholar fools a superior force;
The sailors overwhelm the city's defences!

Chapter 107 209
Song Jiang wins a great victory at Mount Ji;
The Strategist smashes the six flower formation!

Chapter 108 219
The Wizard raises a fog and captures the city;
Mr. Chai stores up ammunition to fight the enemy!

Chapter 109 239
Wang Qing crosses the river and is captured;
Song Jiang completes his defeat of the rebels!

Chapter 110 257
The Prodigy shoots geese at Autumn Woods Crossing;
Song Jiang brings his captives to the Eastern Capital!

Chapter 111 279
White Eel swims to Temple Hill by night;
Song Jiang succeeds in capturing Runzhou!

Chapter 112 295
The Unicorn takes half the army to attack Xuanzhou;
Song Jiang fights a great battle in Piling!

Chapter 113 309
At Lake Tai a small gathering of heroes;
In Suzhou with Song Jiang a major assembly!

Chapter 114 327
In the battle for Hangzhou Song Jiang's plunged in mourning;
White Eel dies at Goldenflood Gate!

Chapter 115 345
The ghost of White Eel captures the Southern Prince;
Song Jiang takes Ninghai Commandery with a trick!

Chapter 116 363
The route to Shezhou falls to the Unicorn;
Song Jiang has a fight at Black Dragon Ridge!

Chapter 117 379
At Muzhou Precious Light is snuffed by an arrow;
At Black Dragon Ridge Song Jiang is helped by magic!

Chapter 118 399
The Unicorn has a great battle at Sundance Pass;
Song Jiang plans to capture the citadel at Bangyuan Gap!

Chapter 119 423
At Zhejiang by the riverside Monk passes away;
Song Jiang returns to his birthplace in a silk robe!

Chapter 120 447
Song Jiang after death goes to Duckweed Marsh;
The Emperor dreams of a visit to Mount Liang!

Acknowledgements

As for the previous volumes, we are indebted to many people's help and encouragement. In particular we would like to thank our editors at The Chinese University Press for their patience and support and especially Esther Tsang, editor of the last three volumes, for many helpful suggestions and exemplary attention to detail.

The illustrations are from two series of old engravings from the Ming dynasty. One is known as the *Rongyutang* 容與堂本, and the other as *Yang Dingjian* 楊定見序本. These illustrations have been published in two different volumes respectively entitled *Rongyutang ben Shuihu Zhuan* 容與堂本水滸傳 (China: Shanghai Chinese Classics Publishing House, 1988), and *Shuihu quanzhuan* 水滸全傳 (China: Zhong Hua Book Co., 1961). We are grateful to Shanghai Chinese Classics Publishing House for granting us free use of these illustrations.

Introduction

The title of this last volume of the *Marshes of Mount Liang* is taken from Song Jiang's panegyric on geese just before the final campaign. When Song Jiang reprimands the Prodigy for shooting the geese at Autumn Woods, he explicitly compares geese to the company on Mount Liang, as close and essential to one another as hand and foot. The shooting of the geese marks the beginning of the decline in the fortunes of Song Jiang and company. For, whichever way you look at it, the 120-chapter version of the novel ends in disaster for the one hundred and eight. Given the ambivalence of their origin and a good deal of their behaviour throughout it seems the only reasonable outcome.

The action divides easily into three parts: the campaign against Tian Hu, the campaign against Wang Qing and the campaign against Fang La. It is in the last of these that the heroes of Mount Liang begin to die. Their demise is as haphazard and casual as the scattering of the flock of geese when the Prodigy shoots them for mere amusement. But the theme of the vanity of human wishes, the emptiness of ambition, becomes prominent earlier. It was discussed in Volume 4 in connection with the Prodigy's friend living in the country, whose views on the undesirability of being honoured in a corrupt world are shared in this volume by the briefly prominent Bountiful when he refuses honours and office and slips off unrewarded in the night. Later the Prodigy will imitate them. White-Water Dragon, Cave Dragon and River Rider are differently motivated but the result is the same: they leave the company at just the time when it seems everyone is to be adequately recompensed at last. First of all the heroes to depart the scene is Taoist Gongsun, when at the end of the Tian Hu campaign Song Jiang has to keep a promise and allow him to return to the Blessed Sage, withdrawing from the world of action. Others at the end of the novel will make a similar choice.

As in Volume 4 we have done what we can to clarify the campaigns and maintain the pace of the narrative. Just as the early part of the novel is held together by the gradual gathering of the company, so its end is dominated by their rather more rapid unravelling. The major virtue of the 120-chapter version is that it shows more of the logic of this trajectory.

It is not however for its overall structure that most people read the novel but for the interest of individual incidents: the tricks, ambushes, escapes and betrayals, the chance meetings, moonlight attacks, anticipated outcomes, the vengeance visited on bullies and cheats, the drunken comedy, the undoing of pompous, boastful or irascible generals. Some of the more lively passages in this volume are those which describe the genesis of the three insurrections and the motivation of their leaders — we note incidentally that these are the three whose names were linked with Song Jiang's in the memorandum in the Emperor's hand found in his palace by Mr. Chai in Chapter 72; there is a certain symmetry here, with the campaigns being fought successively in the north, west and south (the government's earlier struggle with Song Jiang perhaps representing east). The history of each of the three rebels is markedly similar to that of many of the Mount Liang leaders and it would not be difficult to develop from this the idea that Song Jiang himself only differs from them in his devotion to the Emperor and his determination to control his followers and curb their impulse to go for absolute power.

Indeed there are a number of ideas that it would not be difficult to develop, but we have to say in honesty that we find them only hinted at, not clearly articulated, in the novel. This is perhaps one of its important characteristics: that in reading it one senses a quantity of submerged meaning. On the simplest level the motivation of characters is often not made very explicit: for example, we can hope that the reader remembers Short-Arse is a womaniser when he takes up with such alacrity the challenge from Jade

Arrowtip, but the fact is not underlined in the text (though it is not hard to imagine ways it might have been highlighted in an oral performance and we have added a slight verbal reminder). There are other motivations or connections that we, the translators, do not get at all: the moving chair that precipitates Wang Qing's falling foul of the authorities — is it part of a human plot or a supernatural link in the chain of events, or something else altogether? So far as we can see the text does not elucidate it. Perhaps it relates to some stage routine in the performance of an incident which has been partly forgotten or omitted. There are some apparent inconsistencies: the Prodigy is originally introduced as an expert archer but in the incident with the geese archery is apparently a new skill for him (the solution that he is originally expert only with the *cross-bow* does not entirely convince us). On a wider scale there are the suggestions of underlying mythology which are mysterious precisely because they are not clearly developed: the Fire and Water Generals and their troops, personifications of two ancient scourges of China and dressed symbolically in red or black uniforms, seem like characters from science fiction or fantasy. The alliance of such effects with the repetition of circumstantial detail, the down-to-earth description of procedures, is what gives the novel its peculiar flavour.

While we have tried to iron out some minor puzzles or inconsistencies we have avoided trying to get rid of them all because we feel they have something to add. We have hoped to conserve not only the impression of a work which perhaps means more than it says, responding to more than one interpretation and reflecting more than a single vision, but also the sense of a world that exists independently of the words of the narrator. This is why we have emphasized the oral story-telling aspect: it is, we hope, irrelevant whether this corresponds to a reality in the novel's genesis or is a narrative device like the ones other writers have used to organize their fictions.

A final word on the translation. We have already mentioned in earlier volumes the problem with names. There are other decisions to be made about, for instance, narrative and rhetorical conventions: which ones to treat literally and which to transfer into some equivalent. We have been very free with matters like paragraphing and sentence length but have tried to stay relatively close to the way the novel announces or changes its immediate topic, and to follow its extensive use of dialogue.

In style we have tried to move as unobtrusively as possible between a modern idiom for both dialogue and narrative in action passages and slight archaism for such matters as the stylized and formulaic greetings between heores or proverbial sayings. We have also tried to move from a colloquial to a more rhetorical style for passages where the narrator might be supposed to be quoting official history (such as accounts of victory parades or of the establishment of monuments and myths). We have done all we can through so-called elegant variation or sentence rhythm to enliven passages which we feel sure will seem repetitive and tedious to the modern reader. We have followed the modern novelistic convention in trying to present different voices in the dialogue and we have been very free in our use of tense. The onomatopoeic expressions of Chinese are particularly difficult to deal with, but in English alliteration is extremely useful for a heightening effect and its tone can be usefully either serious or comic. Inevitably not all our choices will strike everyone as equally happy. But we believe literary translation is a confidence trick, closer to forgery or larceny than treachery. Antique Chinese heroes speaking modern English are all too easily unmasked. However, we hope, if the reader grants us his or her indulgence, to be able, like the Flea, to get away with a certain amount of walking on rooftops, scaling walls, vaulting fences and doing dodgy deals.

Chapter 91

Song Jiang leads his army across the Yellow River; The Unicorn takes a city by trickery on a dark night!

The campaign against the Liao Tartars is over and Magic Messenger and Madcap have been off on a private jaunt. On their way back to the camp they stop for a drink and their attention is drawn to a stranger who has just told the waiter he is on an urgent mission.

Since the man looked like a policeman and was obviously in a tearing hurry, Magic Messenger asked: "What business are you on exactly?"

The man put down his chopsticks and wiped his mouth before saying: "Have you heard about the insurrection of Tian Hu of Hebei?"

"We know a bit about it," Magic Messenger said.

"This bastard Tian Hu has seized a number of districts and provinces up there in the North and the government troops just can't stop him. Only recently he took Gaizhou and sooner or later he will attack Weizhou. The inhabitants go in fear night and day and in the country the peasants have all fled. The authorities have sent me with an urgent message for the Military Council."

He jumped up immediately, shouldered his pack, collected his umbrella and cudgel, paid the bill and made his exit. As he was going out of the door, he said disconsolately: "A policeman's lot is truly a hard one. I've had to leave all my family back there in the city. I only hope the court will send troops as fast as possible!" With that he hastened off in the direction of the capital.

After hearing this news, Magic Messenger and Madcap also paid up and left. When they got back to the camp, they told Song Jiang what they had heard. Song Jiang discussed it with the Professor. "We're all of us just wasting our time here. It's not good for morale. Wouldn't it be better to ask the Emperor to let us get involved in the action?" he said.

The Professor said: "The best way would be to speak to Marshal Su about it first."

A general meeting of all the leaders was held to discuss the plan and everyone approved. Next day Song Jiang dressed in his official uniform and rode into the city with a dozen horsemen. He went straight to Marshal Su's palace. The Marshal was in his office and he had Song Jiang shown in immediately. Song Jiang prostrated himself and then stood to attention. "What can I do for you, General?" the Marshal said.

Song Jiang said: "Your Excellency, I have heard that Tian Hu of Hebei is in revolt, that he has seized several provinces and declared himself emperor and has even got as far as taking Gaizhou and is expected to attack Weizhou any minute. I and my men have been idle a long while. We would like to take an army to fight the rebels and defend our country. We hope you will be kind enough to obtain authorization for this."

The Marshal was enthusiastic: "It is greatly to your credit that you want to serve your country, General," he said. "I will do all I can to obtain the Emperor's consent."

"We are most grateful. We can never repay you," Song Jiang said.

The Marshal ordered wine for Song Jiang. In the evening Song Jiang returned to the camp and told the others.

Marshal Su went to the palace next day for the dawn audience and saw the Emperor in the Hall of Incense. The Military Council had just reported on Tian Hu's rebellion, how he had occupied five provinces and fifty-six districts and proclaimed a new dynastic name with himself as emperor, how he had just captured another city and how aid was urgently requested. The Emperor was greatly disturbed. He said to his officials: "Which of you is willing to lead an army to suppress these rebels for me?" Marshal Su stepped forward. Clutching a tablet to his chest he bowed and respectfully submitted: "I have been told that Tian Hu has the strength to snap wood and bend poles. This is a forest fire that can only be put out by the efforts of a determined commander with bold troops. General Song Jiang has just returned victorious from his defeat of the Tartars and is camped outside the city. I beg Your Majesty to send him and his men to put down the rebellion. I am sure they will do well."

The Emperor was pleased with this proposal and ordered an official of the Military Council to fetch Song Jiang and the Unicorn to the Hall of Incense for an audience. When they had kowtowed, His Majesty spoke: "I know of your valiant exploits. I now have another commission for you . I wish you to go north to Hebei. You must shirk no hardship and quickly return victorious. I will reward you with promotion."

They kowtowed and said: "We thank you, Your Majesty, for having such faith in us. We shall do our utmost and serve you even unto death."

The Emperor openly showed his pleasure and he appointed Song Jiang Commander-in-Chief of the Northern Pacification Expedition, with the Unicorn as his second-in-command. They were rewarded with imperial wine, with gold and silver, gilt armour and rolls of silk and the other leaders all received silk and silver. Their orders were to put down the rebellion and they were promised rank and honours according to their results. The divisional commanders were all to be paid in silver from the Palace Treasury. A deadline was set for the start. Song Jiang and the Unicorn went once more to express their appreciation of the honour, receive their commission and take leave of the Emperor. After this they rode back to camp and held a meeting in their tent to which all the leaders were summoned. They were told to get their horses and armour ready for the campaign against Tian Hu.

Next day the Treasury paid out the silver and silk for the leaders to distribute among their subordinates. Song Jiang and the Unicorn ordered the water-borne leaders to sail first, proceeding to Yuanwu on the Yellow River, where they were to await the arrival of the main force and ferry them across. The cavalry leaders were ordered to prepare their horses for a joint attack by land and water.

Now this villain Tian Hu was originally a simple hunter. He was very strong, experienced in combat, and addicted to the company of evil youths. His base of operations was surrounded by mountains and well adapted to defence. The people of this area, it being susceptible to flood and drought, were poor and their resources scarce, so rebellion was never far from their thoughts. Tian Hu had profited from the situation to assemble a bunch of ruffians, trump up false rumours and inflame the minds of simple people. At first he simply engaged in plunder; later he seized control of whole districts and the authorities dared not stand in his way.

But why, you will ask, if Tian Hu was just a hunter was he so formidable? Let me explain: in those days government officials were greedy and military commanders cowardly. Although every district had its own garrison of government troops, they were made up of troops who were old and infirm, or just plain fictitious, and all they did was eat up the funds, one man accounting for the entitlement of two or three, or else those who had nothing better to do would simply fork out some silver and buy a stand-in, purchase a proxy, in order to get their hands on government supplies. There were those too who would hire someone to answer for them when the roll was called for training exercises. Since everyone covered up for everyone else it was impossible to unmask them. The government spent a fortune and had nothing at all to show for it. When it came to war, the troops had no idea how to fight. There was no discipline and when they saw the dust of battle or heard the shots they behaved as if they wished their parents had given them two sets of legs. There were one or two commanders who led out armies against Tian Hu, but they hadn't the guts to take him on; all you saw of them was their rears as they fled in all directions. They faked the reports and even killed good men in order to take credit for themselves. Because of harassment by the government troops the people became still more disaffected and flocked to the rebel cause. That is how the rebels had come to occupy five provinces and fifty six districts. Tian Hu had built himself a palace at Fenyang and set up a bogus government, styling himself Prince of Jin. He had keen troops and bold generals and his position was well defended. At present he was advancing with his army in two columns.

Song Jiang picked the day to start and bade farewell to the members of the Military Council. Marshal Su came to see him off in person, and Commissioner Zhao at the Emperor's behest came to the camp to reward the army. The leaders thanked him and then gave the army its marching orders. Three guns were fired and with a brave accompaniment of drums and gongs they set forth, heading northeast.

It goes without saying that Song Jiang gave the strictest orders to his troops to maintain good discipline and not cause the least harm in any of the places they passed through. When they reached Yuanwu district, local officials came out to meet them. Their scouts reported that the boat commanders were already at the river bank waiting to ferry them across. Song Jiang ordered the White-Water Dragon and the other boat chiefs to divide their six hundred sailors into two groups, left and right. They were to commandeer some local boats and load all the horses and carts. One by one Song Jiang and the other leaders were ferried across to the northern bank. The boat chiefs were then ordered to take the battle fleet on and assemble in the Wei River at Weizhou.

On reaching Weizhou Song Jiang's vanguard pitched camp. The local officials had organized a banquet to entertain Song Jiang. When he arrived, they told him: "Tian Hu's bandits are a huge force. It won't be easy to disperse them. Zezhou is defended by Tian Hu's second-in-command Niu Wenzhong. He has sent two of his lieutenants with ten thousand men to attack some of our villages and he is leading ten thousand troops himself against the neighbouring province. We urgently need your help!"

Song Jiang heard them out and then returned to the camp to consult with the Professor about sending a relief force. The Professor said: "Lingchuan is of great strategic importance to Gaizhou. Wouldn't it be better to take a force there to attack it, then we can break the siege in two places at once."

The Unicorn then said: "Inexperienced though I am, I would like to lead the attack on Lingchuan."

Song Jiang thought this a good idea and allotted the Unicorn ten thousand cavalry and five hundred infantry. With him were to go ten cavalry commanders and nine infantry commanders. He set off next day.

Song Jiang was in his tent, still planning the campaign with the Professor. "The bandits are over-confident," the latter said. "The Unicorn should be able to defeat them. The only problem is that this whole region has very rugged terrain, full of mountains and gorges; we should send two leaders to reconnoitre and spy out the land before we attack."

Hardly had he finished when the Prodigy came to the tent and said: "You needn't worry, Professor. I've got a map of the area right here." He took out a hand scroll and unrolled it on the table. Song Jiang and the Professor submitted it to a thorough scrutiny. It depicted every mountain, gorge, walled city and pass in the region. Every detail could be read on it — where you could camp, where an ambush could be laid, where a pitched battle could be fought.

"Where did you get this?" the Professor asked in amazement.

The Prodigy replied: "Remember how we were coming back from the campaign against the Tartars and I ran into my old friend Xu Guanzhong at Double Woods? He invited me to go and stay with him and when I was leaving he presented me with this scroll. He called it just a rough sketch, but when I got back to the camp and had some spare time, I happened to take it out to look at it and realized it was a perfect representation of this whole area."

Song Jiang said: "The day you came back I was just getting ready for my audience with the Emperor and I didn't really have time to ask you much. He looked like a good man, that friend of yours. You've told me a lot about his good qualities; what exactly is he doing nowadays?"

The Prodigy answered: "Guanzhong is a very talented person. He is skilled in martial arts, extremely brave, and has all the lesser accomplishments like music and painting. But he doesn't want to join the government service, so he has retired to the country." He went on in this vein at length, till the Professor said: "It's truly a miracle that such an honest man exists!" He and Song Jiang were hugely impressed.

Now the Unicorn first ordered the Tamer and Colonel Sun, with three thousand men to set up an ambush about two miles east of Lingchuan, and the Tattooed Dragon and the Blue-Faced Beast with three thousand men to take up a position the same distance to the west. "Tonight at the fifth drumbeat," he told them, "we will advance stealthily with the men gagged and no harness bells. Tomorrow we will attack. If the enemy are unprepared and we take the city, we will hoist a signal on the south gate and you will move cautiously into the city to join us. If their preparations are good, we will fire a gun and both supporting forces must join in the attack at once." The four leaders set off.

Before dawn next day the Unicorn rose and breakfasted and led his forces bravely to the walls of the city. There they divided into three units, deployed in a straight line and with waving banners and thundering drums issued their challenge to the enemy.

The guards on the walls raced to report to the commander Dong Cheng and his two lieutenants. This Dong Cheng was Niu Wenzhong's vanguard commander. He was tall and strong and wielded a long wind-splitter of a sword. When he heard that the Song court had sent troops from Mount Liang and that they were already positioned outside the city ready to attack, he hurriedly called a meeting at his headquarters to appoint those who were to counter-attack. One of his lieutenants, Geng Gong, warned: "I have heard that this company of Song Jiang's are not to be taken lightly. We ought to concentrate on defence and send someone to Gaizhou to request reinforcements. If we attack them from two sides we can defeat them."

His commander reacted indignantly: "It is intolerable that those blighters should have the nerve to come here and threaten our city. But they've had to march a long way and they must be tired. Just wait while I go and deal with them — there'll be no survivors!"

He was not moved by anything Geng Gong could say and only responded with: "You stay here then with a thousand men to guard the city. Go up into the gate tower and watch while I slaughter the bastards!" He hurriedly armed and took up his weapon and together with another of his lieutenants, sallied forth to do battle.

The gates were opened, the drawbridge lowered and several thousand troops poured across. They were met with solid fire from the Song army. Heralded by a roll of drums, Dong Cheng rode forward and shouted: "You bog-dwelling scum, prepare to meet your death!"

Whiskers galloped forward from the other side and shouted back: "We are the government forces. I'd advise you to dismount and let us tie you up, double-quick. It'll save us dirtying our weapons!"

To cheers from both sides, the two warriors met in the middle ground. The horses clashed, weapons were raised. They had not fought more than ten bouts when Whiskers whirled his horse about and galloped off eastward. Dong Cheng gave chase. Colonel Hua on the eastern flank levelled his spear and received his charge. They fought over thirty bouts and neither had the advantage. The other rebel commander who had remained close to the drawbridge saw that his chief was not having much success. He whirled his steel lance, slapped his horse and charged to the rescue. Hard pressed now by two opponents, Colonel Hua turned and galloped off to the east, his two opponents following close behind. Then he turned again and resumed the fight.

Within the city Geng Gong saw his two comrades pursuing the enemy and fearing something might go amiss was about to sound the gongs and drums to recall their forces when a bold company charged forward from the Song ranks — it was made up of ten commanders, Iron Ox, Monk, Pluto, the Eight-Armed Ogre and others. Together they raced towards the drawbridge. Before their ferocious onslaught the northerners' resistance crumbled. Geng Gong ordered the gates closed.

Well, it's slow in the telling but happens in a flash: Monk and Iron Ox were already inside the city. When the guards on the gate rushed forward in a body to repel them, Monk gave a triumphant shout and felled two of them with his staff, while Iron Ox whirling his axes knocked down five or six more. Pluto and the others rushed forward and seized the gate, scattering the remaining guards. Geng Gong saw things were going badly and rushed down from the tower. He tried to escape to the north but was caught by the foot soldiers and made prisoner.

Dong Cheng and his lieutenant, who were still engaged with Colonel Hua, heard the outcry from the drawbridge and turned their horses and galloped back. Instead of pursuing them Colonel Hua placed his lance in the rest and taking his bow and an arrow, aimed carefully at the middle of Dong Cheng's back and fired. Dong Cheng plunged from the saddle, legs waving in the air. The Unicorn and his commanders gave the signal and the whole army charged. The lieutenant was transfixed by a thrust from Twin Spears, the majority of the troops were killed and the remainder fled in all directions. All the Song commanders now entered the town. Iron Ox charged around killing everyone he met, devastating as a forest fire. Only when the Unicorn gave the order: "Don't harm the people, brother," did he consent to stop.

The Unicorn quickly ordered his officers to hoist the army's flag on the south gate to inform the troops waiting in ambush, and also ordered a guard to be set on all the gates. In no time the troops from the ambush arrived. The heads of the two dead northern commanders were handed in and Pluto brought in the captive Geng Gong and some others. The Unicorn had them released from their bonds. He raised Geng Gong up and made him sit as guest in the place of honour.

Geng Gong prostrated himself in gratitude and said: "I am a defeated general, yet you treat me so generously!"

The Unicorn raised him up again and said: "You did not come out of the city to fight. You are cleverer than the rest of Dong Cheng's lot. General Song welcomes good men. If you are willing to renew your allegiance to the Emperor, General Song will surely help to secure you a post."

Geng Gong bowed and thanked him again, saying: "Since you have graciously spared my life, you can count me your slave."

The Unicorn, in the best of moods, did all he could to reassure these enemy leaders and at the same time had notices posted to calm the populace. He rewarded his own troops, and laid on wine to entertain Geng Gong and his companions.

When the Unicorn questioned Geng Gong about the strength of the Gaizhou garrison, the latter replied: "Gaizhou is garrisoned by Marshal Niu's men. There's two towns to the west of it, but on the way from here there's only Gaoping, about twenty miles away at the foot of Mount Hanwang. It is defended by Zhang Li and Zhao Neng with twenty thousand troops under them."

On hearing this the Unicorn toasted Geng Gong, saying: "Drink this cup with me, General. This evening I would like you to do something for me. I hope you won't refuse."

Geng Gong said: "In view of your generosity, sir, I am ready to do anything for you."

The Unicorn said: "If you accept, I will give instructions to some of my comrades and their subordinates. If you don't mind I would like to start at once."

He summoned the five or six recently captured commanders, rewarded them with food, wine and silver, promising them more if they succeeded. When they finished the wine, he ordered Iron Ox and Pluto and seven other infantry commanders, with a hundred picked infantrymen, to dress in the Lingchuan soldiers' uniforms and insignia. He also ordered Tattooed Dragon and the Blue-Faced Beast to take five hundred cavalry with muffled harness bells and follow Geng Gong's party at a certain distance. He told Colonel Hua and the rest to defend the town. He himself took three thousand men and followed on in support.

When all the orders had been given, Geng Gong and his party set off according to plan. It was late in the day and by the time they arrived at the south gate of Gaoping dusk had fallen. By the light of the stars they could make out the banners thickly clustered on the walls and hear the sharp beat of the drum sounding the hours. Geng Gong shouted out: "I am Geng Gong, from the Lingchuan garrison. The city has fallen because two of our commanders wouldn't listen to me and opened the gates to attack the enemy. I quickly mustered these hundred men and escaped through the north gate. I got here by taking small paths. Just let me in, will you?"

The guards recognized him by the light of their torches and quickly went to tell generals Zhang and Zhao. These two went up onto the walls themselves whilst their men lit many torches and illuminated the scene all around. Zhang shouted back to Geng Gong: "You seem like one of ours all right, but I'd like to have a closer look." He went down and made a thorough examination to satisfy himself that it was indeed Geng Gong of Lingchuan and all the uniforms and insignia were a hundred percent correct. Among the troops of the garrison there were many who knew the commanders and they pointed them out: "That's so-and-so, that's so-and-so." Zhang confessed himself satisfied and said: "Let them in!"

So the gates opened, the drawbridge was lowered, and thirty or forty troops lined the drawbridge while Geng Gong entered the town. The troops in the rear jostled and pushed, shouting: "Get inside, get inside, they're after us!" They paid no heed to their commander. The guards on the gate shouted: "What's going on? Let's have some order here!"

As this dispute was raging, fires were seen at the foot of Mount Hanwang and a squadron of horsemen advancing, the two leaders in front shouting: "Rebel commanders stand and fight!" Already seven ferocious beasts had mingled with Geng Gong's soldiers — these were Iron Ox, Pluto, Eight-Armed Ogre, Winged Ghost, the Red-Haired Devil, Morbid and Madcap. All now drew their weapons and stormed into the city, a hundred or so strong. Those in the city had no time to act; they couldn't even manage to get the gates shut. Inside and outside the walls the guards were slaughtered by the dozen. The invaders gained control of the gates and Zhang could only curse. When he rushed down from the walls looking for Geng Gong, he ran into Madcap. After three or four bouts Zhang lost heart and fled, trailing his spear. Iron Ox caught him from behind. An axe smashed down and Zhang was cut in two. By now the party of horsemen from the bottom of Mount Hanwang had reached the city and thrust their way in. It was led by the Tattooed Dragon and the Blue-Faced Beast. Each set about killing the northerners on his own account. The second commander was killed in the mêlée and most of the garrison of Gaoping died with him. Zhang's family were all put to the sword. For the people it was as if they had woken in the midst of a nightmare. Their screams rose to heaven. After a while the Unicorn led his army into the city. He ordered a guard to be put on every gate, and deputed a dozen of his men to go about shouting that the people were not to be harmed. At dawn notices were put up to reassure the people, rewards were distributed among the army and a messenger sent to inform Song Jiang.

How had the Unicorn been able to subdue two cities so easily and so fast? The reason was that Tian Hu's forces lacked discipline and recent battle experience. They underestimated the military threat and the valour of Song Jiang's forces. The Unicorn's success was beyond his expectations, but the Professor had calculated that this time he would succeed.

But enough of this. Song Jiang's forces, remember, were camped outside Weizhou. He was holding a meeting in his tent when he heard that the Unicorn had sent a messenger with news and was asking for further orders to attack.

"The Unicorn has captured two towns in succession. We've got them on the run!" he said to the Professor delightedly.

At this moment scouts from the two armies came in and reported: "Two more towns have surrendered, after hearing that Lingchuan has fallen."

Song Jiang said to the Professor: "For astute planning, the world has seldom seen your like!"

He wanted to strike camp at once and march westwards to link up with the Unicorn for a further push. But the Professor said: "There are enemy held cities both right and left of us here in Weizhou, the river is to the south and there is another city on the west. The topography makes it easy to defend, but if the enemy know we are going west, they can move south and cut our forces in two. Then what will we do?"

"You're absolutely right," Song Jiang said. He ordered Scimitar, Twin Rods and Taoist Gongsun to take five thousand cavalry and strengthen the defences of Weizhou. He also ordered the boat captains, White-Water Dragon, the Pilot, White Eel, the Ruan Brothers and the Tong Brothers, to anchor their boats on the Wei River outside the town to protect the flank. These orders were carried out.

In due course Song Jiang and the main army struck camp and set out. Nothing happened on the way. When they reached Gaoping the Unicorn came out to receive them.

"My dear friend," Song Jiang said. "You have subdued two cities, in short order. It's no mean achievement. Everything shall be recorded on the roll of honour."

The Unicorn brought the recently surrendered Geng Gong and introduced him. Song Jiang said: "You have repented the error of your ways and returned to the straight path, General. Join me now in fighting for the country's good. The Emperor will certainly reward you with high office."

Geng Gong prostrated himself in thanks and then stood to attention.

Song Jiang's army was too big so he did not march them into the city but camped outside. The same day he had a meeting with the Professor and the Unicorn to decide where to attack next. The Professor said: "The mountains round Gaizhou are high, the valleys deep, and access is difficult. We have just taken two places in the region and their forces are isolated. If we now take Gaizhou we split them in two. We can then divide our forces and attack on two fronts and Weisheng will fall." Song Jiang said: "That is exactly what I was thinking."

He ordered Mr. Chai and Skyhawk to guard Lingchuan and told Colonel Hua and six others to get ready. The Tattooed Dragon and the Unstoppable were to guard Gaoping. Mr. Chai and three others went off according to instructions. At this point Hotshot made a request: "I have been unwell the last two days. I would like to stay in Gaoping for a while until I am better. I could be available for general duties in the camp."

Song Jiang sent him into Gaoping with Doctor An for treatment.

Next day when Colonel Hua and his party arrived Song Jiang split the army into five divisions. These five divisions bore down on Gaizhou like a dragon rising from the ocean or a tiger emerging from the forest. It was a time when all were determined to gain glory, eager for their part in the spoils!

If you want to know more about the attack on Gaizhou, you must read the next chapter.

Chapter 92

Colonel Hua shows his mastery of the bow; The Professor's clever plan defeats Gaizhou!

Song Jiang's army in five divisions was marching on Gaizhou. When scouts from that city heard about it, they rushed back to report. The garrison commander, Niu Wenzhong, had cut his teeth in the greenwood and prospered there, finding rich pickings among the rivers and lakes. He had put his wealth at the disposal of Tian Hu and aided and abetted him in his rebellion. For grabbing large tracts of Song territory he was rewarded with the rank of marshal. His weapon was a double-edged three-pointed affair and he was exceptionally skilled in its use. He had four valiant commanders to help him run Gaizhou, Lionface Fang, Tigercat An, Wildcat Chu and Bearcat Yu, and each of these four had four lieutenants, so there were sixteen of them in all. The garrison of Gaizhou under Niu and his commanders consisted of thirty thousand northern troops. When they heard that Lingchuan and Gaoping had fallen, they had made their own preparations, while also sending to Weisheng and Jinning for help. On receipt of the latest report Lionface Fang was ordered out with his four lieutenants to engage the enemy. Just before they started, Niu told them: "I want you to know, comrades, that I shall be right behind you, ready to give support."

Lionface said: "No need for you to bother yourself, Marshal. It was only bad luck that those other two towns fell. They got them by trickery. I vow not to return if I don't kill half a dozen of them today."

They put on their armour and rode out of the east gate. The Song vanguard met them. Everyone took up battle positions and the sound of war drums shook the heavens. From the pennants gate in the northern ranks Lionface Fang rode forth, followed by his four lieutenants, banners fluttering on either side. He wore a tall cap, dragon-scale armour and a green brocade robe, a belt with a lion clasp and green boots. Over his left shoulder was a bow, over his right a quiverful of arrows. He rode a dun thoroughbred and held a steel spear. "You bog-dwelling bandits," he bellowed, "how dare you come and steal our cities by trickery?"

From the ranks of the Song army Colonel Sun answered: "Hear this, you rebel scum: the imperial army is here. Are you sure you want to die?" With this he slapped his horse and charged at Lionface. Enveloped in a cloud of dust, the two of them fought more than thirty bouts, until gradually Lionface began to weaken. One of his lieutenants, Zhang, saw that his commander could not get the better of his adversary and reached for his bow. He rode forward and loosed an arrow at Colonel Sun. The latter saw it in time and pulled on the reins. The arrow hit his horse in the leg. He jumped clear and grasping his spear continued the fight on foot. The horse galloped on for a few more strides and then fell. Zhang, realizing he had missed, drew his sword and galloped forward to join the fight. His charge was halted by Thunderclap. Colonel Sun wanted to return to his ranks and get a new horse, but he was hemmed in by Lionface's relentless spear thrusts.

All this was too much for Colonel Hua, the Archer: "So these buggers think they can sneak up and shoot arrows, do they?" he ranted. "Then let them taste one of mine!" He bent his bow to the full, took careful aim at Lionface, and released his shaft. It took Lionface full in the face and he tumbled headlong from his horse. Colonel Sun ran up and finished him off. Then he went back for a new horse.

The fight between Zhang and Thunderclap continued, Thunderclap's cudgel rising and falling only inches from Zhang's skull as the latter defended himself by blocking and parrying. But Lionface's fall had put fear into his heart and gradually he began to lose the battle. Another of his northern comrades slapped his horse and galloped forward to assist him. To fight two at once was nothing to Thunderclap. The three horses formed a T-shape as the fight raged on.

But now Colonel Hua took a second arrow, fitted it to the string and aimed at Zhang's back. He bent the bow to the full and shouted "Take that!" as the arrow sped to its target, hitting with such force that it went right through and pierced the breastplate in front! Head down and heels in the air Zhang plummeted from his mount. His comrade seeing him fall dodged aside, turned his horse and galloped back to his own ranks. Thunderclap was hard on his heels. By now Colonel Sun had found a new mount and joined the others in urging the troops forward. The northerners were thrown into utter confusion. Their three remaining commanders could not withstand the onslaught and hastily retreated.

Now a great roar was heard from behind. This was because Marshal Niu, fearing Lionface might be defeated, had ordered Tigercat and Bearcat into the attack with five thousand cavalry each in two columns. Colonel Hua and his comrades hastily had their troops take up defensive positions just as the three enemy commanders they had been pursuing also turned their troops about and renewed their attack. The Song commanders found themselves under attack from three sides. They pressed on valiantly, but it was obvious they were encircled.

At this point another cheer rose heavenward on the east, causing panic among the northerners again. Two squadrons of Song cavalry, Twin Spears and company on the left flank, the Tamer and company on the right, were charging simultaneously. The northerners were completely routed; it was a massacre. Their leaders struggled back into the city and the gates were bolted. The Song army pursued them up to the walls but were obliged to withdraw, when wooden blocks and ballista missiles started raining down on them.

Soon after this, General Song and the main army arrived at a spot about three miles from the city and made camp. Presiding in his tent, Song Jiang ordered Magic Hand to record Colonel Hua's achievements. Suddenly a gust of wind passed through the camp from west to east, setting all the flags flapping. The Professor said: "This wind is an omen. They'll make a surprise attack on the camp tonight. We must prepare."

Song Jiang said: "Certainly it's something quite out of the

ordinary!" He ordered four of the leaders with three thousand troops to set up an ambush on the left of the camp and four more with a similar force to conceal themselves on the right. Monk, Pilgrim, Iron Ox, Pluto, Eight-Armed Ogre and Winged Ghost with the shield-bearers were concealed in the centre, with five hundred men. A shot was to be fired as signal for them all to attack. When they were all in place Song Jiang and the Professor settled down candle in hand, as if for a chat about military matters.

Now Marshal Niu, who had lost three of his officers and found, when they were counted, that he had lost more than two thousand men, was sitting gloomily in his tent when Tigercat came to him with a suggestion: "You should stop worrying, Your Excellency. That rabble of Song Jiang's have just had a string of successes. They will be feeling very pleased with themselves and they won't be expecting anything. Tonight let me raid their camp. We can carve them up and pay them back for what they did to us today."

"And I will lead the back-up force myself," Marshal Niu said excitedly. "Wildcat and Bearcat will stay and guard the town."

"If Your Excellency is going to be involved," said Tigercat contentedly, "we're bound to capture Song Jiang."

They marched that night in the second watch, Tigercat accompanied by his four lieutenants, with five thousand cavalry in light armour, no bells on their horse's bridles and the troops gagged to prevent talking. When they reached the Song camp they let off a bloodcurdling yell and charged in. They found the gates open and the camp brightly illuminated. Tigercat recognized a trap at once. As he struggled to turn his horse and retreat, the signal gun went off and the Song leaders charged in from left and right. Within the camp Iron Ox and the other five with their shield-bearing troops swept forward. The northerners were routed and fled in all directions. One of the leaders fell to Wu Song's sword, another was killed by Short-Arse. Tigercat and two others found themselves surrounded in the centre. Realizing they were in serious difficulties, Marshal Niu and two of the lieutenants led a rescue attempt. Amid the general confusion, both sides withdrew their forces.

Next day Niu counted his men and found over a thousand missing. He had also lost two more officers and another was gravely wounded, his life in the balance. As Niu was gloomily mulling this over, it was announced that an envoy had arrived from Weisheng with a proclamation. He quickly mounted and rode out of the north gate to receive him. After their return to the city, the proclamation was read: it told how the royal astronomer had recently observed in the night sky a planet which had invaded the field of Jin, heavenly counterpart of Tian Hu's kingdom. It was essential in consequence that Niu strengthen the city's defences and watch out for trouble. Niu in turn told the envoy how the Song emperor had sent Song Jiang to attack them, how the Song army had taken two cities in succession and were now quite close and how there had been fighting the day before and he had lost five officers. Only if reinforcements were sent quickly could the town be saved.

"At the time when I left Weisheng," the other replied, "we had no news of this. It was only when I was half way here that I heard rumours of Song Jiang's army being sent to attack."

Niu entertained the envoy with a feast and presented him with gifts, while at the same time laying up blocks of wood and ballista missiles and preparing bows and crossbows, fire arrows and incendiary materials, for a determined defence until the reinforcements arrived. Of this no more.

Meanwhile the Dandy, Short-Arse and company had completed their rout of the troops who attacked the camp, and had returned victorious. Next day Song Jiang ordered siege carts to be prepared for the assault on the city. He ordered Leopard's Head and three others to take ten thousand troops and attack the east gate, another four leaders with ten thousand troops to attack the south gate, a similar force to attack the west gate. The north gate he left free, for fear that if a relief force arrived and those inside launched a counter attack his own men would be caught between two fires. Another group, four leaders and five thousand troops, were to conceal themselves at the foot of a steep hill northeast of the city and a similar force were to lie in ambush in a dense wood northwest of the city — these would engage any relief force that appeared. Colonel Hua and three others with a thousand cavalry would patrol the perimeter and liaise with the forces attacking the gates. This party would be supported by three hundred infantry under Iron Ox and five others.

Having received their orders everyone went off to carry them out. Song Jiang, the Unicorn and the Professor with some of the minor leaders moved the camp to a position close to the city walls. Green-Eyes and Spots were ordered to prepare siege towers and scaling ladders and supply them to each of the attacking forces.

Leopard's Head and his companions erected their scaling ladders and siege towers outside the east gate and began pushing them up to the walls. Troops in light armour were ordered up into the siege towers, whilst those below shouted encouragement. The city's defenders responded with a shower of fire arrows, thick as a swarm of locusts. The attackers had no answer to this and in no time the siege towers were all ablaze and came crashing down. They suffered five or six dead and a dozen wounded. In the battle on the south and west soldiers were also killed or wounded by fire arrows and missiles. The upshot was that they fought for a week without any result.

In view of this, Song Jiang, the Unicorn and the Professor went themselves to the south gate to superintend the operation. While they were there Colonel Hua and his roving patrol arrived from the west gate heading east. Bearcat and two of his lieutenants were supervising the defence on the gate tower. When they saw Colonel Hua approaching the walls, one of them said: "Two of our commanders were wounded by that one the other day. Now's our chance to avenge them!" He took up his bow, fitted an arrow to it, took aim at Colonel Hua's heart and let fly. Colonel Hua heard the snap of the bowstring and leant backwards in the saddle. The arrow landed conveniently to hand and he wrenched it out and put it between his teeth while he straightened up. He laid his lance in the rest, took the bow in his left hand and fitted the arrow to it, took aim and fired. The arrow hit his opponent in the throat, passing right through and out the other side. Colonel Hua gave a triumphant shout: "Who do you think you are, you

rat, shooting off arrows like that? You shall all die, one after the other!" With his right hand he took another arrow and shot again. There were screams from the tower and several hurtled to the ground. Bearcat and his remaining lieutenant, white with fear, took cover in the nick of time. Colonel Hua laughed contemptuously: "Now you know something about the skill of the Archer!" he shouted, while Song Jiang and the Unicorn applauded loud and long.

"Why don't we all go with Colonel Hua to review the situation along the city walls?" the Professor said. So, closely guarded by Colonel Hua and his company, Song Jiang, the Unicorn and the Professor made a circuit of the city walls.

Later on back in the camp, the Professor summoned the former Lingchuan commander Geng Gong and questioned him about Gaizhou's layout. Geng Gong said: "Niu Wenzhong fancies himself as a military leader. He'll be up on the walls, organizing the city's defence. In the northern sector there are some temples and a large open space with nothing but grass." This gave the Professor an idea, which he explained to Song Jiang. The Flea and Madcap were summoned and given secret instructions. "This is the plan. Colonel Hua will also be given instructions and you will work in concert." Thunderer, Snake and Scorpion were told to take two hundred men and a sufficient quantity of signal rockets of various sizes and proceed in a certain way. Monk and Pilgrim were to have three hundred musicians. The Red-Haired Devil, Morbid, Perilous, and Yellow Dog with two hundred men each, all carrying incendiary materials were to head southeast and northwest, all according to the plan. The Magic Messenger was sent to the contingents on the east, west and south to give them the secret orders. When fires started inside the town they were to attack with all their might. Everyone left to put these orders into effect.

Now Niu Wenzhong had been watching for the relief force night and day, but there was no sign of it and he was extremely anxious. He reinforced the guards and had more wooden blocks and ballista missiles moved up onto the walls. Suddenly at dusk a tremendous shout was heard outside the north gate, while drums thundered and bugles blared. Niu rushed to the north gate but when he looked out from the walls the noise ceased. He could not tell where the enemy were. As he stood there hesitating, shouting broke out on the south, and again a din of gongs and drums that shook the heavens. He told the commander on the north gate to guard it strongly and rushed to the south gate. Again the shouting ceased as soon as he looked out and the drums and gongs were silent. He stared out for a long time, but there was nothing but the very faint sound of a drum beating in the Song position to the south. Otherwise all was quiet, not even a glimmer of light. He slowly descended from the wall. He was about to go back to check the government offices when a string of explosions rang out from beyond the east gate at the same time as shouting and thundering drums at the west gate. Driven thus from east to west and back again, he had no rest till dawn. Then the enemy renewed their attack on the town and did not withdraw till evening. That night at the first drumbeat bugles and drums clamoured again. Niu said: "The buggers are trying to scare us. We'd better ignore them. We'll just make sure our defences are strong and see what they do."

Suddenly at the east gate the sky was lit up, countless torches, siege towers and scaling ladders were being trundled up to the walls. Niu rushed to the eastern wall, where Wildcat and two of his lieutenants were fighting off the attack with fire arrows and ballistas. Then came an explosion that made the mountains and valleys reverberate and even shook the city's watchtowers. The defenders were terrified. For two nights there had been so much disturbance they hadn't been able to close their eyes for an instant and the attacks had been renewed at dawn. Niu himself had been constantly on patrol on the walls.

But now suddenly a host of banners were seen approaching from the northwest and a dozen Song scouts galloped into the main camp. Assuming it was the relief force, Niu ordered Bearcat to prepare to make a sortie to meet them.

Now this force approaching from the northwest belonged to the Jinning governor, who was Tian Hu's younger brother the third prince Tian Biao. He had received Gaizhou's request for help and had sent two of his best commanders, Feng Xiang and Wang Yuan, with twenty thousand troops. As they approached, about three miles out from the city they heard a sudden report and from the densely wooded slopes of the steep hill on either side of them two bodies of troops raced out. This was the ambush set up under Tattooed Dragon and the Tamer. Although there were twenty thousand in the Jinning relief force, they were tired after a long march and no match for these troops who after waiting there over ten days were in fine shape and raring to go, and who now came at them on both flanks. It was a rout. The northern relief force discarded gongs and drums, banners and spears, helmets and armour and a vast number of horses. The majority of the troops were killed. The two commanders escaped with their lives and led the battered remnants of their force back to Jinning. And that was that.

When Niu saw the two columns of the relief force cut off and fighting for their lives, he immediately ordered Bearcat to open the north gate and hasten to their assistance, the north gate, remember, being the one point from which the city was not under siege. But the moment Bearcat crossed the drawbridge he ran into Colonel Hua's roving patrol approaching from the west. The cry went up: "It's the Archer!" So frightened were they that instead of an orderly retreat they piled back into the city in a disorderly mob. Now, Bearcat's morale had already been shattered at the south gate. He had no desire to make a fight of it, but fled back into the city like his men. Colonel Hua's party rode forward and killed a score of enemy soldiers, but let the rest take refuge in the city without pursuing them. The gates were quickly barred.

The Flea and Madcap, dressed in northern uniforms, had now been swept into the city. After passing through the gates they took advantage of the commotion to slip into a small alley. Down this alley they found an ancestral hall with an inscription which read: "Temple of the Local Earth God". They crept inside and found a Taoist warming himself in front of a brazier at the east end. When he saw two soldiers enter, the Taoist said: "What's the news from outside, lads?"

They replied: "Bearcat said as 'ow we 'ad to go an' fight, but we ran into that bloke they calls the Archer an' even Bearcat hisself daresn't take 'im on. Proper pandemonium it was, so we got back inside the city sharpish. Then we took advantage of the confusion to come in 'ere." The Flea took out some loose silver and gave it to the Taoist, saying: "Give us a couple of bowls of that wine what you got stashed away, to keep out the bleedin' cold."

The Taoist responded with a pitying smile: "Don't you know there's a military crisis, has been for days? I haven't even got any incense left. Where would I get wine from?" He tried to give the silver back to the Flea.

Madcap pushed his hand away, saying: "Take it any'ow. We'll see again later. Day after day we been on guard, it's been 'orrible. We 'aven't slept a wink. You let us stay 'ere tonight and get a bit of shuteye, an' we'll push off first thing in the morning."

The Taoist shook his head: "Don't be angry with me. Marshal Niu has given strict orders. They come and inspect all the time. If I let you stay we wouldn't have a chance."

The Flea said: "In that case we'll 'ave to go somewhere else."

Madcap sidled up to the Taoist and squatted by the fire. The Flea took a quick look around to make sure no one could see them and then winked at Madcap. Madcap quietly took out a dagger. Oblivious to the danger, the Taoist went on warming himself. Reaching from behind Madcap ripped the knife across his throat. They bolted the doors of the temple. It was early evening, just before the first watch. The Flea went round the back to the kitchen, where he found a door. Beyond it was a little courtyard where dry grass was piled up under the eaves in two heaps. They carried this in and heaped it over the corpse. Then they unbolted the door. From the courtyard they climbed up onto the roof and concealed themselves on the far side of the ridge.

Half a dozen bright stars appeared in the sky. They waited a while, then slid down from the roof and went to reconnoitre outside the temple. There was no one in the street. They took a few more steps and paused to look around again. Although there were several neighbouring households, all were quiet and had their doors locked. There was only a faint sound of weeping. The Flea went a little further to the south. Beyond the corner of a long mud wall was a large expanse of waste land. There were dozens of piles of combustible materials on it. "This is their ammunition dump," the Flea thought to himself. "How come there's no one to guard it?" The fact is that everyone was up on the walls engaged in repelling the enemy and no one had time to inspect this site. When the watchmen heard that the Song army had scattered the relief column, they reckoned it was all up with the city. They didn't bother about the munitions but were only concerned to save their skins and went off to find somewhere to hide away before the city fell.

The two heroes went back to the temple and got their tinderboxes. They set light to the pile of grass on top of the Taoist's corpse. Then they went to the waste ground, where each piled up half a dozen bonfires. In a moment the whole area was ablaze, flames mounting to the sky. The temple also had caught. One of the people with houses west of the ammunition dump heard the fire and came out with a torch to investigate. The Flea rushed up and snatched the torch away from him. "Let me go and alert Marshal Niu," he shouted. The local saw their uniforms and naturally didn't think of objecting. Waving the torch the Flea, joined by Madcap, sped off southwards, shouting something about warning the Marshal. They started fires under the houses wherever they found a suitable place. Then they threw away the torch and melted into the background. They took off their northern uniforms and went to hide in a quiet place.

Now that fires had appeared in half a dozen streets, the city was seething with alarm. When he heard that the ammunition dump was on fire the Marshal gathered a party and rushed to put the fire out. Outside the city the attackers seeing the fires knew the Flea and Madcap were at work on the inside and redoubled their efforts. Song Jiang and the Professor, with Snake and Scorpion, rushed over to the south. The Professor said: "I noticed before that the city wall was quite low on this side." He directed Thunderclap and his men to move the siege towers up to the wall. Then he told Snake and Scorpion: "The enemy are demoralized, their troops are exhausted. See if you can get up onto the wall!"

Halberd in hand, Snake climbed the siege tower beside the battlements and leapt from it onto the wall; Scorpion followed suit. With a great shout they charged along the parapet, sweeping and stabbing with their weapons. The soldiers were tired and frightened and when they saw Snake and Scorpion bearing down on them so ferociously, they flung themselves off the wall. Tigercat levelled his spear and fought several bouts with the two on the wall till a blow from Snake's halberd struck him through and Scorpion followed up and split his skull.

By now more Song troops had poured into the city from the siege towers, over a hundred of them. Following Snake and Scorpion they charged down from the wall shouting: "Step forward and we'll make mincemeat of you!" They killed two of the commanders, felled the guards on the city gates, took control of the gates and lowered the drawbridge. Immediately Spearsman and his comrades rushed in. Together with Victorious, Spearsman led a charge to the east gate, where Tigercat An failed to stop them and was killed. They took over the gate and let Leopard's Head in. Thunderclap and the Supremo seized the western gate and let in Twin Spears. Three more of the enemy commanders were killed by their own troops. Corpses were draped over the wells, blood filled the gutters. Niu Wenzhong saw the city was lost and took to his horse and galloped out of the north gate, together with Bearcat and some two hundred troops.

They had gone no distance at all when out of the gloom two figures loomed, Iron Ox and Monk Lu Zhishen, a wild warrior and a ferocious monk, and stood in their way.

Truly it is hard to escape heaven's net, difficult to evade earth's pitfalls. If you want to know what became of Governor Niu and Bearcat, you must read the next chapter.

Chapter 93

Iron Ox dreams he is fighting the courtiers; Song Jiang divides his army into two wings!

Seeing the city was lost, Niu Wenzhong had no recourse but to flee. He left Gaizhou escorted by Bearcat and three of the lieutenants and they ran straight into Iron Ox and the Monk, who with their infantry stood blocking the escape route. "We've been waiting for you on General Song's orders, you hopeless fuckers," Iron Ox shouted. "And we've waited a long time!" He came at them, whirling his two axes. The axes rose and fell and two of the lieutenants bit the dust. Niu was so terrified his soul flew right out of his body. Before he could make any move, a blow from Monk's staff smashed down, shattering helmet and skull, and he fell lifeless from his horse. Of two hundred soldiers there were no survivors. Only Bearcat and the remaining lieutenant escaped, dashing off into the undergrowth. "Let 'em go," the Monk said. "The two asses can report what's happened."

The heads of the three commanders were chopped off, according to custom, the horses were rounded up, the armour and helmets collected, and loaded with these spoils they returned to the city.

Song Jiang's main army now entered the city and orders were given out for the fires to be extinguished and the citizens protected. After this the leaders assembled to report their successes. Song Jiang ordered the heads to be displayed on the gates. Next morning notices were posted to restore public order. All three army columns were allowed to camp inside the city and rewards were given out to the commanders. The names of Madcap, Flea, Snake and Scorpion were inscribed on the honours list. A report was produced informing the court of the capture of Gaizhou, the contents of the stores and treasury were transferred to the capital and a full report was sent to Marshal Su.

It was now the end of the last month of the year. Several days elapsed while Song Jiang was reorganizing his army and then Hotshot, now recovered from his illness, returned with Doctor An to present himself for duty. "Excellent," said Song Jiang. "Tomorrow is the fifth anniversary of the reign. We must have a general gathering."

Next day at crack of dawn the company paraded in the garb of servants of the throne and Song Jiang led them in paying homage to the Emperor. When the formal ceremony of obeisance was done they exchanged their court dress for war robes of scarlet brocade and came in perfect order, all ninety-two of them including the recently surrendered Geng Gong, to greet their general with seasonal wishes. General Song Jiang had organized a big feast, a great celebratory banquet, and many a toast did they propose to him. After a good many rounds of wine, Song Jiang addressed them: "Thanks to you all, the nation has regained three cities. And now we are met here to celebrate New Year's Day. It is truly a special occasion. My only regret is that we are without Taoist Gongsun, Twin Rods, Scimitar, the boat captains, and those others who were left to guard the three cities."

The junior commanders were summoned and received their rewards and the same day goats and wine were ordered to be sent to the garrisons of the three cities in further recognition of their achievements. Before this order could be carried out, it was announced that envoys had arrived from these cities to convey congratulations to General Song Jiang on behalf of the leaders whose responsibilities did not allow them to attend in person. Song Jiang said happily: "This gives me almost as much pleasure as seeing them face-to-face." The envoys were rewarded and then everyone settled down to some serious drinking, which did not end before they were all drunk.

Later Song Jiang was planning an excursion to the eastern suburbs to greet the spring, for it was the time of the spring festival. In the evening the wind blew from the northeast bringing in heavily laden clouds, and snow began to fall, filling the whole sky. In the morning they all awoke to find something like this:

> *Soft as willow fluff, smooth as goose feathers; a flock of white egrets floating on high, white gulls swirling over the river; borne on the wind, spinning and eddying into palace courts, brighter than midsummer sun glinting on weapons. A thousand mountains banked high with jade cause the bedazzled woodcutter to lose his way, ten thousand dwellings dressed in white, what poems they have inspired from the recluse! If we have already had the bumper harvest snow portends, what happy omen is this? Many bear arms on the borders; what counts is not numbers but fortune's favour!*

At that time Magic Hand said to the others: "There's quite a number of different names for snow: the smallest kind is known as 'bee swarm'; when the flakes are a little bigger it's 'goose feathers'; then you have the three-lobed flakes or 'triplets'; then the four-lobed 'quatrefoils'; the five-lobed ones are 'plum blossom' and the six-lobed are 'sestets'. This snow is formed from congealed air so you see it's six-lobed, reflecting the magic number six. After the spring festival what you get is always predominantly plum blossom, not the six-lobed kind any more. Although today is the day of the spring festival, we're still at the crossroads between winter and spring and this snow may be either five-lobed or six-lobed."

When Lungs heard this little lecture, he stepped out from under the eaves and began catching the falling snowflakes on the sleeve of his black robe to have a look at them. It was true, they were like six-petalled flowers, but there were some that were not perfectly formed or had sharp corners, and among them were some that were five-lobed. Lungs began crying out "It's true! It's true!" so everyone crowded around to look, with the result that a snort of warm air from Iron Ox melted all the snowflakes, causing general laughter.

Song Jiang wanted to know what was going on: "What are you laughing at?" he asked. "We were trying to look at the snowflakes but Iron Ox's hot breath melted them all," they said.

Song Jiang laughed too. "I've ordered wine so we can all have a party in the Spring Garden," he said.

Just to the east of the town there was a garden called Celebration of Spring. In the middle of it was the Pavilion of Fragrant Rain, screened by a grove of cypress, pine and plum trees. That afternoon they all gathered there and amid much noise and laughter and lively conversation the time passed quickly; soon it was dark and lamps were lit. Song Jiang was merry and kept reminiscing about the old times and the hardships they had passed through and how much he owed to them all. "I was just a local clerk," he said. "Then I committed a serious crime and you lot, fighting against the odds, heedless of personal danger, repeatedly risking your lives, came and rescued me. That time when Magic Messenger and I were taken out to the market place in Jiangzhou, I thought it was all up with us. Now I have become an officer of the crown, fighting for my country. When I look back on those past events, truly it's like a dream!"

At this point he began to break down and the tears streamed down his face. Magic Messenger and Colonel Hua, and others who had shared the hard times with him, were also moved to tears.

Iron Ox by now had drunk rather too much wine and was feeling the effects. In the middle of telling them something his eyes gradually closed and he went to sleep, resting his face on his arms. Suddenly the idea came to him that it was still snowing outside. His body seemed to float mysteriously and he found himself out in the open. When he looked around he was amazed: "There isn't any snow after all! What's the point of sitting indoors? Why don't I go and take a stroll round that temple?" A little way from the garden, just as he was leaving the city behind, he suddenly remembered something: "Heavens! I've forgotten my axes!" But when he put his hand to his belt, there they were. So he marched on, not thinking where he was going nor knowing how far he had gone when he saw a high mountain in front of him. Almost immediately he reached the foot of it and a man appeared before him wearing a scholar's cap and a light yellow Taoist's robe. This person approached and said: "If you're in the

雨香亭

mood for a stroll, Commander, take a turn on the mountain, it's a blessed place."

"What is it called?" Iron Ox inquired.

"It's called the Mountain of the Heavenly Pool," the other replied. "Come back and see me again when you've had your walk."

Iron Ox followed the suggestion and walked all round the mountain. By the side of the path he came upon a little compound. Sounds of a quarrel issued from within. He rushed inside and found a dozen people with staves and cudgels smashing up the tables, chairs and other household items. In their midst was a tall fellow who was shouting: "Hurry up and hand over your daughter for me to marry, you old fool. Don't you dare refuse! You make just the slightest objection and I'll kill the whole lot of you!"

When Iron Ox heard this, he began to boil with indignation: "You fucking bastards," he hissed. "How dare you try to take away someone's daughter by force?"

"What's it to do with you if we want his daughter?" they shouted back.

Iron Ox took out his axes and started laying about him in a frenzy. To his surprise, he knocked down two or three effortlessly with the first blow. Some of them tried to escape, but he pursued them and with half a dozen blows sent seven or eight heads rolling. The ground was littered with corpses. Only one escaped and ran off. Iron Ox tried to go in again, but both leaves of the door were securely bolted so he demolished the door with a kick. Inside a white-haired old man and an old woman were sobbing. When Iron Ox charged in they cried out: "Oh no, they've come for us!"

Iron Ox shouted back: "I saw there was an injustice. I've killed all the bastards, come and see." The old man tottered after him to look. He grabbed Iron Ox's arm and said: "You've killed some villains all right, but I'm the one that'll have to pay for it."

Iron Ox said with a laugh: "Don't you know me, old fellow? I'm Iron Ox from Mount Liang. Along with my leader Song Jiang I've been amnestied and sent to get Tian Hu. My pals are all drinking in the city and I got bored with it so I came out for a stroll. Never mind about those bastards, if I'd killed a thousand or two, what the fuck would it matter?"

The old man wiped his eyes and said: "I suppose it's all right then. Please come in and sit down." When Iron Ox went inside he found a table already spread with wine and food. The old man bade him sit down opposite, filled a bowl of wine to the brim and offered it with both hands, saying: "You have saved my daughter. Please drink this cup."

Iron Ox took it and drank it and the old man offered him more. When he had drunk off four or five, a tearful old woman appeared leading a young girl, who saluted him respectfully with crossed arms. The old woman said: "Commander, since you serve with General Song and appear to be so thrifty, if you don't despise our unworthiness, please take our daughter with you."

When he heard this, Iron Ox leapt to his feet and said: "What a disgusting idea! Do you really suppose I killed those buggers because I wanted your daughter? Shut your fucking noise and don't talk such fucking shit!" With this he kicked over the table and rushed out of the house. Immediately a tall bearded character with a halberd strode after him, roaring out: "You black bastard, stop! What do you mean by killing all my people? What business is it of yours if I want their girl?" Raising his halberd he came charging at Iron Ox. Iron Ox swung his two axes furiously and they fought twenty bouts, till the other, seeing he could not win, knocked the axes aside and fled, trailing his halberd. Iron Ox followed hot on his heels. They came to a little wood where he suddenly saw a number of fine buildings. The other man flung away his halberd and disappeared among a crowd of people. As Iron Ox pondered this, he heard a voice from inside one of the buildings: "Iron Ox must cease this unruly behaviour. Bring him to me!" Suddenly it dawned on Iron Ox: this was the Hall of Culture and Ethics where the day before with his brother Song Jiang he had attended an audience with the Emperor. This was where the Emperor lived! The voice continued: "Down on your knees, quickly, Iron Ox!" He put away his axes. He could make out the Emperor seated on his throne a long way in front of him, with a number of officials lined up in front of the throne. He kowtowed assiduously three times, and then thought to himself. "Oh dear, I've missed one out!"

"Why were you killing people just now?" the Emperor asked.

Still kneeling he replied: "Those villains were trying to force someone's daughter. It made me angry, so I killed them."

"When Iron Ox sees an injustice he seeks to eradicate the evil," the Emperor said. "Your valour is commendable. I shall exonerate you from blame and appoint you to my personal guard."

"How far-sighted the Emperor is!" Iron Ox thought joyfully. He knocked his head on the ground a dozen times and then stood to attention.

In a short while the Grand Preceptor and the three wicked marshals, Tong, Yang and Gao appeared and kneeling before the throne said: "Look at this Song Jiang! He's been given a great army to get Tian Hu and he's just idling away the time instead of attacking, drinking every day. We request that Your Majesty punish him."

Iron Ox heard this and an indescribable rage swelled in his breast till he could no longer contain it and he charged forward with his two axes. With one blow to each he chopped off their heads and said: "Your Majesty don't listen to these villainous counsellors. Our dear leader has captured three cities. He is camped now at Gaizhou and about to launch the attack. How can they tell such lies?"

When the other officials saw Iron Ox kill the four bigwigs, they tried to arrest him, but he waved his axes and said: "If you touch me, you'll meet the same fate!", so no one dared lift a finger. Chuckling to himself, Iron Ox said: "That's great! Those four villains have got their just desserts. I shall go and tell the Leader." With that he strode out of the palace. Immediately he came to a mountain, which he saw at once was the place where he had just met the scholar. And there he was, the scholar, standing at the foot of the mountain. He greeted Iron Ox with a smile: "Did you have a pleasant walk, Commander?"

Iron Ox replied: "I'd better tell you, sir, that I have just killed four wicked ministers."

"Is that so?" said the scholar, quite unperturbed. "I was doing something in Fenjing. Just recently I happened to come here, and knowing of your loyalty and righteousness, I wanted to have a word with you. I have something important to say. At present Song Jiang is pursuing Tian Hu. I have a formula to impart to you that will enable Tian Hu to be captured. You must memorize it carefully and repeat it to Song Jiang." He then intoned to Iron Ox: "To exterminate Tian Hu and his ilk, jade arrowtip must serve your purpose." He repeated this five or six times. What he said seemed meaningful to Iron Ox so he carefully memorized the words. The scholar now pointed towards the woods and said: "There's an old lady over there, sitting among the trees." When Iron Ox turned to look, he found the scholar had disappeared. "That was quick!" he said to himself. "I'd better go and have a look to see if there's someone in the woods." There was indeed an old woman sitting there, and when he approached to take a closer look, it was his own mother! She was sitting on a black rock, her eyes tight shut. He rushed forward and embraced her: "Mother, are you still suffering? I thought you had been eaten by a tiger. But now here you are!"

His mother said: "My son, I was not eaten by the tiger."

Weeping he said: "I've been given an amnesty and now I really am a government official. My brother Song Jiang's army is camped at the northern capital. I will carry you there on my back." At this moment there was a sudden commotion and out rushed a ferocious striped tiger. It roared and waved its tail and sprang. Iron Ox grabbed his axes intending to chop it down but he used too much force and both axes bit the air and then smashed down into the table in the Pavilion of Fragrant Rain in the Celebration of Spring Garden.

Song Jiang and the others had been chatting about everyday events and the talk was at its most absorbing when they saw Iron Ox had dozed off at the table. They thought nothing of it. Suddenly there was this fearful racket. Iron Ox in his sleep was beating the table with both hands, upsetting bowls and dishes, splattering his sleeves with the sauces. He kept repeating: "Mother, the tiger's gone, the tiger's gone!" When he opened his eyes and saw the bright light of the lamps and all his comrades sitting around him still drinking, he exclaimed: "By all that's wonderful, it was all a dream!"

The others laughed and said: "What was a dream? What are you so pleased about?"

Iron Ox told them how he had dreamt of his mother, that she wasn't dead after all, but his conversation with her had been interrupted by a tiger! They expressed their sympathy. Then he recounted how he had killed the thugs and kicked over the table. At this point Monk, Pilgrim and Madcap clapped and shouted: "Bravo!"

"That's not the half of it!" Iron Ox said with a grin. And he told them how he had killed the four evil ministers. They all applauded and shouted out: "That's great, that's terrific! That's the sort of dream that's worth having!"

Song Jiang said: "I don't know what you're making such a noise about. It's only a dream, it's not important!"

But Iron Ox was just getting to the main point. Pulling up his sleeves, he said: "Who says it's not fucking important? I've never done anything more enjoyable in my life. Besides, I had another strange dream. A scholar told me some kind of verse: 'To exterminate Tian Hu and his ilk, jade arrowtip must serve your purpose.' He said this was the secret of destroying Tian Hu and told me to memorize it carefully and tell it to you."

Neither Song Jiang nor the Professor could explain this. When Doctor An heard the words "jade arrowtip" he was dying to say something. but Hotshot gave him a look and he smiled a little and after that did not open his mouth. The Professor said: "This is a pretty strange dream. If the snow clears we can attack." They finished their drinking and went to bed and the night passed uneventfully.

Next day the snow had begun to thaw and in the command tent Song Jiang, the Unicorn and the Professor divided the army into two columns to attack from either side. The eastern force would attack through Kettle Pass and move on to Goodborough to get behind the rebel headquarters; then they would turn back via Dagu to Lin where they would join up with the others. The western force would take Jinning and penetrate to the northwest of Weisheng where they would meet the others at Lin.

Having divided his forces, Song Jiang said to the Unicorn: "From here our two forces will attack from the east and the west. Which side will you take?"

The Unicorn replied: "I shall accept whichever you give me. It is not for me to choose."

Song Jiang said: "Nevertheless, let us test heaven's will. Let us write the two divisions down on ballot papers and each draw one."

So Sterling wrote "east" and "west" on two pieces of paper and after Song Jiang and the Unicorn had both prayed and burnt incense, Song Jiang drew one of them. Now because of the result, a number of valiant commanders were to join the army. And a famous wizard was to appear at the foot of Nine Dragon Mountain. If you want to know which was the assignment that had fallen to Song Jiang, you must read the next chapter.

Chapter 94

Scimitar wins over three leaders; Iron Ox lands them in a mess!

After dividing up the forces in Gaizhou, Song Jiang and the Unicorn draw lots, having first prayed and burnt incense. Song Jiang draws the eastern route, to Fort Kettle and Goodborough, so the western, through Jinning, falls to the Unicorn. They are only waiting for the snow to completely thaw before setting out. The defence of Gaizhou is left in the hands of Colonel Hua and four others with twenty thousand troops. On the sixth of the month, an auspicious day, the two generals muster their troops.

News now came in that two cities, previously beaten into submission by the rebels, had, on hearing of the approach of the government army, overpowered their governors and were handing them over as prisoners. A delegation headed by the elders of these two places had arrived with a tribute of goats and wine. This development was most welcome to Song Jiang: he rewarded them and made a friendly announcement recognizing their return to allegiance. The two governors were executed as a demonstration that the forces of the government were now in control and as an example to other rebels.

That same day the two armies marched out of the north gate. Colonel Hua had organized wine for the send-off. Taking cup in hand, Song Jiang said to Colonel Hua: "After your exploits against the enemy I have every confidence in your ability to defend this city, my friend. The threat is from the north. If the enemy attack, it is necessary to strike back and destroy their morale so they will not intrude south again." Colonel Hua attended carefully to his orders.

Song Jiang again took his cup and addressed the Unicorn: "Today at the start of our campaign we have received this good news of the handing over of the prisoners and surrender of these two cities. You will now be able to attack Jinning straight away, secure a quick victory, capture the rebel leader Tian Hu, inform the court and enjoy wealth and honour thereafter."

The Unicorn said: "It is owing to your reputation, dear brother, that those two cities have surrendered without a fight. You have entrusted me with this task and I shall of course address it with the utmost seriousness."

Song Jiang took the copy of the picture by the Prodigy's friend that he had previously had Magic Hand make and gave it to the Unicorn for his own use. He then established the three divisions of his troops: vanguard under Leopard's Head and three others, rearguard under Colonel Sun and seven others and the main force led by himself and the Professor. The combined force of fifty thousand troops set off heading northeast. His second-in-command the Unicorn bade everyone farewell and with his own forty leaders and fifty thousand troops marched in a northwesterly direction.

After seeing them off Colonel Hua returned to the city. He gave orders for two camps to be set up a mile or two north of the city under the Young Master and Spots each with five thousand troops, provided with crack archers and every kind of incendiary device to foil the enemy. He also, it goes without saying, established ambushes east and west of the city. Please bear in mind that seven other leaders had been left to defend the three previously captured towns.

When Song Jiang and his contingent had marched ten miles he saw a mountain range ahead. It was some while before they reached it. The sight was striking:

Mists, layer upon layer, make dim the light of day.
Peak piled on peak stands in the goose's way;
Glimpses of cliffs like city walls are seen
Mid towering clouds and winding waters green.

As Song Jiang was examining the scene, Iron Ox pointed and said: "Those mountains are exactly like what I dreamed of the other night."

Song Jiang summoned Geng Gong, the enemy general who had surrendered to them earlier, and asked: "You are familiar with the region, you must know all about those mountains. If it is as Guanzhong's picture shows, Mount Fang is east of the provincial capital and this is called Mountain of the Heavenly Pool."

Iron Ox spoke up: "That's the name that scholar used in my dream. I had forgotten it."

Geng Gong said: "It is indeed the Mountain of the Heavenly Pool. Its fallen rocks and cliffs are like a city rampart and in the old days people used to take refuge there. Nowadays the locals say it's haunted. A mysterious red glow is often seen at night. And woodcutters have observed a strange odour there."

"This all seems to confirm Iron Ox's dream," said Song Jiang.

They marched twenty miles that day before making camp. Nothing of note occurred on the way. Soon they were taking up a position just south of Kettle Pass.

Kettle Pass was situated under the mountain's eastern crest, where the terrain was shaped like a kettle. In Han times a customs post had been established here, and it became known as Kettle Pass. To the east was Baodu or Calf Mountain and Kettle Pass lay between the two mountains, some twenty-five miles south of Goodborough and Goodborough Pass. It was held by eight of Tian Hu's commanders with thirty thousand crack troops. One of these commanders, Shan Shiqi, the younger brother of a rich man of the region, was exceptionally talented and skilled in fighting. Because he had killed a man and wanted to escape punishment he joined Tian Hu and after achieving success in battle had been made a general. He wielded a heavy steel staff with great expertise. When Tian Hu heard that the court was sending Song Jiang's forces against him, he sent this Shan Shiqi to Goodborough to pick ten thousand first class troops and join the other seven at Kettle Pass. Once there his orders were to get on with the job and not worry about reporting back for orders.

When Shan Shiqi reached Kettle Pass and heard that Gaizhou had fallen he reckoned it would not be long before the Song army attacked the pass. So he spent each day training his men and feeding up his horses, in readiness for the battle. Suddenly it was reported that Song Jiang's army had made camp only a mile or two south of their position. He mobilized ten thousand cavalry and with three other commanders put on armour, mounted and rode out to do battle.

The two armies were drawn up facing each other. The archers on either side began shooting at the opposing ranks. Martial music struck up on both sides and colourful banners were unfurled. Where pennants marked the opening in the northern ranks Shan Shiqi rode forth: "You marsh-dwelling outlaws!" he roared. "How dare you invade our territory!"

On the opposite side Leopard's Head rode forward and shouted in reply: "You're a bunch of common robbers! The imperial army is here now so what's the point of resisting?" He twirled his lance and gave his horse its head. The two adversaries met in the middle: while two armies cheered, two riders clashed, four arms struck this way and that, four horse's legs became entangled. They fought more than fifty bouts and neither had the advantage. Leopard's Head secretly admired his opponent's skill. One of the northern lieutenants believing his commander could not gain victory by himself galloped to his assistance, whirling his sword; on the other side Hotshot also galloped into action. The fight raged on: four assailants in two pairs. Hotshot and his opposite number fought more than twenty bouts. His strength ebbing, Hotshot turned his horse and galloped away. The other gave chase. Hotshot rested his lance, reached into his saddlebag and took a stone. He twisted in the saddle and with a shout of "Pow!" flung the stone, hitting his opponent square on the nose so that he fell from the saddle streaming with blood. Hotshot took up his lance again intending to finish him off but two other northerners were galloping to the rescue.

When those above on the pass saw one of their champions bested and fearing defeat for the commander sounded the gong for retreat, Song Jiang did likewise. "We got one of their commanders today," he said to the Professor. "It's bound to affect their morale. But the mountain terrain is difficult and their fort appears to be very strong. What's our best plan for defeating them?"

Leopard's Head said: "Let me challenge them again tomorrow. I'm sure I can defeat that leader of theirs. Then you can launch a determined attack."

"Don't be in such a hurry!" the Professor said. "As Sunzi says, 'When you can't win, stick to defence. When you can win, attack!' "

Song Jiang said: "The Professor is quite right."

Next day when Leopard's Head and Hotshot asked permission to engage the enemy, Song Jiang said: "We may have won one battle, but it's still not going to be easy to take the pass. You must have Spearsman and Hasty to back you up."

Leopard's Head and Hotshot with five thousand men advanced to the foot of the pass, banners waving, drums thundering. They hurled challenges and insults at the enemy all morning, but there was no response. Just as they were about to give up, a gun went off in the fort, the gates opened and Shan Shiqi with four of his commanders and twenty thousand men charged out. Leopard's Head said to his companion: "They think they've an advantage because we're tired. We must attack." Hasty and Spearsman now came up from the rear. The armies faced each other and without a word engaged. Leopard's Head found an opponent. When Shan came out, Hotshot took him on with his spear. Hasty with his axe did battle with two others. With both armies roaring encouragement, the seven riders revolved in a cloud of dust, whirling round like shadows on a lantern. Leopard's Head fought till he was drunk with the excitement of battle. Suddenly he let off a cry and struck his opponent from his horse with a thrust of his spear. Hasty's two opponents were running out of strength when they saw their comrade fall. One of them feinted and galloped off. The other, planning to follow suit, tried to parry Hasty's axe but was cut in two.

When he saw he had lost two of his commanders Shan also galloped away towards his own ranks, but Hotshot gave chase. He took a stone and flung it at the retreating general. It landed with a resounding crack on Shan's helmet, frightening him out of his wits. He crouched low in the saddle and fled. The one remaining enemy commander hurriedly ordered his men back to

the pass, but they were caught by Leopard's Head and his cavalry and totally routed. Shan and the remnants of his troops scuttled back into the fort and barricaded themselves inside. Leopard's Head continued the pursuit to the foot of the pass, but there they were assailed with arrows and stones by the defenders and could not gain entrance. Leopard's Head was hit in the left shoulder and gave the order to retreat. Back in the camp Song Jiang told Doctor An to treat Leopard's Head. Fortunately he had thick armour and the damage was slight. Of this no more.

When the roll was called, Shan found that he had lost more than two thousand men, as well as two commanders. It was decided to send a messenger to the Prince at Weisheng to tell him that Song Jiang's army was powerful and would be difficult to hold off and to entreat him to send reinforcements to secure the situation, and at the same time arrange secretly for the commanders on Calf Mountain, Tang Bin, Wen Zhongrong and Cui Ye to march east and cause trouble in the rear of the Song army. A time would be set, with a gun as signal for the defenders to charge down the pass: the enemy would be caught between two fires and surely defeated. Having made the plan, Shan strengthened the guard on the fort, and then there was nothing more to do but wait for Tang Bin's reply.

Meanwhile Song Jiang, depressed that Kettle Pass seemed impregnable and had held them up already more than two weeks, was sitting gloomily in his tent when it was suddenly announced that an envoy had arrived with a confidential letter from Scimitar, who had been left to defend Weizhou. Song Jiang and the Professor hastily opened it. Here is what they read:

> *Tang Bin, commander of the garrison at Calf Mountain was formerly with me in Pudong. Because he is valiant and steadfast, I had a great affection for him. Ill-treated by some influential people he lost patience and killed one of his enemies. The authorities arrested him immediately. He wanted to take refuge on Mount Liang, but south of Pudong the road took him past Calf Mountain and he fell in with robbers. He fought with the two leaders, Wen Zhongrong and Cui Ye, and neither of them could*

defeat him so they asked him to stay and be chief of the stronghold. When Tian Hu seized Kettle Pass he wanted him to surrender. Tang Bin had no wish to do so but he realised he was isolated and had no alternative. He remained on the mountain to cover Kettle Pass' flank. Recently he heard that I was governor of Weizhou and on New Year's Day he rode over to Weizhou, coming secretly and unescorted to explain his true feelings to me. He said he had always respected you for your honour and integrity and that his chief desire was to surrender to you and fight under your banner to redeem his fault. I myself rode back with him to Calf Mountain to encourage the other two, Wen Zhongrong and Cui Ye, to pull their socks up. They have agreed to reform and we now have a secret deal and their word as pledge.

After reading this through carefully Song Jiang and the Professor decided not to make any move but to wait and decide on their strategy after observing developments in the fort.

After Shan had sent the secret message to Tang Bin asking for his support, the soldier returned with this reply: "The moon is full at present. I will not move my forces till it has waned. We do not want the enemy to see what we are doing."

Shan said: "That's reasonable."

There was no attack from the Song army either for the next ten days. Then it was suddenly reported that Tang Bin was approaching from the east with a group of horsemen. Soon Tang Bin reached the fort and went to see its commander: "Tonight in the third watch my two lieutenants with ten thousand men will slip away from Calf Mountain and head east. They will wear light armour and ride without bells on their harness. By break of day they should be behind Song Jiang's lines. You must be ready to play your part with a sortie from the fort."

"We shall have them in a vice," Shan said gleefully. "It's the end of the Song army!" He ordered wine for Tang Bin in celebration.

After nightfall Tang Bin looked out and remarked: "That's funny. There seems to be someone prowling around out there." As he spoke he took two arrows from the sheaf of one of his bodyguards and shot them into the dark. And indeed it was the case that in order to capture the fort Song Jiang had stationed men outside to spy on their activities under cover of darkness. With the arrow he fired Tang Bin had hit one of these men in the right leg, but from its effect it appeared the arrow had no barb. Puzzled by this the soldier examined the arrow and found that some lengths of cloth had been tightly wound around the tip. He realized something was up and sped back to the camp to report to Song Jiang. By the light of the lamp Song Jiang tore off the covering and found several lines of minute spidery script. It was a secret message from Tang Bin: the fort would be handed over to them early next day. Wen and Cui would take up positions behind the General's lines and a gun would be fired as signal for those inside the fort to launch an attack. This would be the opportunity for Tang Bin to seize the fort. He requested General Song to be ready to enter it.

Having read this missive, Song Jiang made secret preparations with the Professor. The latter said: "Scimitar has confidence in all this. But if enemy troops are going to be in our rear, we cannot neglect to take precautions. Send Colonel Sun and four others and ten thousand troops with drums and banners to take up position in the rear. If Wen and Cui do turn up, they must keep them out of the camp until the fort is definitely in our hands. They should not allow them to advance until they hear the report of the big gun. And let Spearsman and Hasty set up an ambush with five thousand men on the east, and Leopard's Head and Hotshot do likewise on the west. When they hear the gun they can come out to back us up and we'll enter the fort together. But just in case there's any treachery they'll be there to help out."

"You think of everything, Professor!" Song Jiang said.

So the orders were given and everyone prepared accordingly.

Up on Kettle Pass, Shan in accordance with what Tang Bin had told him listened for the gun from behind the Song position. Some time after dawn a whole string of reports sounded to the south and a cloud of dust was seen rising to the rear of the Song army amid much waving of banners and general confusion. Tang

Bin said: "Wen and Cui have got there. It's time for us to attack." They set off in order, Shan in the lead, Tang in the second wave. Two commanders stayed behind to guard the fort.

When the Song army sighted the attack they quickly retreated. Shan led the charge, urging his cavalry on. Suddenly a gun fired and two troops of cavalry appeared from the Song left and right flanks and charged. At the same moment Tang Bin ordered about turn and led his troops back up to the pass, where they took up a position with spears at the ready, leaving Shan and his lieutenant to carry on the fight alone. Another gun, and from the Song ranks Iron Ox and the shield bearers poured forward. Shan realized some plan was afoot and ordered a retreat. But the way back to the fort was now blocked: "You must answer to Tang Bin! Kettle Pass is already in Song hands! Dismount and surrender!" he shouted, as he killed the first of the retreating rebel leaders with his lance. Shan was totally nonplussed and could only lead a few dozen of his men off to one side in a desperate attempt to escape. Leopard's Head and Hotshot let them go and continued on forward, wanting first of all to secure the pass.

At this point Iron Ox and company reached the top. Another gun and they joined Tang Bin in killing the guards. The fort was taken. In this action another two rebel commanders had been killed, one in the fort and the other outside. The northerners fled, abandoning helmets, armour and horses. Two thousand were dead and five hundred taken prisoner. The rest surrendered.

Soon Song Jiang and the main army arrived and entered in due order. Tang Bin dismounted, prostrated himself before Song Jiang and said: "My fault is great, but I have heard of your righteousness and humanity. I wanted to join you, but could not find the way, so I was unable to make your acquaintance. Now heaven has granted me this opportunity. This will make me happy for the rest of my life!" Again he prostrated himself.

Song Jiang returned the courtesy and raised him up, saying: "If you are willing to declare your allegiance to the throne and join me in subduing the rebels, I will report it when I return to the court and the Emperor is bound to pardon you."

Colonel Sun now reported back with Wen and Cui, the two outlaws who had marched to the rear of the Song army. Song Jiang had them brought in while Colonel Sun stationed his forces outside the fort. The two outlaws said to Song Jiang: "We would count ourselves lucky to serve under you as your slaves and work like dogs or horses."

Song Jiang said: "You have helped us to capture the pass. This is no small contribution. It will all be clearly noted on the record." A feast was held after this to celebrate with Tang and his two companions. A count was taken of the troops inside and outside the fort: twenty thousand had come over from the rebels and a thousand horses. All the leaders were rewarded for their work. Then Song Jiang asked Tang how many troops there were at Goodborough. "Originally there were thirty thousand," he said. "Shan brought ten thousand here to reinforce the pass. So now there must be twenty thousand, plus the ten commanders."

Tang Bin also said: "Tian Hu relies on Kettle Pass as a shield for Goodborough. Now it has fallen, he has lost a limb. Humble as are my talents, I would like to lead the attack on Goodborough."

Geng Gong, the commander who had surrendered at Lingchuan, was keen to go with him and Song Jiang consented. A little later he said to Wen and Cui: "You used to be on Calf Mountain and know the conditions there. I hear much of your valour. I would like to give you some troops and ask you to fortify it. When we are ready to attack Goodborough we will ask you to join us. What do you say?"

"Your wish is our command," they answered in unison. After wine had been drunk they left for Calf Mountain.

Next day, when Song Jiang gave out orders he sent Magic Messenger to the Unicorn at Jinning to inform him of the military situation and return straight away. While Magic Messenger was performing this duty, Song Jiang discussed things with the Professor and made dispositions for the attack on Goodborough. Tang Bin and Geng Gong with ten thousand men were to attack the east gate, Hasty, Hotshot and another ten thousand the south gate, leaving free access by the west gate for reinforcements from Weisheng, to prevent the besiegers being caught between forces inside the city and others outside. Iron Ox and companions with five hundred infantry would form a roving patrol. Colonel Sun and two others would take their troops up to Kettle Pass to help Demon King and Flautist defend it. This done, he and the Professor with the rest of them struck camp and marched toward Goodborough, camping again just a few miles from it to the south.

Now our story divides. The officials of Tian Hu's defence committee in Weisheng received reports from Shan Shiqi, the commander of Kettle Pass, and from Tian Biao in Jinning and duly informed Tian Hu that the Song forces were strong and posed an imminent threat both to Kettle Pass and to Jinning. When Tian Hu held a meeting with his staff to discuss the sending of reinforcements, someone stepped forward wearing a yellow turban and a cloak of crane's down, like the great general, Zhuge Liang, and said: "Great Lord, I would like to go to Kettle Pass and repel the enemy."

This man's name was Qiao Lie. He was from Jingyuan in Shaanxi. When his mother was pregnant she dreamed that a wolf entered the room, which later turned into a deer. When she awoke she gave birth to Qiao Lie. At the age of eight Qiao Lie was already expert with spear and staff. Wandering in the mountains one day, he met a magician who imparted his secret arts to him and he learnt how to conjure up winds, summon rain, ride the mists and mount the clouds. He went to the Two Immortals Mountain in Jiugong seeking the Way but the Master refused to receive him and sent an acolyte with these instructions: "Your command is external, you have yet to grasp the hidden truth. Turn to good and beat the demons, then you will come to me again."

Visibly angered, Qiao Liu withdrew. Henceforth he relied on his own efforts to achieve knowledge, through his ceaseless wanderings. Because of his reputation for magic, people called him the Wizard. Later he came to the district of Anding. A serious drought occurred there, with not a drop of rain for five months and the authorities published an appeal for a rainmaker, promising a reward of three thousand cash. Wizard Qiao Lie accepted the challenge and went to work. Abundant rain ensued. When the magistrate saw there was a sufficiency of rain, he forgot about the promised reward. That wasn't all. There was a crooked scholar in the town called Ho Cai who was very thick with the local treasurer. When he heard about the affair, he encouraged the treasurer to hand over the lion's share of the reward money to the magistrate and appropriate the rest for himself. Ho Cai then borrowed from him and made a small profit. The treasurer even gave three strings of cash to the Wizard, but said: "With a talent like yours, you really don't need the money. I am responsible for collecting taxes and I can never get it all in. I have to scrape it together here and there. If you take my advice, you'll leave this reward money in the treasury for the time being. Then when you need it you can always come and take it out."

The Wizard flew into a passion. "That reward money was contributed by the wealthy householders of the district. How can you embezzle it? What's in the treasury comes from the blood and sweat of the people and you want to cream it off to buy yourself smiles and pleasures and let affairs of state go hang. I'll kill you, you corrupt and profligate vermin, and get rid of a worm at the heart of the treasury!" He raised his fist and smashed it into the man's face. A debauched degenerate like that, fat and short of breath to boot, could hardly put up a fight. The Wizard punched and kicked him into such a condition that when he had crawled home battered and bruised he took to his bed and lay there in a sorry state for four or five days till he died of his injuries. His wife lodged an accusation with the authorities. The magistrate guessed that the reward money was at the root of the trouble. He signed a warrant and sent bailiffs to bring in the accused, Wizard Qiao Lie, for questioning. When the Wizard heard this, he immediately went back home and packed his things and then went with his mother to seek refuge in Weisheng. Here he gave himself out to be a Taoist sage and exchanged the name Lie for Qing, taking the religious name of Tao Qing.

Not long after all this, Tian Hu started his rebellion and, having heard of this Tao Qing's special gifts, recruited him. The Wizard helped Tian Hu to gain control of many districts by fabricating scandals, making full use of his magic arts and duping simple people. Tian Hu relied on his judgement in everything and named him Holy Sage, Protector of the Land, Marshal of the Army and Deputy Chief Minister. By this time he had changed his name and was called Grand Master Qiao Taoqing.

The Wizard now asked Tian Hu to give him command of an army to reinforce Kettle Pass. Tian Hu said: "You are diligent in my service, Grand Master!"

They had hardly finished speaking when Sun An, one of Tian Hu's ministers, appeared and said: "I would like to take an army to reinforce Jinning." Tian Hu gave them both joint command of the expedition against the southerners and gave each of them twenty thousand men.

The Wizard also said: "The situation at Kettle Pass is serious, so I shall take light cavalry and ride with the utmost speed to rescue them." Tian Hu was delighted and ordered his military council to allot them the troops. This done, the two generals mustered their troops before departing.

This Sun An was the Wizard's fellow-countryman — from the same district, that is. He was tall and strong and a fairly skilled tactician. His energy was exceptional. He had studied martial arts to considerable effect and wielded a finely engraved double-edged sword. He had killed two men in a family vendetta and was relentlessly pursued by the authorities so he fled from his home. He had been a close friend of the Wizard's and when he heard that the Wizard was serving with Tian Hu he went to Weisheng to take refuge with him. After the Wizard introduced him to Tian Hu and spoke of his prowess, he received a palace appointment. Now with ten officers and twenty thousand men he set out to reinforce Jinning.

Meanwhile the Wizard himself set off with his four commanders. They marched by night towards Goodborough and quickly reached a point just a few miles north of the city, when their scouts reported: "Kettle Pass fell to the Song army yesterday. Now they are advancing on Goodborough in three columns."

The Wizard was infuriated. "These fools are impudent. I shall have to show them the power of my art!" He ordered his forces to go forward with all speed. They ran straight into the forces of Tang Bin and Geng Gong who were attacking the north gate.

When they heard that two thousand horsemen had appeared in the northwest, Tang and Geng formed their troops up for battle. The Wizard's forces halted and they faced each other, banners waving and drums beating. Between the northerners and the southerners there was but the length of a bowshot. Surrounded by four officers at the head of the northern troops Tang and Geng could see a Taoist on horseback under a red umbrella. A black banner in front of the horse bore two lines of large gold characters, seventeen in all, which said: "Protector of the Land, Holy Sage and Chief Minister for War, Grand Master Qiao the Wizard, leader of the Expedition against the Southerners." Geng Gong exclaimed in alarm: "This fellow is to be feared!" Before they could engage, Iron Ox with his roving patrol of five hundred men happened on the scene and wanted to attack. Geng Gong said: "This is Tian Hu's right hand man and most accomplished fighter. He knows magic, he is truly formidable!"

Iron Ox said: "What good will his fucking magic do him when I've chopped the fucker's head off?"

Tang Bin also said: "Don't underestimate him!" But Iron Ox wasn't listening. Waving his axes he charged forward. Fearing trouble, his companions Pluto, Eight-Armed Ogre and Winged Ghost followed on with five hundred of their shield-bearers. "The fools must learn some manners!" said their antagonist with a devilish laugh. With the utmost composure he took his precious sword and pointed at the sky, muttered a spell and cried out "Chrrr!" Instantly the clear blue sky filled with black clouds and mist, a violent wind got up and sand and dust began to fly. Black murk swallowed up Iron Ox and his five hundred men. It was like being inside a black lacquer box: no glimmer of light, no chance of moving an inch, nothing but the sound of wind and rain. They knew not where they were.

Well, you may be the bravest of the brave, but you can't grow wings and fly away:

Not even the fiery-headed door god

escapes earth's pitfalls, heaven's net;
Nor does the eight-armed nazha *step lightly forth*
from the dragon's pool, the tiger's den!

If you want to hear what became of Iron Ox and his companions in their predicament, you must read the next chapter.

Chapter 95

Song Jiang remains loyal to his lord; Qiao the Wizard wins by magic!

Now Iron Ox had ignored the words of Tang Bin and Geng Gong and led his forces out in an attack and got into difficulties through Wizard Qiao's use of magic and all his force, five hundred or more, had been taken alive, not a single one escaped. Geng Gong, when he saw things were turning out so badly, turned his horse's head eastward and with two cracks of the whip fled the scene. Tang Bin saw Iron Ox and the others caught and their forces scattered and saw Geng Gong flee, so he thought to himself: "This magic of Qiao the Wizard's is powerful stuff. If I'm caught alive I shall be made a mockery. They say that a soldier should value honour more than life. Anyhow, the way things are now it's better to die!" So furiously brandishing his lance he galloped forward in a desperate charge. Qiao the Wizard quickly muttered a spell and cried: "Chrrr!" and among his ranks a cloud of sand rose up and swept down upon Tang Bin. Completely blinded by the sand, Tang Bin was unable to strike a blow. Caught by the enemy and wounded in the left leg he fell from his horse and was taken alive. There was in fact a rule among the northerners that for every officer captured alive the reward was double, so the leaders were never killed. But among Tang Bin's troops — ten thousand of them all lost in the sand — it was a massacre. They were scattered like chaff and the greater part perished.

Leopard's Head and Spearsman at the east gate heard the noise of a great battle south of the city and rushed over there to give support. The city garrison had recognized the Wizard's banner and quickly opened the gates to receive him. Iron Ox and his comrades were also herded into the city.

Geng Gong was now seen fleeing with the remnants of his force. They were galloping flat out, saddles awry, reins flying, helmets skewwhiff. They only pulled up when they saw Leopard's Head and Spearsman. These two asked where the rest of their troops were. Struggling to speak, Geng Gong finally managed to blurt out a couple of words. Leopard's Head took him back to the main camp and on the way they ran into Short-Arse and Steelbright with a patrol of three hundred cavalry. They went together to inform Song Jiang.

Song Jiang was horrified to hear that Iron Ox and the others had been captured. "Iron Ox and his comrades are done for!" he wailed.

The Professor tried to comfort him. "Don't get so upset," he said. "We'll soon put things right. If they've got magic on their side we must send at once to Kettle Pass and fetch the Demon King to fight them."

"We can do that," Song Jiang said, "but at the same time we must go forward and bargain with those bandits for Iron Ox and the others."

The Professor tried in vain to dissuade him. Leaving the Professor in charge of the camp, he set off at once himself at the head of eight of his most trusted commanders and twenty thousand troops heading north to Goodborough. Hasty and Hotshot joined up with them and with banners waving and thundering drums, shouting and banging gongs, they charged up to the city walls.

Meanwhile the Wizard had entered the city and gone to preside in the court room. The ten military commanders reported to him and were about to hold a welcoming party for him when scouts reported the arrival of the Song troops. The Wizard responded angrily to the news: "The effrontery of the bastards!" He said to the garrison commander: "I'm going to go and get that Song Jiang!" He mounted and with four of his lieutenants and three thousand cavalry rode out of the city to encounter the enemy.

The Song troops were drawn up ready for battle when the gates opened and the drawbridge was lowered and a host of cavalry poured out. At their head was the Wizard, his precious sword unsheathed. The two armies, their banners waving, faced each other. Each set up a heavy fire of arrows and crossbow bolts at the opposing ranks. Trumpets blared and drums rolled on either side. From the Song ranks Song Jiang rode forth, with Perilous bearing his standard and his commanders spread out to his right and left. Half choking with indignation he pointed at the Wizard and shouted: "You rebellious brigands. Quickly return my brothers and their troops to me. If you're not quick about it, I shall take you alive and chop you into a thousand pieces!"

The Wizard replied: "Mend your manners, Song Jiang! If I don't choose to give them back, how do you suppose you're going to make me?"

By way of answer Song Jiang pointed with the stock of his whip and his commanders charged *en masse*. The Wizard through clenched teeth growled out his magic spell, pointed west with his sword and shouted "Chrrr!" In an instant countless warriors appeared in the west and bore down on the Song forces. Then the Wizard pointed north with his sword, muttered a magic formula and cried out "Chrrr!" Immediately heaven and earth went dark, the day was obscured, sand flew and stones rolled, earth shook and the heavens rocked. As Leopard's Head and company charged they could see nothing before them but sand and darkness, no sign of an enemy. They were stopped in their tracks. They sat there on their horses, baffled and bewildered. Then Leopard's Head galloped back to protect Song Jiang and flee with him northwards. The Wizard ordered his troops in pursuit. They caught the Song force and cut it to pieces. It was a rout.

Song Jiang and his commanders fled in confusion but they had not covered more than a few hundred yards when something extraordinary happened: the open plain in front of them became an expanse of tossing billows with no visible shore or limit, vast as the great Eastern Ocean. Even had they possessed wings they could not have flown across it. The enemy behind were catching up, evidently death awaited them. Monk, Pilgrim and the Red-Haired Devil cried out: "Surely we're not going to let ourselves be captured!" They tried to turn and charge. Suddenly there was a clap of thunder and up in the sky appeared twenty or

more spirit knights in golden armour who came on with whirling weapons, overwhelming Monk and his friends. The northern troops followed up and took them all prisoner. Then there was a great shout:

"Song Jiang dismount and be tied up if you want to live!"

Song Jiang gazed heavenwards and sighed: "I do not fear death, it is only that I have not yet repaid my Emperor's favour and I leave my old parents without support. Nor can I rescue Iron Ox and my other comrades. But with things as they are all I can do is fight to the death, to avoid being shamed." Leopard's Head and the other six crowded closely about him and said: "We will follow the Leader in suppressing demons and killing bandits!" In these straits Perilous, hit in two places by arrows, still held aloft the Leader's standard and followed in Song Jiang's footsteps never more than a foot behind. The northerners, seeing the Leader's standard still flying, were wary of advancing.

Sword in hand, Song Jiang and his companions thought about killing themselves. But at that moment a figure was seen approaching. It spoke: "Stop. You have nothing to fear. I am the Lord of the Fifth Stem. I have seen your honour and loyalty and I have come to turn back the evil tide and enable you to return to your camp."

It was an astonishing sight. He bore two horns on his head, his body was black, he was naked but for a pair of yellow trousers and in his left hand he held a bell. He bent and picked up a clod of earth and flung it at the towering waves. Instantly the original plain reappeared. "You must suffer a few days of disaster," he said. "But now the water has gone and you must return quickly to your camp and send someone to Weizhou for reinforcements. Make every effort to defend your country!" With this he changed into a whirlwind and disappeared.

Their amazement knew no bounds. Surrounding Song Jiang to protect him, they headed south. After a mile or two they saw a cloud of dust and another squadron of cavalry appeared. It was a force led by the Professor, coming to their assistance. Song Jiang said to him: "I ought to have listened to your advice. I might not have seen you again, ever!"

The Professor said: "You can tell me about it when we get back to the camp."

They entered the camp in good order and then recounted how a god had come to save them in their predicament.

The Professor put a hand to his head and said: "The Lord of the Fifth Stem is the Earth spirit. Your valour must have impressed the Lord of the Earth. Remember, earth conquers water!" Understanding now the manner of their delivery, Song Jiang and his companions gave thanks to heaven.

Now as evening came on some defeated soldiers returned and told how in the confusion they had been attacked by four enemy commanders from Goodborough, who made a sally that killed many and scattered the rest. A count was made and more than ten thousand were found to be missing. The Professor said: "The enemy are using magic. They've already defeated us twice. We must plan quickly and decide how to defend this camp. Our troops are demoralized for the moment. It is only to be expected that these devilish devices, phantom warriors and the like, will sap their resolve. We must vacate the camp and fix up goats to make the drum sound, whilst we make our real camp a few miles off."

Song Jiang gave out the order and the army withdrew to a certain distance. The Professor also told him to create two camps: a smaller one contained within a larger, connected at the corners in a complex six-lobed pattern. These orders were carried out and when it was all set up the arrival of Demon King from Kettle Pass was announced. He went immediately to see Song Jiang and asked for detailed information about the Wizard. Then he said: "Don't worry brother. It is undoubtedly magic. Tomorrow I will make up a spell and capture him."

The Professor said: "If he does not attack tomorrow, I shall sit tight and wait till Taoist Gongsun arrives."

Song Jiang accordingly sent Hotshot, Short-Arse, Snake and Scorpion and five hundred cavalry, with instructions to ride post-haste by night to Weizhou and bring back Taoist Gongsun to rescue them from this enemy. They saddled their horses, bade farewell to Song Jiang and left. The army then set about laying out barricades of deer's antlers and strengthening the stockades; they strung their bows and unsheathed their swords, laid armour and weapons ready to hand and made sure that bells were rung and there was plenty of noise as, candle in hand, they waited for day.

As for the Wizard, having got Song Jiang into serious difficulties with his magic, he was planning to press home the advantage and capture him. When he saw that the water had suddenly disappeared and Song Jiang had slipped away, he was greatly put out. "My magic spell was something quite out of the ordinary, how did he manage to break it? He must have someone really special in his army." He withdrew his troops to the city and held a meeting with his commanders. They prepared a celebratory banquet in his honour, while the Song captives were brought before him. One of the northern commanders standing on the Wizard's left, started berating Tang Bin when he was brought in. "You turncoat, the Prince of Jin has never let you down!"

Tang Bin shouted back: "Your time is up, all of you."

The Wizard ordered them all to speak their names. Iron Ox just glared at him, held his chin up, stuck out his chest and shouted: "Listen here, you sneaky Taoist. I am Iron Ox Li Kui, otherwise known as the Black Whirlwind."

The others, including Monk and Pilgrim, in response to his questions resolutely refused to open their mouths. The Wizard therefore ordered some of their troops to be fetched. They were soon brought in by the sword and axe bearers and after questioning them one by one the Wizard learnt that Iron Ox and his companions were Song commanders. Then he addressed them, saying: "If you agree to surrender and serve our Prince of Jin, you will all be rewarded with high honours."

Iron Ox replied in a voice like thunder: "What do you think I am? Cut out the fucking shit. If you want to chop me up, that's your business. Cut me a hundred times and if I blink you can call me a coward!"

The others also abused the Wizard: "You perverted Taoist! Stop dreaming! You can cut our heads off, but we won't bend a knee, our legs are iron."

Enraged, the Wizard ordered them to be taken away and executed. Monk laughed out loud: "For me to die is like going home. If I die today, I am following the Way." The sword and axe bearers surrounded them as they were taken down. The Wizard thought to himself: "I've never seen such hard men. I'd best leave them be and think about it." He hurriedly ordered his men to untie their hands and guard them closely. Pilgrim began to shout: "Come on, then, you filthy rebels, cut my head off quickly and be done with it!" The Wizard lowered his head and said nothing as his guards escorted them out.

The Wizard had seen his magic water trick fail and he was already anxious in his heart. He remained in the city and waited to see what the Song army would do. Neither side ventured forth. After five or six days two more northern commanders arrived. They reported to the Wizard and their troops were quartered inside the city. When the Wizard saw that the Song troops had fortified themselves in their camp and were not going to attack, he assumed they must have run out of ideas. He mustered a force and with four of his commanders and twenty thousand men left the city at the fifth drumbeat and camped at Five Dragon Mountain, intending to attack at dawn. He said to his second-in-command: "Today we must capture Song Jiang and take back Kettle Pass." The latter replied: "We have confidence in Your Honour's magic art."

The Wizard launched his attack on Song Jiang's camp with ten thousand troops. When the Song scouts got the news they reported it at once to Song Jiang, who ordered Demon King and the Fire and Water Generals to muster their men, saddle their horses and counter-attack.

The Wizard was observing the Song camp from the top of a knoll. He could not help admiring what he saw. The report of a gun was heard from the camp, the gates opened and troops poured out. On either side now many-coloured banners waved, and the heavens shook to the thunder of the drums. The Wizard came down from the knoll and rode out in front of his lines, his commanders on either side of him. On the Song side Demon King rode out through the gate of pennants. Brandishing his trusty sword, he hurled abuse at the Wizard: "You lying Taoist, how dare you give yourself such airs!"

The Wizard thought to himself: "Most likely this fellow knows some magic. Let's try him out." He shouted back: "Curb your tongue, you hopeless loser! Do you dare pit your martial skills against mine?"

Demon King retorted: "If you want a contest, come out and fight!"

The two armies cheered and the drums rolled. Demon King slapped his horse, pointed his sword and charged. The Wizard likewise urged on his horse, waved his sword and galloped to the encounter. Two swords were raised on high, two demons fought. At first it was just two riders locked together in combat; later each brought his supernatural powers into play and it was two spiralling black clouds swaying this way and that between the armies, to and fro and back and forth. The men of both armies watched open-mouthed. Drunk with the fever of battle, Demon King thought he spied an opening and slashed at his opponent. But his sword bit the air and he almost fell off his horse. The Wizard had drawn him on intentionally, inviting the blow while he himself performed the empty dragon skin trick. Back now in front of his troops he guffawed loudly. Demon King retired chastened to his own side.

Next, two passages formed in the Song ranks, to left and right. From the left the Water General stormed out, with five hundred infantry all in black armour with black banners, carrying shields and javelins, pitchforks and sharp swords; from the right the Fire General rode forth with his fire-masters dressed in scarlet, carrying torches, pushing and dragging fifty fire carts loaded with reeds and other incendiary materials. Tied to the back of each man was an iron gourd, filled with gunpowder and five-coloured smoke powder, which they lit simultaneously. These two columns of troops, those on the right enveloped in black smoke, those on the left with fire spiralling up to heaven, came on at pace, striking fear into the hearts of the northerners, who were on the verge of fleeing. The Wizard shouted: "Deserters will be executed!" With his trusty sword in his right hand he muttered a spell and instantly a black cloud covered the earth, a storm broke out and huge hailstones began to pelt the Fire and Water contingents. The storm intensified and their lights were extinguished. The hailstones battered their formation to pieces and frightened the Water General and the Fire General out of their wits. They scuttled back to their own ranks without having had a chance to strike a blow, their pride squashed flat as a pancake.

In a little while the hail ceased and the clouds withdrew and the sky was as blue, the day as bright as before, but the ground was still covered with countless hailstones smooth as a hen's egg and the size of a man's fist. The Wizard could see the enemy — pates cracked, foreheads bloodied, eyes half closed, noses skew-whiff, slipping and sliding all over the place on the ice. He shouted out in stentorian tones: "Do you have anyone else with special abilities?" Whereupon Demon King, shamefacedly advanced, hair dishevelled, waving his sword and desperately mumbling a spell. A violent wind arose in all four quarters blowing sand and rocks about, while there was darkness over the earth and the sun went out. Urging on his men Demon King charged. The Wizard laughed and said: "What can you hope to achieve with this piddling magic of yours?" He too waved his sword and made magic. He muttered a spell and the wind turned on the Song forces driving them back. There was a loud clap of thunder and countless ghost troops and spirit warriors filled the sky and came charging down on the Song forces. Horses whinnied, men screamed, and there was total panic. The Wizard and his four commanders followed up with a murderous charge. Now his magic had failed him, Demon King gave up all attempt at resistance and fled.

As the northerners harried them and the situation became desperate, a beam of golden light appeared in the Song camp. It scattered the sand storm and caused the spirit warriors to fall flat on the ground. Everyone could now see that they were just cutouts of coloured paper. When the Wizard saw his spirit warriors had failed, he concentrated all his magic powers. With hair flying, he waved his sword and recited another spell: a shout of "Chrrr!" and the Magic of the Three Waters was launched.

Within seconds a vast sea of blackness began sweeping in from the north.

Then a gentleman rode forth from the Song ranks. He brandished an ancient sword patterned like a pine tree, recited a spell and cried "Chrrr!". Immediately a host of yellow-robed spirit warriors appeared in the sky and flew northwards. They dispersed the black cloud. The Wizard was stunned.

When they saw the Wizard's magic defeated, the Song forces gave a shout of triumph: "Qiao you evil Wizard, a greater power than yours is at hand!"

The Wizard flushed to the tips of his ears in mortification and retreated to his own ranks.

That mastery of the spirit world the Wizard had striven so hard for now hangs its head and has lost its impetus. Truly it would be as hard to wash out this occasion's shame as to hold the water of three rivers in the hands.

If you want to know who it was in the Song ranks who defeated the black magic, you must read the next chapter.

Chapter 96

The Wizard takes refuge on Five Dragon Mountain; Taoist Gongsun besieges the Hundred Valleys!

Now the person in the Song army called on to defeat the Wizard's black arts was of course Taoist Gongsun. When he received word from Song Jiang in Weizhou, he came rushing back, accompanied by Short-Arse, Hotshot, Snake and Scorpion. He went to see Song Jiang immediately. This was just when the Wizard was using his magic arts to defeat Demon King. It was the eighth day of the second month, designated by the fifth stem and seventh root. Now the fifth stem corresponds to the element "earth", and Taoist Gongsun asked the Lord of the Heavenly Roots and Stems to subdue those northern waters, sweep back the noxious miasma and restore bright day. When he and Song Jiang rode out in front of the troops, they were able to see the Wizard and his army ignominiously fleeing south.

Taoist Gongsun said to Song Jiang: "We've beaten him, but if we let him get back into Goodborough he'll dig in his heels. Quickly, order Spearsman and Hasty to move east to the south gate with five thousand troops to deny them entry. Short-Arse and Blackface can take five thousand to cut him off on the west. Tell them if they encounter the defeated army simply to prevent them from entering the city and not to engage them." Song Jiang gave the necessary orders and his commanders carried them out.

It was just after nine o'clock when Song Jiang and Taoist Gongsun with six other commanders and twenty thousand men began to advance. The northern commander guarding the Wizard, fought a rearguard action. More troops joined them under two other commanders. They had just reached the camp on Five Dragon Mountain when they heard the Song drums and gongs behind them, and the heaven-shattering cheers of the men as they surged forward. One of the Wizard's lieutenants said: "Stay in the camp, Your Honour, while I and my forces engage them in a fight to the death."

Now the Wizard had boasted in front of the whole army. Moreover, in the practice of his magic he had not hitherto met a rival. To find himself now hard pressed by the Song army was a total loss of face. He answered: "No, all of you stand back and let me deal with them." He deployed his troops in a long battle line behind him, with his lieutenants bunched up on the right and left. "You bog-dwelling bandits," he yelled at the Song army. "What gives you the right to throw your weight about like this? I shall have to hand you out another thrashing!" This Wizard, you see, was from Jingyuan in the far northwest, a very long way from Shandong, and he didn't know Song Jiang and his company at all!

Then the Song army, with much waving of banners, lined up for battle. The two armies faced each other: trumpets brayed, drums thundered. The yellow banner of the southerners was flourished, a passage opened among the pennants and two riders appeared. There sat the Shandong Guardian of Righteousness, Song Jiang the Opportune Rain. On his left hand was Dragon in the Clouds Taoist Gongsun, pointing his trusty sword at the Wizard and saying: "What you have learnt is only the external Tao, you have not grasped the true way, quickly dismount and surrender!"

The Wizard looked closely and saw that it was the one who had broken his spells. "Do you really think I would surrender to you, just because my magic went wrong today?" he answered.

"You still dare to talk about that piddling magic of yours?" Taoist Gongsun said.

"If you think yourself so superior you'd better take another look at what I can do!" the Wizard shouted back. He summoned up all his powers and pronounced a magic formula. He pointed at his lieutenant, whereupon the latter's spear was snatched as if by an invisible hand, wafted through the air like a flying serpent and directed down at Taoist Gongsun's head. Taoist Gongsun pointed his sword at Thunderclap and the latter's wolf-tooth mace rose out of his hand and parried the spear, darting this way, that way, through the air, as if controlled by the wind. Both armies watched in silent amazement. With a loud crash, and an answering shout from the onlooking troops, the shaft of the mace met the spear and knocked it out of the air. It landed with a resonant thud on the northerners' war drum, splitting its skin. The soldier carrying the drum turned white as a sheet. Next thing, the mace was back in its owner's hand, as if it had never left it. The Song soldiers laughed till the eyes disappeared in their faces. Taoist Gongsun shouted: "So you think you can fool around with weapons in front of the master, do you?"

The Wizard responded by conjuring up another spell: he pointed to the north and shouted "Chrrr!". Immediately a black cloud gushed from Five Dragon Mountain behind their camp, and in the midst of it a black dragon with huge scales and billowing mane. As it flew towards them Taoist Gongsun emitted a loud guffaw and also pointed to Five Dragon Mountain. Out shot a yellow dragon, at the speed of lightning, something between cloud and mist in form. It flew at the black dragon and there in the sky they began to fight. "Come forth, green dragon!" the Wizard now shouted and a green dragon raced out from the mountain, but after it came a white dragon opposing it. The armies watched the contest open-mouthed. The Wizard whirled his sword and shouted: "Quickly, red dragon, to the rescue!" Instantly a red dragon appeared and came swirling down. There in the sky the five dragons wove to and fro and it was just as the five elements, metal, wood, water, fire and earth, interact with and counter each other, within a single mass. A violent wind arose and several dozen of the standard bearers in either army were bowled over by its force. Taoist Gongsun transferred the sword to his left hand and with his right tossed his deer whisk into the air, where it performed a somersault and became a great bird like a wild goose and flew off. In seconds it waxed and grew till it reached to the ninth heaven when it turned into a giant roc hovering in the sky like a black cloud before stooping on the dragons. With a splitting sound like thunder the dragons burst asunder, scattering scales and talons in all directions.

You see, this Five Dragon Mountain was a sacred place, where five-coloured clouds were often seen. The dragon god appeared to men in their dreams there, so a temple had been built, within which was displayed an ancestral tablet of the Dragon Lord and the green, yellow, red, black and white dragons of the five directions, formed from clay, gilded and painted in bright colours, were to be seen winding up the corresponding sides of a pillar. The two men had used magic to make these dragons fight as their representatives, and then the big roc Taoist Gongsun had fashioned out of his whisk smashed the five dragons to pieces and the shards rained down on the heads of the northern troops. The soldiers screamed in panic and could find no shelter from those ancient hardened chunks of pottery which left them black and blue and bleeding heavily. In a short space of time more than two hundred were injured and fled. The Wizard found he was bereft of his powers and could do nothing about it. A yellow ceramic dragon's tail falling on him from the heavens nearly cracked his skull and squashed his Taoist cap. Taoist Gongsun pointed once more and the roc softly vanished and the whisk was back in his hand again. When the Wizard made to produce more magic, Taoist Gongsun worked his Five Thunders magic. From his head sprang a yellow-turbaned spirit warrior who shouted: "Get off your horse and surrender, Wizard!" The Wizard tried a spell, but it had no effect whatsoever. Flabbergasted by his powerlessness, the Wizard slapped his horse and fled back to his own ranks.

Leopard's Head now let his horse go, whirled his spear and gave chase, shouting: "Stop, you evil sorcerer!" Two of the northern commanders rode out with readied weapons to stop him and Spots rode to support him. They fought it out in two pairs out in the middle to the cheers of the two armies. Leopard's Head fought more than twenty bouts with his opponent and neither could gain an advantage till Leopard's Head spotted an opening and lunged at the legs of his adversary's horse. The horse fell and Leopard's Head thrust his lance into the other's chest, killing him. The second northerner, at the height of his contest with Spots, saw his comrade fall, dodged aside and galloped off. Spots gave chase and brought his iron club down on the man's head, smashing both helmet and skull, so he fell dead from his horse. Song Jiang pointed with the stock of his whip and the Gardener, Green-Eyes, Steelbright and Auntie Gu charged together. The northerners fled in disarray and there was great slaughter.

The Wizard, surrounded by four of his commanders, now abandoned the camp at Five Dragon Mountain and headed for Goodborough. They had passed the mountain and were only about two or three miles from the city when the sound of a war drum erupted ahead of them and with loud cheers a lively body of men poured out of a small path on the east, led by Spearsman and Hasty. Before the two sides had engaged the two commanders guarding Goodborough saw fighting outside the town and led a sortie from the south gate with five thousand troops. Spearsman and Hasty separated their forces to take them on. Hasty went one way with two thousand troops and his opponent resisted for a dozen bouts before Hasty, furiously wielding his axe, chopped him in two. The second northern commander hurriedly retreated into the town. Hasty galloped in pursuit and killed a hundred northerners, but had to stop when he reached the south gate because the enemy were safely inside and had raised the drawbridge and barred the gates. When wooden blocks and ballista missiles began to rain down from the walls, he was obliged to withdraw.

Meanwhile Spearsman with three thousand men remained to block off the retreat of the main northern army. In spite of having lost one battle the northerners at this point still had twenty thousand men to oppose Spearsman. But two of the commanders had no stomach for the fight and fled westwards with five thousand cavalry escorting the Wizard. The remaining two encircled Spearsman who was greatly outnumbered, until Hasty and Song Jiang arrived from south and north. The northerners could not hold out against attacks from three sides. One of the leaders, wounded in the left shoulder by a thrust from Spearsman, fell from his horse and was trampled into the mud. The other tried to flee but was caught by Hotshot, whose spear transfixed him from the back and brought him crashing to the ground. In the ensuing rout most of the thirty thousand were killed. Corpses littered the fields and blood ran in rivers. Drums, trumpets, banners, helmets and armour were captured, horses were abandoned in countless numbers. The survivors scattered in all directions.

Song Jiang's combined forces now numbered twenty-five thousand. They heard that the Wizard and his two commanders were fleeing north with five thousand and would have set off in pursuit, but it was late afternoon and the troops after battling furiously all day were hungry and exhausted. Song Jiang was about to recall them and return to camp for food and rest, and was pleased to hear that the Professor knowing how long and hard they had fought, had ordered Demon King and the Fire and Water Generals to come to their assistance with twenty thousand troops, equipped with torches and flares. Taoist Gongsun said to Song Jiang: "Now we've got reinforcements, you and the army go back to camp to rest and eat while I and the other three continue the pursuit. It is imperative that we get their Wizard to surrender."

Song Jiang said: "It is thanks to your powers that we have escaped disaster. After your unflagging efforts you should come back to the camp with us and rest. We can finish things off tomorrow. The Wizard is a broken reed; we've nothing more to fear from him."

Taoist Gongsun said: "There is something you should know, brother. My old teacher, the Great Sage, said these words to me many times: 'In Jingyuan there is someone they call the Wizard, who knows the rudiments of Taoism and came to me as a seeker after the Way. Initially I rejected him, because of a certain devilish spirit in him, because he had a base nature with a propensity to evil and because the time was not ripe. Latterly the evil of his nature has been in retreat: a happier destiny has superseded and he has turned to virtue. If haply his path crosses yours, you can reform him and once equipped with my mystic powers there will be profit from him in times to come.' On the way here from Weizhou, in obedience to your orders, I made some inquiries about this enemy with magic powers, and Marshal Zhang told me that the general who surrendered to you, Geng Gong, knows him well. Apparently he is that same Wizard my master spoke of. We have already seen that his magic is on a par with mine. It's only with the Five Thunders method, imparted to me by the Great Sage, that I was able to overcome him. This district is called *Good*borough, which fits in with my teacher's verse: 'Turn to *good* and beat the devils.' If we allow him to escape, most likely he will go to perdition and my master's mantra will not be fulfilled. This opportunity must not be lost. That is why I must continue the pursuit and find a way to make him surrender."

This long speech made all clear to Song Jiang and he was full of gratitude. With the rest of the leaders and troops he withdrew to the camp for food and rest, while Taoist Gongsun with Demon King and the Fire and Water Generals and ten thousand troops pursued the Wizard as proposed.

Meanwhile the Wizard and his two commanders with the remnants of their army, some five thousand men all told, had approached Goodborough from the west. They were heading for the west gate when suddenly drums and trumpets sounded and a fierce squadron of cavalry emerged from behind a thick wood and charged. At its head were Short-Arse and Blackface. They rapidly deployed their five hundred men and blocked his way to the city. The Wizard's two lieutenants led a desperate charge. Their opponents, in accordance with Taoist Gongsun's orders, made sure they could not enter the city but did not actively engage them either and let them get away to the north. The defenders of the city had heard that the Wizard's magic had failed him, that he had suffered defeat and that the Song forces were strong. They were anxious about their defences and reinforced all the gates. They made no attempt to open them and come to their leader's assistance.

Not long after this Blackface and Short-Arse were joined by Taoist Gongsun and his forces. "You two had better go back to the main camp for rest and food," he told them. "I am going to continue the pursuit." They did as told.

It was late afternoon. The Wizard and his companions were hurrying north, like dogs kicked out of the house or fish escaped from the net, with Gongsun and his commanders in hot pursuit.

Taoist Gongsun shouted after them: "Dismount and surrender, it's futile to resist!"

The Wizard shouted back: "Everyone must serve his own master, why do you seek my destruction?"

Dusk had already fallen. The Song troops had lit torches and flares which illuminated the scene as brightly as day. When the Wizard looked about him, he could only see his two commanders and about thirty troopers. The remainder of his force had fled in all directions. He was about to draw his sword and kill himself but one of his lieutenants stayed his arm and said: "You must not do it, Your Honour." He pointed to the mountains which lay ahead of them and said: "We can take refuge up there." The Wizard, at the limit of his powers, followed his two commanders into the mountains. Now, north east of Goodborough was a mountain range called the Hundred Valleys, a spot where the legendary emperor, Shennong, inventor of agriculture, used to test the crops. There was a place there known as Shennong's Temple. This is where the Wizard and his companions set up camp. There were now only some fifteen men with them. The reason why Taoist Gongsun had allowed him to escape into the mountains was that he wanted to force his surrender. If the Song force had caught him they would have killed him, even if there had been not one but five thousand of him. But enough of this. Suffice to say that after allowing him to escape into the mountains Taoist Gongsun divided his men into four sections and posted them on all sides of the Hundred Valleys. In the second watch a host of torches appeared, one lot on the east and another on the west. This was because Song Jiang on returning to base had ordered Leopard's Head and Hotshot out on patrol that night, each with five thousand men. When they joined up with Taoist Gongsun it made a force of twenty thousand in two camps. They had the Wizard thoroughly surrounded, as you can imagine.

When Song Jiang heard next day that Taoist Gongsun had got the Wizard and his forces bottled up in the Hundred Valleys, he made plans with the Professor to attack Goodborough. Orders were given to strike camp and march on the city. But the surrounding water had still not drained away. The defenders of the city had strengthened the moat and after two days it still had not fallen. In his camp south of the city Song Jiang was depressed at the failure. Since the day Iron Ox and his companions were taken prisoner nothing had been heard of their condition and Song Jiang's heart bled for them.

The Professor sought to comfort him: "Stop worrying, brother. The city should fall into our hands for the mere cost of a few pieces of paper."

"What is your idea?" Song Jiang asked eagerly.

Calmly the Professor placed two fingers together and expounded his plan. It was to have important results.

Without bloodshed the city will fall,
Soldiers surrender their weapons, the people be at peace.

If you want to know what the Professor said, you must read the next chapter.

Chapter 97

❦

Commissioner Chen takes over the administration; Princess Jade Arrowtip becomes a leader of men!

Then the Professor said to Song Jiang: "The garrison of the city are weak and vulnerable. Previously they relied on the Wizard's magic. Now he has been defeated and they know they are not going to be relieved; they are bound to be scared. I had a look early this morning from an observation platform and the guards on the walls look demoralized. Now we can take advantage of their distress to open up a new route. Tomorrow the seriousness of their predicament will induce them to surrender and the city will fall into our hands without any bloodshed at all."

Song Jiang was delighted with this: "Your counsel is always invaluable, Professor," he said. After their deliberations, a dozen or so copies of a military dispatch were produced. It read as follows:

Song Jiang, Commander-in-Chief of the Imperial Pacification Expedition to the North
to
The garrison commanders and the citizens of Goodborough:

Tian Hu's crime of rebellion is subject to the full penalty of the law, but his allies and accomplices may be excused. If garrison commanders repent of their errors and return to the right path, and having resolved to turn over a new leaf order their troops and people to open the gates and surrender, I will vouchsafe to petition the Emperor for a pardon. If your commanders remain obdurate, then all and sundry, both the military and civilians, must, as the Emperor's loyal subjects, do what is right by over-powering the military commanders and reinstating allegiance

> *to the Emperor. The leaders will be richly rewarded and may expect honours and rank. If you persist in error or shirk your duty the city will be taken and not a stone will be left standing nor a single person alive. This is our word.*

Song Jiang gave orders for this proclamation to be attached to the heads of arrows that were fired into the city from all sides. He ordered the commanders attacking the gates to relax the pressure and observe developments within. Next day at dawn a huge outcry was heard in the city, following which flags of surrender were raised on all the gates. Two junior officers of the garrison had killed the three commanders and their heads were displayed on poles as a sign to the Song army. Iron Ox and the others were released from the gaol and mounted in sedans; the gates were thrown open and they were escorted triumphantly out of the city. The people then lit incense and candles to welcome the army. Song Jiang ordered the commanders of all units to form up their troops and march in good order into the city. Not a blow had been struck, not a soul had been harmed and the populace expressed their joy vociferously.

Once Song Jiang was ensconced in the government offices, Iron Ox and his companions entered and said: "We had almost given up hope brother! It is only because of you we are able to meet again. It is like a dream!"

Song Jiang and the others wept tears of relief. Later the leaders of the uprising came forward and prostrated themselves. Song Jiang hurriedly returned the compliment and raised them up saying: "You have done the proper thing, your lives are secure. There is no need for this ceremony."

They replied: "Immediate surrender was our only chance to escape punishment. Your graciousness is engraved on our hearts, we owe you our lives." They also gave a full account of how Monk, Iron Ox and the others had never faltered but had steadfastly abused their captors. Song Jiang was moved to tears of admiration.

Iron Ox said: "They tell me that lousy bugger is holed up over in Hundred Valleys. Let me go and chop the fucker up, to relieve my fucking feelings."

Song Jiang said: "Taoist Gongsun and his men have got the Wizard penned in there, because he wants him to surrender. It's something to do with a mantra of the Great Sage's. So hold your horses!"

Monk said to Iron Ox: "Listen to the Leader's orders! You must!" So Iron Ox desisted.

Song Jiang now issued a proclamation to allay the people's fears, rewarded the army commanders and had the exploits of Taoist Gongsun and the leaders of the uprising recorded. He was busy with military matters when it was reported that the Magic Messenger had returned. As soon as he entered Song Jiang asked him the news from Jinning.

Magic Messenger reported as follows: "I went to Jinning as you ordered and found the Unicorn attacking the city. He said to me: 'Wait till I've got the better of this lot, and then you can go back and tell our Leader the good news.' He kept me there three or four days, but Jinning simply would not fall. Then one evening on the sixth of this month there was a thick fog, so thick you couldn't see in front of your nose, and the Unicorn ordered his men to place sandbags surreptitiously under the walls. Around midnight, when the sentries on the northeast had grown careless, our troops crept up by means of the sand bags onto the city walls and killed a number of guards. Tian Biao fled via the north gate. His remaining commanders surrendered. More than five thousand war horses were taken and over twenty thousand troops gave themselves up. A considerable number were killed.

"The Unicorn now had control of Jinning. When daylight came the mist lifted. As the pacification process was proceeding it was suddenly reported that Tian Hu's deputy chancellor Sun An and ten lieutenants had arrived on the scene with a relief force of twenty thousand and had taken up a position only a few miles from the city. The Unicorn ordered Thunderclap and three others out to oppose the Chancellor and himself led the reserves. Thunderclap and the Chancellor fought sixty bouts but it was a stalemate. When the Unicorn arrived with his troops, he was impressed by the Chancellor's valour and ordered the gongs sounded to break off the fight. The Chancellor did likewise and everyone returned to camp.

"The Unicorn told everyone that such a brave antagonist would have to be defeated by guile, not force. Next day he laid an ambush and then rode forth himself to challenge the Chancellor. When they had fought some fifty bouts the Chancellor's horse suddenly stumbled and threw him. 'That does not count,' the Unicorn shouted to him. 'Quickly, get yourself a new mount!' The Chancellor found himself a new horse and they fought another fifty bouts. Then Unicorn feigned defeat and galloped off luring his opponent towards the edge of a wood. A report rang out and from either side the troops who had been waiting in ambush rushed out. The Chancellor had no time to act: his horse stumbled on the trip wires and the troops rushed up and seized both man and horse. Three other northern commanders dashed to the rescue, but were halted by the Blue-Faced Beast, Golden Wings and Redeye. As they fought it out, three pairs of riders, the Blue-Faced Beast gave a sudden cry and lunged with his spear, knocking his opponent from his horse. Golden Wings tricked his adversary into thrusting with his sword and dodged aside so that the blow hit only the air, and before he could recover Golden Wings' spear had pierced his heart. The third northern commander, seeing his two comrades fall, slapped his horse and galloped back towards his own ranks. But Redeye gave chase and brought his axe down on his head, smashing both the helmet and the skull inside. The Unicorn now urged his troops forward and the northerners were routed. Four or five thousand were killed and the rest ran three miles or more before making camp.

"Our troops returned victorious to the city. Some of them brought in the Chancellor, bound hand and foot. The Unicorn personally released his bonds and received him with the utmost courtesy, urging him to renew his allegiance to the Emperor. When he found the Unicorn's treatment so honourable, the Chancellor was willing enough to cooperate. He said to the Unicorn: 'There are still seven commanders and fifteen thousand troops at large. Will you allow me to go and negotiate their surrender?' The Unicorn could see no objection to this. The Chancellor rode by himself to the northern camp and talked the seven into surrendering. The Unicorn was delighted to see them and entertained them with wine. The Chancellor said: 'I marched out of Weisheng at the same time as the Wizard, who headed off to relieve Kettle Pass. This fellow has magic powers. I am afraid General Song may have some trouble with him. The Wizard and I are fellow countrymen. On account of your generosity towards me I would like to go to Kettle Pass and find out what is going on. I will try to persuade the Wizard to surrender.' The Unicorn gave his consent and sent me along with the Chancellor to report the victory. He told off the Son-in-Law and three others with twenty thousand troops to reinforce the garrison at Jinning. He is taking the remainder to attack Fenyang. We left only yesterday but I let the Chancellor do the magic walking with me. Today on the road I learnt that you were besieging Goodborough and that you had the Wizard surrounded. Just before we got here I heard that you had taken the city so I came here at once. The Chancellor is waiting outside."

Song Jiang was very pleased and told Magic Messenger to show the Chancellor in.

When the latter entered, Song Jiang saw it was someone quite out of the ordinary, of noble mien and dignified bearing. He came down to welcome him.

"I deserve a thousand deaths for opposing you." The Chancellor said, kowtowing respectfully.

Song Jiang returned his greeting and insisted: "You have changed your ways and returned to the right path, help me to subdue Tian Hu and when we return we will petition the court. You are sure to be rewarded with office." The Chancellor thanked him and stood up. Song Jiang bade him be seated and poured wine for him.

"The Wizard's magic is dangerous," he said. "It is fortunate that Taoist Gongsun was able to defeat it."

"Taoist Gongsun wants him to surrender, so he can put him back on the right track," said Song Jiang. "He has been holed up there for three or four days, but he still shows no sign of surrendering."

"We are good friends," said the other. "I must go and tell him to surrender."

Song Jiang sent him off by the north gate with Magic Messenger to Taoist Gongsun's camp. When the Chancellor explained his intentions, Taoist Gongsun was pleased and gave him permission to climb the mountain and seek out the Wizard. He rode off up the mountain alone.

The Wizard, remember, was hiding out with the two commanders and fifteen soldiers in the Shennong temple where they survived by sharing the Taoists' vegetarian food. There were only three Taoists at the temple and the Wizard and his party had soon eaten up all the food it had taken them months to collect from the faithful, but since they were outnumbered they had to put up with it. The Wizard heard the hubbub that day in the city below and climbed a ridge to see what was going on. When he saw soldiers all round outside the walls and people coming and going through the gates, he knew it had already fallen to Song Jiang. As he was lamenting this, he noticed a woodcutter emerge from a wood on the hillside below, with an axe stuck through his belt and a staff over his shoulder. Slowly and deliberately the man wended his way up the mountainside, singing to himself:

On the way up: hauling a boat.
On the way down: go with the flow.
Hauling a boat: nowt but a chore.
Go with the flow: please thyself.
On the way up is not so bad:
Get to the top, 'tis all the way down.

As he listened to this little woodcutter's ditty, the Wizard felt uncertain. "Do you know what the news is of the city?" he asked the man.

"The deputy governor has been killed by his two subordinates and the city has gone over to the Song," the man replied. "Song Jiang's force captured it without striking a blow."

"So that's the way it is," said the Wizard. The woodcutter completed his ascent and having reached the top headed off round the shoulder of the hill. A man on horseback now appeared, also

making his way up the hill towards the temple. The Wizard was surprised to recognize Chancellor Sun An. What was he doing here? The Chancellor dismounted and made obeisance. "You were leading the relief column to Jinning, Chancellor," the Wizard said. "Why are you here on your own? It's swarming with troops down there. Why did they let you through?"

"Let me explain, brother ..." the Chancellor said. Noticing that the Chancellor failed to address him as Lord Protector, the Wizard realized something was wrong. "Let us go into the temple," the Chancellor said, "and I will tell you everything."

After the Wizard's two commanders had been introduced, the Chancellor recounted the fall of Jinning. The Wizard was struck speechless. "Do not be mistrustful, brother," the Chancellor said. "General Song is completely just, and if we enter his service and renew our allegiance to the Emperor, we will not be losers by it. I have come here to find you. Did you not once seek knowledge from the Great Sage?"

"How did you know about that?" the Wizard asked.

"The Great Sage would not receive you and sent an acolyte to tell you that you should 'Turn to good and beat the demons', am I right?"

"Yes, yes," the Wizard replied eagerly.

"Do you know who it was who broke the power of your magic?" the Chancellor asked.

"My adversary! I only know that he is one of Song Jiang's people. I know nothing of his background."

"He is the Great Sage's disciple, his name is Gongsun Sheng and he is one of Song Jiang's deputies. It was he who explained that mantra to me. This place is called Zhaode or Goodborough. Don't you see how the collapse of your magic power accords with the saying: 'Turn to good and beat the demons'? Gongsun Sheng has the Great Sage's injunction to reform you and set you back on the right path. That is why he has you surrounded here but has not come up to capture you. He has the means to overcome you and if he wished you harm what would stop him? Please see the truth."

These words effected in the Wizard a great awakening and

with his lieutenants he duly accompanied the Chancellor down the mountain to where Taoist Gongsun was camped.

When the Chancellor announced him, Taoist Gongsun came out to welcome him into the camp. The Wizard prostrated himself and asked for pardon: "You show me such mercy as I do not deserve. After the trouble I have given you, it makes my guilt even greater."

Taoist Gongsun returned his greeting with alacrity and entertained him warmly. Seeing the other treated him so honourably, the Wizard said: "I was blind not to recognize a good man. If I am permitted to serve you I shall be happy all my life."

Taoist Gongsun now called off the siege and his commanders on all sides packed up and followed him back into the city. Song Jiang also received them most courteously and spoke conciliatory words. The Wizard, seeing Song Jiang's friendliness, was even more pleased. The other Song commanders arrived and Song Jiang ordered them all to be quartered inside the city. Wine was served in celebration. During the banquet, Taoist Gongsun said to the Wizard: "This magic of yours, at the highest level it can't compare with the Nirvana that the Boddhisattvas for aeons past attest to, the sense of being at home in mystic knowledge. And at the ordinary level it's no more than what the thirty-six immortals of Fairyland can achieve when years of exercises have enabled them to practise the art of metamorphosis, transcending the world of appearances and knowing the joy of creation. All you've got is a few borrowed spells which allow you to usurp natural powers and call ghosts and spirits to your aid, what in Buddhism they call sorcery and in Taoism we call necromancy. If you think this knowledge will enable you to transcend the mundane and achieve pure spirituality, what a huge error that is!"

When he heard all this the Wizard felt as if he had woken from a dream. He prostrated himself before Taoist Gongsun and called him master. The others too after listening to the Taoist's explanation of these secret mysteries were awed by his spiritual prowess. Finally the party broke up and they all went to bed. The night was uneventful.

Next day Song Jiang told Magic Hand to write out a report informing the court of the capture of Jinning and Goodborough and requesting Marshal Su to appoint officials to fill the vacant posts in the six captured cities as quickly as possible so the rest of them could get on with the campaign. As soon as this document had been satisfactorily drafted it was entrusted to Magic Messenger to deliver, with orders to start at once.

Magic Messenger packed his bags, chose a fleet-footed orderly to accompany him, bade farewell to Song Jiang and with his magic walking reached the Eastern Capital next day. He went straight to Marshal Su's palace to hand in the report and was lucky enough to catch the Marshal in his office. He spoke to one major-domo Yang, to whom he gave some small monetary gifts, asking him to see that the report reached the Marshal. Yang took it in and a few minutes later returned to say: "The Marshal orders you to attend on him." Magic Messenger followed him inside. He found the Marshal ensconced on his throne reading the report. When Magic Messenger had paid his respects the Marshal said: "This is a critical juncture and your arrival is most timely. The other day the Grand Preceptor and his gang in the presence of the Emperor brought accusations against your leader of incurring heavy losses of commanders and men, betraying public trust and shaming the country. They launched this campaign of defamation to persuade the Emperor to impose heavy penalties. The Emperor prevaricated. Then Deputy Chief Minister Chen memorialized him, accusing the Grand Preceptor and company of making false accusations against good men and picking on the innocent. He said that you had broken through Kettle Pass and asked for your accusers to be punished for bearing false witness. This only made the Grand Preceptor more determined to secure Chen's downfall. Yesterday he told the Emperor that Chen was author of a slanderous book, *In Praise of Yao*: Yao was supposed to represent the Emperor Shenzong and in some way this implied a criticism of himself. He wanted Chen punished for slander. Fortunately the Emperor has not yet pronounced judgement. This report of victory you bring will not only save Chen's bacon but also take a lot of pressure off me. I shall report this at tomorrow's dawn court." Magic Messenger thanked him and went to find somewhere to rest and await the outcome. Of this no more.

Next morning Marshal Su attended the dawn court, which was held in the Hall of Culture and Ethics. Immediately after the acclamation, Marshal Su announced Song Jiang's victories and told how he was in hot pursuit of Tian Hu and had won control of six provinces, as reported by a messenger who had just arrived from him. His Majesty expressed his complete satisfaction. Marshal Su also said: "As for the accusation that Deputy Chief Minister Chen wrote *In Praise of Yao* to represent the former emperor as Yao and Your Majesty as Shun, since when was praising Yao a crime? Minister Chen is honest and straightforward. He deals with affairs in a forthright manner and is brave and resourceful. I request that he be promoted and sent to Hebei to oversee the army. He is sure to achieve good results." The Emperor gave his consent and issued a proclamation saying: "Minister Chen is hereby promoted to Marshal and entrusted with the Northern Pacification Campaign. Imperial Commissioner Chen is to proceed with twenty thousand imperial guards to Song Jiang's headquarters to take over the running of the campaign. He is to take silver to pay them and reward commanders and men."

The court broke up and Marshal Su returned to his residence and summoned Magic Messenger to receive the reply. Magic Messenger after learning the outcome bade the Marshal farewell, and left the capital. Doing his magic walking he reached Goodborough next day. The whole trip had only taken him four days.

Song Jiang was busy arranging his forces and discussing the next campaign. When Magic Messenger returned he asked at once for news of the mission. Magic Messenger delivered Marshal Su's reply. When he had read it Song Jiang gave a full account to the other leaders. They all said: "That Commissioner Chen's a brave man! We'd better not just sit here twiddling our thumbs!" Song Jiang announced that the next attack would start as soon as they received the imperial edict. They all took note and remained in their quarters in the city. Of this no more.

Now north of Goodborough in the same province was the

town of Lu. When Chi Fang, commander of the garrison there, heard that the Wizard was cut off, he sent a messenger to Weisheng by night with an urgent report for Tian Hu. The head of Tian Hu's bogus administration received it and was just about to take it in when the news suddenly broke that Jinning had fallen and that Third Prince Tian Biao was fleeing for his life. Hard on the heels of this news came the arrival of Tian Biao himself.

The Third Prince went in with the minister and prostrated himself before Tian Hu. He broke out into a loud wailing: "The Song army are too strong. They have captured Jinning and killed my son. I only just managed to escape. I have betrayed the trust you placed in me. I deserve a million deaths!"

The Third Prince continued to weep as the minister also reported his news: "I have also received a report from the commander of Lu saying that the Wizard is cut off by the Song forces and the fall of Goodborough is imminent."

Tian Hu hastily summoned all his officials, including the president, the vice-president and the army commander to discuss the situation. "Song Jiang has violated our borders, seized two of our main cities, killed many of our troops and is presently besieging the Wizard, what are you all going to do about it?"

At this point the Royal Brother-in-Law Wu Li spoke out: "There's no need to worry Your Majesty! I know my duty to my country, I shall raise an army and set off for Goodborough and in short order capture that Song Jiang and his rabble, and restore the cities to your rule."

This Royal Brother-in-Law was originally just a rich man of Weisheng. He was profoundly skilled in the use of spear and staff and immensely strong. He was a good shot too with the bow and wielded a fifty catty wind-splitter of a sword. Tian Hu was captivated by the beauty of his young sister and married her. He subsequently made the brother Grand Marshal, with the title "Royal Brother-in-Law".

The Royal Brother-in-Law went on: "My daughter Qiongying recently dreamt that a spiritual being had instructed her in the martial arts. When she awoke she found she was endowed with outstanding strength. Not only is her martial skill exceptional but she also has another miraculous talent. She can throw a stone and kill a bird ten times out of ten. People have taken to calling her 'Jade Arrowtip' I shall make her commander of my vanguard and I am confident she will achieve great things."

After the Emperor had confirmed their appointment and the Royal Brother-in-Law had thanked him, army commander Ma Ling announced: "I would like to lead a force against the enemy at Fenyang."

Tian Hu was pleased and granted him a seal and a general's banner, as well as jewelry. The Royal Brother-in-Law and Ma Ling each received thirty thousand troops and rapidly prepared to march.

We shall say nothing of Ma Ling and his force as they march towards Fenyang, but turn our attention to the Royal Brother-in-Law as, armed with the King's commission, he goes down to the parade ground to select thirty thousand troops, and organize arms and equipment for them. Returning to his residence he gave his daughter her orders as leader of the vanguard, took leave of Tian Hu and mustered his troops for the march.

So Jade Arrowtip under her father's command marched on Goodborough. The intervention of this woman warrior was to have consequences.

A chaste maid feels hatred beyond endurance;
A hero discovers the joys of matrimony.

If you want to hear what happened when the woman warrior went into battle, you must read the next chapter.

Chapter 98

Hotshot meets his destined bride; The Professor plans to poison the Royal Brother-in-Law!

The Royal Brother-in-Law has made his daughter Jade Arrowtip commander of the vanguard and is himself following on behind with the main army.

The girl was just sixteen, a lass beautiful as a flower. She was not his real daughter. Her original name was Qiu and she was the daughter of a man called Qiu Shen. Her home was in a little Fenyang village called Flossdown. This incidentally was the same Flossdown that was famous in the days of Duke Jin of the Spring and Autumn period. Her father, who was quite a rich man, attained the age of fifty without having a male heir. Happening to lose his wife, he took a second wife — a girl from another village — and she gave birth to Jade Arrowtip. When the girl was ten, her grandfather passed away and her mother had to go back to her native village with her husband Qiu Shen for the funeral. This village was in the next district, more than twenty miles away. Since it was so far, they were obliged to leave the child behind in the care of their butler Ye Qing and his wife. When they were half way there, a band of robbers suddenly materialized and killed the husband, scattered the retainers and kidnapped the wife. The retainers made their way back and told the butler, Ye Qing, what had happened.

Now although this Ye Qing was only in service, he was what could be called a man of honour and knew something of spear and staff play. His wife besides was a sensible woman. When Butler Ye Qing told his employer's relatives, the latter appealed to the police to catch the robbers and buried the body. But the Qius' only real concern was to secure the inheritance for one of their own, and the butler and his wife were left to take care of their young mistress.

A year or more later when Tian Hu's rebellion broke out, he seized Weisheng and sent out the Royal Brother-in-Law to plunder. When the latter got to Flossdown and started grabbing all the riches and kidnapping men and women, the Qiu heir was killed by Tian Hu's rebels and Butler Ye Qing and his wife together with Jade Arrowtip were all seized.

Now the Royal Brother-in-Law had no children. Struck by Jade Arrowtip's beauty he took her to show to his wife, whose name was Ni. Never having had a child of her own, Mistress Ni loved Jade Arrowtip at first sight and treated her as a daughter. From the start Arrowtip was extremely clever and had a hundred pretty wiles. Realizing she could not run away, since she had no relatives to turn to, and knowing Mistress Ni loved her, she persuaded her adoptive father to take Butler Ye Qing's wife An into his employ. As a result the butler's wife and Arrowtip were inseparable.

When he was first arrested, Butler Ye Qing had thought about escaping. But Arrowtip was still young and he and his wife were virtually all she had left in the world, and he realized that if he ran away there was no knowing what would become of her. It was fortunate his wife was there for her and if the opportunity presented itself he would try to get them all to safety. His master had met his end, he was no more. Then there was nothing for it but to serve the Royal Brother-in-Law.

After a successful campaign the Royal Brother-in-Law gave Butler Ye Qing his wife back, but she continued to come and go in the governor's residence and report the news to Jade Arrowtip. The Royal Brother-in-Law petitioned Tian Hu and Butler Ye Qing was given an official position.

Later the Butler was sent by the Royal Brother-in-Law to the Stonehouse Hills to fetch timber and stones. A member of his military escort pointed at the cliffs and said: "There is some beautiful rock there that is white as snow, absolutely flawless. The local inhabitants tried to carry it off and there was a tremendous clap of thunder and some of those who were trying to take it fainted from terror and did not come to for quite a while. Now they all bite their fingers and pray and daren't go near it."

When the Butler went with them to look, everyone cried out in amazement: "How extraordinary! Before it was just a block of white stone, now it's turned into a woman's body!"

The Butler went up to it and had a good look. Truly it was extraordinary. It was the body of his late mistress. The face was quite unharmed, but the skull was shattered, as if she had fallen off the cliff. He shed tears of horror and amazement, but this was not the time or place for explanation.

At this point a soldier stepped forward: he had been one of Tian Hu's grooms and he gave a detailed account of Mistress Song's capture and death. "It was back in the first days of the Prince's rebellion, in a place called Jiexiu, that he kidnapped this woman, intending to make her his concubine. She persuaded him to free her from her bonds. When they got here she threw herself down from the top of the cliff and died. Seeing she was dead, the king told me to strip off her clothes and jewellery. I actually lifted her onto my horse and took off her clothes, I got a very good look at her face, there can be absolutely no doubt that it's her. That was over three years ago, and the body is still in perfect condition."

The Butler wept copiously at this tale. Turning to the soldier he said: "I recognize her too. It's Mistress Song, the daughter of my neighbour." He ordered the soldiers to bury the body, and lo and behold, it was a block of white stone again. Everyone was full of wonder as they went off to complete their business fetching stone. When the Butler returned to Weisheng he told his wife how Tian Hu had kidnapped Mistress Song and how she had killed herself to preserve her chastity. He asked her to inform Arrowtip discreetly.

When Arrowtip heard this it was as if a thousand arrows pierced her heart. All the time she had to repress her tears and grieve in secret but not for a moment did she abandon her thoughts of revenge. When she closed her eyes one night a spirit appeared to her and said: "If you want to avenge your parents, let me teach you martial arts." She was a clever girl and when she awoke she remembered everything. She secretly got a staff, bolted the door of her room and practised. After quite a while she was expert. Gradually the winter of the fourth year of the reign drew near. One evening Arrowtip happened to fall asleep with her head resting on the table. Suddenly there was a rush of wind and a strange scent assailed her nostrils. A scholar appeared, wearing a turban, accompanied by a young warrior in a green robe, whose role was to teach her the art of throwing stones. The scholar said to her: "I went all the way to Gaoping to invite the Unshakeable Star here to instruct you in magic skills that will save you from the tiger's den and enable you to avenge your family. This gentleman is also your destined partner from a previous incarnation." These last words were a cause of such embarrassment that she quickly covered her face with her sleeve. In doing so she brushed the knife. The clatter it made woke her to the cold moonlight and a dying lamp. It was like a dream and not a dream. She sat there for a long time in a daze before she lay down to sleep again.

Next day she remembered about the art of throwing stones. She picked up a round stone the size of a chicken's egg outside her window and without thinking threw it at the upward-pointing finial on the ridge of the roof. It was a direct hit and with a crash the tile shattered into a thousand pieces which fell in a cloud to the ground. The noise brought Mistress Ni, her adoptive mother, running to see what had happened. Arrowtip artfully explained: "Last night I dreamt that a god came to me and said: 'Your father has a royal destiny. I have come to teach you the mystic arts of battle, to help your father in his ambition.' Just now I picked up a stone and threw it without thinking and it broke the tile on the roof."

Mistress Ni was astonished. She reported the tale to her husband who refused to believe it and summoned Arrowtip for questioning. When she was tested in the handling of spear, sword (long and short), halberd, cudgel, staff, trident and harrow, she was found to be proficient in them all. As for the art of stone-throwing, she never missed! The Royal Brother-in-Law thought to himself in amazement: "I am indeed destined to fortune. Some kind of heavenly spirit is aiding me." The upshot was that he ordered Arrowtip to practise her horsemanship and swordplay and news of her prowess spread throughout the household and the people of Weisheng also became excited. They dubbed her "Jade Arrowtip". The Royal Brother-in-Law wanted to find a husband for Arrowtip but she said to his wife: "I won't marry anyone but a stone-thrower. If you try to marry me to anyone else, I shall kill myself." Mistress Ni told this to her husband, who decided the whole business was too difficult and gave up the idea.

The two words "royal destiny" burgeoned in the Royal Brother-in-Law's mind and he made Arrowtip commander of his vanguard. His idea was that a split between two factions would allow him to take the middle ground and assume the rule himself. He picked his troops carefully, instructed his officers and marched out of Weisheng. He allotted five thousand picked troops to Arrowtip in the vanguard, whilst he himself followed on with the main army.

We shall leave the Royal Brother-in-Law and his adopted daughter Jade Arrowtip as they advance, and turn to Song Jiang and company who were waiting for the arrival of Commissioner Chen in Goodborough. After ten days it was announced that he had come. Song Jiang led the others a long way out of the city to meet him and escort him to his quarters in the governor's residence which for the time being was to serve as military headquarters. They all paid their respects. The Commissioner knew all about Song Jiang's virtues but happened not to have met Song Jiang face to face. Now that he saw his modesty and generous spirit he felt even more respect for him. "His Majesty, who has heard of your repeated successes, has sent me here to supervise operations. I come with carts loaded with gold, silver and silk to reward you all."

They prostrated themselves in thanks and said: "We are grateful, Your Excellency, for all you have done on our behalf. We know it is you who have won us this reward. The Emperor's favour comes to us as a result of your merit and even if we lay down our lives for you we can never adequately repay you."

The Commissioner said: "You have done sterling work. When you return to the capital the Emperor will find you important posts."

Song Jiang again prostrated himself and said: "May it please you, Your Excellency, to undertake the administration of Goodborough, so that we are free to deploy our forces and attack Tian Hu in his lair and disrupt his forces."

The Commissioner said: "Before I left the capital I mentioned to the Emperor that the cities you have captured lack administrative officers and a time limit was set for them to start their duties. They should arrive any day now."

Song Jiang distributed the reward among the army and at the same time composed a dispatch with which he sent Magic Messenger to every district and village ordering his commanders to await the arrival of the new officials and then hand over to them and report back for duty with their troops. He sent to Fenyang for news of the situation there. He informed the Commissioner of the contribution made by Tang Bin who had surrendered in Hebei, and recommended the two leaders of the uprising in the city for the command at Kettle Pass and Calf Mountain, in order to release Colonel Sun and Whiskers for further duties. The Commissioner agreed to everything.

Suddenly an urgent report came in from the scouts. "Tian Hu has sent Ma Ling with a relief force for Fenyang and the Royal Brother-in-Law and Princess Jade Arrowtip are marching on Xiangyuan from the east."

After consulting the Professor, Song Jiang organized a force to meet the enemy. At this point the Wizard said: "Ma Ling possesses magic powers and has a method of magic walking. He carries a metal block which he throws with deadly accuracy. I have received many favours from you but I have not yet done anything for you. I would like to go with my master, Taoist Gongsun, to Fenyang and persuade Ma Ling to surrender."

Song Jiang was well pleased and ordered two thousand troops to accompany them. The two of them bade him farewell and set off at once.

Song Jiang now ordered Hasty with six other leaders and twenty thousand troops to attack Lu, while Short-Arse with Steelbright, Blackface, Auntie Gu and a thousand cavalry were to carry out reconnaissance and ascertain the position of the northern troops.

He himself bade farewell to the Commissioner and marched out of Goodborough heading north with the main army, together with Chancellor Sun An, who had come over to them just recently, and thirty five thousand troops.

On reaching a point north of Mount Wuyin in Xiangyuan district Short-Arse and his patrol came upon the advance guard of the northern army under two commanders, one of them being the Butler. The two forces clashed, with drums thundering and waving banners. At the forefront of the northerners was the other commander, Sheng Ben. On the Song side Short-Arse galloped forward to do battle. Without a word he slapped his horse, twirled his spear and charged. A shout went up from both sides as Sheng Ben galloped to meet him. When they had fought a dozen bouts Steelbright rode out with whirling sword to support her husband. Two opponents at once was too much for Sheng Ben and he turned his horse and galloped off. Steelbright galloped in pursuit and cut him down with a blow of her sword. Short-Arse and his men charged and the Butler, unable to face them, hurriedly retreated. The Song forces gave chase and killed five hundred or more. The remainder scattered in all directions. The Butler, with no more than a hundred horsemen, fled to somewhere about eight miles south of Xiangyuan. Jade Arrowtip and her forces were encamped here.

Just six months before, Tian Hu had sent the Butler with General Xu Wei to the garrison of Xiangyuan. When the Butler heard that Jade Arrowtip, whom he had served so faithfully, remember, after her true parents were killed, had been made commander of the Royal Brother-in-Law's vanguard, he requested permission to take his troops out on reconnaissance hoping for a chance to meet up with his mistress. The Prince sent another of his officers, Sheng Ben, along with him and he was the one killed by Steelbright. The Butler now was fortunate enough to make contact with Jade Arrowtip's forces.

When the Butler came into the camp, he saw how his mistress had grown up: although a woman, her appearance was dignified and imposing and she bore herself like a true leader. The moment she saw who it was, she dismissed her aides and said to him: "Although I've escaped from the tiger's den, I've only got five thousand men. How am I going to avenge my parents? If I run away it seems like a betrayal. I am in a quandary and I was waiting for you."

The Butler said: "I have been thinking about it but I can't see any way. If I think of something, I'll let you know." He had hardly finished speaking when it was announced that the southerners were attacking. Jade Arrowtip armed at once and marched out to meet the enemy.

The two armies faced one another, banners and drums responding to each other on either side, the troops drawn up in battle formation. In the opening of the northern ranks a beautiful young woman warrior appeared, seated on a silver charger. On this young woman's standard it was clearly written: "Princess Jade Arrowtip, Leader of the Vanguard for the Expedition against the Southerners." Even the Song troops exclaimed in admiration. Stirring martial strains were heard on either side while brilliantly coloured embroidered banners blotted out the sun.

When Short-Arse saw it was a beautiful woman, well, naturally, he drove his horse forward, levelled his lance and charged. To cheers from either side, Jade Arrowtip slapped her horse, twirled her halberd and rode to meet him. After a dozen bouts, Short-Arse simply couldn't control his thoughts and his work with the spear became confused. Arrowtip thought to herself: "This man's disgusting!" She feinted and then slashed him in the left leg. His legs waved in the air and he fell headlong from his mount.

When Steelbright saw her husband wounded, she gave a furious shout: "You dirty bitch! What are you playing at?" and charged to the rescue. Arrowtip levelled her halberd and received the charge. Short-Arse was still floundering on the ground and the northerners surrounded him and took him captive. But Blackface and Auntie Gu snatched him away from them. Auntie Gu saw Steelbright could not get the better of Arrowtip and rode to her assistance, wielding her two swords. Imagine that encounter! Three women, six arms, four swords and a halberd, all whirling about like a snowstorm, like a shower of shattered crystal, like a blizzard of flower petals! So fast was the movement that to the eyes

of the onlookers in the two armies it became just a blur! After twenty bouts Arrowtip feinted, then put up her halberd and fled, while the other two gave chase. Arrowtip switched the halberd to her left hand and in her right took a stone. She bent her willow waist, screwed up her eyes, took aim at Steelbright and let fly. It caught Steelbright on the wrist of her left arm. The pain caused her to drop one of her swords and she turned her horse and galloped back to her own ranks. Auntie Gu abandoned the chase and rode to help her comrade. Arrowtip reined in her horse and turned to chase them. Blackface furiously charged, waving his two rods. But before he arrived, a stone from Arrowtip clattered on his helmet of hardened bronze. That was enough for him. He abandoned the attack and galloped back to his own ranks. They all retreated with the wounded Short-Arse and Steelbright.

As Arrowtip was preparing to follow up, a loud report rang out. It happened to be the end of the second month, the time of year when there are willow branches in bud waving in the breeze and horses neighing restlessly in the meadows. Down the hillside raced a squadron of men: Leopard's Head and the Chancellor, together with Iron Ox and his infantry in support. The two groups met with thundering drums, waving flags and a continuous uproar. Eight-pointed lance at the ready, Leopard's Head led his troops forward. Opposite, Jade Arrowtip twirled her square halberd and urged her horse on. When Leopard's Head saw it was a woman he shouted: "What makes you think you can oppose the imperial army, you wretched female?"

Jade Arrowtip answered not a word but twirled her halberd, slapped her horse and charged. Leopard's Head rode to meet her. The horses clashed, the weapons were raised. After countless bouts Jade Arrowtip was too exhausted to block the blows so she dodged aside with a wild sweep of her halberd and turned her horse and fled eastwards. Leopard's Head galloped after. The Chancellor who was also out in front saw her banner and shouted: "Don't follow her commander, it's probably a trick." But a redoubtable warrior like Leopard's Head was not going to listen to that. He strove all the harder to catch her. Over the springy turf eight hooves clattered with the sound of upturned cups, as they flew like the wind.

Jade Arrowtip waited till Leopard's Head closed on her, then took the halberd in her left hand and reached into her saddlebag with the right, took out a stone, twisted in the saddle and launched the stone directly at his forehead. Leopard's Head was sharp-sighted and agile and he parried the stone with the butt of his spear. Seeing she had missed, she took another and it flashed through the air like a shooting star. With awesome accuracy it sped towards Leopard's Head. Too late he tried to dodge. The stone hit him in the face and the blood spurted out. He put up his lance and returned to his own side, pursued by Jade Arrowtip.

The Chancellor was just about to go forward when the men in his ranks made way and outpoured five hundred battle-hardened infantrymen led by Iron Ox, Monk, Pilgrim, Snake and Scorpion. Brandishing his axes Iron Ox charged forward shouting: "What's that bloody woman playing at?" Jade Arrowtip grasped another stone and flung it at Iron Ox, catching him square on the temple. Iron Ox had a shock but luckily his skin was tough and his bones strong. and though the wound was painful there was no serious damage. Seeing she could not knock him down, Jade Arrowtip galloped back to her own ranks. Iron Ox, tiger's whiskers bristling with indignation, eyes bulging in fury, roared into the attack. His comrades, fearing for his safety rushed after him. The Chancellor tried unavailingly to stop them. Jade Arrowtip saw them all coming and knocked Snake to the ground with another stone, whereupon the other three rushed to pick him up. Iron Ox was still out to get her, so she waited till he was close; her next stone caught him on the temple. This second hit drew blood. But Iron Ox was made of steel. Painted red with blood, that swarthy face seemed on fire. Whirling his axes he burst upon the northern ranks and began wreaking havoc.

The Chancellor had seen Jade Arrowtip return to her own ranks and mustered his men for a charge. But at this moment the Royal Brother-in-Law along with General Xu Wei and eight junior officers arrived with the northerners' main army and there was confused fighting on all sides. Monk and Pilgrim rescued Snake and then returned to the fray. Scorpion took charge of his brother and was trying to get him away from the fighting when they were overtaken by the enemy, bound and dragged back to the other side. Iron Ox's infantry were repulsed. But the Chancellor, fighting with desperate courage, cut one of the northern commanders down from his horse with a single sword blow. The Royal Brother-in-Law was also hit in the neck by an arrow fired by one of the Chancellor's men and fell from his horse. The General made a desperate charge, rescued him and put him on a horse.

When Jade Arrowtip and her commanders saw the Royal Brother-in-Law hit by an arrow, they hurriedly sounded a withdrawal. By now more Song troops were coming up from the south. This time it was Hotshot, who had received an urgent dispatch in the camp from which he learnt of a stone throwing woman warrior among the northerners who had wounded Steelbright and others. He wondered greatly at the report and begged Song Jiang to let him go at once to reinforce them, because he wanted to see this woman warrior for himself. But Jade Arrowtip had already withdrawn from the field. Escorting her adoptive father, the Royal Brother-in-Law, she was riding off towards Xiangyuan, skirting the great forest. Hotshot stared after her. The poem says:

Proudly she turns her horse and rides away,
Surrounded by the bustle and pageantry of war.
She enters the forest and is lost to view,
Among multitudes of flowers, a flower's easily concealed.

When the Chancellor saw Snake and Scorpion taken and Monk, Pilgrim and Iron Ox charging into battle, he would have liked to muster his troops and join in, but it was getting dark and he and Hotshot were obliged to protect Leopard's Head and order their troops back to camp.

Song Jiang was in his tent where Short-Arse's wounds were being attended to by Doctor An. Short-Arse turned out to be not only wounded in the foot, but also cut about the face. When Doctor An had finished treating him he turned his attention to Leopard's Head. Song Jiang was extremely upset when he heard

Snake and Scorpion had been taken and the whereabouts of Iron Ox and the others were not known. In a little while the Pilgrim and Iron Ox appeared, muddy and bloodstained. "When I saw how excited Iron Ox was," said the former, "I was determined not to hold back. Together we murdered them, smashed right through them till we reached the city walls. There we found they had Snake and Scorpion tied up and were just about to take them inside. We killed the escort and grabbed our two comrades. But their general came up with the main army and recaptured them. We fought our way out and came back empty-handed. We don't know where Monk has got to."

Song Jiang's eyes filled with tears. He ordered search parties out in all directions to listen for any sign of Monk and told Doctor An to attend to Iron Ox. Night had now fallen. Song Jiang ordered a roll call and it was found they had lost more than three hundred. The defences were strengthened and alarms set up. Nothing happened that night. When it was reported early next morning that there was no news of Monk, Song Jiang grew still more gloomy. He sent Lungs and three others out to search, each with a detachment of light cavalry. He would have liked to attack the city himself, but too many of his leaders were wounded and he was obliged to rest his forces. Those in the city had barred and bolted their gates and did not come out to fight. After two days Perilous caught a spy and brought him in. The Chancellor recognized him as the northern superintendant, Butler Ye Qing. He said to Song Jiang: "From what I hear this is a brave man. He ventured out of the city all on his own. There must be something behind it." Song Jiang had the man's bonds released and told him to come forward. The Butler kowtowed repeatedly and said: "I have a secret matter to discuss. Please dismiss your aides and I will explain myself."

Song Jiang said: "These are all my friends. We have no secrets from each other. You may speak freely."

The Butler then said: "In the battle the other day, the Royal Brother-in-Law was hit by a poisoned arrow. He has become delirious and the doctors in the city can do nothing for him. On the pretext of looking for a doctor I have come out to make certain inquiries."

Song Jiang asked: "What are you doing about the two leaders of ours you captured the other day?"

"I didn't want any harm to come to them. Since the Royal Brother-in-Law's mind is not clear I have been giving the orders for him. For the time being the two commanders have been locked up and they are quite safe there."

The Butler told them what Tian Hu had done to Jade Arrowtip's true parents and all the rest of her story. When he finished he was overcome with grief.

Song Jiang remained uneasy. Since the Butler was a northerner, he feared a plot. As he was hesitating, Doctor An stepped forward and said: "Truly it must be a stroke of fate. This is no accident!"

Then he explained. "Last winter commander Zhang, our Hotshot that is, dreamed that a scholar asked him to go and teach a young woman how to throw stones. He also told him that this girl was destined for him as his wife. When he awoke he appeared to have lost his wits. That was when you sent me away with him to Gaoping for the rest cure. I took his pulse and realized it was some kind emotional disturbance. I questioned him at length and finally he confessed the cause of his illness and I was able to proceed with the cure. Now that we have heard this story of the Butler's, does it not sound exactly as if it refers to Hotshot?"

Song Jiang again asked the surrendered Chancellor, who replied: "I had certainly heard that Jade Arrowtip was not the Royal Son-in-Law's real daughter. One of my officers and the Royal Son-in-Law's aide are close friends, so I have heard quite a lot about the girl. The Butler's story could well be true."

The Butler said: "My mistress Jade Arrowtip is resolved to have vengeance and wipe out the disgrace. I have witnessed her ferocious courage in battle. I fear that if the city falls it will be reduced to rubble. I have risked death to come here. I implore you to help us."

The Professor stood up and took a long, hard look at the Butler. "His distress seems genuine," he said to Song Jiang. "I am sure he is honest. Heaven will favour your purposes and allow a filial daughter to have vengeance!" Then he lowered his voice and said to Song Jiang in confidence: "Although our forces are divided into three columns to attack, if Tian Hu joins up with the Jin, we will be caught between two fires. If the Jin refuse to take the field and Tian Hu's plan fails, he will surrender to them. Then how will we pacify the region? What I have in mind requires inside help. This is an opportunity. Given this match of Hotshot's, we need only do thus ... and thus ... Then Tian Hu's fate is in Jade Arrowtips's hands. The spirit Iron Ox saw in his dream is a harbinger of this. Don't you remember the lines he was told to memorize: 'To exterminate Tian Hu and his ilk, jade arrowtip must serve your purpose'?"

Song Jiang suddenly got the message and nodded enthusiastically. He summoned Hotshot, Doctor An and the Butler and explained the secret plan. They set off in accordance with their instructions.

Well, the commander of the garrison at Xiangyuan saw the Butler returning and heard him shout: "Quick, open the gates! I am Superintendant Ye Qing. I was sent to fetch doctors Quan Ling and Quan Yu and we've just arrived!" One of the guards reported it to the guard commander and shortly afterwards the order came back to open the gates. The Butler entered the city with his two doctors in tow. They went straight to the palace. From within came the order for them to enter and get to work. The Butler went in first with Quan Ling and asked among the staff and attendants for his mistress Jade Arrowtip, to whom he introduced the doctor. When they arrived at the Royal Brother-in-Law's couch they found him scarcely breathing. The doctor took his pulse and applied some ointment and gave him a tonic to take. In three days the patient's skin gradually regained a healthy colour and his appetite began to return. In just five days, although the wound had not fully healed his appetite was normal. He was delighted and told the Butler to bring the doctor in to see him. "Thanks to your brilliant treatment," he said to him, "my wound has healed. One day when I come into my own, you shall share in my fortune."

The doctor prostrated himself and said: "My skill is slight and unworthy. But I have a brother who was with me a long time in the rivers and lakes and who picked up some skill in martial arts.

He is expert in making up medicines. I beg Your Excellency to give him advancement."

The Royal Brother-in-Law gave orders for the doctor's brother to be admitted. Since his appearance was quite out of the ordinary, the Royal Brother-in-Law was well pleased with him and told him to stay outside the palace and be ready for orders.

The two brothers kowtowed and left. Four days passed and then it was suddenly reported that Song Jiang was advancing on the city. When the Butler went to report this to the Royal Brother-in-Law he impressed on him that Song Jiang's forces were powerful and bold and only the Princess would be able to repel them. The Royal Brother-in-Law ordered Jade Arrowtip down to the parade ground to organize an army. At this point the Doctor's brother said: "I am here at your service, Your Excellency. I have heard that the enemy are approaching. My ability is slight, but if you give me an army I will endeavour to see the enemy so beaten that nothing survives, not so much as a scrap of armour." Then the Butler feigning a great anger said to him: "Since you've got such a big mouth, do you dare test yourself by fighting me?"

Quan Yu replied with a laugh: "I studied the eighteen weapons from childhood, I am certainly your match."

The Butler requested the Royal Brother-in-Law's permission, which was granted, together with arms and a horse. The two men armed and mounted and went to it on the parade ground in front of the saluting post: backwards and forwards they fought, sculpted into a single block, moulded into a single mass, man against man, horse against horse. They fought forty or fifty bouts and neither had the advantage. All this time Jade Arrowtip was standing on the sidelines studying Quan Yu's face. Suddenly she exclaimed: "He looks like someone I saw before; his technique with the spear is just like mine." After pondering this for a while, she suddenly remembered: "The person in my dream, who taught me to throw stones, had a face like that. I wonder if he can throw stones too." Grasping her halberd she galloped forward and interposed it between the two combatants. She was afraid, you see, that the Butler might injure Quan Yu. She didn't know they were really both on the same side. With her halberd she aimed a blow at Quan Yu and he met it with his. They fought fifty bouts. Suddenly she turned her horse and galloped back towards the pavilion. Quan Yu raced after her. She grasped a stone, turned and flighted it towards the pit of his stomach. He saw it coming and stuck out his hand and caught it deftly. Marvelling at his dexterity, she took another stone to throw. As he saw her raise her arm, he also took a stone and threw it. There was a loud crack as the two stones met in mid-air and broke into splinters which fell to the ground.

The commander of the garrison, General Xu Wei, and most of the others were all manning the gates that day and there were only some junior officers at the parade ground. Some of these suspected Quan Yu might be a spy. But when they saw that their mistress Jade Arrowtip, who was a princess, was prepared to compete with him and since it was the Royal Brother-in-Law's own confidential aide Butler Ye Qing who had brought him in, it was impossible for anyone to raise objections. Evidently there was nothing to be done about it and they thought best to trim their sails to the wind. Anyway, Tian Hu was destined for defeat and heaven hid the truth from the Royal Brother-in-Law. He called Quan Yu in and presented him with robes, armour and a horse and gave him command of two thousand troops to go out and meet the enemy. Quan Yu thanked him and led his troops out of the city promising he would repulse the enemy and report victory when he returned. The Royal Brother-in-Law was delighted. Having rewarded Quan Yu he retired for the night, which passed uneventfully.

Next morning the Song troops had arrived and the Royal Brother-in-Law sent Quan Yu out with three thousand troops to engage them. From early morning till noon the attacks continued and Quan Yu put the Song commanders to flight with his stone throwing. He led his troops in a charge to occupy Mount Wuyin and Song Jiang's army were pushed right back and retreated to Goodborough. Quan Yu returned in triumph to the city and announced his success.

The Royal Brother-in-Law was tremendously pleased. "Now that you have this person," the Butler said to him, "and also Jade Arrowtip, there's no need to worry about how fierce the Song commanders are. How can we not prevail?" He also said: "Previously my mistress expressed a wish. She said she would only marry someone who could throw stones. This man is so valiant, he would not disgrace her."

The Butler persisted and finally the matrimonial union became a reality, settled and sealed irrevocably. The Royal Brother-in-Law having given his consent, the sixteenth of the third month was chosen as being an auspicious day, the appropriate ceremonies and feasting were laid on and Hotshot was welcomed into the family as son-in-law. There was music, singing and merriment that day, mountains of brocades and embroideries, meats and wine galore; it goes without saying that the bridal chamber was resplendent with lights. The best man conducted the ceremony. Side by side Hotshot and Jade Arrowtip dressed in their wedding finery did homage to the earth god and then to the Royal Brother-in-Law, her bogus father. Swelling music rose to heaven, rare perfumes tickled the senses. The couple made a solemn vow as they entered the bridal chamber. The Jade Arrowtip whom Hotshot observed in the light of the lamps was quite different from the one on the parade ground.

There is a poem about this:

Her fingers are soft as lotus in the pool,
Her waist more flexible than branches of the willow on the belvedere,
Her gliding steps' allure
A thing more rich than men's ability to find a price for.
Now as she turns her head under the lamplight,
It's an immortal you see,
Floating among heaven's peaks.

From then on Hotshot and Jade Arrowtip were like fish and water, clasping each other close as lacquer or rubber, it goes without saying.

That night in bed Hotshot divulged to his bride his real name. He was in fact Hotshot Zhang Qing, a commander of the Song forces and Quan Ling the doctor was Doctor An, also of the Song army. Jade Arrowtip likewise recounted all her troubles. The sound of their voices went on all night. The plot was hatched in two days' time. The Royal Brother-in-Law was poisoned, General Xu Wei was inveigled into the palace for a secret meeting and also killed. The rest surrendered. Hotshot and Arrowtip ordered total secrecy in the city: anyone who betrayed the secret together with all his friends and family would be put to death. Any who opposed the uprising, military or civilian, would be liquidated. Thus the news was prevented from leaking out. Snake and Scorpion were released from prison and with Hotshot and the Butler took command of the four gates. Doctor An escorted by the Butler's men returned to Goodborough to inform Song Jiang. The Professor ordered Iron Ox and Pilgrim to take Magic Hand by night to see Hotshot and Jade Arrowtip in Xiangyuan, where he was to study samples of the Royal Brother-in-Law's handwriting and forge a letter telling Tian Hu how he, the Royal Brother-in-Law, had acquired a live-in son-in-law. The Butler was instructed to deliver this to Weisheng and see what happened. The Butler duly bade farewell and set off for Weisheng.

Back in Goodborough, after Magic Hand and Doctor An had left, Song Jiang heard that Hasty and the Spearsman had captured Lu. The messenger who reported the victory said: "When Hasty and his troops invested Lu, their commander barred the gates and refused battle. Spearsman and his men devised a plan: they stripped naked and taunted the defenders, working them up to such a pitch that they were desperate to fight and the commander had no alternative but to open the gates and attack. The northerners streamed out in all directions in a frenzy. Our men fought them and retreated at the same time, luring them on till they were scattered and far from the city. Then Tang Bin charged from the east and Spots from the west. Under pressure from both sides they could not get back and close the gates and Spots and Tang Bin fought their way inside and seized control. Spearsman ran the commander through with his lance and as for the others, some died and some fled. More than five thousand northerners were killed, three thousand war horses were taken and ten thousand troops captured alive. When Hasty and his party entered the city they reassured the people and sent off this report."

Song Jiang was delighted with the news. He composed a report for Commissioner Chen and recorded the exploits of Hasty and company and gave out rewards. He also wrote out a military order, requiring all units to return to base so they could launch a combined attack. The messenger returned to Lu.

In Weisheng the members of Tian Hu's military council kept getting reports of the Wizard and the Chancellor surrendering and Goodborough and Lu having fallen. Tian Hu had a shock when they informed him. As he was discussing with them what to do, it was reported that the aide to the commander of Xiangyuan, Butler Ye Qing had arrived with a letter from the Royal Brother-in-Law. Tian Hu had him shown in at once. Now this visit was to have important consequences. Weisheng would be razed to the ground and the robbers would gather there, a certain usurping prince would be taken alive. If you want to know what reply Tian Hu gave after reading the Royal Brother-in-Law's supposed missive, you must read the next chapter.

Chapter 99

The Monk is delivered from the well of karma; White-Water Dragon floods the town of Taiyuan!

Now Tian Hu had received a letter delivered by Butler Ye Qing. He broke the seal and handed it to one of his officials who could read and had it read out to him. Here is what it said: "I, the Royal Brother-in-Law, have taken in a son-in-law named Quan Yu. This individual is extremely brave and has routed the Song army, forcing Song Jiang to retreat to Goodborough. I have today sent my daughter Jade Arrowtip with him to attack Goodborough. I venture to send my servant Ye Qing with this good news and as to the business of the marriage I beg Your Majesty to forgive my fault in arranging it without authorization."

After reading this Tian Hu looked somewhat relieved. He issued an order confirming Quan Yu in his status of royal son-in-law and sent the Butler back accompanied by two of his own officials with the order and also a gift of red patterned silk, brocades and silver for the new royal relative. The Butler took his leave and with his two companions set off for Xiangyuan.

Previous to this Magic Messenger on Song Jiang's orders had conveyed his military order to all districts and areas, before proceeding to Fenyang to find out how the Unicorn was faring. The new administrative officials had been arriving in the districts in a continuous stream. Accordingly the army commanders had been handing over the reins of government to them and reporting back to Goodborough in turn. First came the commanders of the Weizhou garrison, Scimitar and Twin Rods, together with Colonel Sun and his companions from Kettle Pass and Wen and Cui from Calf Mountain. When they had reported to Commissioner Chen and Song Jiang, it was announced that the water-borne chief White-Water Dragon and the rest of his commanders, having received intelligence of the fall of Lu, had sailed the fleet from the Wei via the Yellow River to Lu Water and were assembled there ready for action. Song Jiang ordered a celebration, at which there was much wine and excited talk. Next day he ordered Scimitar and company to Lu, with the boat commanders to back them up, and sent Hasty and company to attack two other towns behind enemy lines and stir things up in their rear. He wanted to waste no time, fearing that the enemy in desperation might surrender to the Jin.

In due course all the other garrison commanders handed over to the new civilian administration and returned to base with their troops. After greetings had been exchanged they heard how Colonel Hua had fought another engagement with the northern commander Shan Shiqi in which two thousand enemy troops were killed, the commander surrendered and the other officers fled. When they brought Shan Shiqi in there was wine to celebrate.

Song Jiang and the army now stayed put in Goodborough in order to reinforce the deception involving Hotshot and Jade Arrowtip and convince Tian Hu that he was too scared to venture forth. Of this no more.

The Unicorn had by now overcome Fenyang. Tian Bao as he fled had happened to meet up with Ma Ling's company. This Ma Ling was practised in magic. He could ride both on wind and fire and, like a good horse, a hundred mile journey meant nothing to him, a fact which had earned him the name of Magic Steed. He made expert use of a metal block, with which he could inflict terrible damage. It was also believed that in battle a magic eye would appear in the middle of his forehead, for which reason he was also know as God of Fire. He was second only to the Wizard in his magic powers. He had two lieutenants Wu Neng and Xu Jin, who had also acquired some of his arts. Magic Steed now joined forces with Tian Bao to form an army with eight other commanders and thirty thousand troops. They marched to a point a few miles north of Fenyang and made camp. The Song commanders judged it unwise to engage them there and retreated into Fenyang. Not only did they not dare attack the northern army; they were also concerned that the northerners might attack them.

As the Unicorn and his companions were considering their predicament, a guard from the east gate rushed in and reported that Song Jiang had sent Taoist Gongsun and the Wizard with ten thousand troops to their assistance. The Unicorn immediately had the gates opened to admit them. The Unicorn invited Taoist Gongsun to sit in the place of honour, with the Wizard next to him, and offered them wine. "The powers of this Magic Steed are prodigious," he told them. "He has already wounded Sergeant Lei, and half a dozen others. I am stuck here, helpless, and you've arrived in the nick of time."

The Wizard said: "I and my master, Taoist Gongsun, asked General Song to send us here to capture him." As he was speaking a guard rushed in and said that Magic Steed was attacking the east gate, his two lieutenants were at the west gate and Tian Bao with four others was at the north gate. Taoist Gongsun said: "I will make a sally from the east gate and deal with Magic Steed, the Wizard will go from the west gate and capture Wu Neng, while you attack from the north gate and take on Tian Bao."

The Unicorn ordered four others to assist the Wizard. Magic Messenger asked to join Taoist Gongsun because he had heard that Magic Steed could do magic walking. The Unicorn gave his consent. He also ordered River-Jumper and others to back up the Wizard. He himself with Thunderclap and company sallied forth from the north gate and attacked Tian Bao. Outside Fenyang waving banners veiled the sky to north, east and west that day as the battle raged.

We shall ignore for the moment the progress of the Wizard and the Unicorn and tell how Magic Steed's men, waving their banners, beating their drums and shouting taunts and challenges outside the city, saw the gates open, the drawbridge descend and the southern army pour out. They formed up in a line like a long snake. Magic Steed levelled his halberd and shouted out: "You rotten band of fucking losers, give us back our city at once. One moment's delay and you're done for!"

Golden Wings and Redeye rode forward and shouted back: "Your time has come, the day of your death is here!" Then they brandished spear and mace, slapped their horses and charged Magic Steed, who came to meet them. After more than ten bouts, Magic Steed got out his metal brick and took aim at Golden Wings. But Taoist Gongsun had already ridden forward and began to do magic with his sword. As Magic Steed raised his arm, Taoist Gongsun waved his sword and there was a sound like a clap of thunder: a red light burst out, and Taoist Gongsun's sword blazed with fire. Magic Steed's block fell to the ground, rolled about and melted. Taoist Gongsun had the true Taoist magic and in an instant the ranks of the southerners and their weapons were all blazing with light and had formed into a flaming crocodile, like a fire dragon. Magic Steed's metal magic was defeated by Taoist Gongsun's fire magic.

Taoist Gongsun now flourished his whisk and the whole army advanced together. The northerners suffered a huge defeat: smashed to bits, they were, turned inside out! Two thirds of the men were lost. Magic Steed fled for his life. It was lucky for him that he had his brand of magic walking, enabling him to run away eastward, borne on wind and fire. Magic Messenger who had already strapped on his amulets for magic walking gave chase, halberd in hand. But soon Magic Steed had done a dozen miles to Magic Messenger's ten and was out of sight. However, as he sped onward he came upon a fat monk who ran straight at him and knocked him down with a blow of his staff. Easily as one might drive a sheep the monk made Magic Steed captive.

As this monk was questioning his prisoner, Magic Messenger caught up with them. He took in what had happened and as he drew near he recognized the monk as Lu Zhishen the Flowery Monk, who had marched with the other army, Song Jiang's that is, on the eastern route. "However did you get here, Father?" he asked in amazement.

"Where is here?" Monk replied.

"We're east of Fenyang," Magic Messenger said. "This is the northern commander Magic Steed. There's just been a battle in which Taoist Gongsun broke his magic spells and I was chasing him. The bugger can certainly move! It's like a miracle from heaven that you were here to stop him."

Monk said with a grin: "Well, I'm no miracle from heaven. Actually I came out of the ground!"

Together they trussed Magic Steed up and with plain earth-bound steps made their way back to Fenyang. Magic Messenger asked Monk again where he had been and as they walked the latter explained: "The other day Tian Hu sent this fucking woman to attack outside Xiangyuan, near Goodborough. She was good at stone throwing and she wounded many of our commanders. I was at the front of a charge, intending to capture the bitch. I wasn't watching out and there was a concealed pit in amongst the undergrowth. I went right in with both feet and ended up sitting on the bottom. Fortunately I wasn't hurt. I looked around and found an opening on one side. When I explored this, a strange thing happened: I seemed to see the sky and the moon. There were farms and cottages and there were crowds of people, all busy at their work. When they saw me they laughed. I didn't stop to ask why; I just kept on going. Beyond the human habitations I came to a completely deserted area. Eventually I found a thatched hut. Coming from inside it was the tock-tock of the wooden fish. There was a monk in there just like myself, sitting cross-legged and reading the scriptures. I asked him the way and he answered with a smile: 'Where you come from is where you must come from, where you go is where you must go.' This didn't make much sense to me and I began to get annoyed. He just went on smiling and said: 'You know where you are.'

"'How the fuck should I know where I am?' I said.

"Again he said: 'At best you should think of combating evil; at the lowest level there is fear of hell. It is very big, the universe, it is vast, what mind can encompass it?' Then he went on: 'All men have a mind; where there is mind there is desire. Hell and heaven, all are born from desire. The three worlds therefore are nothing but mind, the ten thousand laws are but mental phenomena. If there is no desire, reincarnation ceases, the cycle of rebirth is broken.' When I heard his words I was enlightened. I gave a great shout of acclamation. Still smiling he said: 'You have entered the well of karma and it is hard for you to escape from illusion. I will direct you.' He led me out of the hut. We took but a few paces and then he said: 'Here we must part, but we will meet again!' Pointing to the way ahead he said: 'Proceed straight on and capture the magic steed.' When I turned round he was gone. There was a flash of light, and suddenly the scene changed. This man appeared. I saw him hesitating and I knocked him down with my staff. But I have no idea what I am doing here. Obviously the seasons are quite different here from Goodborough; the peaches and plums are in full leaf, no sign at all of any flowers."

Magic Messenger was amused. "Spring is over," he told him, "the peach and plum blossom has all fallen."

The Monk did not believe him. He protested: "It's not the end of the second month yet. It was only just now I fell down the well. I was there just a short time. How can spring be over?"

Magic Messenger found all this very puzzling. But soon with their captive they were back in Fenyang.

By this time Taoist Gongsun had completed his rout of the northern army and recalled his troops to the city. The Unicorn and his group had killed three of the enemy commanders and after pursuing Tian Bao and Duan Ren for several miles had scattered the northerners. Tian Bao and his remaining commanders took their defeated army north. The Unicorn withdrew with his forces to the city and met the Wizard and his company returning from their pursuit of Wu Neng and Xu Jin. The northerners had suffered defeat and heavy losses at the hands of the combined Song forces. Wu Neng had been knocked off his horse and killed by a blow from the White-Spotted Snake's sword and Xu Jin had been run through by Hound. Many horses were captured, together with a vast quantity of uniforms, armour, gongs, drums, saddles and bridles.

The Unicorn and the Wizard now combined their armies and made a triumphal entry into the city. Just after the Unicorn reached the government offices Monk and Magic Messenger arrived with their captive, Magic Steed. Delightedly the Unicorn asked Monk: "How did you get here? And what is the news of the Leader's campaign against the Royal Brother-in-Law?" Monk retold the story of his falling in the well and Song Jiang's battle with the Royal Brother-in-Law and all of the Unicorn's commanders marvelled at his account.

Then the Unicorn himself untied Magic Steed's bonds. Magic Steed had already heard what Monk said on the road and now seeing the Unicorn was so honourable he prostrated himself and indicated his will to surrender. The Unicorn rewarded the whole army. Next day the commanders left in charge of Jinning reported for duty to Fenyang, having been replaced by the new officials. The Unicorn sent Magic Messenger off to tell Song Jiang of the victory and held a discussion with his second-in-command the Strategist, about how to continue the campaign and so on.

Magic Steed meanwhile had passed on his method of rapid walking to Magic Messenger and they both reached Song Jiang's camp within a day to give a full report of the victory. When Song Jiang heard about the Monk he was as pleased as he was astonished. He went himself to report it all to Commissioner Chen. Of this no more.

Back now to Tian Bao and his lieutenants: creeping like curs kicked out of the house, darting like fish escaped from the net, they scurried into Weisheng. As Tian Bao, weeping, confessed his shameful dereliction, an official of the usurper's War Council rushed in and said: "For two days, Sire, we have been inundated with reports of defeat — of Magic Steed captured, of the troops of Scimitar and Twin Rods besieging this town, of the Unicorn having taken that town. Only from the Royal Brother-in-Law in Xiangyuan does there come the good news that the Song troops are too scared of him to attack."

Tian Hu was too devastated by the situation to take any decision. Some of his military and civil officials discussed things and proposed surrendering to the Jin to the north of them. But a deputy chief minister named Lucky Bian intervened, saying: "The southerners only have three armies. Weisheng is surrounded by mountains, we have supplies enough for men and livestock for two years. Your Majesty's crack guard number over twenty thousand. There are two towns east and west of us with fifty thousand troops in each. To our rear are four more cities strongly defended, with ample supplies to enable them to hold out for a good while. There is an old saying: 'Better face a crowing cock than a buffalo's backside.'"

Tian Hu was hesitating about what to say to this, when it was announced that Butler Ye Qing had arrived. When Tian Hu had him shown in, he prostrated himself and said: "The Princess and her consort, whose repeated successes have given them supremacy in the field, are attacking Goodborough. They were about to lay siege to the city, when the Royal Brother-in-Law fell sick and was unable to direct the operation. They beg Your Majesty to send a replacement commander and some picked troops to help them win Goodborough back."

Another of the usurper's officials, Superintendent Fan Quan, now stood up and said: "I have heard that the Princess and her consort are very brave. The Song army dare not face them. If Your Majesty would lend his own weight to this attack, supported by brave soldiers and intrepid commanders, it is certain to succeed. If you leave the young Prince to govern in your stead, I could assist him."

Tian Hu agreed to this proposal. In fact Fan Quan's daughter had been a stunning beauty and he had given her to Tian Hu who favoured her greatly. He had therefore no reason to mistrust Fan Quan's words. The latter had taken large bribes from the Butler, however. He also understood the strength of the Song army and had made up his mind to sell his country.

Tian Hu sent Lucky Bian with ten commanders and thirty thousand troops to oppose the Unicorn and Colonel Hua. He also ordered Marshal Fang Xuedu with a force of the same size to confront Scimitar and his troops. He himself with two of his ministers, two field-marshals and two generals was to lead an army of a hundred thousand picked troops. Sacrifices to flag and leaders were performed, oxen and horses slaughtered and the army rewarded. Another edict was promulgated appointing Tian Hu's younger brothers Tian Bao and Tian Biao with Fan Quan and a number of other officials, civil and military to advise Prince Tian Ding in governing the country.

When the Butler heard this he secretly sent someone he could trust to ride post haste to Xiangyuan and inform Hotshot and Jade Arrowtip. Hotshot sent Snake and Scorpion out of the city by means of a rope to inform Song Jiang, with orders to return at once.

Lucky Bian waited while his commission was made out and the troops selected. He wasted three days on this. Then with his commanders and thirty thousand troops he marched out of Weisheng's east gate. His force was in two divisions: the vanguard had three commanders and five thousand troops. They had reached a place called Mount Floss, where a forest ran along the foot of the mountain; the leading troops were just skirting the forest, when there was a sudden clamour of gongs and a squadron of cavalry burst out from behind the shoulder of the hill. What had happened was that on receiving the report from Hotshot, Song Jiang had told Colonel Hua and others to ride here at speed with a force of five thousand cavalry in light armour and with horse's bells removed. One of these commanders now rode to the front with a spear in either hand. This was the Song commander Twin Spears, leading exponent of the cavalry charge. He shouted out: "What troops are you? Surrender at once, what are you waiting for?"

One of the enemy shouted back angrily: "You swamp-dwelling outlaws! Why are you attacking our towns?"

Twin Spears replied: "We are the imperial army. Resistance is pointless!" Slapping his horse and levelling his two spears he charged and the enemy commander rode to meet him. After twenty bouts the northerner began to tire and could no longer parry effectively. Twin Spears ran him through the throat and he fell lifeless from his horse. His comrade, enraged, galloped at Twin Spears, but Colonel Hua rode out to cut him off. After more than ten bouts Colonel Hua turned away and his opponent gave chase. Colonel Hua took an arrow and fitted it to his bow. Twisting in the saddle he took aim and fired, hitting his enemy in the face. The helmet fell, the legs kicked in the air and the rider crashed to the ground. Colonel Hua turned and finished him off. Twin Spears and the others swept the enemy back, killing two more of their leaders. The northerners were defeated and the better part of five thousand men were killed, the rest fled. They captured many gongs, drums and horses and pursued the enemy a couple of miles until Lucky Bian's army arrived on the scene.

Now Lucky Bian was originally a farmer and the strength of a water buffalo was in his shoulders and arms. He was an experienced fighter and had been head of a robber band. The two armies met and faced each other, banners waving, bugles blaring and drums thundering. Lucky Bian rode in front of the northern forces, wearing a bronze winged helmet and fish-scale armour. He was a tall man, with a thick growth of whiskers surrounding his mouth, square-jawed, broad-shouldered, with straight eyebrows and round eyes. He rode a powerful charger and shouldered a mountain-splitter of an axe. He had four lieutenants on either side and other officers behind to protect him. His troops were drawn up in perfect order.

From the Song side the Tattooed Dragon rode out: "Who do you think you are?" he shouted. "Dismount at once and let us tie you up to avoid dirtying our weapons!"

Lucky Bian laughed scornfully. "Pitchers and jugs have ears, don't you have any? Do you mean to say you haven't heard of Lucky Bian?"

Tattooed Dragon replied: "You peasant! This is the imperial army, what chance do you think you have against us?" With that he slapped his horse, levelled his three-pointed double-bladed weapon and charged Lucky Bian, who came to meet him whirling his axe. Two horses met, two weapons were raised. Sword and axe clashed, horses' feet tangled. They fought more than thirty bouts but there was no victor.

Colonel Hua was so impressed by Lucky Bian's martial skills that he thought it dishonourable to use an arrow, impersonal as that is, so he slapped his horse, levelled his spear and joined the fray. Lucky Bian fought bravely with the two of them and still there was no victor.

The northern leader feared their man might lose and sounded the gong for withdrawal. Since it was getting late and they were outnumbered, Colonel Hua and Twin Spears made no effort at pursuit. They withdrew to the south and the two armies camped about three or four miles apart.

That evening a big wind got up from the south, thick clouds descended and at midnight a great rainstorm broke. Tian Hu by this time was more than thirty miles from Weisheng, with all his officials, commanders and troops. At nightfall they made camp. The camp-followers and concubines were in the tents and Tian Hu was relaxing with Fan Meiren, his concubine, in his tent. That was the night the rain came. The downpour continued five days without stopping. It was difficult for the soldiers to cook or even to stand on their feet. Above them heaven seemed continually weeping, below them was always the sound of water gurgling.

Of this no more.

Meanwhile Hasty and others met up with Scimitar's party and the water-borne leaders and their boats and conferred. Leaving the Water General and the Fire General to defend Lu, Scimitar advanced with his army by land and water. He captured Yushe and left it in charge of Hasty and Spots. Then he pressed home his advantage, taking Dagu and killing the senior garrison commanders, whose subordinates surrendered in droves. He calmed the populace, rewarded his troops and sent a messenger to Song Jiang to report the victory. Next day Scimitar and his group also encountered the rain storm, which pinned them down in their camp. Suddenly it was reported that the Unicorn had left the Son-in-Law and others to settle Fenyang and attacked and taken two other towns where he left Victorious and the Supremo and the Kong brothers in charge respectively, and was now investing Taiyuan with the main army. But because of the rain he was unable to attack it. The White-Water Dragon chanced to hear this report and rushed to Scimitar to say: "This incessant rain that the Unicorn has run into means we can't afford to delay. What if the enemy should make a desperate sally from the city? But I have an idea. I'd like to go and discuss it with the Unicorn." Scimitar gave his consent.

So the White-Water Dragon left, appointing the Tong Brothers, Cave Dragon and River Rider, to take charge of the boats in his absence. He took the Pilot, White Eel and the Ruan Brothers with him, and two thousand sailors. Wearing straw hats and wooden clogs they braved the storm and made their way with all speed to the Unicorn's camp. Despite the weather they talked for a long time. The Unicorn was excited, and ordered his men out to brave the elements and cut down trees and build rafts, while the White-Water Dragon and his party made their own preparations, of which we shall say nothing here.

Now Tian Hu's officials in Taiyuan, garrison commander Zhang Xiong and his two subordinates were real monsters. These three were the cruellest among all the rebels. The soldiers under their command were wild and licentious and the people of the town, persecuted beyond their endurance, had abandoned homes and possessions and fled in all directions. Seventy or eight percent of them had left. Though surrounded, Zhang and his gang were still confident they could hold out. He and his pals reasoned as follows: with all this rain the Song army had no chance of plunder, they had no advantage by land or water, firewood was scarce, they would have no heart to make a long stay of it, a quick counter-attack would certainly bring victory. It was the beginning of the fourth month and Zhang Xiong was just about to attack out of all four gates when he suddenly heard the thunder of gongs on all sides. He hurriedly climbed the watchtower, whence he was able to observe the Song army struggling through the rain in clogs, clambering onto the high ground. Whilst he was wondering what this meant, he heard a thunderous roar from the Zhibo Drain and from east and west of the town: it was as if thousands of men and millions of horses were charging. A moment later a huge wave swept down on them, a raging torrent, like the great neap tides of September or the floods when the waters of the Yellow River spill over. Truly they had no more chance than three planks put there to shore up a collapsing dyke or a couple of sandbags that are meant to stem a river in spate.

If you want to know how this flood ended you must read the next chapter.

Chapter 100

Hotshot and Arrowtip work in tandem; Song Jiang and the Commissioner jointly announce victory!

So White-Water Dragon working in concert with the Pilot, White Eel and the Ruan brothers and all their company of sailors had taken advantage of the deluge and the surging waters to flood Taiyuan by breaching the Zhibo Drain and Jin Water. Instantly the water came boiling out:

> *The water gushes forth, a great wave rears up. Soldiers ride in on planks and rafts, commanders advance on the flying flood. Gods howl, ghosts weep, the day is plunged in sightless murk. Peaks shake, mountains crumble, the vast wave roars like an angry beast. City walls come tumbling down, there's no more shelter anywhere. Banners vanish on the tide, their green and red tangled with the soldiers' spears. Frothing and foaming, the rushing waters have gone berserk. Corpses wallow like fish or turtles, hot blood bubbles through the waves. In a moment trees are uprooted, in an instant rafters are hobnobbing with the waters.*

A tremendous hubbub arose in the city. When they saw the water rushing towards them soldiers and civilians clambered onto walls and rooftops or clung to planks and beams. The weak, the elderly, the obese could only climb onto chairs and tables. But moments later even benches and tables were swept away as houses collapsed and they all went to join the fishes and the turtles. White-Water Dragon, the Pilot and White Eel and the Ruan brothers rode the floodwaters towards the city and fetched up on a level with the city wall. Their men leapt out onto it, cutlasses in hand, and began killing the guards. Other troops attacked on rafts.

Under this onslaught resistance could only crumble. Up on the watchtower the commander, Zhang Xiong, cursed his luck ceaselessly as he watched the two brothers, Pilot and White Eel, halberd in hand, leap with a shout from their craft, land on the walls and race up the tower. They slaughtered a dozen guards in quick succession. The rest fled in confusion. There was no escape for Zhang Xiong. The Pilot knocked him down with a blow of his halberd, while White Eel rushed forward and struck off his head with a loud crunch.

By the time the waters began to recede, countless numbers of soldiers and inhabitants were dead, either drowned or killed in the fighting. The south wall was left encumbered by beams, pillars, leaves of doors, window handles and the like, and floating corpses. The only building still standing in the city was the summer palace built by Emperor Shenwu of the Northern Qi dynasty, which had very solid foundations. Those who were near it rushed up the steps in a jostling, trampling crowd. More than two thousand people died, and even on that eminence and on the city walls the survivors numbered only about one thousand. Outside the city the Unicorn had secretly warned the people in advance that when a gong was struck they were all to go up onto the high ground. Moreover outside the city there was more open space, so the waters dispersed faster and the people did not drown.

The west gate was seized by White-Water Dragon and his sailors, the north by the Pilot and White Eel, the east by Ruan the Second and Ruan the Fifth, and the south by Ruan the Seventh. So the Song flag now flew over all four gates. In the evening when the water receded and the land was revealed again, White-Water Dragon threw open the gates and invited the Unicorn in. No cock crowed, no dog barked inside the city and the corpses were heaped in mounds. Although the wickedness of Zhang Xiong and his cronies was manifest, White-Water Dragon's treatment of them was exceedingly cruel. Thousands knelt everywhere in the mud and water, kowtowing like people offering candles at the temple, and begging for mercy. After examining them the Unicorn found that only a dozen or so were soldiers, the rest were just ordinary people. Two of the commanders had climbed into the branches of a tree next to a building behind the government offices. When they saw the waters receding they crept down but were captured and taken before the Unicorn. He ordered them to be executed and the corpses displayed. He had the money in the treasury distributed to relieve the common people who had suffered from the floods inside and outside the city. He sent a messenger to Song Jiang to report the victory, ordered his troops to bury the dead and repair the walls and buildings and commanded the people to stay in their homes.

We shall say no more about how the Unicorn settled Taiyuan, but return to the time before the city's fall when Tian Hu with an army of a hundred thousand was forced by the rain to halt and make camp south of Brass Key Mountain. His scouts reported that the Royal Brother-in-Law was dead and that the Princess and her consort had retreated to Xiangyuan to bury him. Shocked by this news, Tian Hu sent a messenger to Xiangyuan with orders for Jade Arrowtip to fortify the city strongly and for her consort Quan Yu to report to him for duty. He also wanted to know why the people he had sent to Xiangyuan had not reported back.

Next day the rain had ceased and at dawn despatch riders came in with news that Song Jiang was sending the Chancellor and Magic Steed with troops against them. This report threw Tian Hu into a passion: "Those two received the highest favours from me," he ranted. "Now they turn traitor! It is not to be endured! I shall have to go and have a word with them myself! The rest of you must spare no effort. Anyone who captures them will be richly rewarded with gold and honours."

The army advanced under Tian Hu's personal command and encountered the Song forces. From the enemy's banners the northerners could see that the commanders they faced were Colonel Sun and the Flautist. At the front of the northern army were massed soldiers with clubs, axes, swords and lances; amid the paired banners, under a yellow ochre umbrella with a nine-coiled flying dragon, seated on a silver-maned white horse with jade trappings and gold saddle, was the great rebel prince Tian Hu, personally directing the engagement. From the rear of the southern ranks now came Song Jiang who was also personally in command, with the Professor and others at his heels.

When Tian Hu heard Song Jiang was there he wanted to start the battle at once and capture Song Jiang. But just then a messenger arrived to say: "Scimitar and his forces have taken two more cities and in the west the Unicorn has also taken two more. They have flooded Taiyuan and no one is left alive there. Deputy chief minister Lucky Bian was halted at Mount Floss by Colonel Hua and others, while the Unicorn came up from Taiyuan to attack from the rear. Lucky Bian could not hold out against this attack from two sides and was defeated and captured by the Unicorn. The Unicorn has now joined forces with Scimitar and they are surrounding Qinyuan and have it in an iron grip."

This report left Tian Hu petrified and he immediately decided to retreat into Weisheng again.

One of Tian Hu's ministers, Li Tianxi, held the position while the other four retreated with him. But then a report sounded from Brass Key Mountain and Monk with four others and a picked force of infantry secretly deployed there by Song Jiang began to advance in two columns. Tian Hu hurriedly ordered his royal guard into action but they were immediately met by Magic Steed and the Chancellor, coming in on their flank from the east. Magic Steed bestriding wind and fire attacked the northerners with his metal block, while the Chancellor cut and thrust with his two swords. They went through the northerners' ranks as if there were no one there, slicing the army in two. The Professor had used his forces so cleverly that although there were a hundred thousand of the northerners they made mincemeat of them, scattering them to the four winds and inflicting a massive defeat. As minister Li Tianxi and the others fled east with Tian Hu in their midst they found themselves opposed by Monk and his company with their stout staves and the shield bearers with their javelins and knives, who cut a bloody swathe through the enemy troops, scattering their commanders and forcing them to flee west. Although Tian Hu had the pick of the royal guard under his command, now they had to face the imperial army they found they had never met such fierce opponents. How could they be expected to put up a fight?

Only a few of Tian Hu's staff now remained — two commanders, one official and the chief of police, with about five thousand demoralized troops. Clustering around him they retreated.

Then, when the danger was already extreme, another body of cavalry charged in from the east. When Tian Hu saw them he raised his eyes to heaven and said with a sigh: "Now it's the end!" The leader of this troop was a bold young commander wearing a blue turban and green uniform and grasping a wooden lance, seated on a tall charger with a white curling mane. On his standard it said clearly: "Quan Yu, Leader of the Campaign against the Southerners". The Butler who was following close behind Tian Hu saw this banner and explained it to the King. Tian Hu immediately sent word to the Princess's consort, for that is who it was, that his help was needed. The Royal Consort came forward, dismounted, knelt and said: "Sire, I am in full armour and I cannot make proper obeisance. I deserve to die for such disrespect."

Tian Hu said: "That is no fault, my dear friend."

"The situation here is desperate," the Consort said. "I beg Your Majesty to take refuge in Xiangyuan. When the Princess and I have repelled the enemy, we will invite you to return to the palace in Weisheng and devise a plan to return things to their former glory."

Tian Hu was well pleased with this. He gave the orders and they set off for Xiangyuan, the Consort taking up the rear to guard against attacks from pursuers. As they reached the city a hubbub arose behind them. When the guards saw who it was they quickly opened the gates and lowered the drawbridge. As one of Tian Hu's commanders led the troops forward, the soldiers heard pursuit behind and there was a rush to get into the city in which no respect at all was paid to the King. As soon as they were inside there was a loud report and on either side the concealed troops sprang forward forcing the northern commander and his men into some concealed pits, where they were indiscriminately massacred with long spears. Less than half of the unfortunate three thousand men survived. A cry went up: "We want Tian Hu alive!" Realizing the city had turned and it was all a trap, Tian Hu hurriedly reined in his horse and fled north. The Consort, alias Hotshot of course, and the Butler gave chase. But Tian Hu's horse was swift and they couldn't catch him. When he was already a bowshot ahead a gust of wind suddenly arose in front of his horse and a girl appeared and called out: "Tian Hu you swine, you killed my family, where do you think you can run to?" Then from where she stood another gust of fateful wind caught him head-on, and next thing she was gone. Tian Hu's startled horse shied and whinnied and he was thrown to the ground. Hotshot and the Butler now caught up. Leaping from their horses they pressed forward with their men and made him prisoner.

One of Tian Hu's last remaining guards commanders charged to the rescue, but Hotshot hurriedly remounted, grasped a stone and let fly, hitting the northerner square in the face and knocking him from his horse. "I'm no bloody Prince Consort," he roared. "I'm Hotshot, a warrior in the Song army under General Song Jiang."

Simultaneously Iron Ox and Pilgrim charged out of the city at the head of five hundred infantry, scattering the Palace guards and the police superintendent's two thousand men like chaff. After dispatching the guard commander, Hotshot tied Tian Hu up and drove him back into the city. The gates were then locked, and orders given that they were not to be opened again until Song Jiang had destroyed all the northern forces and Tian Hu could be handed over.

Monk now came on the scene. When he saw Tian Hu had already been taken, he and his followers turned west again and continued to harry the enemy till they reached the foot of Brass Key Mountain. The time was now around five o'clock.

Song Jiang had fought the northerners all day and killed more than twenty thousand of them. Leaderless now they fled in all directions. Fan Meiren, Tian Hu's concubine, and the other female attendants were all killed by the soldiery. Four of the commanders including minister Li Tianxi and thirty thousand troops were holed up on Brass Key Mountain, where Song Jiang had them surrounded. When Monk came to report that Hotshot had captured Tian Hu, Song Jiang clasped his hands together in joy and immediately sent an urgent dispatch to Xiangyuan instructing Pilgrim and company to make sure the gates were securely bolted and keep Tian Hu under the closest guard. He also ordered Hotshot off to Weisheng to assist Jade Arrowtip.

Now Jade Arrowtip had received secret instructions from the Professor and was lying in wait on the slopes of Mount Shipan outside Wuxiang, with Snake and Scorpion and six others and five thousand cavalry all in northern uniforms and insignia. When they received news that the battle with Tian Hu had begun, they marched with all speed to Weisheng. That evening, at sunset, with a crescent moon hanging in the sky, Jade Arrowtip approached the city walls and sang out sweetly: "It's the Princess. I'm escorting the Prince. Open up, quick!" The guards rushed to the palace to report. The brothers Tian Bao and Tian Biao mounted and galloped to the southern ramparts. They raced up to the top of the gate tower to look: there was the yellow ochre umbrella, and beneath it, seated on his lively grey with the embossed saddle, the Prince. In front of him stood a young woman warrior, with "The Princess Jade Arrowtip" in large characters on her standard. Behind was a long train of ministers and officials stretching into the distance. In ringing tones Jade Arrowtip called out: "We have been defeated by the Song army. I have rescued the Prince and brought him here. Come out to receive him at once!"

Having seen the Prince, they opened the gates and went out. As they halted before his horse, the Prince shouted out: "Seize those two villains for me!" His officers leapt forward and arrested them.

"But we are guiltless!" they cried, struggling to free themselves. But the officers bound them. In fact this "Prince" was the Professor's invention: he had the Chancellor select from the ranks of the southern army a soldier who resembled the Prince, and dress him up as Tian Hu. The ministers and officials behind were Snake and Scorpion and their men in disguise. Now they all drew their swords, while Fleetfoot and some others with five hundred men marched Tian Bao and Tian Biao off to Xiangyuan. When those in the city saw their leaders arrested and marched away southward, they realized it was a plot. But they were prevented from charging out of the city and attacking because Arrowtip, determined to get the young Prince Regent, Tian Ding, boldly forced her way in with Snake and Scorpion. The first of the guard commanders to oppose her was knocked over by one of her stones. Six or seven of them suffered the same fate, while Snake and Scorpion fought alongside her. Outside the city Lungs and Yellow Dog ordered their men to remove the northern insignia and show themselves in their true colours, and then joined in the attack and seized the south gate. After scattering the northern resistance they raised the Song flag.

The city was in tumult. A number of the usurper's officers and ministers together with some of the royal family led a counter-attack. Jade Arrowtip and her four thousand had penetrated deep into the dragon's lair by now and were seriously exposed. But Hotshot arrived with eight thousand men and seeing Jade Arrowtip, Snake and Scorpion engaged in a desperate struggle attacked with his stones, putting out four northern commanders in quick succession and beating back their forces. "Don't go any further: we're too isolated," he told Jade Arrowtip.

"I've got to avenge my father," she replied. "They can tear me limb from limb, but I won't leave off!"

"I've captured Tian Hu already," Hotshot replied. "He's being held in Xiangyuan."

Only then was she satisfied.

They were about to retreat from the city when something happened that was truly a judgement of heaven on wrongdoers. The Unicorn arrived, having taken Qinyuan. Seeing the flag on the gate, he marched his army straight into the city and joined Hotshot in the attack. Thunderclap and his companions took the east gate, Golden Wings and some others the west gate, the Tamer and his men the north gate. Morbid and Madcap and others with the infantry hacked their way with swords and axes into the royal palace. Another group of infantry commanders entered through the back gate. Of the wives and concubines and the royal entourage countless numbers were killed. The Prince Regent, when he heard what was happening, killed himself. All the Song commanders on the spot now joined in the slaughter of the usurper's ministers and officials, his family members, and all the rest of the gang. For indeed:

On palace steps the bodies lie;
The blood streams out through royal gates.
War takes no account of low or high:
The soul its own outcome dictates.

The Song troops went on killing in Weisheng till the corpses littered the streets and blood ran in the gutters. Finally the Unicorn gave out an order that no one was to harm the people and sent someone to tell Song Jiang the news. Only near dawn did the fighting cease. Many enemy commanders surrendered.

At daybreak the Unicorn had a roll call taken. Leaving aside the Strategist, who had remained in charge of the garrison at Qinyuan, all his commanders had come through the battle unscathed. The only casualty was Geng Gong, the enemy commander who had come over to them previously — he was trampled to death in the mêlée. When the leaders came to report their successes, Nameless brought in the corpse of the Prince Regent. Snarling with hatred, Jade Arrowtip drew her sword and hacked off the head and dismembered the body. The Royal Brother-in-Law's wife was already dead but Arrowtip wanted to find Mrs. Ye, the Butler's wife, who had brought her up, so she took leave of the Unicorn and went with Hotshot to Xiangyuan to take Tian Hu to Song Jiang's camp. The Unicorn was just settling some military matters when a scout reported that Fang Xuedu had Hasty and Spots bottled up in Yushe. The Unicorn sent Scimitar and some others to rescue them.

Next day Song Jiang overcame minister Li Tianxi on Brass Key Mountain and sent someone with a report to Commissioner Chen: "The rebel's stronghold has been taken and the leader captured alive. Please come to Weisheng and take command." When Song Jiang arrived outside Weisheng with the main army, the Unicorn and his men went out to welcome him. Song Jiang issued a proclamation to calm the people. The Unicorn brought the prisoner

Lucky Bian to him. Song Jiang was so impressed by his manly bearing that he loosed his bonds with his own hands and treated him courteously. Seeing Song Jiang was so honourable Lucky Bian was filled with gratitude and surrendered. Next day Jade Arrowtip, Hotshot and the Butler brought the three Tian brothers in prison carts and handed them over. Arrowtip and Hotshot paid their respects to Song Jiang side by side. Arrowtip apologized to Short-Arse and the others for the offence she had done them. Song Jiang ordered Tian Hu and his brothers to be locked up together until such time as the army withdrew, when they would take them to the Eastern Capital and hand them over. He ordered wine to be served in honour of Jade Arrowtip and Hotshot.

That same day the enemy commander of Wuxiang surrendered to them with all the personnel, military and civilian, under his command, handing over all the records and supplies. After recompensing him, Song Jiang reappointed him. When Song Jiang had been two days in Weisheng, scouts reported that Scimitar and his party had reached Yushe and together with Hasty and Spots caught the northern commander Fang Xuedu between two fires and killed him, as well as five thousand of his men. The rest had surrendered. Song Jiang said to them all delightedly: "Thanks to the efforts of all of you, we have successfully put down the uprising." Everyone's exploits were faithfully recorded as was Jade Arrowtip's and Hotshot's part in capturing the leader and attacking the rebel stronghold. After three or four days Scimitar returned and the arrival of Commissioner Chen was announced.

Song Jiang marched out of town with all his commanders to welcome the Commissioner, who praised him saying: "In only five months you have performed wonders. I hear that you have captured the rebel leader. I am forwarding the report of your victory to the capital immediately. The court is sure to reward you with high honours." Song Jiang thanked him again.

Next day Jade Arrowtip came to make a request. She wanted to go to Stonehouse Mountain in Taiyuan to find her mother's body and give it burial. Song Jiang told Hotshot and the Butler to accompany her.

Song Jiang asked the Commissioner to burn down Tian Hu's

palace with all its ostentatious halls and luxurious apartments. He also proposed that the contents of the government granaries should be given out to assist the many whose homes had been burnt down by the soldiery. He then drafted a report for Marshal Su to present to the court and sent Magic Messenger off with it immediately.

Bearing this report, Magic Messenger caught up with the man sent by the Commissioner and they entered the Eastern Capital together. They went first to Marshal Su's palace and handed the report to Yang, his chamberlain. Marshal Su was delighted and next morning at the dawn court read out the Commissioner's report to the Emperor. His Majesty openly showed his pleasure and gave orders for Song Jiang and the others to make all necessary provisions and then march the army back to the capital, where high honours awaited them. With this news Magic Messenger set off again the same day, after bidding Marshal Su farewell. Shortly after noon next day he reached Weisheng and reported to the Commissioner and Song Jiang. These two ordered all members off the puppet government who had been captured alive, with the exception of the Tian Hu and his brothers who were to be sent separately to the capital, to be taken to the execution ground and beheaded.

A few villages in Jinning had remained uncaptured. Half of the rebels' henchmen and lackeys in these places disappeared when they heard that Tian Hu was taken, the rest gave themselves up. The Commissioner spared them all, reinstating them as loyal subjects. He had notices posted everywhere to calm and reassure the people. Others who had worked for the rebels but done nobody any harm and surrendered voluntarily were told to go back to their villages and take up their normal agricultural occupations. The work of pacification complete, garrisons were posted to protect the boundaries and maintain the peace. Of this no more.

The Emperor issued an edict and sent a special envoy to Hebei to deliver it. After that a full meeting of the Military Academy was called, which the Emperor was to attend, and the Grand Preceptor spoke beforehand on military affairs and they listened respectfully.

But there was one official there who sat staring at a corner of the room and paid him no attention. The Grand Preceptor was highly indignant and demanded to know the man's name. It was indeed a case of "One person left out means trouble for all". For after the Grand Preceptor asked this man's name:

Heavenly stars and earth stars will spread their wings;
Brave leaders and fierce troops pacify Hubei.

If you want to know who this man was, you must read the next chapter.

Chapter 101

The theft of a burial plot leads on to rebellion; A stroll on a fine spring day provokes dalliance!

After some inquiries, the Grand Preceptor learnt that this official who had ignored his discourse on tactics, pointedly fixing his gaze on a corner of the room, was called Luo and was from a military family of Yunnan and a graduate of the Academy. But when the Grand Preceptor's indignation was on the point of exploding, the Emperor was announced. He was obliged to shelve the matter and lead the members out to welcome His Majesty. They escorted the Emperor inside and performed the ceremony of obeisance.

Well, after the Emperor had spoken of military affairs, this Luo, before the Grand Preceptor can even open his mouth, jumps up and launches into the following tirade: "As a humble member of Your Majesty's military academy I know I am risking my life by this, but I must speak to Your Majesty of the dangers of the bandit Wang Qing's insurrection west of the river Huai. The turmoil Wang Qing is provoking beyond the Huai has been going on for five years now and the government forces have proved incapable of ending it. Marshal Tong Guan and Cai the Younger, the Grand Preceptor's son, were entrusted with the campaign against these rebels but their whole army disappeared. They tried to cover up by lying to Your Majesty. They said they had ordered a ceasefire because the climate was unfavourable to the troops. They even said the army was affected by some epidemic. Meanwhile Wang Qing's viciousness grows ever more unbridled. Last month he defeated the forces of my home state of Yunnan. What do we see? Plunder and rapine, licentiousness, horrors that scarce bear repeating. Eight military commands have been seized and eighty-six districts. The Grand Preceptor is supposed to be the chief prop of your reign, yet his own son suffered ignominious defeat and betrayed the country's trust in him. Before Your Majesty entered just now he was trying to lecture us on military matters. This is presumption beyond endurance, this is madness, this is insanity. I beseech Your Majesty to reprimand the Grand Preceptor and his cronies, the whole pack of corrupt, cheating officials, and appoint commanders and an army to put down the rebels as soon as possible, in order to save the people from their devastation, in the interests of good government and for the people's welfare. The whole world will rejoice!"

The Emperor was moved to anger by what he heard and severely reprimanded the Grand Preceptor and the rest for the cover-up, but the latter, with their glib tongues, talked him round and he finally retired to the palace without having imposed any sanctions. Next day the governor of Bozhou, Hou Meng, arrived in the capital on official business and also gave a frank account of how Tong Guan and Cai the Younger had failed in their duty and disgraced their country. At the same time he extolled Song Jiang's strategic skill and multiple achievements, pointing out how he and his men had subdued the Tartars and settled Hebei and were now ready to withdraw and make a triumphant return to the capital. Now that Wang Qing was on the rampage, the Governor begged His Majesty to order Song Jiang's company first of all be given due honours and then sent beyond the river Huai where they would undoubtedly achieve great results. The Emperor gave his consent and the order was sent to the Military Council to bestow appropriate ranks on Song Jiang and his commanders.

The Grand Preceptor and his colleagues discussed the matter and made the following recommendation: "Wang Qing has taken Wanzhou. Recently three more districts, all close to the capital, have asked for help. We request Your Majesty to order Commissioner Chen and General Song Jiang not to return to the capital but to move their army rapidly to Yuzhou. We will appoint Marshal Hou Meng as Commander-in-Chief of this expeditionary force. Academician Luo too is a skilled tactician so we will send him along as well to serve in Commissioner Chen's force. Song Jiang and his followers will be fully occupied putting down the rebellion, there is no need to give them official rank until they have successfully dealt with the situation beyond the river Huai. It will be time enough then for celebrations and honours."

Of course the Grand Preceptor knew this Wang Qing was a force to be reckoned with, he had discussed it all with Marshals Tong and Yang and Gao the Ball. He knew what he was doing sending Hou Meng and Luo to Commissioner Chen. He was hoping Song Jiang and company would get themselves defeated — and if Hou and Luo should pass on as well, who cares? Would it not be killing two birds with one stone?

But enough of this. Suffice it to say that the Emperor consented to all the schemes of these four villains: the orders were written out, Marshal Hou and Academician Luo were instructed to leave immediately for Hebei and deliver them to Song Jiang and company, together with a reward of gold and silver, bales of silk, robes, armour, horses, imperial wine and suchlike. The new officials who were to fill all the vacant posts in the province were ordered to proceed there at once and take up their duties by a given date. This business concluded, the Emperor was carried off again by his friends Wang Fu and Cai the Younger to the Model Mountain Pleasure House.

Marshal Hou Meng led his party off on the road north with the Emperor's edict and the thirty-five carts fully loaded with the bounty for Song Jiang and his commanders. Nothing occurred on the journey and without losing any time they crossed Kettle Pass and Goodborough and were soon approaching Weisheng. Five or six miles from the city they ran into the Song detachment escorting the captive rebel leaders. The fact was that Song Jiang had received the order to withdraw just as Jade Arrowtip returned from burying her mother. He wrote a detailed report of events for the court, including an account of Jade Arrowtip's integrity and honour, her exploits in capturing the rebel leader, the surrender and return to the Emperor's service of the Wizard, the Chancellor and the rest and the good service they had done. He then sent Hotshot, Jade Arrowtip and the Butler off in advance with the captive rebels.

Hotshot, who was in the lead, first met Marshal Hou Meng and Academician Luo. When they had told him of their mission he sent a messenger back to inform Commissioner Chen and Song Jiang, who rode out to meet the imperial envoys. The embassy bearing the imperial edict entered the city and a special altar was set up to burn incense. Song Jiang and the Commissioner with all their commanders lined up in orderly ranks knelt with their faces to the north whilst Sterling called out the acclamation. Marshal Hou Meng facing south stood on the left of the imperial altar and read out the proclamation:

> *Hear our will: In accordance with the respect due to heaven and to the ancestors, in administering this great kingdom I have inherited, I am compelled to request the services of great men in the furtherance of affairs of state. Recently there have been many alarms on the frontier and disturbances in the country at large. General Song Jiang and his men, traversing much rough terrain and many dangerous regions, have successfully performed the task of pacification, secured the payment of tribute by the rebels and shown themselves to be fully worthy of our trust. I now send Marshal Hou bearing my edict, to reward Commissioner Chen, Song Jiang, the Unicorn and the rest with gold and silver, robes, horses, armour, imperial wine and the like in recognition of their services. But now once more, by reason of the insurgency of the bandit Wang Qing west of the river Huai, order is disturbed, injury inflicted on my people, my lands invaded and my western capital in tumult, and I must call again on the services of Commissioner Chen as civil governor, Song Jiang as Commander of the Pacification Expedition, the Unicorn as his deputy, with Marshal Hou Meng as Commander-in-Chief of the Expedition. On receipt of this edict, they are to lead the army out and march with all despatch to the relief of Wanzhou. If they work diligently to subdue the rebels and restore peace we guarantee that the army will be amply rewarded. Commissioner Chen will be instructed to draw on the rich treasury of Hebei and make out an official register and everyone can count on our favour. This is our decree.*

Afterwards they gave three cheers for the Emperor and prostrated themselves again in thanks. Then the Marshal brought out the reward. Names were called out in due order and each received his portion. The Commissioner, Song Jiang and the Unicorn each got five hundred catties of pure gold, ten bales of silk brocade and a set of robes, a horse and two bottles of imperial wine. The Professor and the other thirty-four principal leaders got two hundred catties of silver, four bales of coloured silk and a bottle of imperial wine. The Strategist and the rest of the seventy-two secondary leaders got a hundred catties of silver and a bottle of imperial wine. The rest of the gold and silver the Commissioner had distributed among the men. When this was all done, Song Jiang repeated his orders to Hotshot, Jade Arrowtip and the Butler to proceed to the capital with the captives. Taoist Gongsun came and requested Song Jiang to set up five images in the Temple of the Dragon Lord on Five Dragon Mountain. Song Jiang agreed and sent craftsmen to carry out the work.

Song Jiang sent Magic Messenger and the Magic Steed to tell every garrison commander to muster his troops as soon as the new officials arrived to replace them and rejoin the main army for the campaign against Wang Qing. He spent several days making his own preparations, and by this time the new officials had all arrived at post and the garrison commanders and their troops were coming back one after the other. After handing out their rewards to them, Song Jiang told Hand and Craftsman to engrave a tablet commemorating all these things. At midday on the fifth day of the fifth month he told his brother Iron Fan to arrange a feast to celebrate the peace, with Commissioner Chen presiding and all the new civilian governors, together with Marshal Hou and Academician Luo and all the assistant magistrates and other officials according to their rank, and his own company of one hundred and seven commanders (Hotshot being absent in the capital), as well as the Hebei leaders who surrendered, viz, the Wizard, the Chancellor, Lucky Bian and others, a total of seventeen, all seated in two orderly rows. During the banquet, the Commissioner, Hou and Luo praised the achievements of Song Jiang and his men. Song Jiang and the Professor thanked them.

Conversation was about the court or about matters dear to their hearts, candles and torches burned brightly, and the party did not break up till after midnight.

Next day Song Jiang and the Professor conferred and organized their forces. They bade farewell to the other officials and with the Commissioner set off southward. They caused absolutely no trouble in the places they passed through, where the people lined their route with incense, candles and flowers and thanked them for having put down the bandits, and made it possible for them to enjoy heaven's mercy again.

We shall now leave Song Jiang to his southern campaign and turn to Hotshot who with Jade Arrowtip, the Butler and the prisoners confined in their carts had reached the capital. First he delivered Song Jiang's missive to Marshal Su with the money and presents. Marshal Su conveyed this to the Emperor, who was full of praise for Jade Arrowtip's virtue and filial piety and gave orders for a posthumous title to be conferred on her mother and a shrine dedicated to her in the local temple to celebrate her exemplary constancy, with offerings made in spring and autumn. Jade Arrowtip was also awarded a title, and Hotshot was promoted and a reward of fifty taels of pure silver was bestowed on them. Hotshot also got back his old post.

The three of them were commanded to go back and join Song Jiang in the march westward beyond the Huai and bid for further glory. The Emperor gave the order for the rebel King and his brothers to be taken to the execution ground and put to death by slow cuts. Jade Arrowtip handed small images of her parents to the executioner and asked him to hang them up at the execution and place an altar before them. At three minutes past midday when Tian Hu had been cut to pieces she laid the remains on the altar, offered the blood as a libation to the spirits of her mother and father and wept noisily. News of Jade Arrowtip's activities had spread and a crowd had turned out to watch. She wept so bitterly that there were none that were not moved to tears. Afterwards with Hotshot and the Butler she gave thanks, kowtowing towards the capital. Then they set off for Wanzhou to join Song Jiang in the campaign against Wang Qing. Of this no more.

Now you must try to store this in your memory, friends, because here comes a digression about Wang Qing's life, from childhood to the time of his growing up, in order that all shall be clearly known. Wang Qing had been a humble police sergeant in the Kaifeng district of the capital. His father was a rich man of the capital addicted to litigation, who would stir up trouble and then sue, commit an outrage and bring trouble down on his own head, and set traps for honest citizens. For this reason people gave him a wide berth. On the word of a fengshui expert, he coveted a certain piece of land which was supposed to ensure him an illustrious son. This plot was the burial ground of a family to whom he was related. With the help of the fengshui merchant he plotted their downfall. He got his way forcibly by trumping up charges against the family and bribing the officials. The family lost their patrimony and, powerless to defend themselves against him, they left the capital and went to reside far away. Later after the rebellion, when all Wang Qing's clan were exterminated, this family alone were allowed to survive because it was found that Wang Qing's father had ruined them. After he had taken over the coveted plot and buried his own father and mother there, his wife was delivered of a son in the last month of the year. He dreamt that a tiger entered the house and squatted down west of the hall, but was driven out by a lion. When he woke up, Wang Qing was born.

From his earliest days Wang Qing was profligate. At sixteen he became very strong. He wouldn't study but spent his time at cockfights and the horses, or practising with spear and staff. He being an only son his parents loved him dearly and of course spoiled him. No wonder they had no control over him when he grew up! All he did was gamble, sleep with prostitutes and drink. When they admonished him he would blow up and swear at them, nothing they could do would stop him, he had to have his own way. After six or seven years the family fortune was exhausted and on the strength of his ability he got taken on as a sergeant in the constabulary. As soon as he had some money in his hand he was everyone's friend and would spend freely on food and drink. When hard times returned he would resort to his fists and look for a fight. People regarded him therefore with a mixture of fear and admiration.

One day, then, Wang Qing went to attend the roll call, and when it was over went to stroll south of the city in the Jade Ford Gardens. It was the sixth year of Huizong's reign, a beautiful late spring day. There were swarms of people strolling about and hordes of cavalry:

Flowers in the gardens, girls on the embankment;
Strolling groups that paint the scene with grace.
Cavaliers a-canter, sweetness of fresh grass.
They're tipsy in the teahouse — blossom scents the air.

Wang Qing wandered about by himself for a while and then went and leant against a weeping willow that stood beside a lake in the garden, waiting for an acquaintance to turn up so they could go and have a few drinks together. Before long he saw on the north shore of the lake a group of a dozen or so young stewards or the like, gathered about a sedan chair inside which sat a young woman beautiful as a flower bud. She wanted to look at the scenery and she had dispensed with the bamboo screen. Wang Qing was a great admirer of feminine beauty and the sight of such a splendid girl had him with his tongue hanging out. He recognized that group of stewards as belonging to the household of Marshal Tong. He followed at a distance until they reached the Model Mountain which was in the northeast district of the capital. Here the Emperor Daojun had contrived an artificial landscape of dramatic peaks and weird stones, ancient trees and rare birds, innumerable pavilions, plants, lakes and rustic taverns. It was bounded by a red wall and gate, like that in the palace, and like the palace too there were guards inside so that ordinary strollers would not presume to set foot there. Here the bearers put down the sedan-chair, the serving maids helped the lady out and they passed through the gate, chattering merrily to each other.

The guards all made way for them and let them enter, for the lady was in fact the daughter of Tong Guan's younger brother, who was Marshal Yang's daughter's son. Marshal Tong had brought her up as his own daughter and destined her for the Grand Preceptor's grandson in marriage. She was called Jiaoxiu and she was just sixteen. Today she had persuaded Marshal Tong, taking advantage of the fact that the Emperor was spending two days of pleasure with Lily, to let her visit the Model Mountain. The Marshal had first given orders to guards, so of course they let her in. After four hours she still had not emerged. Wang Qing hung about outside watching for her. He was getting very hungry so he wandered off to a wine shop in East Street to get some wine and food. He hurriedly downed six or seven cups but he was afraid he might miss her, so without even asking for the bill he threw down a heavy piece of silver on the counter for the waiter, saying: "I'll be back in a minute to settle up." He returned to his former post and waited there a while. Suddenly the girl came out with her attendants, walking slowly. She did not get into the sedan. She began admiring the scene outside. As he strolled towards her, Wang Qing saw that she was truly lovely. In fact her beauty made such an impression on him that his heart seemed to hammer uncontrollably, his bones and flesh turn to jelly. He was melting like an ice lion in the fire, instantly he was overcome!

As for the girl, she too had noticed Wang Qing in the crowd. She looked and liked what she saw. Then one of the stewards got the people to move back, her nurse pushed her into the sedan chair which, with the attendants gathered about it threaded its way through the crowd to the Temple of the Sacred Peak outside the Gate of Wild Jujubes, where she stopped to light incense. Wang Qing followed her in. The temple was packed, it was impossible to move, but when the crowd saw it was Marshal Tong's people, they made way for them. When she got down from the chair to do the incense, Wang Qing pushed forward. But he could not get very near and besides was afraid the stewards would shout at him. So it occurred to him to pretend he was a familiar servant of the temple god, and help her light the candles and incense. Now their eyes met, he staring fixedly at her and she returning the gaze with equal urgency. Now, the Grand Preceptor's grandson had been born a simpleton and, since the girl had several times heard the matchmaker saying it was so, she was constantly bemoaning her fate. Now when she saw Wang Qing's elegance and good looks the little idiot's mind filled with romantic ideas. Then one of the stewards, who had been observing, recognized Sergeant Wang Qing. He went straight up and smacked him one in the face! "This is not something for the likes of you!" he shouted. "You, a common Kaifeng policeman, you've got a nerve! Who told you to worm your way in here? If His Excellency gets to hear about this, that ass's head of yours won't be secure on its neck any longer!" Wang Qing dared not reply. He hung his head and sneaked off, sighing and cursing himself: "What a fool I am! How can a warty toad like me expect to dine on wild swan's flesh?"

Wang Qing returned home crestfallen that evening, hiding his anger and disappointment. But the amazing thing was that the girl, when she got home, went on thinking about him night and day. She bribed her maid to go and find out all about him from the Head Steward. The maid was friendly with the Head Steward's wife; they did a spot of pimping together. They got Wang Qing in secretly by a back door and in utter secrecy an affair started between Wang Qing and the Marshal's adopted daughter. Wang Qing was in seventh heaven and gave himself up to drinking every day.

Time doesn't stand still, however, and three months soon passed: extreme joy always gives way to sadness. One day when Wang Qing had got himself drunk as a lord he blurted it all out in front of his commanding officer. Subsequently the affair was bruited abroad and inevitably Marshal Tong came to hear of it. He was furious. That he wanted to punish the offender and get him cashiered goes without saying.

So after this Wang Qing felt he dared not go back to Marshal Tong's residence. One day while he was sitting idly at home — it was near the end of the fifth month and a blazing hot day — he got a bench and placed it in the courtyard of his house to catch the breeze, then went back inside to get a fan. He suddenly saw the legs of the bench move and it followed him inside from the courtyard...."Good heavens!" he exclaimed, and launched a kick at it with his right foot. "Ouch!" he screamed.

Well if he hadn't kicked the bench, many things would have been different. As soon as he did kick it he was in trouble. Truly, as the heavens have unpredictable storms, so is man ever threatened by catastrophe.

If you want to know why Wang Qing screamed like that when he kicked the bench, you must read the next chapter.

Chapter 102

Wang Qing is punished for his adultery; Gong Duan takes a fighting instructor!

When the bench began behaving so strangely, Wang Qing went up and gave it a kick. Only he used too much force, because he pulled a muscle and could do nothing but squat there shouting: "Help, help!" He was quite unable to move. His wife heard the cries and rushed out to see what was happening. She saw the bench lying on its side and her husband in a heap on the ground so she went up and slapped his face, saying: "You useless thing, you! You spend all the day outside and never think of coming home. Now when you are here you have to play silly games!"

Wang said: "Don't laugh at me, dear. It's no joke. I've done my back in. It's very painful."

The woman helped him up. Leaning on her shoulder and shaking his head, he cried out through clenched teeth: "Aiya! It hurts like hell!"

"You profligate," she scolded. "You fucking good-for-nothing. When you're off on one of your sprees you're always ready to lash out with your feet and fists, and now look at you, the joke's on you!" Realizing what she had just said was not exactly appropriate, she put her silk sleeve in front of her mouth and giggled. Wang Qing also, when he heard "the joke's on you" applied to such a painful situation, could not help laughing and let out a guffaw. She boxed his ears again for him, saying: "You crazy fucker, what've you been up to?"

When she finally got him onto the bed, she pounded a dish of walnuts for him and warmed a jug of wine. Then she went and bolted the door, spread the mosquito net and lowered the curtain for him to sleep. It goes without saying that with that pain in the ribs he could not stir. The night passed uneventfully. Early next morning the pain was still just as bad and he could see no way of getting to the roll call in front of the government offices. As midday was approaching his wife packed him off to see if he could get hold of some ointment and he hobbled as best he could to a place near the government offices where Old Qian, who was an expert in sprains and pulled muscles, had a shop. There he bought two medicinal patches to stick on his back. Old Qian said: "If you want it to heal quickly you should take a couple of doses of a healing potion to increase the blood flow." So saying, he mixed the potion and handed it to Wang Qing, who took out a piece of silver about two or three tenths of a catty in weight. He asked for a piece of paper to wrap the money in. The old fellow saw what he was doing and pretended to look away. Wang Qing handed him the packet, saying: "Please do not think I am disrespectful. You can buy some watermelon to eat."

The old man said: "One doesn't make money out of one's friends, sergeant. I can't allow it." Even as he spoke he took the packet in his right hand, opened his medicine cabinet and popped it inside.

Wang Qing picked up his medicine and was about to leave when a fortune-teller appeared round the corner of the street west of the Government offices. He wore a cap pulled down over his eyebrows and a robe of brown cloth and was carrying a sunshade from which was suspended a sign with big characters that read "Secrets of the Other World" and on either side of this some smaller letters that read: "Li Zhu of Jingnan, ten dollars a time, every word guaranteed, compares with the finest."

When Wang Qing saw it was a fortune teller, his mind being full of this business with the girl and the strange happenings of the day before, he shouted out: "Mr. Li, come in and sit down!"

"What can I do for you sir?" said the fortune teller. As he spoke his eyes slid over Wang Qing exploring him from head to foot.

"I'd like to hear my fortune," Wang Qing replied.

Mr. Li lowered his sunshade and entered the apothecary's. He greeted Old Qian with joined hands, saying "Please excuse the disturbance." Then from within his robe of rough brown cloth he produced a red sandalwood box. He took off the lid and took out a large copper coin which he presented to Wang Qing, saying: "Go and say a silent prayer to heaven, if you will sir."

Wang Qing tried to make a deep obeisance to the sun's flaming red disk, but it hurt so much he couldn't bend. He was stiff as an eighty- or ninety-year-old and all he could manage was a little bob, something between a bow and a nod, after which he raised his eyes to heaven and prayed. Observing this, the fortune-teller said quietly to Old Qian: "If he's using your medicine no doubt he'll be better soon. I assume he's injured himself in some way?"

"There was some funny business with a bench," the old man said. "He kicked it and strained his back. When he came in just now he couldn't even speak properly. He's used two of my patches and already he's able to bend his waist again."

The fortune-teller said: "Just what I thought."

After completing his prayers, Wang Qing gave the coin back to the fortune-teller. The latter asked him his name, then waved the divining tube in the air and intoned:

> *The day is auspicious the time is right, the Sage casts the sticks, let that which is hidden be revealed. The Tao is all-embracing and universal, it connects all things; it unites the virtues of heaven and earth, combines the brightness of sun and moon, gives motion to the cycle of the four seasons, relates the good and ill luck of gods and ghosts. This gentleman, Mr. Wang of the Kaifeng district of the Eastern Capital, would purchase from heaven his fortune. On this day in this place he entreats all the great Sages, every god and saint, by all that is most sacred, most holy, most blessed, most spiritual to point the way to the lost one, to make manifest his destiny.*

The fortune-teller cast the sticks twice for a double divination, what he called a water and thunder divination. Observing the disposition of the six lines, he asked: "What exactly is it you want to know about?"

"Domestic matters," Wang Qing replied.

Li nodded and said: "Don't be upset if I speak frankly. It's hard, very hard. You will have many troubles, but things will improve later. There are some verses that you should remember." He began to wave about a pleated fan of oiled paper on a bamboo frame and recited: "Home's in a mess, strange events portend disaster, there is no peace to be had there. I see trouble with an old temple, a dangerous bridge, a malicious attack, an official injustice or a serious illness. When there is no proper order, how can one prosper? See honour fierce fright, litigation connected. When people are not at ease, accidents occur. When the limbs are weak, a man is insecure. A change can bring improvement. Meet tiger-dragon-chicken-dog day means more trouble."

Wang Qing was sitting facing Li. He couldn't abide the strong smell of lacquer from the fan so he held his silk sleeve across his nose as he listened. After his recital Li said: "I said I would be frank. There are yet more strange events lying in wait for you at home! You had better move house, if you want to be safe. Tomorrow is a dangerous day. Watch out!"

Wang Qing heard the warning but didn't know how to act on it. He took out some money to pay Li. Taking up his sunshade Li walked out of the shop and went east. At that moment half a dozen constables from the district office spotted Wang Qing and said: "What are you doing loafing about here?"

When Wang Qing explained about the strange happening and spraining his back they all had a good laugh. "Friends," he said, "if His Excellency asks for me just cover up for me, will you?"

"We'll take care of it," they said, and went away.

Wang Qing went home and got his wife to brew the medicine. He was determined to get better so he kept on taking the tonic and chased it down with several cups of wine. What he didn't realize was that this concoction was a heating potion, and when he went to bed that night and his wife snuggled up to him, his ardour was aroused. The trouble was, he was in such pain he couldn't move. But the woman had suffered weeks of neglect all the time Wang Qing had been involved with the Marshal's daughter and constantly away from home and her desires were burning like fire. She wasn't going to let him off, no way! So she climbed on top of him and they reversed the roles of pleasure.

They got up late next morning. After washing, Wang Qing was

starving and he warmed some wine for himself. He was just in the middle of breakfast when a voice outside called out: "Is the sergeant at home?" His wife looked over the fence and said: "It's two policemen." Wang Qing was nonplussed, but he had to put down his rice bowl, wipe his mouth go and out to greet them. "What can I do for you gentlemen?" he asked.

"Nice work if you can get it, sergeant," they said. "Look at the colour on you — drinking at this hour of the morning! The guv called the roll this morning and when you weren't there he was right pissed off. We told him that stuff about seeing something strange and hurting yourself but he didn't buy it. He made out a warrant and told us not to come back empty-handed." They handed the warrant to Wang Qing.

"How can I go and see him when I'm flushed from drinking like this?" he said. "Just wait a bit, then I'll go."

"Nowt to do with us," they said. "But the guv is waiting for you. If you don't go at once, we'll be in trouble too. Come on, get a move on!" They started to pull him. When his wife came out to see what was happening he was already out of the door. The dragged him all the way to the government office where the magistrate was sitting on a leopard skin chair. "We brought Wang Qing, like you ordered, sir," they said.

Wang Qing made the obligatory four kowtows and the magistrate shouted: "Wang Qing, you're one of my officers. Why are you shirking, why didn't you report for duty?"

Wang Qing told his story again, adding: "I really am in pain, I can't sit or lie comfortably, I can't walk properly. I wouldn't dream of deceiving you, Your Excellency. Please be lenient."

But the magistrate saw his face was red and he yelled: "You idle bastard, getting drunk is all you're good at. You got involved in all that hanky-panky and now you're inventing a pack of lies, think you can fool your superior!" He shouted to the guards to take him out and beat him. Wang Qing didn't even have time to open his mouth. They beat him till the blood ran to make him confess his story was a fabrication, and that he was hoping to deceive the credulous with seditious intent. Wang Qing after being manhandled by his wife the night before and now tortured by the police was truly like a block of wood between two axes, or a corpse revived. Able to hold out no longer, he was obliged to make a false confession. The magistrate recorded his statement and ordered his officers to put him in irons and throw him in the death cells, whilst the death penalty was demanded for the fabrication of evil tales and seditious plots. He was taken down.

Of course Marshal Tong had sent a secret message to this magistrate with orders to this effect because he was determined to pay Wang Qing out and get rid of him; this mysterious event had cropped up most opportunely! Everyone in that government office knew about the liaison with the Marshal's daughter and they were all spreading it around that: "Wang Qing has been punished because of that affair. He won't get out of this alive." However, the Grand Preceptor and his son did not much like the sound of this: they felt that if Wang Qing were put to death the affair would gain in notoriety and the scandal would be even greater. So they quietly got some officials they could trust, who were also friends with the magistrate, to tell him he should quickly banish Wang Qing to a distant frontier where he would be lost to view. They also appointed a day for the girl to be betrothed, firstly in order to save Marshal Tong's face and secondly to put an end to the gossip. The Grand Preceptor's grandson was something of a simpleton and would not know whether the girl was a virgin or not, so that was no problem.

In deference to the Grand Preceptor's wishes confidentially imparted to him, the magistrate convened his court. Wang Qing was brought up from the cells, the cangue was removed and he was sentenced to twenty strokes of the cane. A tattooer was summoned to brand his cheeks, the distance of his banishment was calculated and he was assigned to the prison camp at Shanzhou. The court ordered a full ten catty cangue for him, which was fitted and sealed, a warrant was made out and two guards or escorts, Sun Lin and Ho Ji, assigned to deliver him. As the three of them left the court, Wang Qing's father-in-law approached and took them to a wine shop on South Street opposite the court room. He told the waiter to bring them wine and food, and after a few cups and some dishes, he took out a bundle of silver and offered it to Wang Qing, saying: "Here's thirty taels of silver for your travelling expenses."

Wang Qing reached out his hand, saying: "Most kind of you, father-in-law."

The other pushed away his hand, saying: "Not so fast. I'm not giving you the money for nothing. You're being sent off to Shanzhou, that's hundreds of miles, over rough roads and mountain passes, who knows when you'll be back. You've been fooling around with someone's daughter and you've had no time at all for your wife. Who's going to look after her for you now? You've no family, land or property to your name. You've got to sign a divorce certificate and let her marry again. It will avoid problems later. If you do this, you can have the money."

Wang Qing was always a spendthrift. He was thinking that he hadn't an ounce of silver in his pocket, how was he going to manage the journey to his place of banishment? Whatever way he looked at it, he needed that money. He took a deep breath and said: "All right, I'll sign the paper."

His father-in-law took the certificate with one hand as he handed over the money with the other. Then he left.

Wang Qing went home with his guards to pack his bags. His wife had already been taken away by her father and the door was locked. He went and borrowed an axe from a neighbour and broke the door down. He found all his wife's clothes were gone and all her jewellery. It made him half angry and half sad. He got a Mrs. Zhou who lived next door to come and prepare some food and wine for the policemen. He gave them ten taels of silver and said: "It still hurts a lot from the beating. I can't walk properly. I would like a few days to rest before we set off." They'd had the money, so of course they agreed. It was in vain that the Grand Preceptor's son sent friends round to urge the policemen to get going. Wang Qing sold off all his household possessions and rented his house to a Mr. Hu, a man of substance.

Wang Qing's father, who had gone blind as a result of his son's behaviour, lived somewhere else. When his son visited they always quarrelled. Now, hearing that his son had got into trouble with the authorities and been banished he found it surprisingly painful. He got a lad to lead him to his son's house. "You never listened to my warnings, my son," he said. "That's why you've ended up like this." The sightless eyes filled with tears as he spoke. Wang Qing, who from childhood had never been accustomed to use the word "father", now at the moment of final split-up felt a sudden pang and cried out: "Father, I've been so cruelly used by corrupt officials and so insulted by my father-in-law who made me sign a divorce before he would give me money."

His father said: "They'd never have treated you like that if you'd loved your wife and shown respect to your father-in-law."

This censoriousness infuriated him. He paid no further attention to his father but packed his bags and left town with the two policemen. His father tore his hair and beat his breast and said: "I should never have come to see the ungrateful wretch!" The boy led him back home and that was that.

After leaving the capital Wang Qing and his guards took lodgings in a lonely spot so he could recuperate for another ten days or so. When his wounds were better the policemen insisted he set off. Moving slowly they headed for Shanzhou. It was the beginning of August and the weather was blazing hot, so they could only do about fifteen miles a day. They suffered the usual discomforts of travel, sleeping in beds people had died in, eating suspect food. After more than a fortnight on the road they passed Mount Song. One day one of the guards pointed to a mountain range far off in the west and said: "That's the Northern Mang Mountain." Talking as they went and making the most of the morning cool, they covered another twenty-six miles and then they came to a town on the eastern end of the mountain set in a rich country. Thither they directed their steps. East of the town, where dwellings were few, there was a T-shaped grove of tall poplars. Under the trees they found a crowd of people, jostling and craning their necks and there in the shade a fellow stripped to the waist and calling people to come and see his exhibition of staff play. They decided to take a rest under the trees. Wang Qing was soaked with sweat from the walking, his whole body dripping. With his cangue round his neck he pushed his way into the crowd and stood on tiptoe to see the fellow with the staff. After a moment he smiled involuntarily and said: "It's not serious stuff, what he's doing." The man was working himself up to a climax and when he heard this he put down his staff to see who had spoken. It was just a convict! He was outraged. "You bloody felon!" he shouted. "My staff play is renowned far and wide. What right have you to open your fucking mouth? Who said you can criticize me and talk such shit?" Throwing down his stick he squared up to Wang Qing and punched him in the face. Immediately two young men in the crowd stepped forward and separated them, saying: "Stop it!" They asked Wang Qing: "Are you an expert then?"

Wang Qing replied: "I spoke without thinking. I didn't mean to make this gentleman angry. I do have a little knowledge of staff play."

The other continued to rail against him: "You bloody convict, I bet you don't dare to take me on!"

The other two said to Wang Qing: "If you're willing to and can beat him, then these two strings of stolen cash are yours."

Wang Qing said with a grin: "It's no problem." He made his way through the crowd and borrowed a staff from one of the guards. He took off his shirt and rolled up his robe. Then he took a firm grip on the staff. The bystanders said: "You've got that cangue round your neck, how can you manage the staff?"

"That's the whole point," Wang Qing answered. "If I can beat him with this cangue on, there'll be no doubt about my skill."

"You'll certainly deserve the silver if you can beat him with the cangue on," they all cried. Everyone made way for him. His opponent was ready for him, staff in hand, and giving it a flourish shouted: "Come on, let's have you!"

Wang Qing said to the crowd: "Please don't be too critical. I only hope I won't disappoint you, gentlemen."

His opponent, hoping to take full advantage of the fact that Wang was hampered by the cangue, performed a move known as "the python swallows the elephant". Wang Qing countered with a move called "the dragonfly skims the water". The other gave a shout and lunged. Wang Qing took a step back. The other followed, raising his staff and aiming a hefty blow at Wang Qing's forehead. Wang Qing swayed to the left and his opponent's staff hit nothing but air. His recovery was too slow and as he tried to dodge Wang Qing struck him on the wrist and his staff fell to the ground. Luckily Wang had moderated the full force of the blow, but even so the wrist was broken. The crowd all laughed. But Wang Qing rushed forward and taking the other's hand in his said: "Forgive me for the blow!" The man made an attempt to scoop up the money with his left hand, the right hand being too painful. The crowd scolded him: "He's beaten you. It was just agreed this money was for the winner." Now the two young men who had come forward before grabbed the money and gave it to Wang Qing, saying: "Please, we would like to invite you to our house for a chat."

The staff play merchant could hardly dispute the matter with all those people so he had to pack up his things and head back to the city. After that the crowd dispersed.

The two young men led Wang Qing and his guards south past some woods, all of them wearing straw hats to keep off the sun, till they reached a village. Here among the trees was a manor house surrounded by a mud wall in a grove of willows. Outside the house the sound of cicadas filled the trees, inside the beams were alive with the twittering of swallows. They were led into the thatched hall and after formal courtesies had been exchanged they all took off their sweat shirts and hemp sandals and seated themselves. Their hosts said: "From your accent, you're from the capital, gentlemen?" Wang Qing told them his name and explained how he had been unjustly sentenced by a venal magistrate. He politely asked the other two their names. "I am Gong Duan," said the elder, "and this is my younger brother Gong Zheng. This is our ancestral home and the place is called Gong Village." He told a retainer to take away the visitors' wet shirts and dry them and then after drawing some cool water to relieve their thirst, take them up to bathe. Tables were laid first in the hall with freshly made dimsum, following which chickens and ducks were killed and some beans were boiled and peaches picked to offer them with the wine.

Then the retainers re-laid the tables: first a dish of peeled garlic and a dish of chopped chives. Then tea and vegetables were brought in, fruit and nuts, and fish, chicken, duck and so on. They seated Wang Qing in the place of honour with the two policemen next to him. The brothers took the host's place, while servants poured the wine. "I am a convicted criminal," Wang Qing said. "I am most grateful for your kindness, but I really do not deserve so much honour."

Gong Duan said: "Nonsense. Who can say he never gets into trouble? And who carries wine and food with him when he travels?"

They played guessing games and forfeits that evening and wine flowed till they were half tipsy. Gong Duan opened his mouth and said: "This little village of ours has about two hundred souls, all told. For some reason they insisted that we should be their leaders. It's true we're quite handy with fists and staves and can beat most people. Well, this spring in the second month at our local temple festival they put up a stage and had some performances and my brother and I went along to see. There was a quarrel over some betting and we got pretty badly beaten up by this chap from our village called Huang Da. We can't defeat him and he's been boasting to everyone about how he's the strongest. It's driving us crazy, but we've had to swallow our pride. Now we've seen how complete your technique is and we'd like you to be our teacher. If you would agree to train us we'd be extraordinarily grateful to you."

Wang Qing was only too happy to oblige and accordingly they prostrated themselves in the show of respect due to a teacher. They all got thoroughly drunk that evening, and then went to bed to get the benefit of the cool night air. Next morning Wang Qing was up betimes and took Gong Duan, the elder brother, down to the threshing floor to practise his footwork. As they were thus engaged a tall man strode in with his hands behind his back and shouted: "What's this bloody convict doing here trying to cheat us over his skill?" Now the appearance of this man was to have important results: further calamities would befall Wang Qing and Gong Duan would conceive an even greater hatred. Truly

A life of misrule begets only disaster;
What do gamblers win but disgrace!

If you want to know who the man was, you must read the next chapter.

Chapter 103

A warden loses his life because of his brother-in-law;
A prison official removes his cousin's scar!

Now while Wang Qing in the Gong brothers' compound was enjoying the start of a sunny day, cooled by a gentle breeze, training the elder brother in the art of attack and defence with the staff on their threshing floor shaded by the willow trees, a tall man marched in. The top of his head was shaved but he had no headgear and the remaining hair was tied back in a pigtail; he wore a short loose-fitting gown of brown cloth with plain silk trousers and open straw sandals, and he carried a triangular fan. As he marched in with his head held high, arms crossed behind his back, he saw this convict conducting the training session. He had heard the day before about a convict who defeated the expert performing in East Mang, and was afraid that the Gong brothers were learning some new moves, so he shouted to Wang Qing: "If you're a convict, what are you doing hanging around here to cheat people, instead of getting on with your journey?"

Wang Qing thought this must be some relative of the Gongs' so he didn't like to answer back. In fact it was Huang Da, their enemy. He too had come out to enjoy the morning freshness and was on his way to the house of Old Liu on the western end of the Gong village to collect a gambling debt, when he heard some noise up at the Gongs'. He was familiar with them, which is why he marched in uninvited.

An indescribable rage filled Gong Duan's breast when he saw who it was. The feeling rose towering and irrepressible, and he burst out: "You scoundrel! You piece of ass and ox shit! The other day you cheated me of my wager, how dare you walk in here and try to bully people!"

Huang Da equally annoyed riposted: "Go stuff your mother's arse!" He threw down his fan, raised his fists and rushed at Gong and punched him in the face. Wang Qing when he heard them giving vent to their feelings like this, guessed this must be Huang Da and rushed forward to help. He aimed a blow at Huang Da's ribs and Huang Da came crashing down. Before he could recover the Gong brothers and two of their retainers had pinned him down and began pounding him with their fists and feet in the back, chest, shoulders, ribs, flanks, cheeks, head and four limbs. There was nowhere their fists or feet did not reach except perhaps the tip of his tongue! He received an infinity of blows. His gown and trousers were in shreds. "That's enough, that's enough!" he kept shouting. He was now completely naked, not a scrap of clothing left to cover him. Only when the two guards of the prisoner's escort intervened did the Gongs at last stop.

After such a pounding Huang Da could only lie there gasping, there was no thought of resistance in him. Gong Duan told some of his farm workers to carry him half way to East Mang. They left him there on the grass where he lay naked in the sun for half the day. Eventually some neighbouring farmers came out to get fodder and found him. They carried him back home and he took to his bed. He got someone to write an accusation and take it to the local authorities. Of this no more.

Having fought all the first part of the morning, the Gongs told their retainers to bring some refreshments and invited Wang Qing and his guards to breakfast.

"That fellow will be back looking for revenge one of these days," said Wang Qing.

"If the lousy bastard wants to try something on, there's only his wife on his side, the neighbours were just scared of him, that's all. Now they've seen him beaten up, they won't back him. If he dies, we can pay a retainer to say he's responsible, take the beating and keep his mouth shut. If he doesn't die, then it's only a case of fighting. Anyway, I've had my revenge, entirely thanks to you, master, so please drink some wine and stop worrying. Once you've taught us fencing, we will have to repay you properly."

Gong Duan took out two silver ingots, each weighing five taels, and gave them to the guards, to persuade them to stay a little longer. With the money in their hands they could only say yes. They stayed more than ten days, in fact, and each day Wang Qing practised moves with spear and staff with the two brothers. The guards went on insisting they should leave, and when they heard that Huang Da had sent someone to the local government office to lodge a complaint, Gong Duan took out fifty taels of silver and gave them to Wang Qing for the journey to Shanzhou. They rose in the night and packed their things and left the house before daylight. The elder told his younger brother to carry the silver he had just given Wang Qing and accompany him on the journey.

The journey was uneventful and without any delay they reached Shanzhou. The two guards took Wang Qing to the government office and handed in the warrant from the Eastern Capital. Having acquainted himself with the facts, the magistrate accepted Wang Qing and signed the receipt which he gave to the escorts to take back. Of this no more. He then dispatched Wang Qing to the prison camp, while the guards returned to the capital with their receipt.

Gong Zheng then went off to see someone he knew there and gave him the money to give to the warden of the gaol for Wang Qing to buy some things he might need. This warden's name was Zhang Shikai. After receiving the money he had Wang Qing's cangue removed and excused him the serious flogging. Wang Qing was not given any work. He was given his own room and allowed to come and go as he pleased.

Gradually two months passed and it was late autumn. One day as Wang Qing was sitting idly in his cell, a guard came in and said: "The Warden wants to see you."

Wang Qing went with him to the reception room and kowtowed. The Warden said: "You've been here some time now, and I haven't yet asked you to do anything. I want to buy a good Chenzhou bow. Since you're from the capital and Chenzhou is in the same province, you ought to be able to tell whether the price is right." He took a package from his sleeve and handed it to

Wang Qing saying: "Here's two taels of the best silver. Go and get me a bow."

"I'll take care of it," Wang replied. He took the package to his cell where he opened it and found it to be indeed pure silver. He weighed it and it was a fraction over the weight. He left the camp and headed for a shop that sold bows, where he bought a real Chenzhou bow for only one seventy. When he got back to the camp with it, the Warden was not in his office, so he gave it to one of the officials of his household to take it to him. Happily there were thirty cents left over. Next day the Warden called him in again and said: "You are very efficient. The bow you bought yesterday is excellent."

Wang Qing said: "You should apply heat in its box to season it, Your Excellency."

"You don't need to tell me that," the Warden said.

From then on the Warden sent Wang out every day to buy things, only it was not like before. He did not advance him any money, but gave him an account book and told him to note down in it what he bought each day. But of course the shopkeepers would never let him off paying. He was obliged to draw on his own capital so he could buy the things and deliver them to the Warden's office, and the Warden always found fault, so it was always curses and beatings. After ten days when he presented the accounts and asked to be paid not a cent was forthcoming. When it came to the monthly balance, all he received from the Warden would be ten strokes, or twenty, or thirty. All in all he must have received a good three hundred and his legs were black and blue. The fifty taels of silver Gong Duan had given him had all been used up on these expenses.

One day Wang Qing went to the shop of one Doctor Zhang, maker of pills and mixer of beverages for internal and external applications, concoctor of medicines and seller of ointments, by the eastern corner of the triumphal arch west of the camp, because he wanted a cream to rub on his sores. The doctor talked while he applied the ointment for him: "An uncle of that prison warden of yours was here the other day, buying an ointment for his wrist. He said he'd had a fall in East Mang. But it looked more to me as if it had been broken by a sharp blow."

"How come I've never seen him in the camp?" Wang Qing asked eagerly.

"He's the brother of the Warden's minor wife," the doctor said. "His name is Pang Yuan. This Mistress Pang is the Warden's favourite. Her brother is a dreadful gambler and is also fond of spear and staff play. He owes everything to his sister who looks after him."

When he heard this Wang Qing was practically certain it was this Pang Yuan whom he had beaten the other day in the shade of the poplars. Small wonder the Warden was out to get him. When he went back to the camp he secretly got some wine and food and invited one of the junior turnkeys and gave him money and slowly questioned him about Pang Yuan. What the man told him confirmed what Doctor Zhang had said. Two things in particular he said: "You injured this Pang Yuan the other day at East Mang and he has complained about you to the Warden. I'm afraid you can't escape the thrashings!"

Truly we can say:

Be not too keen to win the race;
Better to yield and know your place!
From a single blow the quarrel's made;
With interest it will be repaid!

Back in his room, Wang Qing sighed and said: "As they say, don't fear justice, fear those who hand it out! The other day instead of keeping my big mouth shut I told that bugger I could beat him with the staff. How was I to know he was the younger brother of the prison Warden's sweetheart! If he's so determined to get me I'd better start by keeping out of his way and think of a plan later." He went out surreptitiously and bought a sharp knife which he secreted on his person just in case. Ten days passed and luckily there was no trouble. His wounds had healed somewhat.

Then one day the Warden ordered him to buy two rolls of silk. This had to be taken seriously, he could not put it off. He went at once to the shop and made the purchase. When he got back the

Warden was sitting in the reception room and he went straight there and reported. The Warden objected that the colour was wrong, that it was not long enough and the pattern was old-fashioned. "You cheeky beggar," he shouted. "You're a convict, you ought to be carrying water and shifting stone. Or maybe you should be locked up in solitary! This work I've given you is far too good for you. You just don't know when you're well off, you idle bastard."

Wang Qing bore it all in silence, kowtowing like someone laying out candles and asking for mercy.

"For the time being we'll postpone the beating. Go and get it changed quickly. If you don't bring it back by this evening, if you're a second late, then watch out for your life!"

Wang Qing had to take off his own clothes and pawn them for a couple of strings of cash in order to pay extra for changing the silk. This all took time and when he returned it was already after lighting up time and the camp gates were shut. The duty officer said: "How can I take it on myself to let you in after dark like this?"

Wang Qing said: "I'm on a mission for the Warden." But the duty officer didn't want to hear. Wang Qing had to give him all the money he had left before he would let him in and he still held him up a long time. Carrying his bundles of silk Wang Qing went to the door of the residence. The doorkeeper said: "His Excellency has had a big quarrel with his first wife. He's gone to the second wife's room, and the mistress is fuming. I daren't pass on your message, it's more than my life's worth!"

Wang Qing was thinking to himself: "He said I had to bring it back by tonight. Why put all these obstacles in my way? It's all meant to get me into trouble. How can I get out of the beating tomorrow? My life is really in that villain's hands. I've been beaten three hundred times. Isn't that enough to satisfy his taste for revenge? Previously he had all the money from Gong Zheng. Now he's changing his face and persecuting me like this!"

Now from his childhood Wang Qing had been an awkward cuss and even his own father and mother had been scared of upsetting him. When his rebellious spirit was aroused, he seemed proof of the saying "Gentlemen hate passionately, it's manly to express your anger". The thing was now, he could neither do it nor refrain from doing it. He had reached the limit. While everyone in the camp, convicts included, was asleep, he quietly crept round to the back of the residence, climbed a low wall, silently drew back the bolt on the rear door and hid on one side. By starlight he could see that inside the wall on the eastern end there was a stable and on the west end a very small shed which on closer inspection turned out to be a privy. Wang Qing picked up a set of wooden palings that were inside the stable and leant them against the wall by the two-leaved gate, climbed onto them and thence onto the wall, pulled up the palings after him and leant them inside, and carefully slipped down to the ground. First he drew back the bolts on the two doors and hid the wooden palings. There was another wall within and from behind it came the sound of laughter. He crept over to this wall and pressed his ear to it. Straining to hear, he recognized the Warden's voice and a woman's voice. There was also another man's voice. They were drinking and gossiping inside. After stealthily listening for some while, he heard the Warden say: "Brother-in-law, that villain will report back to me tomorrow and then his life will be forfeit to the cane."

"I reckon all the bugger has is used up by now," said the other man. "I hope you'll get on with it and finish the fucker off!"

The Warden said: "The day after tomorrow you'll have what you want!"

The woman said: "That's enough, now! Don't you two ever stop?"

The man said: "Who asked your opinion, sister? It's none of your business!"

Wang Qing listening outside the wall could get about one word in three, but the meaning was clear. A vast anger arose in his soul, an indescribable fire, towering into the sky, impossible to restrain, and he was involuntarily filled with the strength of a door god, till he was ready to throw down that plastered wall and charge in and kill the scoundrels. Indeed so far as they were concerned it was a case of

Illness strikes when all seems well.
Calamity looms when life's at the full.
Till autumn's winds the grasshopper plays.
The Reaper's waiting to end your days.

Just when he could bear it no longer, he heard the Warden say: "Boy, bring a lamp to light me to the privy." Immediately Wang Qing pulled out his knife and crouched down in the corner behind a plum tree. Then with a creak the door swung open, and casting a glow like the setting sun the boy emerged with a travelling lantern, the Warden following. They proceeded, unaware because of the dark that there was someone hiding there, watching only where they set their feet, till they reached the double doors and a curse resounded: "The incompetent oafs, not one of them pays attention. Why can they never remember to bolt the doors?"

The boy held the doors open and watched while the Warden exited through them. Wang Qing quietly crept up behind. The Warden heard steps behind him and turned just in time to see Wang bearing down on him with the knife in one hand and the fingers of the other splayed out. The Warden's heart and other organs flew heavenward as he cried out: "A thief!" It's slow in the telling but happens in a flash. Wang Qing's knife descended, carving a gash from ear to collarbone, and his victim crashed to the floor. The boy, though in the normal way of things he got on well enough with Wang Qing, when he saw him with the knife glinting in his hand, in the process of performing the dreadful deed, was naturally terrified. He would have fled, but his legs were as if nailed to the ground. He tried to scream, but he had been struck dumb and no sound came out. He was literally scared out of his wits. As the Warden lay writhing on the ground Wang Qing threw himself on him and finished him off with a stab in the back.

Pang Yuan, drinking in his sister's room, heard muffled noises outside and without waiting to light a lamp ran out to look. When he saw someone coming, Wang Qing delivered a kick to the boy with the lantern and both boy and lantern disappeared. Pang

Yuan thought it was the Warden beating the boy so he called out: "Why are you beating him, brother-in-law?" As he came forward, Wang Qing charged and stabbed at him in the dark, catching him in the ribs. Pang Yuan let out a screech like a stuck pig and fell to the floor. Holding the head up by the hair, Wang Qing cut it off.

The woman had heard the screams outside: she told one of the maids to light a lantern and they rushed out to see what was going on. Wang Qing thought to kill her too. What a scene that was! Words are not adequate to describe it! Anyway, Wang Qing saw in a flash that there were a dozen maids behind, all carrying makeshift weapons and screaming. Springing into action, he fled the scene. He opened the back door, scrambled over the wall of the prison compound, removed his bloodstained clothing, and wiped his knife and put it away. The watchman's drum sounded the third watch. Taking advantage of the fact that the streets were empty he approached the city wall. Shanzhou had an earthen wall and it was not very high nor was the moat very deep. He was able to cross both.

We shall leave him to make his escape, and describe how the Warden's wife Mistress Pang with two of her maids came out with a lantern to investigate. None of the others came with them. First she came upon her brother's bleeding head, lying on the ground in one place and the body in another. The women stared at each other in utter terror, feeling as if their skulls had been split open in eight places and a bucket of ice-cold water poured over the top. For a long time they stood and no words came out. Then stumbling and shaking with fear they ran back in again. They shouted to the other servants inside and to the guards on duty outside. Torches were lit, weapons grasped, and everyone went to the back to see. Outside the double doors they found the Warden's body and the boy lying on the ground gasping for breath and spitting blood. It was obvious he was not long for this world. Seeing the back door open they assumed it was a thief who had got in at the back. They rushed out to look and found the two bundles of silk thrown down on the ground and with one voice they all said: "Wang Qing!" They hurriedly called a roll of the convicts and found that Wang Qing alone was missing.

The whole camp was in an uproar, and also the people who lived around it on every side. Outside the back wall the blood-stained clothing was found and careful examination showed it to be all Wang Qing's. They discussed what to do and agreed that the matter must be reported to the magistrate before the opening of the city gates. Someone was sent at once. By now it was the fifth watch. The magistrate was shocked and sent the district police chief immediately to obtain details of the victims and ascertain the whereabouts of the murderer. It was ordered that the gates remain closed for two days and a state of emergency be maintained while a thorough house-to-house search was conducted, but no trace was found of the murderer. The magistrate published a notice and had it distributed to all the villages in his jurisdiction, requiring village elders to carry out searches and apprehend the murderer. The notice gave details of Wang Qing's place of origin and age; it contained a description of his appearance and build, together with a picture, and announced a reward of a thousand strings of cash. Anyone who knew anything of his whereabouts was obliged to report it and would receive the reward. Anyone harbouring the criminal or giving him food and lodging would be prosecuted as an accomplice and suffer the same fate as the criminal. Neighbouring districts for miles around were put on the alert.

After climbing the city wall that night, Wang Qing had made a bundle of his clothes and waded across the moat. He was thinking: "I've got out of it with my life, but where can I go now?" Winter was approaching. The leaves had fallen the grass withered, and he had to find his way with only the stars to light him. He followed several small paths and finally came to a main road. He moved along at a smart pace and by the time dawn was showing red in the east he had done a good twenty miles, but he continued on, heading south, till he came to a populated area. He remembered he still had a little money on him and decided to approach and find something to eat and drink and give himself time to think where he was going to go. In a little while he came to a market. It was still early and the wine shops and eating house were not open yet. There was just one eastward facing house under whose eaves hung a battered lamp, announcing it to be a rest house for travelling merchants. The place had not been properly closed up the night before and the door was half open. Wang Qing advanced and pushed the door, which swung open with a creak. The man who appeared from inside was still unwashed. Wang Qing recognized him. It was his first cousin, Fan Quan. In his youth he had been a successful broker with his father in Fangzhou, and had been made superintendant of the district's two prisons. This spring in the third month he went to the capital on official business and stayed several days in Wang Qing's house. "Cousin, how've you been keeping?" Wang Qing called out.

"Can it be cousin Wang Qing?" the other replied. Startled by his appearance and by the two golden seals tattooed on his cheeks, he did not at first know what to say. Wang Qing looked around to make sure no one was near and then knelt before him and said: "Cousin, save me I beg you!" Fan Quan hurriedly raised him up and said: "You really are Wang Qing then?"

Wang Qing waved a hand and said: "Keep your voice down!"

Fan Quan caught on at once and taking him by the sleeve pulled him inside. Luckily the night before he had chosen a single room. Quietly but urgently he asked: "Why are you looking like this?" In a whisper Wang Qing told him all about the injustice he had suffered and the banishing to Shanzhou, after which he told of Warden Zhang's cruel treatment and what had happened just the day before. Fan Quan was so shocked he could not at first think what to do. Then he quickly washed and shaved, had breakfast, and paid the bill for food and lodging. Having decided that Wang Qing must pretend to be a gaoler's assistant, they left the inn and headed for Fangzhou. As they went Wang Qing asked his cousin how he came to be there. "My governor sent me to deliver some papers to the governor of Shanzhou," he said. "Yesterday I received the reply and set off. But it was getting late so I stopped here for the night. I had no idea you were in Shanzhou or that all this had happened."

They continued their journey all night till they arrived in Fangzhou. Two days had passed and in Shanzhou the notices were out for the arrest of the murderer Wang Qing. Fan Quan returned home anxiously and told Wang Qing: "You're not safe here in the city. I've got some cottages out in the country, east of Mount Ding, on a piece of land I bought for myself last year. I've settled a few farm hands there to cultivate it. You'd better go and hide there for a few days. Later you can decide what to do."

He waited till dark and then took Wang Qing to the cottage at Mount Ding. They decided to change his name to Li De. Fan Quan thought the tattoos on Wang Qing's cheeks didn't look too solid. Luckily he had previously been in Jiankang and having heard a lot of Doctor An, had gained his confidence by means of generous gifts. Doctor An had shown him a way of removing tattoos. He used an acid on Wang Qing's cheeks and afterwards an ointment to heal them. At first the treatment raised a red welt but the tattoos disappeared. In two months even the scar was gone.

Since time is ever fleeting, a hundred days soon passed and it was the spring festival of the first year of the reign. The Government pursuit of Wang Qing had come to nothing. His face now bore no trace of the tattoos and gradually he began to go about more confidently, wearing the clothes that had been donated to him by his cousin. One day as he was sitting bored in the cottage, he heard a certain commotion in the distance. He asked some of the peasants what the excitement was all about.

"There's some people called Duan, Mr. Li, lives just west of us here. Well these Duan brothers have got a singer to come from the capital, They've put up a stage and all. There's going to be a performance, with all kinds of music. They say she's the latest thing, a top-notch artist. She's expected to pull in a huge audience. You ought to go along and take a look."

After this build-up, Wang Qing was never likely to resist. But because he went there, certain things would happen. A young lady of the district was going to marry a convict, the people would suffer a load of misfortune at the hands of a fierce beast.

If you want to know whether there really was a performance or not when Wang Qing went there, you must read the next chapter.

Chapter 104

At the Duans' a bridegroom is welcomed; The chief on House Mountain fights two opponents!

When Wang Qing rushed over to the next village, Mount Ding, he found a crowd of five or six hundred gathered there. The stage was set up on the threshing floor outside the village. The artist had not yet made her entrance, but around the stage there were some thirty or forty tables. People were crowding around, throwing dice and placing bets. Others, a group of twenty or so, were squatting on the ground tossing coins.

That's how it was: some shaking the dice and shouting out the combinations — pairs, straight, flush, full house, and so on, others tossing coins and calling heads or tails. There was laughter and curses and even serious fights. The losers took off their shirts and pawned their clothes, ready to lose all they had and ruin their business, forgetting to eat and sleep. This was losing indeed, going the whole hog! Those who were winning were in expansive mood, strutting and swaggering about, marching this way and that in search of drinkers willing to continue the game, their purses, bags, and sleeves overflowing with money. But when the final reckoning came, they would find they had really won very little. They gambled their winnings away or had them eaten up by the gaming master's rake-off.

Besides the gambling scene there were also all the countrywomen who had abandoned the hoeing and watering of their crops and come flocking in droves, and who stood there, brown faces upturned and gold teeth glinting, waiting expectantly for the actress to appear. There were also mothers and fathers and their offspring. She was really smart and fashionable and many people had come to see her. Not only the locals from the village were there; people from the city had come to gaze too. A huge area of that green countryside had been trampled bare.

Well, to cut a long story short, Wang Qing became restless after watching this scene for a while. As he glanced round the throng beside the stage his eye was taken by a large bewhiskered gent sitting on a bench and leaning his arms on the table. He had round eyes and a big head, broad shoulders and narrow waist. Five strings of cash were piled on the table, a dice cup and six dice, but he had no takers. "It's about ten months since I fell foul of the law," Wang Qing was thinking. "In all these months I haven't had a go at this. I've got that money Fan Quan gave me the other day for my living expenses. Why don't I test my luck, try a few throws with this fellow? I'll just make enough to buy myself something special to eat." He took out his money and threw it down on the table, saying: "Let's give it a go."

The other man took a good look at him and said: "Come on then." As he spoke another man emerged from the crowd around the table in front. He had a long thin face and bore a distinct resemblance to the one who was sitting. He said to Wang Qing: "Is that all you've got? You won't get far with that. Have some money from me. I'll only charge you two percent on your winnings."

"Fair enough!" Wang Qing said. He took two strings of cash from the man, who set aside twenty cents from each. "That'll do," said Wang Qing, and announced he was going to try for a full house. After the first few throws, another man approached and put down a stake. Now Wang Qing was accustomed to gambling in the style of the Eastern Capital: he believed in his luck, but he also knew a trick or two and was a master of bluff and deception. The man who had lent him the money took the opportunity to slip round to the other side of the table, while the newcomer encouraged him to give the dice a "good whirl".

Straight off Wang Qing won two strings of cash. Having won, he went on throwing and his luck held. He was about ready to leave off, but the other man impatiently renewed his stake, seemingly determined to go on to the bitter end. When Wang Qing threw a nine, the other man only threw eight. In not much more than an hour he had lost five strings of cash and was cleaned out. From his winnings Wang Qing made up two strings of cash with a piece of twine and put them on one side. He strung together the rest of the money to his satisfaction and was about to lift it onto his shoulder when the man who had lost cried out: "Where are you taking that money? I reckon that's still too hot from the stove — you're going to burn your hands!"

"You lost to me," Wang Qing replied angrily. "Cut it out!"

The other man glared at him and said: "You son of a bitch. Can't you see I'm your superior?"

Wang Qing replied in kind: "You motherfucking peasant! If you hit me in the stomach you'll never get your fist out! How can you stop me taking the money?"

The other put up his fists and aimed a blow at Wang Qing's face. The latter swayed to one side and caught the other's arm, thrust his right elbow into the pit of his stomach and tripped him with his right leg. The man's strength availed him nothing, he could not break the hold and he crashed over backwards and lay flat on his back, face to the sky. The onlookers all began to laugh. The man struggled to rise but Wang Qing pressed him down and subjected him to a regular going over. Now the one who had first put down the money came and without a word of either reproof or encouragement scooped up all the money on the table. Furious, Wang Qing left the man on the ground and raced after the other. Suddenly a woman appeared from the crowd and began shouting: "He won't get away with it, the blighter, he's got me to reckon with!"

This is what she was like:

There's a ferocious glint in her eye, a malignant expression on her face. Her waist and limbs are thick and coarse; she lacks all feminine charms. Her skin is rough; she relies on thick make-up to cover the blemishes. She boasts a headful of weird hairpins, and offers glimpses of two arms covered in most ordinary looking bangles. When it comes to moving the stone mortar, she laughs at the way others pant and strain; picking up the rail of

> *the well she is proud that it costs her no effort. If it's needlework you're after, she hasn't a clue; but for kicking and fisticuffs she's a real artist.*

She was around twenty four or five, this woman. She removed her outer garment rolled it up and threw it down on the table. Inside she wore a tight short-sleeved robe of parrot green silk and underneath wide breeches of padded silk. She strode forward, raised her fists and shaped up to Wang Qing. Well, since she was a woman and he could see a weakness in her guard, Wang Qing thought he was going to have some fun. He deliberately refrained from using fast kicks, and instead took up a wrestler's stance, adopting an open posture and waiting for her to attack.

By now the actors had come on stage to perform their comic sketch, but the people had all gone off to watch this fight between a man and a woman and were crowding around them in a tight circle. The woman saw that the man was going to confine himself to blocking and parrying, but she hadn't enough strength to force the issue. So she waited for an opening and then performed a "black tiger", aiming one fist at his heart. He swayed to one side and she struck only the air. Before she could recover her balance he grabbed her and upended her with a twist. As soon as she hit the ground he lightly picked her up in a move called "the tiger grabs a head". "Be careful," he said, "you'll get your clothes dirty. Forgive me for being a bit rough, but you did start it." She was not the least bit put out. "You're pretty nifty," she said. "That's a good hold."

Now the man who had lost money and been beaten, together with the one who had first put up money and then grabbed the winnings, pushed through the crowd and began shouting: "You lecherous bastard, you've got a nerve! How dare you interfere with our little sister!"

Wang Qing shouted back: "You're a fucking bad loser. You stole my money, and now you're making filthy insinuations." He rushed at them with his fists flying. Then another man came out of the crowd and got between all three of them. "Mr. Li, enough of this!" he shouted. " Duan brothers, stop it! We're all neighbours.

If you've got something to say to each other, then say it nicely!" It was Wang Qing's cousin, Fan Quan. The three men stopped fighting. Cousin Fan Quan hurriedly said to the girl: "Please forgive him."

The girl bowed and said: "Is Mr. Li a relative of yours?"

"He is my cousin."

"He's a terrific fighter!"

Wang Qing said to Fan Quan: "I couldn't bear to see that villain lose and then call in his accomplices to steal the money!"

Fan Quan said pleasantly: "To them it's a business, why did you have to come and make trouble?"

The Duan brothers were watching their sister expectantly. She said: "Out of respect for Mr. Fan you mustn't fight with him any more. Give us the money."

In deference to his sister, who was evidently something special, Duan the Fifth was obliged to admit that he had lost the money fairly and hand it over to her. She gave it to Fan Quan, saying: "Here is the original sum. Please take it." With that she hustled her brothers away, while Fan Quan likewise took Wang Qing back home.

Fan Quan made no secret of his annoyance: "For my mother's sake I lay my life on the line, letting you stay here. If an amnesty comes up we can do some business together. Why the devil do you have to be so restless? Those Duan brothers are real troublemakers. And the girl is even worse. They've nicknamed her 'Big Beast'. I don't know how many young gentlemen she's ruined. When she was fifteen she was married to a squire who was an old idiot and before a year was out she'd burnt him to death. Relying on their strength she and her two brothers earn themselves a dishonest living by going around creating disputes like that. In all the villages round about they're afraid of them. Their speciality is getting people to gamble. That gaming table is the bait, don't you see? It was just asking for trouble to go there and stir things up, my friend! If you've been noticed, we're going to be in a real mess!"

Wang Qing kept his mouth shut during all this.

Fan Quan stood up and said: "I've got to go and report for

duty at the government office. I'll come back and see you tomorrow."

We shall leave Fan Quan to go off to Fangzhou, and tell of Wang Qing, who went to bed quite late and passed an uneventful night. Next morning when he had just completed his toilet, one of the farm workers entered and said: "Squire Duan has come to see you."

Wang Qing went out to receive the guest who turned out to be a wrinkled silver haired old gentleman. After the exchange of courtesies Squire Duan took the place of honour. He looked Wang Qing up and down from head to foot and muttered to himself: "What a giant!" He asked Wang Qing about his family background and what brought him to the neighbourhood, what was the relationship between him and Fan Quan and whether he was married or not. Wang Qing responded to this interrogation by telling him a pack of lies to throw him off the scent: "I'm from the Western Capital, my parents are both dead, and my wife also, Fan Quan and I are first cousins. Last year he came to the Western Capital on business and saw I was all alone with no one to look after me so he invited me back here. I know a bit about fighting and I'm watching out for an opportunity here to advance my fortunes."

Squire Duan seemed satisfied with this. After asking Wang Qing what his sign was, he said goodbye and left. After a certain while as Wang Qing was wondering about all this he had another caller. "Is Mr. Fan at home?" he asked. "And is this Mr. Li I'm speaking to?" They stared at each other in amazement, both thinking: "We've met before." They exchanged courtesies and were just about to start a conversation when Fan Quan turned up. When the three of them were seated, Fan Quan said: "What brings you here, Mr. Li?"

When Wang Qing heard that name, he suddenly remembered: "It's Mr. Li the fortune-teller!"

For his part the fortune-teller was thinking: "It's that chap from the Eastern Capital, name of Wang, who wanted me to tell his fortune." He said to Fan Quan: "I have never been to your home before, sir. May I ask you, is it true that you have a relative called Li?"

Fan Quan pointed to Wang Qing and said: "But this is my relative, Mr. Li."

Wang Qing leant towards him and said cannily: "Li is my original name. Wang is the name of the family I married into."

The fortune-teller smiled and said with a wave of the hand: "I was right then. I thought it was Wang. We met before in the Eastern Capital, didn't we?"

Wang Qing could see that he remembered exactly. He lowered his head and said nothing. The fortune-teller said: "After I left you, when I went back to Jingnan I met a stranger who taught me the ancient secrets of swordplay. Recently in Fangzhou I heard there was something going on here and came here in the hope of earning some money. The Duans know how I can handle a sword and wanted me to teach them so they invited me to stay in their house. Just now Squire Duan came home and gave me your sign to do your horoscope. When did I ever see such a good fortune? Some day you'll be rich beyond words! Right now a great marriage is in the offing, a most fortunate affair. Miss Duan and her father have much pleasure in inviting you to bcome part of the family. Since it is an auspicious day I took the liberty of calling as their representative. Miss Duan's fortune is splendid. It is really suitable that you should get together. Like steel bowl and iron broom, it's a union made in heaven. May I look forward to drinking the betrothal wine?"

After listening to this long speech, Fan Quan sighed to himself and thought: "Those Duans are a troublesome lot. If I stand in the way of this alliance or try to prevaricate, there's going to be no end of trouble. I'd best go along with it." To the fortune-teller he said: "So that's how it is! I'm most grateful to the Squire and Miss Duan for their kind thoughts. The only thing is, this cousin of mine is not much of a catch. Are you sure he's good enough?

"Aiya!" exclaimed the other. "Don't be so modest. Miss Duan never stops talking about him!"

Fan Quan said: "That's excellent then! I can be his guarantor." He took out a five tael silver ingot and gave it to the fortune-teller saying: "Here in the country we haven't got the means to entertain you properly. This is just a little something to prepare some refreshments, in token of my gratitude."

The fortune-teller said: "There's no need."

Fan Quan said: "It's nothing! There is just one condition. You must not mention that he has two names. I hope everything will go well."

Li Zhu was like any other fortune-teller: once he had the money in his hand he left with many professions of gratitude and went back to the Duans. What did it matter to him whether the man had one name or two, or what kind of person he was? His business was to secure the match, get the wine flowing, earn himself some money. Especially since the girl herself had set her sights on the other party and they were all afraid of her, even the Squire himself wouldn't want to cross her. The affair was as good as settled.

As the fortune-teller went to and fro he was hoping to talk up the betrothal money, to the greater benefit of the go-between. But Fan Quan was afraid the question of money would arouse difficulties and urged that both sides should minimize the costs. This was pleasing to Squire Duan, who was a thrifty man, and no time was lost fixing the day. They settled on the twenty-second of the same month. Sheep and pigs were slaughtered, fish and frogs caught, there would be big bowls for the wine and big dishes for the meat. A few relatives were invited to the wedding banquet, musicians were hired and the bridal chamber decked with flowers, all at minimum cost. Fan Quan had a new set of clothes made for Wang Qing. Because of his official duties he himself had to leave early. Wang Qing and the girl went through the official introductions and drinking from the betrothal cup and so on, all as quickly as possible. The Squire had the banquet laid in the main hall, and together with twenty or so relatives, his own children, the groom and the matchmaker, they feasted all day long and the party did not break up until nightfall. Then the relatives who lived nearby said thank you and left. The ones remaining because they lived too far away were the girl's uncle and aunt, the Fangs, the family of her cousin Qiu, and Duan the Second's brother- and sister-in-law, the Shis. The three men were to sleep over in the east wing. The three ladies, who were all bright young things, prepared some food and wine for the newly weds to warm up the bridal chamber. With much giggling they continued drinking for a while, then everyone prepared for bed. At this point an old servant came to make up the beds and turn down the covers in the bridal chamber and invite the new master and his wife to go to rest. She then bolted the door of the chamber on the outside and took herself off.

Miss Duan had been domineering and headstrong even as a child. She was in no way inexperienced and knew the ways of the world. Nor was she troubled by shyness. She had already taken her hair pins out and removed her outer garment. Wang Qing was a man of the world and since his sentencing, which was ten months now, he had known no woman. Miss Duan had beetling brows and big eyes, it is true, and had nothing like the sweet allure of his former lover the Marshal's daughter or his wife, but seen now by lamplight her swelling form, her red stomacher unlaced to reveal the soft white breasts naturally aroused his lust and he rushed forward to embrace her. She boxed his ears roundly and said: "No hanky-panky, let's get that clear!" But when they embraced on the bed and slipped between the covers, then they shared the bliss of the common pillow:

> *One a country girl of easy virtue, the other a rough convict; both have skin a foot thick and great clodhopper feet! One is panting urgently like an ox resting under a willow; the other sweetly utters coarse words, like the oriole among flowers. There are no momentous oaths and treaties here, yet there is a great fluttering of flags; no trembling or reluctance greets the clouds and rain, for here compacted lie ten thousand bewitchments.*

Outside the bedchamber that night there was a deal of lewd talk and laughter. The ladies, Mistresses Fang, Qiu and Shi, were all youthful and they had all drunk enough to turn their cheeks bright red, so instead of going to sleep they enlisted the wives of the two Duan brothers and all together crept up to the bridal chamber and put their ears to the wall to listen. They could hear every sound plainly. Wang Qing was an experienced lover well versed in the arts of the bedchamber. When he saw his new wife was more than willing, he did all he knew how to satisfy her. The group of young women outside, hearing all the sounds, found that their silk knickers were soaked through.

There, then, was this bevy of females outside the room, engaged in sniggering and lewd commentary, nudging and pinching each other, when Duan the Second burst upon them, shouting: "This is a fine thing! Are you senseless, all of you, fooling around like this?" This stopped them in their tracks. They had nothing to say for themselves. "Sister, sister, get up!" Duan the Second shouted. "You've invited calamity into your bed!"

The woman, in the midst of her pleasure, reacted furiously: "What're you doing, kicking up such a row in the middle of the night?"

"You're in for a bloody shock!" he shouted back "You're in deep trouble!"

Now Wang Qing was no fool. He told his wife to get dressed and they both came out to find out what was going on. The other women had fled. The moment Wang Qing appeared Duan the Second grabbed him and dragged him off to the main hall where they found Fan Quan cursing fate, frantic as an ant on a hot plate with nowhere to go. Soon the Squire joined them, with his other son and his daughter. Apparently back in the Gong village their enemy Huang Da had recovered from his beating and after inquiries had traced Wang Qing to his present whereabouts. The previous day he had arrived in Fangzhou and informed the Governor. The latter had issued a warrant and sent a captain with troops of the local militia to arrest the murderer Wang Qing, together with Fan Quan, guilty of harbouring him, and the Duan family. Because he worked in the government office Fan Quan was friendly with the registrar of cases, who had leaked the news to him. He abandoned everything and raced back to say government troops would be there any minute, they were all for it! There was a general stamping of feet and beating of breasts, as if a henhouse had been overturned, a great deal of commotion, and everyone began to accuse Wang Qing of ruining Miss Duan. In the midst of all this the fortune-teller turned up. He stepped forward and said: "Ladies and gentlemen, if you want to get out of this, you'd better listen to me!"

They all crowded forward to hear what he had to say. "The damage is done," he said. "There are thirty-six things you can do in a crisis, but the best is always running away."

"But where can we go?" they clamoured.

"Mount Fang, House Mountain, is only a few mile west of here," he said.

"But that's the robbers' hideout," they said.

"Are you stupid, or what?" he said scathingly. "Do you really think you can go on as respectable citizens, as if nothing had happened?"

"Then what are we to do?" they said.

"I know Liao Li, the leader of the band there, quite well," he said. "He's got five or six hundred troops and the government forces can't catch him. You'll have to act fast. Pack up all your valuables and go there to join the band. It's the only way out."

Mr. Fang and the others were also afraid they'd eventually be implicated and were persuaded by Wang Qing and his wife to join them. All of them saw no other solution but to follow this path. Everything of any value on the estate was collected and packed up. Thirty or forty torches were lit. Then having completed their preparations nine of them — Wang Qing and his wife, her two brothers, Messers Fang, Qiu and Shi her relatives, the fortune-teller and Fan Quan the government official — buckled on swords and took up spears and halberds. The retainers were summoned and over forty of them said they wanted to go too, so they packed their things. The party would proceed with Wang Qing, Fortune-teller Li and Fan Quan in the lead, the ladies in the middle and Fang, Qiu and Shi bringing up the rear. Luckily the ladies had sturdy farmer's legs and could keep up with the men. The Duans were the last to leave and went round setting fire to their farm. With much cheering they shouldered their weapons and set off westwards. The people round about regarded these Duans with as much dread as a tiger so when they saw them passing with torches and cudgels and didn't know what was going on they simply bolted their doors. No one thought of interfering.

They had only gone a mile or so when they ran into the captain of militia and Huang Da who had joined forces to arrest them. The captain who was leading soon fell: Wang Qing's sword cut him in two and the rest of the party surged forward and scattered the militia men. Wang Qing also killed Huang Da.

They reached House Mountain a little before dawn. The fortune-teller proposed to go up the mountain first alone in order to explain what they wanted, before taking the rest of them up to join the band. Scouts in the stronghold saw the lights down below and reported it to their chief, who assumed it was government troops. Accustomed to think of them as useless, he rose quickly, armed himself and went down with some of his men to deal with them. Wang Qing saw lights coming down the mountain and then a body of men, and made preparations. When the robber chief got to the bottom and saw the people he realized they were not government troops. He levelled his spear and shouted: "What the fuck are you buggers doing disturbing my fortress? Don't you know you're tempting fate?"

The fortune-teller stepped forward and bowed. "Great prince, it is I, your friend Li Zhu," he said. He proceeded to explain about Wang Qing's crime and the killing of the governor and government troops. But when the chief heard him describe Wang Qing's qualities and saw he had all the Duans in support, it occurred to him that he was on his own and he began to fear that later on they might oppose him. So he turned to the fortune-teller and said: "There isn't room for all of you in this place of ours."

This in turn gave Wang Qing an idea: "They've only this one chief. If we get rid of him, what alternative will his troops have?" He raised his halberd and attacked. The bandit came angrily to meet him, twirling his lance. Fearing for her husband's safety Miss Duan joined in with her halberd. These three fought ten bouts before one of them fell.

What they say is true, it's near the well that the pot gets broken, the strong man dies by the sword!

If you want to know which of the three it was that fell, you must read the next chapter.

Chapter 105

***Song Jiang gives his men a break;
The Wizard sends the fire right back!***

The robber chief had only fought half a dozen bouts with Wang Qing and his wife when Wang Qing spotted an opening and ran him through with his halberd. Miss Duan rushed in and finished him off. This man had ruled his little world like a king, but now it was all a vain dream! Wang Qing put up his weapon and announced: "If there is anyone who objects, the same fate will be his!" None of the troops, seeing their leader dead, was prepared to argue. They switched their allegiance forthwith.

Wang Qing led the way up the mountain. By this time light was beginning to show in the east. All around the mountain were natural rock formations shaped like houses, whence its name of Mount Fang or House Mountain. Wang Qing made arrangements for everyone, organized the troops and inspected the camp's provisions and assets of cash and valuables. Oxen and horses were slaughtered, the troops rewarded, and wine was laid on for a general celebration. Wang Qing was elected leader. Thereafter arms were manufactured and the troops received training to prepare them for taking on the government forces. Of this no more.

Now some of the militia men and officers sent to arrest Wang Qing and defeated that same evening had managed to escape with their lives and went back to report to the governor of Fangzhou. "Wang Qing had been forewarned," they said. "They attacked us and killed the captain as well as the accuser Huang Da. They made off to the west."

The Governor was greatly disturbed. Next day a count was made of the militia and it was found that over thirty had been killed and another forty wounded. The Governor held a meeting with the officers of his garrison and ordered the bandit suppression force and troops of the garrison to pursue and capture the miscreants. The resistance was fierce and more government troops were killed. The bandits of House Mountain, with Wang Qing and his friends, began making regular forays down the mountain to pillage and burn. In the face of the bandits' unbridled savagery the Governor issued a proclamation ordering all districts to contribute troops from their own defence forces to aid in suppressing them. He also planned a campaign against them with his own defence chief, General Hu, who selected troops from the garrison, chose an auspicious day and set out on the campaign. But there was a sudden disturbance among the troops of both camps. The reason for this was that for two months they had not had any rations or pay and were half-starved. In this condition, how could they be expected to catch bandits? When news of the mutiny reached the Governor he was obliged for a start to supply a month's pay and rations. However this handout only made things worse! Why so? Well, the authorities were normally very stingy. Now that the troops found they only had to make a fuss and they were generously rewarded, they became quite overbearing. There was also a more trivial aspect. The forms of respect for authority had been neglected, becoming weaker and weaker until they dwindled to nothing. With the breakdown of discipline mutiny suddenly flared among the troops and they killed their general. The Governor decided things looked bad and, pausing only to rescue the official seal, fled the scene.

There was now no authority in the city. All the local vagabonds joined forces with the rebellious army and began looting and burning the houses of loyal citizens. The bandit Wang Qing, seeing the city in revolt, took the opportunity of marching his troops down to capture it. The rebellious troops and the malefactors in the city enlisted with the bandits. Thus Wang Qing gained advantage and was now able to make Fangzhou his base. In the end the Governor did not escape either — they killed him too.

Wang Qing seized all the contents of the Fangzhou stores and treasury and ordered Li the fortune-teller and the two Duans to muster troops on House Mountain and elsewhere, and lay in

stores of fodder and grain. Villages were plundered far and wide. Vagabonds and disaffected folk poured into the city. The two Gong brothers, Wang Qing's former pupils in swordsmanship, who had been denounced by Huang Da and had all their property confiscated, heard that Wang Qing was raising an army and came to join up. Neighbouring cities were only concerned to defend themselves. No one there had a thought of coming after the rebels. Within two months the rebels had enlisted twenty thousand men and captured three more cities.

Nearby cities reported all this to the court and the court ordered the arrest of the rebels. But the Song army was short of supplies and the troops ill-trained; the men did not respect their commanders and the commanders did not know their men. Whenever the alarm was sounded, reports of the rebel strength grew to alarming proportions: the troops were paralysed with fear and the people's morale was shattered. The eve of a battle found the officers quaking in their boots and their forces weak and irresolute. Then of course Wang Qing and his lot threw everything into the attack and the government troops were bound to lose. So the disturbance caused by Wang Qing grew ever greater and he captured Nanfeng as well. When the court appointed a general, he had to present gifts to the Grand Preceptor and Marshal Tong and bribe Marshals Gao and Yang and even when they all had their bribes nothing got done. The general, having spent his own money and got power into his own hands, would act shamelessly, hanging on to the stores, discriminating against men of integrity, allowing the soldiers to rape and loot, antagonizing the local population and driving honest citizens into the arms of the rebels.

Thus the power of the rebels grew continuously and their territory began to expand. Fortune-teller Li, being originally from Jingnan, came up with a plan whereby he resumed his fortune-teller's garb, entered that city and secretly organized the riff raff into a resistance which, coordinated with the attack from outside, handed them the city. He was duly appointed military adviser and styled himself Prince Chu. Subsequently the rebels were joined by some important pirates and bandits.

Within three or four years the rebels had overrun six Song

commands. Wang Qing built himself a great palace in Nanfeng, complete with courts and towers, and assumed a false imperial title. He copied the Song administrative system with its civil and military officials, its burocracy, palace ministers and generals. He gave important posts to all the founder members of his movement, including Fortune-teller Li, his in-laws the Duans, his relative Fan Quan and those former pupils in the art of the sword the Gong brothers. The former Miss Duan was now the imperial consort. In the spring of the fifth year of the Emperor's reign — during the time Song Jiang was in Hebei dealing with Tian Hu and on the day of the battle at Kettle Pass — Wang Qing's forces captured Yun'an and Wanzhou. They had now overrun eight military commands.

But once Wang Qing attacked Wanzhou, which was very close to the Eastern Capital, the Grand Preceptor and his cronies could no longer conceal everything from the Emperor. They requested him to order Cai the Younger, the Grand Preceptor's son, and Marshal Tong to attack Wang Qing and relieve Wanzhou. These two maintained no proper discipline: the ordinary soldiers were treated with the utmost harshness and their morale was at rock bottom. Therefore Wang Qing's forces were able to inflict a great defeat on them: Wanzhou was lost and the Eastern Capital came under serious threat. The two government generals were afraid they would be held accountable and withheld the truth from the Emperor. The rebels, followed up their success by besieging two more cities.

Song Jiang's army, having just pacified Hebei, now had to go and deal with the situation west of the river Huai. It was truly a case of "no time to enjoy the feast, the horse's hooves don't stop". With this great army of more than two hundred thousand they were moving south. They had crossed the Yellow River when a directive arrived from the War Council urging Commissioner Chen and Song Jiang to rush to relieve the two cities under siege. They urged their sweating mounts on through the summer heat, taking great care not to harm the local population in any way. The rebels heard of their approach and lifted their siege.

At this time Hotshot, Arrowtip and the Butler, after witnessing the execution of Tian Hu, had received the imperial favour and were hurrying to rejoin Song Jiang in the campaign against Wang Qing. A fortnight after they left the capital they met up with him. After the greetings they gave a full account of the Emperor's gracious treatment. Everyone was greatly impressed. Song Jiang told them to be ready for service.

Song Jiang requested Commissioner Chen, Marshal Hou and Academician Luo to set up their headquarters in the nearby town, which was unsuitable for quartering the army. He ordered the army to make camp at Mount Fangcheng, where the cool shade of the forest would provide protection from the heat. Because they had travelled hundreds of miles many of the men were suffering from sunstroke and he ordered Doctor An to prepare medicines for them. He also ordered them to erect awnings for the horses and instructed Redbeard to treat the horses and trim their manes.

The Professor said: "If the army camps in the forest there is a danger that the enemy might use fire."

Song Jiang said: "We'll have to take the risk." High up on the mountain he had them construct a small mountain refuge with shelters made of bamboo matting in a cool place under the trees. Then Qiao the Wizard, who had surrendered in Hebei, came to him and said: "I owe you a great debt for your magnanimity. I would like to suggest a way to protect the camp."

Song Jiang was pleased and when he had heard the plan in secret he sent the Wizard off to the mountain refuge. He selected thirty thousand strong men and told Hotshot and Arrowtip to take ten thousand cavalry to the foot of the east mountain to lay an ambush. The Chancellor and Lucky Bian were to lay an ambush with ten thousand cavalry under the west peak. When they heard the main force fire the big gun they were to attack. All the stores and fodder were to be piled up on the south, guarded by Skyhawk and Mr. Chai with five thousand men.

After these orders had been given Taoist Gongsun suddenly came and said: "It's a good plan, brother, but with the weather as hot as this the men always get sick and if the enemy made a sudden and determined attack our troops would have a hard time of it, even if they were ten times better than normal. Let me practise my art a little to get us all some respite and refresh the troops so they can regain their strength." He began to wave his sword and tread out the pattern of the Dipper, in his left hand the thunder seal, in his right hand the magic sword. Concentrating his mind and thinking deeply, he turned toward the southeast aspect and taking a deep breath, intoned a spell. In a moment a cool breeze began to blow, and clouds filled the sky and released their load on the mountain. The whole of Mount Fangcheng was streaming with water. Two hundred thousand men and horses breathed in the freshness with joyous relief. Everywhere else except just here on the mountain it was hot as a furnace, the cicadas whirring and birds and animals all hiding away. All of Song Jiang's men were delighted and exceedingly grateful for Taoist Gongsun's special powers. In less than a week Doctor An had put everyone back on their feet and Redbeard had got the horses back into shape; men and horses were all restored to full strength. Of this no more.

Now the rebel commander of Wanzhou was one of their best tacticians. They had dubbed him Uncle Know-all. When he learnt that Song Jiang's army were camped in the forests on the mountain to avoid the heat, he said: "That lot are all bandits from the marshes, they know nothing about military tactics. They don't amount to anything. Let me just put a little plan of mine into action. I'll make sure that of the two hundred thousand not half survive!" He gave his orders, selecting five thousand of his best troops equipped with fire arrows, rockets and torches. Two thousand carts were also marshalled and loaded with dry reeds and firewood, together with gunpowder and other incendiary materials, with four men to propel each cart. It was the seventh month, the beginning of autumn, when Uncle Know-all with his four commanders led out this force, taking ten thousand armoured cavalry in support, the riders in light armour and the horses without bells, and leaving two of his deputies to defend the city.

It was towards evening that they rode out and a strong breeze happened to get up. "It's a sign! Song Jiang is destined to lose this battle," Uncle Know-all exclaimed delightedly. By the third watch they were close to the southern slopes of Mount Fangcheng. Suddenly the valley was filled with mist. "Heaven is definitely on our side," said Uncle Know-all. He ordered the troops in the rear to assist by drumming and shouting. Then he ordered five thousand men to bombard the forests on the mountain with their fire arrows, rockets and torches and set fire to them. He ordered two of his commanders to roll the carts forward and set them on fire and then propel them towards the stores on the mountain. Everyone now charged forward. Then suddenly there came a cry: "Watch out!" It was extraordinary! The south wind that had been blowing strongly suddenly veered round to the north. Reports like thunder began to roll down from the mountain. Under the influence of the Wizard's power over wind and fire, the fire arrows and such all began to fly south into the ranks of the rebels. Like a million golden snakes and fire dragons twisting and turning, their own weapons flew towards them. There was no hope of dodging. The Song army celebrated this occasion with a verse making fun of Uncle Know-all:

A military scheme is hard to assess;
The rebels have landed themselves in a mess.
The fire that they used becomes their own pall.
Uncle Know-all, you see, does not know it all!

Song Jiang had told Thunderer to fire a signal shell: the shell climbed high into the sky and burst with a shattering roar. Then from the east Hotshot and Arrowtip, from the west the Chancellor and Lucky Bian, came charging out with their troops and the rebels were routed. One of their commanders was cut in half by the Chancellor, another was knocked from his horse by one of Jade Arrowtip's stones and finished off by Hotshot with his spear. A third was transfixed by Lucky Bian and a fourth was killed by his own troops. Most of the twenty-three thousand rebel troops were burnt to death. The remainder scattered and melted away. All the two thousand fire carts were destroyed by fire. Only Uncle Know-all and three or four hundred men got back alive to Wanzhou. The Song army lost nothing to the fire, not even its firewood. Not a soldier was injured. They took huge quantities of horses, uniforms, gongs and drums. After their victory Hotshot, the Chancellor and the rest returned to the camp to report their success. They presented the heads of the defeated rebel commanders, and Song Jiang rewarded them all for their efforts and mentioned the Wizard's contribution and the achievements of the others in his report.

The Professor said: "Your excellent plan, brother, has done for the rebels' morale, but the Wanzhou region is awkward terrain for us. It is an eminently fertile plateau, and if the rebels throw in more troops and defend it in force, we won't get control of it in a hurry. Now that the cool breezes and dews of autumn bring respite from the summer and the troops have recovered their strength, we should make the most of the fact that our strength is increasing while they are weak, and strike while the iron is hot. I am sure we can win."

Song Jiang approved and ordered Scimitar with nine others and thirty thousand cavalry to take up a position east of Wanzhou and prevent the rebel forces from the south reinforcing it. Leopard's Head also with nine others and thirty thousand cavalry were to take up a position west of Wanzhou and block the enemy forces from the north. The commanders went off to carry out these orders. Then the Chancellor with the seventeen others who had surrendered in Hebei came and said: "We are all very grateful to you for choosing us. As a small repayment of our debt of gratitude we would like to lead the attack on the city." Song Jiang accepted this proposal and ordered Hotshot and Jade Arrowtip to join them with fifty thousand cavalry. These commanders marched on Wanzhou.

Song Jiang, the Unicorn and the Professor, in command of the main contingent, struck camp and headed south from Mount Fangchen. They made camp a few miles from Wanzhou. Green-Eyes, Spots and the Nine-Tailed Turtle were put in charge of building defences and manufacturing arms. Hotshot and his friends were sent ahead on reconnaissance. They were stopped by the water around Wanzhou. Uncle Know-all, who had escaped, remember, from the Song trap, the moment he reached Wanzhou had sent a messenger to Wang Qing at Nanfeng and also requested reinforcements from all the neighbouring provinces. Now the city was surrounded by the Song army and he ordered his troops to defend the city strongly and make no attempt to counter-attack until the reinforcements came.

The Song army strove for nearly a week to take the city but its defences were solid and not to be broken down in a hurry. The rebel commander of Yuzhou to the north sent set out with a relieving force of twenty thousand but he was killed by Leopard's Head and all his troops scattered. The same day reinforcements approached from the south and were defeated by Scimitar. Their commanders were sent to Song Jiang to deal with. Many from both armies were executed.

At this time Green-Eyes was put to producing siege equipment, while the Chancellor, Magic Steed and their men laboured to fill sandbags and pile them up on all sides, pushing them up to the walls of the city. Daring and agile solders were chosen to cross the moat by means of flying bridges and windlasses. The troops fearlessly scaled the walls and took the city, capturing the commander Uncle Know-all alive. More than twenty of his officers were killed in the fighting and over five thousand troops. Ten thousand surrendered.

Song Jiang and the army entered Wanzhou. Uncle Know-all was executed and his head exposed as a lesson to the people. The deeds of Scimitar, Leopard's Head, Hotshot, the Chancellor and others were recorded. A report was sent to Commissioner Chen and a request that he come and take charge of the city.

The Commissioner was delighted with the news and soon arrived, together with Marshal Hou and Academician Luo. Song Jiang and the army welcomed them and the Commissioner of course was full of praise for their achievements.

Ten days passed while Song Jiang reviewed the military situation. It was already the beginning of the eighth month and the heat of summer had retreated. Song Jiang said to the Professor: "Which city should we attack first?"

The Professor said: "If we go south from here we come to Shannan, which gives access to their southernmost limit and also commands another city to the north. It is of great strategic importance to the region. If we take it, we have cut the enemy forces in two."

Song Jiang said: "Exactly what I was thinking." He left Colonel Hua and some others with fifty thousand troops to assist the Commissioner in defending Wanzhou. The Commissioner also retained the services of Magic Hand. The White-Water Dragon and the other boat commanders were told to take their boats and men and sail down the river, meeting up with them north of Shannan. The land army was divided into three. They bade the Commissioner farewell and with a hundred and fifty thousand men marched on Shannan. Truly it was an example of

A great host on the march affrighting heaven and earth;
Battalions of warriors to make gods and ghosts quake.

If you want to know how they attacked Shannan, you must read the next chapter.

Chapter 106

A scholar fools a superior force;
The sailors overwhelm the city's defences!

Song Jiang has given orders for a combined land and water attack on Shannan, boats and cavalry working in conjunction. The land forces have been divided into the usual three columns. Scouts of the vanguard report that Wang Qing already has intelligence of their advance and has sent another twenty thousand troops under four commanders to oppose them. On hearing this Twin Spears orders the Chancellor and Lucky Bian to set up an ambush with five thousand men on his left flank and Magic Steed and Tang Bin to do likewise on his right flank and to attack when the signal is fired.

By the time these arrangements have been completed, the enemy are already advancing with flags and drums and a great deal of shouting. The two armies face each other, in full battle array, drawn up north and south. Each side keeps up a heavy fire of arrows and crossbow bolts. First of the rebel commanders is Mi Sheng, wearing a bronze helm, his bow painted with magpies and his arrows flighted with eagle's feathers, his face puce and his eyes fixed in a brazen stare. He carries a long-handled mountain-splitter of an axe and is seated on a tall chestnut with a curly mane.

"You bunch of robbers from the marshes, why have you joined forces with the unjust and despotic Song emperor, and why do you come here to die?" Mi Sheng shouted out.

On the Song side the drums thundered in response and out rode Hasty and yelled: "Watch your language, you rebel bandit! I'm going to give you a hundred blows of my axe!" Brandishing his gilt axe, he slapped his horse and charged.

A continuous roar arose from both armies as the two leaders met in the middle. Horses clashed, axes rose and fell, they fought fifty bouts and neither had the advantage. This enemy commander, Mi Sheng, was truly brave!

In the Song ranks Thunderclap saw that Hasty could not prevail and rode forward to join the fight, waving his wolf's-tooth mace. Another enemy leader met him with his halberd. These four fought it out in a cloud of dust and just as the fight was at its most furious a report sounded and the Chancellor and Lucky Bian attacked. They were met by another of the enemy commanders, while Magic Steed and Tang Bin charged from the right flank and also encountered an enemy commander. Jade Arrowtip now came forward on the Song side and surreptitiously took out a stone and threw it. It caught Thunderclap's antagonist on the nose and knocked him from his horse. Thunderclap rode up and with a blow of his mace smashed both helmet and skull. On the left flank the Chancellor fought ten bouts with his opponent before his sword chopped the man from his horse. On the right Tang Bin also ran his opponent through. The rebel leader Mi Sheng, seeing his companions thus disadvantaged, thrust aside Hasty's gilt axe, slapped his horse and galloped off.

Hasty, the Chancellor and Magic Steed urged their followers to give chase and the rebels were routed. They pursued the enemy commander round the side of the hill, but there the enemy had laid an ambush of ten thousand cavalry, concealed in a dense wood, and two enemy leaders led this force out in support of the fleeing Mi Sheng, who now turned about and led the charge. Among the Song ranks Wen Zhongrong, one of the two robber chiefs of Mount Calf who had defected from Tian Hu's forces in Hebei, was eager for glory and charged to meet him. After ten bouts Mi's axe cut him in two. Maddened by the sight, his comrade Cui Ye galloped into the attack. When they had fought six or seven bouts Tang Bin slapped his horse and rode to his friend's assistance. Preferring not to face two at once, Mi Sheng gave a great cry and chopped Cui down before riding at Tang Bin.

At this point the husband and wife pair of Hotshot and Jade Arrowtip decided to intervene. Hotshot took a stone and launched

it at Mi Sheng. The latter had a good eye and quick hands. He parried with his axe. Sparks flew and the stone clattered to the ground. Seeing her husband had missed, Arrowtip hurled a stone. Mi Sheng saw the second stone and ducked. It clanged on his bronze helmet. Now Spearsman and Twin Spears came out from the Song ranks in a furious charge. Faced by such a throng of enemy commanders, Mi Sheng blocked Tang Bin's lance, turned his horse and fled once more. Tang Bin gave chase, but the other two enemy commanders stood in his path and unfortunately Mi Sheng got away. They had to content themselves with killing the other two enemy commandeers and scattering their troops. Vast quantities of horses, drums and gongs, armour and uniforms were taken. Twin Spears ordered his men to retrieve the bodies of Wen Zhongrong and Cui Ye for burial. Tang Bin wept bitterly for his two companions and personally supervised the interment. Twin Spears and the others made camp with their men somewhere south of the mountain.

Next day Song Jiang and the other two columns arrived and joined up with Twin Spears and his men. Song Jiang was saddened by the loss of two allied commanders. Libations were poured and then he conferred with the Professor over their plans to take the city. The Professor and the Strategist mounted a siege tower to observe the city's defences. When they came down they told Song Jiang: "There is nothing to be gained by attacking such solid defences directly. We should let them think that we intend to attack, but just await developments." Song Jiang ordered the siege equipment to be withdrawn and sent out sharp-witted scouts to listen for news.

We shall leave Song Jiang there and tell how Mi Sheng with a mere two or three hundred horsemen had fled to Shannan. The garrison commander was Wang Qing's brother-in-law, Duan the Second. When Wang Qing heard that the court was sending Song Jiang there he had made Duan Commander-in-Chief of the eastern plain and sent him here to strengthen the city's defences. Mi Sheng now told him that Song Jiang's forces were redoubtable and that they had lost five of their own commanders and the army was no more. He begged him to provide troops so they could retaliate. Now Mi Sheng had been sent out by Wang Qing himself, that is why he dared to ask for troops. Duan was outraged: "Although you are not under my command, I will have you executed for suffering defeat and losing leaders!" He called his aides to come and carry out the sentence. At this point someone popped up and said: "Calm yourself, Marshal, and leave him alone!" The speaker was Wang Qing's special envoy, Zuo Mou. Duan said: "Why should I pardon him?"

"I have heard that he is very brave, and has killed two of the Song generals," said Zuo. "Song Jiang's forces are truly very strong. It will take reasoning to defeat them, not just brute force."

"What do you mean by reasoning?" Duan asked.

"All of Song Jiang's supplies are stored in Wanzhou, and have to be brought from there. I have heard that Wanzhou is weakly defended. You must send some of your people secretly to the commanders of the neighbouring towns and fix a date for them to attack Wanzhou from the south. I will select some crack troops here and put them under Mi Sheng's command. He will attack Wanzhou from the north and have a chance to redeem his fault. When Song Jiang hears about it he will withdraw his forces to protect Wanzhou. We will take advantage of this to attack from here and catch him between two fires. We will be able to capture him!"

Duan was a countryman, what did he know of military strategy? He accepted Zuo's plan without demur and sent people off immediately to the neighbouring towns of Jun and Gong to secure their cooperation. Then he put twenty thousand troops under the command of Mi Sheng and two others. They left by the west gate under cover of darkness with banners furled and drums silent and headed for Wanzhou.

Song Jiang at this moment was engaged in thinking about how to capture Shannan when his boat captain, White-Water Dragon, arrived and said: "The boats are all now tied up on the Han River or Xiang Water. I have come to know your wishes."

Song Jiang invited him to his tent and they were drinking a few cups of wine, when a scout came in with a report on something that was happening in the city and how the enemy had sent troops to attack Wanzhou. Somewhat alarmed, Song Jiang called in the Professor to discuss this.

The Professor said: "Commissioner Chen and Colonel Hua are brave and resourceful men, there is no need to be concerned about this development in Wanzhou; on the contrary it provides us here with the opportunity to take the city." He went on for a long time, expounding his secret plan to Song Jiang. Song Jiang was satisfied with it and passed on secret instructions to White-Water Dragon, also ordering the infantry commander Pluto with twenty other leaders and two thousand men to go with him that night under cover of darkness.

Meanwhile Mi Sheng and the other rebels were marching on Wanzhou. A scout reported the fact in Wanzhou and the Commissioner ordered Colonel Hua and Leopard's Head out with twenty thousand men to repulse them. As they were leaving the city a scout came in with an urgent report. "The rebel general Mi Sheng has arranged for reinforcements from Jun. There's thirty thousand of them just a few miles north of here." The Commissioner ordered Little Duke and the Halberdier to take twenty thousand troops out to counter this new threat. In less than two hours further urgent news arrived: "Two enemy commanders from Gong with thirty thousand men are approaching our west gate!"

They all looked at each other in horror. "We've only two military commanders left in the city, the Son-in-Law and Hound," they were thinking: "We've ten thousand troops, but half of them are old and infirm. How can they defend us?"

Then Magic Hand spoke: "No need to worry, Commissioner. I have a plan." Folding two fingers together, he proceeded: "We do thus and thus and thus … and we've got them!" Everyone from the Commissioner down nodded approval. The Commissioner gave the necessary orders and told the Son-in-Law and Hound to choose five thousand strong men and lay an ambush at the west gate to attack the enemy when they were retreating. They left to carry out his instructions. He also told the old and infirm soldiers that they were not needed to defend the city. Their job was to hide all the flags and banners until a shot was fired from the west gate tower, when they should raise them all at once. They were to remain under cover and not leave the city. He next had wine and pots of food carried to the west gate tower and a banquet laid out there. Then with Marshal Hou and Academician Luo he went up into the gate tower where they put on a show of drinking, with much laughter and animated talk, after telling their men to open the gates wide for the enemy. After quite a while, the two enemy commanders with ten of their lieutenants arrived in a tumultuous throng. They saw the gates wide open and the three officials and a scholar up in the gate tower drinking amid sounds of merriment and loud music. Not a flag did they see flying on any of the walls. General Ji from Jun hesitated. He was afraid to advance. The second commander said: "They must be ready for us. We'd better withdraw at once, or we'll be caught in their trap." Ji gave the order, and as he did so a gun went off in the tower with a thunderous report and drums shattered the silence, while countless banners rose on the walls. The rebel troops had heard what their commanders were saying and it had made them nervous. Now they saw what was happening in the city they panicked, without a blow having been struck. When the Ugly Son-in-Law and Hound charged out of the city the rebels fled, abandoning countless drums and trumpets, uniforms, arms, horses and armour. More than ten thousand were killed. The two generals were killed by their own troops in the stampede and the remaining officers fled for their lives. The Son-in-Law and Hound recalled their troops and returned victorious to the city. To the north Colonel Hua and Leopard's Head had already killed the other two rebel generals and scattered their troops. Only Mi Sheng got away.

Just as this contingent were returning victorious to the city, it was reported that two more rebel columns were approaching. The western force had already been broken up by Magic Hand's cunning plan. To the south, where Little Duke and Halberdier were fighting, the issue remained in the balance. Colonel Hua's force were ordered south immediately to assist Little Duke and the Halberdier, who were involved in fierce fighting. They knocked the rebels for six, scattering them to the four winds, killing and capturing many. More than thirty thousand died that day from the three rebel columns and countless numbers were wounded: the fields were littered with corpses, the ditches running with blood.

Leopard's Head and his companions called in their troops and entered the city. Along with the Ugly Son-in-Law and Hound they went to the government office to report their success. Commissioner Chen and the other officials were delighted and Magic Hand's clever plan came in for special praise as well as the bravery of Colonel Hua and his comrades. These heroes modestly kept quiet.

The Commissioner ordered a celebration feast for the commanders, while their troops were rewarded. The exploits were recorded in despatches and the city's defences put in order. Of this no more.

As for Duan the Second, the night after he had sent his troops out of the city, he climbed the watchtower to have a look at the besieging Song army. It was getting on for the middle of the eighth month and the moon nearly at the full, illuminating the scene as brightly as daylight. He saw a flurry of flags and banners hurriedly retreating north. He said to his aide: "Song Jiang must have heard about the threat to Wanzhou so he is withdrawing."

"You're right," said the aide. "We can send out a force of armoured cavalry to attack them."

Duan appointed two commanders with twenty thousand troops to harry the Song forces. They saluted and left.

Looking westward from the city, Duan noticed flood water reflecting the moonlight and shining light everywhere. Over this expanse Song supply ships were slowly being poled northward. Now Duan was a robber at heart and when he saw so many loaded boats sailing past, with no sign of a military guard, just a crew of six or seven to each boat, he quickly ordered his men to open the west watergate and told his boat commander to take five hundred warships and attack the transports. The Song troops on the boats responded by hurriedly lining them up alongside the shore and jumping out. As the rebel commander bore down on them, some kind of loud signal was emitted from the boats and hundreds of little fishing boats began pulling away, each

with two men rowing and three or four bearing shields and javelins or short halberds. As these came flying towards them, the rebel commander ordered his men to fire rockets and fire arrows at them. Apparently deterred by this, the crews of the fishing boats leapt into the water with loud cries and disappeared.

Having apparently won the contest, the rebels seized the boats and their commander told the sailors to row them into the city. The first boat was just in when the order came that all boats were to be searched before they entered. The commander told them to begin by searching the boat that was already inside, and about half a dozen men went on board. But when they tried to remove the decking, it seemed to be made of solid timber and they couldn't shift it. The commander began to smell a rat: "It must be some trick!" he said. He ordered axemen to break the deck open and see what was inside. "Don't take any of these boats into the city," he was saying, when three or four of the rearmost transports outside the city began to move forward, without human agency, as if drifting with the current or propelled by the wind. Now he knew it was a trap and he tried to jump ashore, but a dozen men with cutlasses in their mouths emerged from the water. It was White-Water Dragon and his seven companions White Eel, the Pilot, the Ruans, Cave Dragon and River Rider. The rebels tried to draw their weapons but White-Water Dragon blew a whistle and the infantry commanders and their men concealed on the hindmost boats broke open the decking and sprang out with a shout. They were armed with short spears and there were twenty leaders and a thousand infantrymen. They went to work at once, leaping out onto the bank and slaughtering rebels. The latter offered no serious resistance but fled in disorder. Their commander was killed by Cave Dragon. The greater part of the sailors were killed by White-Water Dragon's men outside or inside the city and the water ran red. They seized the watergate. Pluto and his savage company guarded Thunderer as he let off the signal shell with a shattering roar and then went off killing and burning on their own account. The city was in a frenzy all this time, brother calling to brother, sons searching for fathers, lamentations rising to heaven. Duan heard and rushed with his troops to the rescue but he ran into

Pilgrim and company. He was wounded in the leg by a blow from Fleetfoot's halberd and taken alive. Monk, Iron Ox and ten others raced to the north gate, scattered the guards there, and opened it and lowered the drawbridge. Hearing the uproar and the shells Song Jiang's army attacked. They met the other two rebel commanders and a fierce battle ensued. Lucky Bian killed one of the rebels and the other was knocked down by the Wizard and trampled into the mud. The best part of the thirty thousand armoured cavalry were killed. The Chancellor, Lucky and Magic Steed led their forces into the city through the north gate. The rebels were routed, the city taken, and Song Jiang was invited to enter with the main army.

It was now the fifth watch. Song Jiang gave orders for the fires to be put out and no harm done to the people. As soon as it was light a proclamation was issued to restore peace and the commanders presented their trophies. Fleetfoot brought in Duan the Second, bound hand and foot. Song Jiang sent him under escort to the Commissioner to be dealt with. The commander of the city garrison had already been killed by his own men. Many others were killed and over ten thousand of the rebel garrison surrendered. Song Jiang had oxen and horses slaughtered to reward his army and recorded the exploits of White-Water Dragon and his comrades. Magic Steed was sent off to report the victory to the Commissioner and to obtain news of the rebel movements. Not many hours later he was back and reported: "The Commissioner is delighted and has sent off a report of his own to the court." He went on to tell them about Magic Hand's scheme and Song Jiang was alarmed. "What if the enemy had seen through it? That's typical of a scholar!" He ordered the grain stores to be opened up to relieve the people whose property had been burnt by the soldiers. When all the military affairs had been settled, he conferred with the Professor about how to attack Jingnan. Suddenly word came from the Commissioner that rebel bands from the Western Capital were running amok, infringing on districts of the Eastern Capital, and that Song Jiang was to pacify the Western Capital first before attacking Wang Qing's base. He had also appended a note of his own critical of the Military Council.

Song Jiang and the Professor now discussed how to divide their forces so they could simultaneously attack Jingnan and the Western Capital. Then the Deputy Commander-in-Chief, the Unicorn, with the generals who had come over to them in Hebei, volunteered for the attack on the Western Capital. Song Jiang approved this and appointed twenty-four leaders and fifty thousand troops under the Unicorn for the job.

The Unicorn and his force set off the same day. Song Jiang left Tattooed Dragon and some others in charge at Shannan. He told him: "If the enemy come, just concentrate on defence." He himself led eighty thousand troops to attack Jingnan.

Then this great force swept forward like a river in flood, men and horses swift as the wind. Truly you could say

A host of banners and pennants paint the sky red;
Swords and lances glitter like a vast field of snow.

If you want to know how they attacked Jingnan, you must read the next chapter.

Chapter 107

Song Jiang wins a great victory at Mount Ji; The Strategist smashes the six flower formation!

So Song Jiang and his army advanced on Jingnan. They covered twenty miles a day before stopping for the night. In the places they passed the people suffered not the slightest aggravation. The cavalry finally made camp in the region of Mount Ji.

Mount Ji, north of Jingnan, had great strategic importance. It was guarded by a bandit named Li Rang with thirty thousand troops under his command. He was a relative of Li the fortune-teller and Wang Qing had appointed him District Commander. When he heard that Song Jiang had taken Shannan and captured Duan the Second, he sent an urgent messenger to Nanfeng informing Wang Qing and his relative the fortune-teller as follows: "The Song army is very strong. They have already taken two main cities. Now they're advancing on Jingnan and a detachment under the Unicorn is headed for the Western Capital." Greatly disturbed by this news, Fortune-teller Li entered the palace to tell Wang Qing. A palace attendant went in and reappeared a moment later to say: "Please wait, General. His Majesty will be out in a moment." Fortune-teller Li waited and waited and nothing happened. He made inquiries of one of the palace officials who was a friend of his and was told: "The King and his consort have just had a big fight!"

"What about?" he asked.

The official whispered in his ear: "The King hasn't been to her apartments for ages, because she's ugly. She's mad at him!"

He waited a while longer. The attendant came out again and said: "His Majesty asked me to come and see if you're still here."

"I've been waiting hours!" he said. The attendant went back

inside and in a little while, closely surrounded by a bevy of ladies-in-waiting, Wang Qing came out and ascended his throne in the outer chamber. Fortune-teller Li bowed low and said: "Sire, my cousin Li Rang reports that Song Jiang with a strong army has captured Wanzhou and Shannan and is now advancing in two columns, one to attack the Western Capital and the other to attack Jingnan. I entreat Your Majesty to send a relief force."

Wang Qing was outraged. "What, that bunch of robbers from the marshes!" he exclaimed. "What's so terrible about them?" He gave orders for General Du Bo with twelve officers and twenty thousand men to relieve the Western Capital and Marshal Xie Yu with a force of equal size to relieve Jingnan. These two took their warrants, picked their troops and prepared their arms. The bogus military council made out the appointments and put Quarter-Master General Gong Zheng, elder of the two Gong brothers, with two assistants in charge of supplies. They all took leave of Wang Qing and set off on their separate routes. Of this no more.

Meanwhile Song Jiang's army had halted and made camp a few miles north of Mount Ji and were preparing for the attack, when scouts returned with news of the enemy's movements. Song Jiang discussed things with the Professor and then told the others: "We have heard that Li Rang has brave men under his command and Mount Ji is of great strategic importance to Jingnan. Although we outnumber them, their position is strong, whereas ours is overlooked by the mountain and is dominated by them. This Li Rang, what's more, is a cunning bastard. If you get into a fight with him you will have to watch out. Don't take anything for granted."

Then he gave the order: "Go back into camp, secure the gates and clear the decks. Any unauthorized moving about or shouting will be punished. Failure to carry out an order immediately will be punished." From then on discipline was strictly maintained. Song Jiang sent Magic Messenger with orders for White-Water Dragon and his company to guard the transports closely and bring them up gradually to supply the army. He sent an envoy to challenge Li Rang to a showdown the following day. He appointed eight leaders with twenty thousand men to lead the assault.

To another four leaders and two thousand men he gave the task of cutting down trees to clear a route for their advance and form a battlefield. The rest would remain with him to defend the camp.

Next day they breakfasted before dawn. By the time men and horses had all had their fill it was daylight and they were ready for action. Li Rang with his five lieutenants and twenty thousand troops came charging down from the mountain. These five were the boldest among the rebels and Wang Qing had made them his special strike force. They now came face to face with Thunderclap and his colleagues. They lined up at the foot of the northern slope, with reinforcements above them on the mountain. There was much waving of signal flags now among both armies as they formed up for battle. Both loosed volleys of arrows at the opposing ranks, while the drums thundered and many-coloured standards dazzled the eye. An opening appeared among the rebel ranks and Commander Yuan Lang rode out. He had a helmet of weathered bronze, and black chainmail. He rode a black charger with a curly mane. His face was red and his hair brown. He carried two hammers of polished, hardened steel, the one in his left hand weighing fifteen catties, the one in his right hand sixteen. He shouted out: "Which of you bog-dwelling outlaws dares step forward and face death?"

From the Song ranks two of the commanders who had come over to them in Hebei, Huang and Jin, wanting to have some achievement to their names, galloped forward and hurled abuse: "You traitorous villain, how do you dare show your face?" One of them whirled his windsplitter of a sword, the other twirled a spear of pure steel, as they charged. The rebel commandeer came to meet them. The three horses and riders fought in a T-shape. After thirty bouts Yuan Lang parried and then turned his horse and galloped off. As the Song commanders rode in pursuit, he suddenly turned his horse. Jin, who was in front, struck out with his sword, but the rebel raised his left arm to block the blow and Jin's sword missed its mark. Before he could recover, the hammer in Yuan Lang's right hand struck right through the helmet and shattered his skull. He fell from his horse. His companion Huang now arrived and thrust with his spear at Yuan Lang's heart.

The latter was sharp-eyed and quick of hand and swayed aside so that Huang's spear met only air and slipped harmlessly past his ribs. Yuan Lang tucked the hammer under his left arm and with the right hand grasped the shaft of his opponent's spear. He gave it a tug and Huang started to fall towards him. Catching him with his right hand round the waist and holding onto his horse, he threw him to the ground. The troops applauded and rushed forward to take Huang prisoner, while the horse galloped back riderless to the Song ranks.

Now Thunderclap, seeing these two commanders lost, was moved to anger. Forcing his horse forward and whirling his wolf's tooth mace, he attacked the rebel. The latter advanced to meet him, spinning his hammers. When they had fought more than fifty bouts, Jade Arrowtip galloped out to join Thunderclap, on her silver grey charger, square halberd at the ready. On her head was set a purple and gold winged cap; she wore a war robe of finely embroidered red silk and was encased in armour of silver chainmail interlaced with gold.

Another of the rebel leaders, seeing it was a woman attacking them, laughed and said: "You can see Song Jiang and his friends have no breeding! How can they let a woman ride into battle?" So saying he went to meet Arrowtip's attack brandishing his three-pointed double-bladed sword. After ten bouts Arrowtip knocked aside his blade with her halberd and galloped back towards her own ranks. With a shout he urged his horse after her. Reaching into her embroidered saddle bag she surreptitiously took out a stone and bending her willow waist took aim at the rebel and let fly. It hit him square in the face causing terrible lacerations. Blood poured out and he fell headlong from his mount. She abruptly turned her horse and finished him off with a blow of her halberd.

When the brother of Arrowtip's victim saw him die at the hands of the woman warrior, a great anger rose in his breast. He slapped his horse and rode at her, whirling a jointed tiger's eye chain. Twin Rods galloped to intercept him. Everyone stopped to watch them go at it. There was really nothing to choose between them, it was six of one to half a dozen of the other! Twin Rods had a steel helmet with a towering crest, a yellow silk headband shot with gold, a black silk robe with seven stars and oiled black chainmail. He rode a black charger with white socks. The other also had a crested helmet, a red silk headband, a black silk robe patterned with blue flowers, oiled black chainmail threaded with gold and he rode a fiery chestnut. Twin Rods also had his octagonal rods of burnished steel. The pair of them traded blows in front of the armies, coming and going, this way, that way, and after fifty bouts there was still no victor.

Thunderclap and his opponent by now had fought a hundred and fifty bouts. Watching from the top of a knoll the rebel bandit leader Li Rang had seen the woman warrior with her deadly stone throwing knock out one of theirs and ordered a retreat. Thunderclap and Twin Rods did not give chase. Their two opponents carefully guarding their backs returned to their own ranks and the rebel force withdrew up the mountain.

Thunderclap called in his troops and returned to camp. He reported that the enemy commanders were very brave, that they had taken the lives of two of his commanders and that but for Hotshot's wife his troops would have been completely demoralized. Song Jiang was exceedingly disturbed. "How are we ever going to capture Jingnan then?" he said to the Professor. The latter, crossing two fingers, expounded a plan. "The only way is to do thus … and thus … and thus."

Song Jiang accepted the plan and ordered the Monk and thirteen others together with Thunderer and five thousand brave infantrymen to go by night with the moon dark, wearing light armour and carrying short weapons, bucklers, throwing knives and javelins, and make their way by the small trails to the other side of the mountain. They set off.

Next morning Li Rang sent down his war declaration. Song Jiang and the Professor discussed it. The Professor said: "They must have something up their sleeve. Monk and his party should have got themselves into position by now. We must prepare for battle at once."

Song Jiang accepted Li Rang's challenge immediately and a soldier was sent up the mountain with his reply. Thunderclap and company were instructed to lead the attack as previously.

帥
轅門

They would attack with twenty thousand troops, with bows and crossbows in the outer ranks and halberds and shields on the inside, war carts going in front and cavalry behind in support. Tamer and three others were to wait in the camp with ten thousand men; Skyhawk with a similar force was also stationed inside the camp. "When you hear our signal from the front line, bring your men up on the east and west flanks." Scimitar and six others with twenty thousand cavalry and infantry were stationed behind the camp to prevent reinforcements reaching the rebels. The whole operation was directed by Song Jiang himself, the Professor and Taoist Gongsun. The rest of them would guard the camp. Early in the morning the Professor mounted a siege tower to observe. The terrain was rough and difficult and he hurriedly ordered the army to pull back a little way to allow the relief columns room for manoeuvre.

They were just completing this operation when the rebel leader Li Rang with his four lieutenants and twenty-five thousand troops appeared on the slopes of Mount Ji. One of these lieutenants had told his men to display the remains of Huang on bamboo poles. There were five thousand armoured cavalry. The riders all wore full helmets and chainmail so that only their eyes showed. The horses also had full armour and only their hooves were exposed. This was because Li Rang had seen the day before how the woman warrior wounded one of his commanders with a stone. Like this even if stones were thrown the armour would give protection. The cavalry were in threes, two archers supporting a spearsman. They charged and the main force followed behind in two columns. The onslaught was too fierce for the Song forces who were pushed back. Song Jiang hurriedly ordered the signal to be fired. Already a hundred or so soldiers pushing the carts had been wounded, but it was as well the carts were there because they prevented the armoured cavalry from getting through. On the other hand, the cavalry behind the carts were unable to charge.

At this critical moment a string of reports sounded from the mountain. It was Monk and his party who had scaled the ridge and now launched their attack. The enemy camp was only defended by five thousand superannuated soldiers and a deputy commander. Monk and his men killed them all and the camp was in their hands. When Li Rang saw his camp had fallen to the enemy, he tried to retreat, but he ran into Tamer and Skyhawk, advancing in two columns. Song Jiang also ordered the artillery to fire on the armoured cavalry and the rebels were routed. Monk, Iron Ox and their companions now poured down the mountainside and set on the enemy, scattering them to the four winds. The unfortunate Yuan Lang, a brave leader, was killed by a shell; Li Rang was killed by Monk; two others died in the mêlée and only one escaped. Vast quantities of helmets and armour, gongs and drums and horses were taken. Most of the thirty thousand troops were killed. Corpses littered the mountainside. When Song Jiang recalled his troops and they were counted, they were found to have suffered over a thousand dead. As night was now approaching they made camp there north of the mountain.

Next morning Song Jiang marched up the mountain. After appropriating all the gold and silver and stores, they set fire to the camp. The commanders were rewarded and the exploits of Monk and his companions and of Jade Arrowtip were recorded. Then the army was ordered to march. They next made camp five miles outside Jingnan. The Professor was consulted about how to attack the city. Of this no more.

Here our story divides. We must go back to the Unicorn's column, which we left advancing on the Western Capital. They forged ahead, surmounting all obstacles. One of the places they passed through was Baofeng, where the rebel commander Wu Shun and his men came out with incense and candles and surrendered the city to them, expressing their desire to renew their allegiance to the Emperor. The Unicorn proclaimed peace and reappointed Wu Shun as governor of the city. All the rebel leaders were grateful and gave evidence of their gratitude by abandoning their wicked ways and returning to the path of righteousness. After this, for the Unicorn and his men the troubles seemed to be over. They moved rapidly and without wasting a day reached a point ten miles south of the Western Capital, a hill known as the Watchtower, and made camp. They learnt that the city was under the command of Gong Duan, second of the Gong brothers, and his deputy Xi Sheng and a crowd of brave officers. This Xi Sheng was a good tactician and also versed in magic arts. When the Unicorn conferred with the Strategist to devise a plan for taking the city, the latter said: "I have heard that Xi Sheng is a passable soldier and he will certainly attack us. Let our army take up a position and then wait till the enemy attack. We will not rush into it."

"Excellent advice!" said the Unicorn and ordered his army to take up a position on the plain south of the mountains in the revolving ring formation.

As they waited the enemy were seen advancing in three columns, red banners in the centre, blue banners on the left and red banners on the right. When they came within range of the Song formation the rebel commander split off the blue and red banners on the left and right and had them take up positions on either flank. He mounted a siege platform to observe the enemy and when he saw they were drawn up in the revolving ring, he came down and said: "That formation is old hat. I'll show them a formation that'll put the wind up them!" He mounted the platform again, ordered the drums to beat and with two signal flags directed the deployment of his army. When the left and right flanks were properly lined up, he came down again, mounted his horse and with his commanders rode out in front to parley with the Unicorn. Reining in his horse in front of his troops, he shouted: "Who do you think you can fool with that revolving ring formation of yours? Do you know what my formation is?"

Realizing it was a competition in strategy, the Unicorn went up onto a siege platform with the Strategist to look. The enemy formation was based on threes — three men to a squad, three squads to a platoon and five platoons to a company, forming a square on the outside and a circle on the inside, with the bigger units enclosing the smaller, making it all continuous and interdependent.

The Strategist said: "This is Doctor Li's 'Six-lobed formation'. The good doctor cut Zhuge Liang's original eight lines to six. The rebel leader thinks he can scare us with a formation we don't know. He doesn't realize that this eight line formation of ours can turn into eight by eight, giving sixty-four, in other words Zhuge Liang's eight line formation, which can smash his six-lobed one."

The Unicorn rode out in front and called out with a laugh: "Do you really believe this paltry six-lobed formation of yours can cause us any surprises?" He returned to the army and the Strategist went up onto the dais and began waving the signal flags this way and that and the eight line formation began to change. Then he told the Unicorn to give the order for the Blue-Faced Beast, the Chancellor and Lucky Bian to lead two thousand armoured cavalry into battle. The sign for the day was metal so the troops that were thrown into the attack had to be brought up from positions on the south, the direction of fire.

When Blue-Faced Beast received the command he ordered three rolls of the drum and then advanced against the enemy's western position. At this point the Unicorn led Magic Steed and others in a charge on the left flank. They raced forward and routed the enemy.

In their advance Blue-Faced Beast and company clashed with Xi Sheng. The latter fled north, protected by a group of brave commanders. The Chancellor and Lucky Bian were eager to acquire merit and rushed after them, not realizing they were riding into a trap. Suddenly there were thunderous reports from the mountain and a troop of horsemen raced out. The Blue-Faced Beast's company tried to turn back but it was too late. Truly it was a case of:

Charging men and horses lost under the green cliff;
The boat that can ride the waves founders among green rushes.

If you want to know what troops these were and how the Chancellor and his friends fared against them, you must read the next chapter.

Chapter 108

The Wizard raises a fog and captures the city; Mr. Chai stores up ammunition to fight the enemy!

Racing towards Watchtower Mountain in pursuit of Gong Duan's general Xi Sheng, the Blue-Faced Beast and company fail to observe an enemy ambush behind the shoulder of the hill. Ten thousand rebel cavalry rush out and engage them in a fierce fight, while the troops they are pursuing escape to the safety of the city.

The Chancellor did his utmost and two of the rebel commanders were killed, but with only a thousand men the Song detachment were totally outnumbered and got driven deep into a ravine. Surrounded on all sides by sheer cliffs they had no way out. The enemy closed off the entrance with tree trunks and rocks and reported back to the city's governor, Gong Duan, who stationed two thousand troops at the mouth of the ravine. Unless they grew wings there was no way they could escape.

We shall leave Blue-Faced Beast bottled up in there and return to the Unicorn who defeated Xi Sheng's six-lobed formation — largely thanks to Magic Steed's skill with the metal block, which he employed to knock down a considerable number of the enemy, as well as to the bravery of the others — and secured a great victory, killing three of the rebel leaders. He pressed home the advantage by taking Dragon Gate Pass, with the loss of over ten thousand of the enemy, capturing besides vast quantities of horses, helmets and armour, gongs and drums as the enemy retreated into the Western Capital.

When the Unicorn's forces were counted, only the Blue-Faced Beast and his companions were missing, with their one thousand cavalry. The Unicorn ordered Snake, Scorpion, the Forester and

Rhinoceros, with a thousand men each, to spread out and search in every direction. But by nightfall they had still found nothing.

Next day the Unicorn stayed put and ordered the search to be continued. Snake and his party scaled cliffs and conquered heights, scrambling up through the undergrowth till they reached the highest peak of Watchtower Mountain on the east. Looking west from the summit, they thought they could make out a group of men and horses deep within a hidden valley, but so thick were the trees and vegetation they could see nothing clearly and they were so high above that no sound would carry. Snake ordered them to descend, looking out on the way for locals whom they could question. They saw no one. The inhabitants had all been forced out of their homes by the fighting. Eventually they came to a level area in a very remote corner of the mountain where there were a few houses belonging to some impoverished peasants, who huddled together in terror when they saw troops. Snake said to them: "We are soldiers of the imperial army, sent here to arrest bandits." This only increased their consternation. Snake said soothingly: "We serve under General Song Jiang."

"Would that be the one as killed the savages, captured Tian Hu and never did no harm to the locals?"

"That's him!" said Snake.

They knelt and said: "You're not come here to take our chickens and steal our dogs, then? Last year when government troops come to catch bandits they behaved worse nor bandits theirselves. That's why we come here, to get away. Uncommon glad to see you we be sir!"

Snake told them about the disappearance of the Blue-Faced Beast and his thousand troops and that hidden valley west of the peak.

"Windy Valley, that's what it be called," they said. "There be only one way in." They took Snake and his men to the mouth of the valley. As luck would have it, Forester and Rhinoceros got there at the same moment. They joined forces and attacked the rebel guards, putting them to flight. They set about clearing the logs and rocks together and then Snake and Forester advanced into the valley. The season was autumn so you can just imagine what the valley was like!

A gloom is cast o'er cliffs and vales,
The trees are chilled by autumn's breath;
Above, the vapour smokes and swirls,
Below, the woods are dark as death;

Blue-Faced Beast and his forces, men and horses, were lying about exhausted under the trees, but when they saw the search party they leapt to their feet. After Snake had distributed the dry rations he had brought, to allay the pangs of hunger, they made their way out of the valley. Snake took the villagers with them to meet the Unicorn. The latter gratefully gave them silver and grain to relieve their wants. They kowtowed in thanks and departed calling down blessings on his head. Later Scorpion also returned to camp. By then it was late and they went to bed and passed an uneventful night.

Next morning the Unicorn was discussing with the Strategist the disposition of troops for attacking the city. Suddenly a messenger arrived to say that Wang Qing was sending a relief force under general Du Bo, with twelve officers and twenty thousand troops and they were only ten miles away. The Unicorn told the Strategist and six others to take twenty thousand men and position themselves in front of the camp to prevent any sortie from the city. Snake and three others were given five thousand troops to defend the mountain stronghold on Mount Ji. He himself would take the rest, thirty-five thousand troops, to meet the enemy.

Then the Prodigy spoke up. "You should not get involved in this battle yourself, sir."

"Why do you say that?" said the Unicorn.

"Last night I had an unlucky dream," he said.

"The things that come to you in sleep are not to be trusted. Danger is of no concern when one serves one's country."

"If you are determined to go, please give me five hundred infantrymen to do something."

The Unicorn laughed. "What do you plan to do, lad?"

"You needn't worry about that. Just give me the men."

"All right then, I will. I can't wait to see what you do with

them!" said the Unicorn. He went on laughing at the Prodigy after the latter led his command away.

The Unicorn now set out with the main army. When they crossed the bridge over the river Ping, where there were many strange stones that had been there since the days of the Tang, they saw the Prodigy and his men cutting down trees. Although the Unicorn thought this was pretty odd he was impatient to start the battle so there was no time to stop and ask questions. He marched to a few miles west of Dragon Gate and drew his troops up in line to the west and waited for the enemy. Two hours later they appeared. Drums thundered and shouts rose to the sky as the two armies faced each other. On the west the rebel second-in-command, Wei Ho flourished his long-handled sword, slapped his horse and rode out in front. On the Song side Shan Shiqi, one of Lucky's comrades, received his attack without a word, seated on his prancing steed, his lance at the ready. They fought it out for thirty bouts and then Shan's lance caught Wei's horse in the hind leg. The animal lashed out with its hind legs and threw its rider. With another thrust of his spear Shan killed him.

Among the rebel ranks Feng Tai was enraged and whirling a pair of steel rods he slapped his horse and charged Shan. They had fought ten bouts or more when Lucky Bian, seeing his companion could not get the better of his adversary, readied his lance and joined in. Feng gave a great roar and thrust with his lance knocking Shan from his horse and putting an end to him with a second thrust. Then he turned on his new assailant. But Lucky was a tougher proposition. As Feng's horse drew level he gave a shout and thrust his spear into Feng's chest, killing him in the saddle. A cry went up from both sides. The rebel commander Du Bo, seeing he had now lost two of his commanders, felt a fire in his breast, he was smoking with anger. He levelled his long lance and rode into battle himself. From the other side the Unicorn also advanced and fought fifty bouts with him and neither had the advantage. That long serpent lance of Du Bo's was enough to scare a ghost. The Chancellor saw the Unicorn could not win this fight and galloped to assist him. The rebel leader Zhuo Mao rode at him whirling a wolf's-tooth mace. Before they had completed five bouts the Chancellor's greater experience took effect and he knocked his opponent from his horse. Then he turned and rode at Du Bo. Du saw him kill Zhuo and before he could strike a blow himself the Chancellor's sword fell on him too, cutting off his right arm and hurling him to the ground. The Unicorn finished him off. Now the Unicorn and his companions pushed the enemy back, inflicting a great defeat on them.

Suddenly a troop of horsemen appeared from a small path to the southwest. At the head of them was a rider of swarthy complexion and uncouth appearance, with flourishing whiskers and short hair, wearing a Taoist's cap of iron and a travelling robe and mounted on a fiery chestnut. Grasping his sword and waving his troops on, he made his horse caper and bounded forward. The Unicorn and his men could see his rebel insignia and they urged their men to charge. He made no attempt to engage them but began to mutter the words of a spell. Then he slashed with his sword to the south and instantly fire spurted from his mouth. Moments later the whole waste ground between the armies was on fire and the flames were racing towards the Song side. The battle was lost before the Unicorn could do anything about it. Abandoning drums, gongs and horses, his men fled in disarray. Those who were too slow had their heads and foreheads seared. More than five thousand died like this. Surrounded by his commanders the Unicorn raced back to the River Ping Bridge.

Just as the first of the men set foot on the bridge to cross, it collapsed in ruins. It was indeed fortunate that the Prodigy had cut down trees on either side and constructed a pontoon bridge so they were still able to make the crossing and twenty thousand survived. The Unicorn and Lucky Bian fell behind in the race for the crossing and just as they reached it the enemy commander caught up with them and spat fire at Lucky, whose whole body was engulfed in flames. He fell flaming from his horse and was killed by the enemy troops. The Unicorn was fortunate to make it to the floating bridge and escape.

As the pursuing enemy were coming up, the foremost troops informed the Wizard. The latter rode out alone sword in hand to meet the enemy leader. When the enemy leader saw him, he again shaped a blow with his sword toward the south and the fire he breathed this time was fiercer than before. The Wizard composed a secret formula and pointed with his sword to one side to summon the three water spirits. In an instant flocks of black clouds streamed across and disgorged foaming cascades of water which fell in a billion, billion drops like tiny pearls or specks of jade dust, drenching the rebel leader and dowsing his fire. When he saw his magic had failed, he turned his horse and galloped away, but the horse trod on a wet stone and stumbled, throwing its rider to the ground. The Wizard raced after him and cut him in two with his sword. Of the five thousand cavalry more than five hundred were trampled down. The Wizard waved his sword and shouted out: "Surrender at once or you'll all lose your asses' heads!"

It was too much for the rebels! They dismounted and surrendered their weapons, begging for mercy. The Wizard reassured them with kind words and had the head of the rebel leader exposed. He presented the prisoners to the Unicorn, who was profuse in his thanks and also praised the Prodigy's contribution. On questioning the prisoners they learnt the name of the rebel leader. He was known as a practitioner of fire magic and was exceedingly ugly: people called him Scorcher. He had helped during the original uprising but had disappeared for two years. Recently he had come to Wang Qing and said: "The Song army is powerful. Let me get rid of them for you." Wang Qing sent him off immediately to the Western Capital.

The two enemy commanders had seen the relief force destroyed and dared not come out. They simply reinforced the guard on the city walls.

The Wizard said now: "This place is strongly fortified. We will not be able to break down the defences. You must let me practise a little of my magic tonight to help you succeed. I want to repay your kindness."

"Tell me what you propose," said the Unicorn.

The Wizard whispered in his ear: "We will do this and this and this.... We will do it thus and thus and thus...." The Unicorn was delighted and made certain appointments and the commanders went off to prepare for the attack. Instructions were also given concerning the burial of Shan Shiqi and Lucky Bian, the former Hebei commanders. The Unicorn himself made the libation.

That night in the second watch the Wizard drew his sword and made magic. Soon a fog arose, cloaking the whole city in darkness. The guards could see not an inch in front of their noses, could not even see each other. Screened by this darkness the Song troops hauled themselves up by means of windlasses and climbed onto the battlements. A sudden report and the fog immediately lifted. On all the walls now stood Song soldiers, every man carrying a lighted brand, spreading a glow that lit everything below clearly, revealing all. The troops of the garrison were struck dumb with fear and stood rooted to the spot. Then the Song troops drew their swords and the massacre began. Multitudes of rebels were cut down. The two rebel commanders saw the sudden change and rushed with their troops to the rescue. But the Song army now held all four gates. The Unicorn's main army poured inside and the two rebel commanders were killed by their mutinous troops. The other officers of all ranks surrendered, along with thirty thousand men. The ordinary people were exonerated.

At dawn the Unicorn issued a proclamation restoring peace, recording the Wizard's achievement and rewarding the army. He sent Magic Steed to tell Song Jiang the news. At evening Magic Steed returned and said: "Song Jiang has fought with the enemy for several days at Jingnan and defeated Nanfeng's relief force and taken the leader Xie Zhu prisoner. Because of the strain he has become ill and is confined to the camp. For some time now the Professor has been in charge of military affairs."

Disturbed by this news the Unicorn immediately made all necessary military arrangements and handed over the defence of the Western Capital to the Wizard and Magic Steed. Next day he bade them farewell and with the Strategist and twenty others set off with all haste for Jingnan. They wasted no time on the way and soon reached the main camp north of the city. They were relieved to learn that, thanks to the treatment of Doctor An, Song Jiang was sixty or seventy percent recovered from his illness.

They were just talking about the question of the rebels when a fugitive soldier burst in and said: "I were with Tang Bin escorting Magic Hand and his party. We'd only got ten miles when two of them generals from Jingnan, Generals Mi and Ma, come at us with ten thousand troops out of a small mountain trail. They'd heard the commander-in-chief were ill like and were 'oping to attack our camp from the rear, but they ran into us. We was outnumbered and couldn't do nothing against two of them at once, especially seeing as that General Mi is particular brave. Tang Bin got hisself killed and Magic Hand, Craftsman and Sterling got taken. Them two enemy leaders were going to continue on here and attack us when they heard as how the Unicorn and his army had arrived. So they cleared off with their prisoners."

Song Jiang involuntarily let out a cry. "I fear for their lives!" he lamented and immediately suffered a relapse. The others tried to animate him. The Unicorn asked him: "Where was Magic Hand going?"

"When he heard I was ill, Magic Hand left Commissioner Chen to come and see me. He also brought instructions from the Commissioner for the Craftsman and Sterling to go to Wanzhou where they were needed to inscribe a tablet and examine a scroll. I sent them all off today with Tang Bin and an escort of a thousand men. I did not mean them to be captured by the enemy. I fear they will be killed!"

Song Jiang now told the Unicorn to help the Professor to take the city, capture Mi and Ma and exact revenge on them. They joined the army north of the city. After exchanging courtesies with the Professor, the Unicorn immediately told him about Magic Hand. The Professor said: "Alas! They're done for!" He ordered the troops to surround the city and attack it fiercely. The commanders acted accordingly. The Professor also ordered men up onto the siege towers to shout out towards the city: "Send out Magic Hand, Sterling and the Craftsman to us at once! If you're not quick about it your city will be destroyed and all of you, civilian or military, are dead men!"

The garrison commander in the city, also appointed governor by the rebel administration, merely strengthened the defences.

The two generals, Mi and Ma, who had shunned an engagement with the Unicorn, had taken refuge within. After capturing Magic Hand and his companions they had been able to call for the gates to be opened because at that point the Song army had not yet tightened its grip on the city. They presented their three captives to the Governor. The latter had heard of the fabulous Magic Hand and he ordered the men to release him from his bonds, thinking that he would declare his submission. All three captives simply glared back and abused them roundly: "You stupid rebels, what sort of men do you take us for? Quickly, give us a couple of chops and be done with it! Don't imagine these knees will ever get anywhere near the ground! Another day when Song Jiang comes and takes your city the whole pack of you will be sliced to pieces, you rats!"

"Beat the dogs into submission!" cried the Governor, beside himself with rage.

The guards took up cudgels and battered the prisoners to the ground, but not one of them would consent to kneel. Rather they continued to shout imprecations. The Governor said: "You want to be finished off with just one cut, but I shall settle your hash infinitely slowly!" He shouted to the guards: "Take these dogs and fix them up at the gate and beat their legs for them. When their legs are smashed they'll have to be kneeling." They guards took them away, fitted them with cangues and beat them black and blue.

Now among the members of the public, soldiers and civilians, who came to see the Song captives, was one who became exceedingly angry. This was a manly looking fellow with beetling brows. He was called Bountiful and he had lived for years next door to the stationer's in South Street opposite the government office. An ancestor of his had been governor of Jingnan during the Northern and Southern Dynasties, and when the river broke its banks had personally led his officials in a rescue operation. It rained heavily and the current was strong and the officials asked him to take a rest. He said: "Wang Zun stopped the flow with his own body. How can I do less?" He persevered and the waters retreated. That year there was a bumper harvest, producing grain six-fold, and it was in memory of this that Bountiful had been given his nickname. When he happened to come to Jingnan, the people honoured him greatly because of his ancestor. He was noble, far-seeing, wise and exceedingly strong, skilled in martial arts and thoroughly brave. When he met a brave man, whatever his rank or station, he would make friends with him. When Wang Qing started his rebellion and attacked the city, Bountiful had presented a plan for defeating the rebels but the authorities rejected it, and that is why the city fell. Under the rebels, the people were ordered into the city and no one was permitted to leave. Bountiful lived there thinking and planning night and day, but you can't make cloth from a single thread. Now he saw the rebel soldiers beating up the three prisoners and heard that the Song army was attacking fiercely on their account and that both the people and the military were in a state of complete panic. After thinking about it for a while, he said to himself: "Now is the time. It's the only chance of rescue for the city." He rushed home. It was late afternoon. He quickly had a servant grind some ink and at the stationer's next door bought a quantity of strong paper. Then by the light of the lamp, carefully loading his brush, he wrote with a flourish in big characters:

> *You citizens are all loyal subjects of the Song. It cannot be with willing hearts that you aid the rebels. General Song is the court's loyal commander, who killed the Tartars and caught Tian Hu; no one dares to take him on. Under his command are one hundred and seven bold leaders, all of one heart and mind. From those three men you saw being beaten outside the gates of Government House you can tell the calibre of Song Jiang's commanders. The rebels have tortured those three, but the troops in the city are weak and their commanders incompetent; sooner or later the city will fall, and then even the stones will burn. Any of you who want to save your skins, join with me in fighting the rebels!*

After he had written out these broadsheets, Bountiful made some discreet inquiries. When he learnt that people were staying in their homes lamenting, he said to himself: "If that is how the people feel, my plan will work." He waited till just before dawn and then went out and dropped his broadsheets in all the town's busy places.

Soon it was light and people began picking them up and reading them, one after another. A crowd quickly gathered. Before long the members of a patrol confiscated one of the broadsheets and rushed to inform the Governor. The latter had a shock and immediately sent an official with orders for the guards to watch the doors of Government House closely as well as the barracks. He also instigated strict measures to catch the enemy agents. As for Bountiful, he equipped himself with a sword, which he kept hidden, and mingled with the crowd. He also picked up the broadsheet and read it out in ringing tones for all to hear. The public looked on uncertainly as the Governor's official bearing the government order galloped up to the barracks with four or five soldiers in attendance. Bountiful stepped forward and with a great shout slashed at the horse's legs. The official was thrown from his horse and Bountiful cut off his head with one blow. With the head in his left hand and the sword in his right he shouted out: "All who want to save their lives follow me and we'll kill the rebels!"

Bountiful was well known to the guards in front of Government House and they knew him to be a man of iron. In a moment he was the centre of a mob of five or six hundred. Seeing the soldiers had joined him, he cried out with redoubled vigour to the people: "Come and join us if you've got the guts!" His voice carried many hundreds of yards. All around people responded by grabbing sticks and cudgels, tearing up palings, breaking off chairlegs. In a twinkling they were five or six thousand. They set up a continuous roar and led by Bountiful burst into the government office. The Governor was accustomed to bully his officers and persecute the men of his personal guard and they all nourished an intense hatred of him. When they heard of the uprising they joined the mob. Charging inside they slaughtered the Governor and all his family. By the time Bountiful led them out again, the mob had grown to twenty thousand. They released Magic Hand, Sterling and Craftsman from the stocks and removed the cangues.

Bountiful told three men with strong backs to carry them. Led by Bountiful and bearing the Governor's head, they rushed to the north gate, killed the guard commander and scattered his troops, opened the gate and let down the drawbridge.

The Professor had just reached the north gate to personally direct the attack when he heard the uproar in the city. When he saw the gate being opened he thought the enemy were about to make a sortie. He hurriedly ordered his troops to pull back three or four bowshots and form a defensive line. Then he saw Bountiful, bearing the head, with three soldiers behind him carrying Magic Hand and his companions. As soon as the drawbridge was lowered they rushed out. Magic Hand shouted to the startled Professor: "Professor, we have to thank this brave man who has incited the people to kill the rebels and save our lives!"

The Professor was as delighted as he was amazed. Bountiful said to him: "The situation is urgent, there is no time for ceremony. Please move your army into the city immediately!"

Beside the drawbridge there was already a crowd of soldiers who all shouted in unison "Let General Song Jiang enter the city!"

Seeing such a variety of people all gathered there, the Professor ordered his commanders to march their men into the city, with instructions that if any man killed someone the whole platoon was to be executed. When they heard this the rebel guards on the north all laid down their arms and came down from the walls. The news also reached the guards on the south, east and west and they tied up their officers and opened the gates, welcoming Song Jiang's army with open arms. Only General Mi was courageous enough not to give in and escaped through the west gate, breaking through the encirclement and getting away.

The Professor sent an urgent despatch to Song Jiang, whose gloom and despondency were almost entirely dispelled by the news. Briskly he gave the marching orders. When the army reached Jingnan, Song Jiang took over the government office and issued a proclamation restoring peace and rewarding his commanders. He summoned Bountiful, asked him his name and assisted him to a seat. He greeted him most courteously and said: "You, sir, have eliminated the rebels and made life secure for the people, subdued the city without bloodshed and rescued my three brothers, I bow down before you."

Bountiful likewise bowed repeatedly, saying: "It is not through my efforts but through the power of the ordinary soldiers and people." His words impressed Song Jiang even more. The other leaders then paid their respects to Bountiful. The rebel commanders in the city were brought in and Song Jiang offered an amnesty to all who surrendered. There was great rejoicing in the city and ten thousand or more gave themselves up.

Now the water-borne forces under White-Water Dragon arrived in the river Han and came to report. Song Jiang ordered a banquet in honour of Bountiful. He offered him the cup with his own hands saying: "When I return to the court I shall tell the Emperor of your great talents and virtue and you will certainly be promoted."

Bountiful said: "That is not what I would wish. I did not act out of desire for fame or riches. I have always had an undisciplined nature and the people at home do not have a high opinion of me. I have little talent and no real experience. Nowadays we see that calumny reigns in high places and good men have no credit. Besides, though a man's nature be forbearing and his conduct amenable, yet will it not enable him to obtain enlightenment. I observe that there are many driven by ambition to bear the insults of office whose activity is not beneficial. And those who strive to maintain a family find their virtue is sapped and they have delivered themselves into the power of evil men. As for me, having no burden of office, am I not like the crane that rides the clouds, enviably free to fly where I will?"

Neither Song Jiang nor any who served under him could resist a sigh on hearing this long speech. Taoist Gongsun, Monk, Pilgrim and all the rest who were present sat there nodding appreciatively at Bountiful's words. That evening when the party broke up Bountiful bade farewell and left the government office. Next morning Song Jiang after sending Magic Messenger to tell the news to Commissioner Chen, went himself to Bountiful's house to pay his respects. He found it empty. Pinned to the wall was a note which said: "This morning before dawn I packed my belongings, bade my family farewell and set off, I know not whither."

When Song Jiang went back and told the others how Bountiful had slipped away in the night, every one of them breathed a sigh. That evening Magic Messenger returned and told them that the as yet unpacified districts of Shannan and Wanzhou facing the campaign organized by Commissioner Chen and Marshal Hou with Leopard's Head and his companions had all sued for peace. The court had sent a good many new officials and all had taken over. The Commissioner was on his way with all his commanders and would arrive soon.

Song Jiang decided with the Professor that as soon as the Commissioner arrived to take charge they would start their campaign against the leadership of the rebellion. Song Jiang rested at Jingnan five or six days more till he was fully recovered. Then one day it was announced that the Commissioner had arrived and they went out to welcome him.

The Commissioner rewarded the army commanders handsomely. After that the acting governor of Shannan, Tattooed Dragon, arrived with his men, having handed over to the new officials. Song Jiang requested the Commissioner to take over the city, bade farewell and set off with his land and water-borne forces to seize the rebel's stronghold at Nanfeng. Now all one hundred and eight leaders were together again, plus those who had surrendered in Hebei, viz the Chancellor and eleven others with two hundred thousand troops. They had fought and won countless battles, their strength kept on growing and everywhere they went the rebels surrendered at the mere sight of them. Song Jiang was able to report the recovery of many districts to Commissioner Chen, and the Commissioner sent Academician Luo with troops to take control of them.

Song Jiang and his water-borne forces advanced as far as the borders of Nanfeng. Scouts came in with the intelligence that Wang Qing had made Fortune-teller Li his Commander-in-Chief and had raised a water-borne force of fifty thousand, while there were another three columns of local troops, twenty thousand in each, under some local commanders. A dozen brave officers, then, with hundreds of thousands of troops were advancing on them, and Wang Qing himself was directing the operation.

Song Jiang consulted the Professor about all this: "The enemy have turned out in full strength; it seems they have decided on a showdown. How can we get the better of them?"

The Professor said: "In battle as they say numbers aren't everything. We're all of us here now. Let us divide our forces and attack before they have a chance to settle down." Song Jiang gave orders accordingly.

On the first day Skyhawk and Mr. Chai led six others and five thousand men to escort the supply carts and carts filled with silk and ammunition in the army's rear. At a place called Dragon Heights at the foot of the mountain they found a village surrounded by cliffs like earthen ramparts with three access roads. The people lived in a hundred or so rough huts but they had all fled because of the fighting. That evening a strong wind blew from the northeast and black clouds piled up. Because the sky was so menacing, Skyhawk and Mr. Chai were afraid rain might damage the supplies and ordered their men to open up the huts and drag the carts inside. They were about to start preparing a meal for themselves when a patrol led by Pill Monger arrested a spy and came to report to Mr. Chai: "Under interrogation this spy told us that General Mi with ten thousand picked troops plans to burn our supplies tonight in the second watch. At present they are concealed on the mountain."

This place Dragon Heights, you see, had two cliffs that faced each other forming a kind of gate barely wide enough for a boat to be rowed through; the sides were clad in impenetrable scrub. Skyhawk immediately said to Mr. Chai: "I'll go to the village and wait for the bastards and give them such a drubbing not a scrap of their armour will survive whole."

Mr. Chai said: "That General Mi is a true soldier. You won't beat him just by strength. Besides we haven't enough troops. Let me try a little plan of mine first. We'll need five or six gun carts with explosives and a hundred or so carts of firewood. We'll avenge Tang Bin and company and annihilate the treacherous swine." He had his men bring the supplies, ammunition and carts

and ordered Skyhawk to guard the stores with three thousand troops equipped with fire arrows. At dusk they all left the narrows and headed south, leaving behind hundreds of carts loaded with firewood, lined up on the lower ground southwest of the village. Among the hundred or so empty carts, drawn up in a number of different places, they deliberately placed some supplies so that they were visible. Explosives were hidden everywhere underneath together with firewood primed with gunpowder. He told the Young Master and three others to take two thousand men and set up an ambush along the East Peak road and Water General to do likewise along the road south from the village, in preparation for the enemy attack. All was done thus and thus and thus, according to plan. Mr. Chai himself with the Fire General and three hundred infantrymen equipped with incendiary materials, concealed themselves among the trees and scrub on the mountainside.

At nine o'clock General Mi with his two lieutenants and more than ten thousand troops in light armour, the horses with muffled hooves and harness bells, with banners furled and drums silent, approached the southern pass. The Water General ordered his men to light their torches and attack. After four or five bouts with Mi, he slapped his horse and led his troops in retreat. General Mi, who was a brave and unsuspecting soul, raced after them. The Young Master and the Pill Monger seeing fire on the south road left a thousand troops to their two companions and galloped toward the village to close off the road. By now the rebels were streaming into the village. They attacked the higher ground on the northeast and found nothing but empty houses, no supplies anywhere. They searched about and found that on the lower ground there were several hundred carts of supplies with only five or six hundred soldiers to guard them. The latter saw them coming and with shouts of alarm scattered and ran for it. General Mi said: "They can't have much in the way of supplies!" He ordered his men to light torches so they could see. At intervals among the supply carts there would be a couple loaded with silk brocade. When the rebels saw this they fell to plundering them. General Mi was trying to put a stop to this when from above them on the mountainside fire arrows and firebrands began raining down, setting the carts with firewood ablaze. A shout rose from the rebels as they tried to take cover but the fuses were already lit to fire the charges and with a roar like thunder they went off. Before the rebels could take evasive action they were mown down by the shells.

Well, the fires blazed and the cannon roared as though the heavens were falling in or earth splitting. In a moment all the thatched huts were hidden in clouds of smoke or converted into balls of fire. General Mi was killed by a shell, as were most of his men. Many suffered terrible burns. Then the Water General and the Young Master attacked with their three columns killing the other two enemy generals. Of the ten thousand rebel troops only a thousand or so escaped with their lives.

When daylight came Mr. Chai's unit joined up with Skyhawk's and brought the supply train up to the camp. Song Jiang was in the headquarters tent making the dispositions for his troops, cavalrymen were saddling their horses, the infantry putting their weapons in order. Indeed

Flags and banners painted the sky red;
Swords and spears glittered like snow.

If you want to know how Song Jiang and his friends attacked the rebel stronghold, you must read the next chapter.

Chapter 109

Wang Qing crosses the river and is captured; Song Jiang completes his defeat of the rebels!

So Song Jiang sat in his tent that day and his commanders paraded to receive their orders. A gun was fired, music played and the flag was raised. At the signal the guard commanders fell in outside the tent, standing to attention, to hear the orders. A fanfare and the orders were read out, after which they kowtowed and went to stand on either side.

Next the platoon leaders knelt to hear the disciplinary arrangements: all insolence or disorder in the ranks, all insubordination or questioning of orders, all wavering in the face of the enemy were to be stamped out.

For every twenty or so men there was an ensign. To them Song Jiang spoke personally: "Discipline is your responsibility: if any man fails to advance or is neglectful of his orders you are to punish him." The ensigns stood down, the music sounded again and everyone returned to their companies to proceed as commanded. Finally Song Jiang gave out the orders for the boat commanders.

The drummer was to give the orders with a handclap: one, form up; two, raise banners; three, forward march! Next to the band the five directions flag was raised and a gun fired. The signal was given to strike camp and all was ready for battle:

The thunder of the drum shakes the mountain peaks;
Banners fill the sky dismaying gods and ghosts.

Wang Qing meanwhile was planning his battle formation. He appointed the leaders of the vanguard and the left and right flanks. He himself would command the main army with a number of his aides and police chiefs to protect him. Fortune-teller Li was head of the army. The troops were drawn up in perfect order with Wang Qing in overall command of the operation. The horses had protective armour, the men chainmail. The bows were strung. Three beats of the drum and all stood to. Forward march!

They had not gone more than a few miles when a cloud of dust announced the approach of a Song patrol. Thirty riders appeared, all wearing blue scarves and green battle robes, and there was a great jingling of harness bells as they rode forward. Their horses were decked with scarlet tassels, their harness hung with dozens of bells; they sported pheasants' feathers, the hafts of their spears were bound with silver rings and they carried light bows and short arrows. The leader of this band, bearer of the Emperor's commission after winning back his honour, was that paragon of warriors Hotshot. He wore a gold-embroidered blue turban and a special war robe of blue brocade. His waist bound with a crimson sash, slippers of soft leather on his feet, he bestrode a horse with a silver saddle. On his left was another imperial appointee, the chaste and filial Jade Arrowtip. She wore a crimson cap with a golden pattern and a war robe of crimson silk brocade. About her waist was a sash of many colours and on her feet small winged slippers. Her mount was a grey thoroughbred. On the right, a little lower down, bearing the flag, was that worthy servant the Butler, also a recipient of the Emperor's favour. This party rode on till they were quite close to Fortune-teller Li's company, not more than a few hundred paces separating the two forces, before they turned their horses and rode back.

The two leading rebel commanders urged their horses forward in a charge. Hotshot slapped his horse, levelled his spear of seasoned wood and rode at them, Jade Arrowtip following behind, square halberd at the ready. When these four had fought a dozen bouts, Hotshot and Arrowtip knocked aside their opponents' weapons, turned and galloped off. The rebels gave chase, but there were shouts from their companions on either side: "Don't follow them. Those two have got masses of stones in their saddlebags and when they throw they don't miss!"

The rebel leaders reined in their horses at once. Then on Dragon

Heights a drum thundered and a company of five hundred infantry appeared, with four marching in front: Iron Ox, Demon King, Eight-Armed Ogre and Winged Ghost. As they came on their men spread out in a long line under the mountain, with the shield bearers thickly clustered on either side. The rebel commanders urged their men forward and Iron Ox and Demon King split their force into two columns, which turned and using the shields to cover their backs retreated towards the mountain again.

By now the main rebel army with Wang Qing and Fortune-teller Li had come up and they all advanced together. Iron Ox and Demon King had raced up the mountain and disappeared over a ridge into the forest. They were nowhere to be seen. Fortune-teller Li ordered the rebel troops to form up on the level wasteland.

Suddenly a loud report from the mountain and a column of men was seen racing forward on the south with three leaders in their midst: Short-Arse, in the centre, Colonel Sun on the left and the Gardener on the right. They rolled forward with five thousand cavalry and infantry. Wang Qing was just about to deploy troops to oppose them when the gun on the mountain fired again and another column of troops raced out on the north with the three women warriors: Steelbright in the centre, Auntie Gu on the left and the Ogress on the right, also with five thousand cavalry and infantry. The rebel commanders on the right received this charge, while Short-Arse and company clashed with the rebels on the left. They fought a dozen bouts before the Song commanders turned their horses and galloped off to the east, Steelbright and company following suit.

When Wang Qing saw them retreat he said with a sneer: "If these fuckers are all Song Jiang's got, how can we go on losing to them?" He led the main army in pursuit. They had not gone more than a couple of miles when the crash of a gong rang out and the four infantry commanders who had previously retreated began to advance from the thickets on the left flank of the mountain. Four more had now joined them: Monk, Pilgrim, the Red-Haired Devil and Nameless, with five hundred infantry, all armed with round shields and short swords. The rebel second-in-command

immediately detached two thousand troops to engage them. After a few bouts Iron Ox and company feigned defeat and retreated in two separate columns, covering their backs with their shields as they fled into the forest and disappeared. The rebels gave chase, but Iron Ox and company were too fast for them and in an instant they had vanished. Fortune-teller Li hurriedly told Wang Qing: "Do not follow them, Sire. It's a trick. We should form up and wait for them to attack."

Before Li had completed this manoeuvre there was a thunderous report on the mountain and the whole of the main Song army poured forth to take up a position in the centre. Wang Qing ordered those on his right and left to stand guard while he mounted the observation platform. Here is what he saw:

To the south: troops with red banners, red armour, red robes, vermilion tassels and chestnut horses massed behind a command banner that is red with gold embroidery, and beside it, among a crowd of red pennants, a tall leader. This is Thunderclap, with the Water General on his left and the Fire General on his right, all fully armed and mounted on chestnut horses.

To the east: troops with blue banners, blue armour, blue robes, blue tassels and blue-grey horses following a blue command flag with gold embroidery and another tall leader. This is Scimitar, with the Son-in-Law on his left and Hound on his right, all fully armed and mounted on blue-grey horses.

To the west: troops with white banners and so on. In front of them Leopard's Head, with Tamer on his left and Colonel Sun on his right.

To the rear of these: troops all in black behind Twin Rods, with the Supremo on his left and Victorious on his right.

To the southeast: troops with blue banners and red armour, led by Twin Spears, with Golden Wings on his left and Redeye on his right.

To the southwest: troops with red banners and white armour led by Hasty, with the Dandy on his left and Flautist on his right.

To the northeast: troops with black banners and blue armour, led by the Tattooed Dragon with River-Jumper and White-Spotted Snake.

To the northwest: troops with white banners and black armour, led by Blue-Faced Beast with Panther and the Big Chief.

These forces offer protection on eight sides like an iron bucket. They are all in their proper units, cavalry with cavalry, infantry with infantry, all armed and provided with their banners, an awe-inspiring sight. In the centre of the octagon is a cluster of yellow banners, among them sixty-four depicting all the figures of the *Book of Changes* outlined in gold, in four groups. South of the central section are cavalry, with two senior leaders: Whiskers and his subordinate Sergeant Lei, their forces all in yellow. On the east of the central section is the Little Master, on the west Whitey, on the south Door-God and on the north Pill Monger.

Grouped behind the yellow flags, the artillery, with its commander, Thunderer, and twenty of his gunners standing around their guns. Behind these a contingent with hooks and ropes, and behind them some banners of various colours with the twenty-eight heavenly mansions represented on all sides.

Among the gold embroidered banners is the goose yellow command banner, worked in felt and bordered with real pearls, with gold bells along the bottom edge and surmounted by a pheasant's feather. Guardian of this is an impressive giant of a man with a cap secured by a fishtail pin, and dragon scale armour. This is Perilous. Beside the banner are two ensigns, both mounted, dressed identically and holding steel lances: the two brothers, Comet and Red Star. In front of and behind their horses twenty-four armoured guards with wolf's-tooth maces. Behind, two signal flags and on either side twenty-four halberdiers. Two riders in the midst of them: Little Duke and Halberdier. In the midst of the halberds a thicket of tridents with two powerful commanders, identically dressed: Snake and Scorpion, both with three-pronged forks, protecting the central army. Behind them two horsemen with silver saddles: Magic Hand and Sterling. Behind them soldiers dressed in red with hemp-bound swords and in their midst the two executioners, Strongarm and Blossom.

At the very back are ranks of spearsmen with gold spears and silver spears, one lot under Spearsman, the other under Colonel Hua. Behind these row upon row of padded uniforms, coloured turbans, crimson robes, padded jackets, then two shimmering, glittering walls of green streamers and blue screens, crimson pennants and yellow-shafted halberds with white animal tails hanging from them, preceding three ranks of halberds, axes, whips and hammers.

In the midst of these, under three gilt umbrellas, seated on precious saddles, the three chiefs: on the right, with his star cap and crane's feather cloak, Dragon in the Clouds, Taoist Gongsun Sheng, on the left, with his silk kerchief and feather fan, the Beacon of Learning Professor Wu Yong, in the centre, on the famous horse Moonlight with a gold saddle, that humane and virtuous general, scourge of brigands and rebels, Shandong's Opportune Rain, Song Jiang the Guardian of Righteousness. In front of his horse on the left stands the Magic Messenger, master of flying despatches, military intelligence and troop dispositions. On the right is the Prodigy, protector of the main army and entrusted with special missions. Behind his horse are ranks of pikes and halberds, horses with embroidered saddles, thirty-five junior officers on horseback with lances, a company of archers. Also the musicians playing for all they are worth. To the rear of the whole army are two companies of roving troops waiting on either side to protect the flanks: the Guv and Nine-Tailed Turtle with three thousand infantry on the left and Irrepressible and Unstoppable with three thousand on the right.

The whole formation is drawn up in perfect order. Truly it can be said that:

Many the troops are, the battle plan mighty;
Like tigers the men, their horses pure dragon.
Bent on their task of subduing the West,
The leaders shout threats that spell death to the rebels.

And so this hedge king, this upstart Wang Qing stood on the observation platform with Li the fortune-teller and surveyed the opposing force, which before his eyes took on this formation based on the nine mansions of the *Book of Changes*. The troops were fierce enough, the leaders brave enough, the expressions grim and the weapons sharp-edged enough to frighten his soul out of its body, to cause his spirits to plunge. Despite himself he had to say: "No wonder we keep losing to them. Who'd have thought an army could be so imposing!"

The drums on the Song side kept up an incessant thunder. Wang Qing and the fortune-teller descended from the platform, mounted their horses and rode out with the security chiefs on either side and a crowd of palace attendants behind. Wang Qing gave the order for his vanguard to attack. The opposing armies were lined up facing east and west, and wood was the sign for the day. The Song ranks on the west opened and Leopard's Head sped forward. Both armies cheered. He reined his horse in, rested his eight-pointed serpent lance and shouted at the top of his voice: "You rebellious fool, you mad dog conspirator, the imperial army is here, why have you not surrendered? If you wait till I've ground you to dust, it'll be too late then for regrets!"

In the rebel ranks Fortune-teller Li, who knew the laws of cause and effect, hurriedly gave the order for the two commanders on the left flank to take the red-banner troops into action. This order was carried out, to much shouting from the armies and thundering music. Leopard's Head took on one of them and four arms rose and fell while four horse's hooves clattered on the ground. The antagonists, hidden in a cloud of dust, surrounded by the chill of death, went this way and that, swooping to the left and spinning to the right. They fought fifty bouts and neither had the advantage. This rebel leader was one of their bravest. When his comrade saw he was not winning, he raised his sword and charged to the rescue. Faced by two opponents, Leopard's Head gave a great shout and making a supreme effort thrust the first of them through with his lance, flinging him from his horse. His deputies, Tamer and Colonel Sun, galloped forward. Tamer dealt the second leader a great blow with his deadly sword: the blood gushed and there was the helmet rolling under the horse's legs.

When the second rebel leader died, his troops scattered and the enemy ranks were broken. Wang Qing heard he had lost two of his commanders and immediately ordered a retreat. But just then a gun going off in the Song army was the signal for frenzied activity as, white leading black, black leading blue, blue leading red, they changed their formation into a long snake and then a winnowing basket, effecting a complete encirclement. Wang Qing and Fortune-teller Li moved their troops this way and that, attacking in different places, but they were just running their heads against a brick wall; they simply couldn't break out. What a battle that was, between the government forces and the rebels!

> *Weapons clash, horses and riders dash against each other. Spear foiling sword: the sword aims to split the skull, the spear darts like a swordfish to meet it; the sword strikes from below, the spear bears down like an earth-borer; the sword sweeps along the ground, the spear blocks it like the fringe of a corselet. Sword countering spear: the spear lunges at the heart, the sword makes a five-flower defence; the spear seeks to prick the eye, the sword parries. Halberd defeating shield: the shield advances like a spinning top, the halberd sweeps it aside like the wind; the shield bores in from the side, the halberd stands athwart; the shield comes crowding forward, the halberd draws back and jabs defensively. Shield countering halberd: the halberd closes, the shield ducks and weaves; the halberd presses hard, the shield responds with a block. The naked blade hidden in silk feigns defeat, pretends surrender; the steel trident thrusting upward, sweeping downward, feints and ripostes. The sniper on horseback watches his opportunity; in front of carts men with billhooks wait for the horses. Rods, darts, maces, hammers, broadswords, halberds, lances, bucklers: here the conflict raging unabated, there the fortunes ever in the balance. Blood soon runs in rivers, corpses are piled in mountains.*

Fierce fighting continued for a long time, but eventually the rebels were routed and the government forces prevailed. Wang Qing gave the order to withdraw into Nanfeng, hoping to make new plans. But then a gun went off in their rear and a messenger galloped up and reported: "Sire, there are more enemy troops behind us!" The hero leading this contingent was none other than the Unicorn, armed with his lance of hardened steel, with Morbid on his left and Madcap on his right and ten thousand battle-ready troops. They charged furiously at the rebels' rearguard.

Morbid knocked one of the commanders off his horse, Madcap ran the other one through, as the impetus carried them on through the rebel ranks.

In the midst of this crisis, Wang Qing heard another loud report and the Monk marched out from the left with seven other leaders and a thousand infantry, equipped with cudgels, cutlasses, axes, pikes, swords, javelins and round shields; they cut through the enemy like someone slicing a melon or chopping vegetables. On the right the Gardener, Short-Arse, Blackface and Hotshot and their respective wives, with a thousand cavalry, armed with spears and lances of weathered wood and bronze, square halberds, double-edged swords and daggers attacked the rebels' left flank, bowling them over, going through them like a knife through rotten wood, scattering them to the four winds.

The Unicorn, supported by Morbid and Madcap, took on the main army, killing the commander, routing the flanking troops and pressing on with the intention of capturing Wang Qing. Instead he found the fortune-teller, who was an excellent swordsman and came at him with his sword darting at the speed of lightning. The Unicorn was unable to cope with this and retreated into the lee of Song Jiang's main army. The commander on the right was Taoist Gongsun, who advanced muttering a spell. He cried out "Chrrr!" and the sword flew out of Li's hand and dropped to the ground. The Unicorn galloped up to him and stretching out his long arms and twisting his supple waist wrenched him off his horse and handed him over to be tied up. Then he slapped his horse and readied his lance and charged off again in search of Wang Qing, like an eagle stooping on a swallow or a tiger devouring a lamb. The rebels abandoned drums and gongs and threw down their halberds and spears. There was complete havoc; it was one of those days when fathers mourn sons, sons search for fathers and brothers lose each other. The greater part of a hundred thousand troops were killed. The field was littered with corpses, blood ran in rivers. Thirty thousand gave themselves up. Apart from a few who managed to run away, the rest ended up more dead than alive, trampled underfoot by men and horses, battered to pieces, rendered into mincemeat. Two fearsome rebel commanders had their horses killed under them by Nameless, who dragged the riders off and killed them too. Arrowtip knocked the rebel Li Xiong down with one of her stones and finished him off with her halberd. Another rebel commander was accounted for by Fleetfoot, the latter's halberd knocking him from his mount and spitting him as he attempted to flee. Many of the upstart's officials, ministers, security chiefs and officers of all kinds never made it to safety. Apart from the fact that the chief rebel himself was missing it was a complete victory for the Song forces.

Song Jiang had the gong sounded to recall his troops and they made for Nanfeng. He sent Hotshot and Jade Arrowtip off on reconnaissance with five thousand cavalry. He also sent Magic Messenger ahead to gather news of the Chancellor's attack on Nanfeng. The Magic Messenger used his magic amulets, so he overtook Hotshot and Arrowtip. The journey took him all morning and when he returned he gave this account: "When he got your orders, the Chancellor dressed himself as one of the western army to try and deceive the city, but they saw through it. They dug a pit just inside the gates. Then they opened the east gate and let his troops in. Seven of the officers under the Chancellor's command, and five hundred men with their horses charged through the gate and all, men and horses, plunged into the pit. There were troops hidden on either side who with long spears and pikes stabbed all five hundred or more of them to death. Luckily the Chancellor was at the back. He waited his moment and then charged through and got his men to fill in the pit. They continued on into the city and the guards fled. He seized the east gate, but later the enemy counter-attacked on all sides and got them surrounded in there. As soon as I heard this I raced back here. On the way I met Hotshot and Jade Arrowtip and told them and they are rushing there with their troops."

Song Jiang immediately mobilized the main army and marched them with all speed to surround Nanfeng. Hotshot and Arrowtip by now had reached the East Gate and reinforced the Chancellor. They were engaged in fierce fighting. Song Jiang and his army also entered by the East Gate and captured the city, putting the rebels to flight. They raised the Song banner on all the gates. Many of the usurper's officials in the city, civil and military, were executed, including Fan Quan — Wang Qing's cousin and erstwhile government official. The usurper's consort, formerly Miss Duan, when she heard the government troops were in the city, having been always strong and an accomplished horsewoman, girded herself and rode forth at the head of a hundred or so of her bravest attendants. They left the palace through the rear court, heading for the west gate with the intention of joining the rebel forces at Yun'an. But they ran into Jade Arrowtip, who at that moment was attacking the palace from the back. Miss Duan brandished her sword and urged her horse forward in one last desperate charge. One of Jade Arrowtip's stones caught her in the face. Bleeding profusely she fell from her horse. Troops rushed up to tie her up and make her prisoner. Her maids were all killed. Jade Arrowtip pressed on into the palace garden. All the palace maids, when they heard the Song army had entered the city, either hanged themselves or threw themselves down wells or stabbed themselves to death or threw themselves down steps, almost all dying by their own hand. The remainder were tied up by Arrowtip's troops and taken before Song Jiang in his tent. He was well pleased and ordered Miss Duan and her attendants to be locked up until Wang Qing was captured and then sent off to the capital. He again sent out detachments in all directions to hunt for Wang Qing.

Wang Qing with only a few hundred armoured cavalry left to him had broken out of the encirclement and fled to the east of Nanfeng. When he saw fighting in the city he was frightened half out of his wits. The main Song army was at his back and there was no chance of fleeing northwards. Looking about he found he had barely a hundred men. The remainder, even those he trusted most, had fled in the face of defeat. With those remaining he headed for Yun'an. On the way he spoke with those nearest him: "I still have Yun'an, Dongchuan and Ande. This region east of the river is not large, but surely it will suffice for a kingdom? What hurts me is that those courtiers who were happy to take my salary, have deserted me now in my time of need. As soon as we have driven off the Song troops, I will arrest those ungrateful traitors and have them sliced into little pieces."

There was no rest for horses or men as they galloped on till dawn. They were relieved when they saw Yun'an before them. Wang Qing said happily: "They are well prepared. See how bravely the banners are flying and how well camouflaged the guns." He spoke as they were hastening towards the city.

But one of his followers who could read and write said: "Sire, something is wrong. Why is the city full of Song flags and ensignia?" Wang Qing looked again and it was true: on the east gate was a banner, visible from afar, which had large gold embroidered characters: "General Song's Commander of Water-borne Forces in the West, White-Water…". Below were three lines which could not be made out because of the way the wind was blowing the flag. When he saw this Wang Qing's heart went heavy as lead, his whole body numb, and for a long time he was quite unable to move. Indeed it was as if the Song forces had fallen from the sky. Finally one of his close aides, who was an astute fellow, said: "Sire, there is no time to lose. I beg you to remove your royal insignia and flee to Dongchuan. I fear this city has changed hands."

Wang Qing said: "You are right, my friend." He took off his towering crown and divested himself of his imperial dragon robe embroidered with figures of the sun and moon, removed his jewel-encrusted belt and his slippers and changed into a simple turban, ordinary clothes and soft leather shoes. His followers also removed their outer clothing and then, like dogs kicked out of the house or fish escaped from the net, they fled away by small paths, passing Yun'an by and heading for Dongchuan. They travelled till men and horses were exhausted and every stomach empty. The people had suffered so long at the hands of the rebels that when they heard of great battles, they had all taken to the road and there was no sign of human habitation at any of the important places along the route. All was silent: no cock crowed, no dog barked. You could not even get a drop of water, let alone find a place to buy wine and food.

By now some sixty or seventy of Wang Qing's personal

attendants had absented themselves, saying they had to go to the toilet or needed a pee. The party, now consisting of thirty, rode on till evening when they came to Kaizhou, still in Yun'an province, where a river blocked their path. This was the river Clearwater, which rose in a lake in Dazhou. The water was indeed especially clear, hence the name. Wang Qing said: "If only we could find a boat to take us across!" One of his retinue pointed and said: "Over there, Sire, look, where the reeds are thinner and the geese are landing, there are some fishing boats."

They all went down to the river bank. It was the depths of winter but the day was bright and clear. There were about a dozen fishing boats: some of the men were fishing and others were drying their nets. Out in midstream there were some boats where the fishermen were playing the guessing fingers game and drinking from large bowls. Wang Qing sighed and said: "Look at those fellows, how happy they are! How different from my lot. They are my subjects, but they know nothing of the hardships their prince must suffer!"

One of the attendants shouted: "Ahoy there, fishermen! Bring some of your boats over here to ferry us across. You'll be handsomely paid for it."

Two of the men set down their bowls and the boat came creaking across the water. A fisherman in the bows poled the boat in to the bank. He looked Wang Qing up and down from head to toe and said: "Look lively about it then. We've still got more drinking to do. Get in, get in!"

Wang Qing's attendants helped him aboard. The fisherman was a big fellow with shaggy eyebrows, big eyes, iron-grey whiskers and a voice like a gong. He held the pole in one hand and with the other helped Wang Qing aboard. Then he gave one shove with his pole and the boat shot away from the bank a metre or more. This caused a great commotion among the attendants left on the bank. "Hey, bring the boat back here at once," they cried out in unison. "We all want to go across!"

The fisherman glared at them and said: "And where do you plan to go to then?" Then he put down his pole, planted a hand on Wang Qing's chest, pulled on his arms and threw him to the

deck with a crash. Wang Qing tried to struggle but the man with the oars put them down and leapt up to help pin him down. The fishermen who were drying their nets jumped ashore and fell on the attendants, making them prisoner one after another.

The big fisherman with the pole was of course the White-Water Dragon, and the one rowing was Cave Dragon. The fishermen were all members of the Song water-borne force. White-Water Dragon had received orders from Song Jiang to sail his fleet to engage the rebel fleet. They had fought a big battle at Gautama Narrows where they'd killed the rebel commander and taken his deputy, Hu Jun, prisoner, inflicting a heavy defeat on the enemy. Recognizing him from his bearing as exceptional, White-Water Dragon had courteously released his prisoner. In gratitude the latter had contrived to open the water gates of Yun'an for him and he had captured it, killing the garrison commander. Anticipating that the rebels after being defeated and scattered by the main army would attempt to flee back to their base, he left White Eel and the Pilot in charge of the city and went with Cave Dragon, River Rider and their men disguised as fishermen, to set a watch for the returning enemy. He posted the three Ruan brothers also at three other river crossings to keep watch. When he saw Wang Qing approaching, riding at the head of a crowd, he assumed he was an enemy leader, though he did not know it was the chief villain of all. After interrogating his followers he learnt that it was Wang Qing and he clapped his hands with joy. He recalled the Ruan brothers and the Tong brothers to help guard the city and with the former enemy commander, Hu Jun, took Wang Qing and his followers to Song Jiang. They learnt on the way that Song Jiang had taken Nanfeng. On entering the city they took Wang Qing to the government office. Song Jiang was somewhat downhearted at the time, because of their failure to capture Wang Qing, and he could scarce contain his joy when he heard the news. When White-Water Dragon entered, he was loud in his praises: "Dear Brother, this is a major achievement," he said. White-Water Dragon presented Hu Jun to him and said: "This is the man who deserves the credit." Song Jiang asked him his name and enquired about his part in the taking of Yun'an.

After Song Jiang had distributed rewards and compensation, he conferred with them all about how to capture the two cities still in rebel hands, Dongchuan and Ande. The newly surrendered Hu Jun said: "Don't worry about it, General. I can tell you something which will take care of both places, it's a cinch!"

Song Jiang was delighted to hear this. He took Hu aside and respectfully asked him what his plan was. Hu bowed and said a few words which were to have important consequences: without a shot fired the cities were recaptured, the army subdued and the rebels forced to surrender.

If you want to hear what Hu Jun said, you must read the next chapter.

Chapter 110

The Prodigy shoots geese at Autumn Woods Crossing; Song Jiang brings his captives to the Eastern Capital!

Now when Song Jiang asked General Hu Jun what was his plan for capturing Dongchuan and Ande, the latter replied: "The garrison commander at Dongchuan is my younger brother Hu Xian. Out of gratitude to Commander Li for sparing my life, let me go to Dongchuan and order my brother to surrender. When the garrison at Ande find they are alone, they will have no alternative but to give themselves up."

Song Jiang was pleased and ordered the White-Water Dragon to go too. He now made his dispositions, deploying troops to pacify the districts that had not yet surrendered, and sent Magic Messenger to request the court to declare the campaign successfully concluded, and to deliver a report to the Commissioner for forwarding to Marshal Su. With the army he went to Wang Qing's imperial palace to impound all valuables in the treasury and burn down and destroy all the topless towers and splendid halls, all the weapons of war and uniforms. He likewise sent word to Pilot in Yun'an ordering him to burn and destroy all the armaments in the palace there.

Magic Messenger went first to the Commissioner in Jingnan. The latter added a report of his own. Magic Messenger went next to the capital and handed the reports in to Marshal Su together with some gifts. Marshal Su presented the report to the Emperor for his scrutiny. The Emperor expressed great satisfaction and immediately ordered the drafting of an edict for the Western region whereby the rebel Wang Qing was to be sent to the capital for sentencing, and the usurper's concubines, officials and hangers-on executed in the local market-places and their heads exhibited.

The people had suffered cruelly at the hands of Wang Qing and there was to be an indemnity of cash and rations, distributed to each needy household to relieve poverty. The surrendered Hebei commanders who had died in battle were rewarded posthumously by gifts to their followers. The temporary administrations were to hand over to new officials as soon as possible. Where local officials had first sided with the rebels and later returned to their allegiance, their conduct was to be judged by Commissioner Chen and dealt with on merit. All who had contributed to the putting down of the rebellion would be rewarded with official posts on the army's return to the capital. Magic Messenger went on ahead in order to tell them about the edict. Commissioner Chen and company were all in Nanfeng. Hu Jun had by now got his brother to surrender and the people of Dongchuan had handed over all the local registers and treasury accounts and come to await their sentence. The rebels of Ande in trepidation followed suit. Thanks to the efforts of White-Water Dragon these three places, Yun'an, Dongchuan and Ande, had all been pacified without the farmers having to leave their work in the fields or the merchants their shops. All of the eight cities and eighty-six districts seized by Wang Qing had now been recovered.

Some ten days after Magic Messenger returned to Nanfeng from the capital, the Emperor's envoy arrived bearing the decree. Commissioner Chen and his officials received it and one by one all the instructions were carried out. The envoy returned to the capital early next morning. The Commissioner had the Duans, Li the fortune-teller, and all their accomplices brought out of the gaol and after sentencing they were beheaded and the heads exposed on the gates as a lesson. Miss Duan, who had been rebellious from childhood, had insisted on arranging her own marriage and had committed a capital crime, had not only lost her own life in the process but implicated many of her relatives. Her father had died earlier in the camp on House Mountain.

Anyway, to be brief, after recording the exploits of the White-Water Dragon and the rest, Commissioner Chen and Song Jiang had notices posted in every district to reassure the people. Eighty-six districts had been returned to the Emperor's control and their inhabitants' loyalty could be counted on again. All the other followers of the insurgency were left unharmed and told to return to their former trades or to farming. In due course the Wizard and Magic Steed came from the Western Capital, new officials having arrived to take over the administration there. Other leaders who had been seconded to local administrations began to arrive from all over. After White-Water Dragon and his comrades handed over their administrative duties and came to Nanfeng, the Commissioner with all the officials and Song Jiang's one hundred and seven commanders and the surrendered commanders from Hebei, celebrated the peace with a banquet, in honour of all the military commanders and civilian officials, and to reward the army. Song Jiang put Taoist Gongsun and the Wizard in charge of a religious ceremony which was to last seven days and nights, to ease the passage of the souls of the dead commanders and of all who had suffered an unjust death in the West.

Shortly after this it was announced that the Chancellor had caught some infection and died in the camp. Song Jiang was very upset. He arranged the funeral and the body was buried at Dragon Heights. The Chancellor's death affected the Wizard deeply and he said to Song Jiang: "He was my countryman and my close friend. He committed a crime in order to avenge his father and had to throw in his lot with the rebels. When you enlisted him I hoped that his fate would improve. Who'd have thought that he would suddenly die like this! The fact that I joined you is due to his having set me straight. You can imagine my feelings now he is dead. The kindness of yourself and the Unicorn is engraved on my heart and I can never repay it, but I would like to ask you to allow me to take myself off to the wilderness; I need to husband what remains to me of the life force."

When Magic Steed heard about this he too went to Song Jiang and said: "Please allow me to go with the Wizard."

Song Jiang was exceedingly reluctant but since they were adamant he had to let them go. A farewell party was held, at which Taoist Gongsun was notably silent. The two of them said goodbye and then went to take leave of the Commissioner, after which they departed contentedly. Later they would both proceed to where the Great Sage was and sit at his feet and follow the Way till they reached the end of their days.

The Commissioner calmed the fears of all the people in the West, civil and military, and provided them with aid. This was the region beyond the Huai River, which is why in the days of Song they called it West of the Huai, or the West. The Commissioner now ordered all his commanders to pack up and return to the capital. Song Jiang ordered the main army to escort Commissioner Chen and the other two on the journey and told the waterborne leaders to sail on ahead to the capital first in their boats, tying up and awaiting orders when they got there. He instructed Magic Hand to compose an inscription and the Craftsman to carve a stone tablet to commemorate these events. The monument was placed to the east of Nanfeng at the foot of Dragon Heights, where it stands to this day. A send-off was organized for the Hu brothers; when Song Jiang returned to court he told the Emperor how they had turned over a new leaf and made an important contribution to the victory and got them appointed as waterborne commanders in Dongchuan, but that was later.

Song Jiang now divided the army into five columns and fixed the time of departure. As well as the troops left to guard each district, there were also a number who asked leave to return to farm their land. Nevertheless there were more than a hundred thousand who left Nanfeng and headed for the capital. They had strict orders not to cause any disturbance in the regions they passed through, and the people came out to greet them with incense, lamps and candles. After several days' march they came to the place called Autumn Woods Crossing, at the foot of the Autumn Woods range. The landscape around here was particularly beautiful, full of streams and rocks, and Song Jiang looked around him as he rode. Raising his eyes to the sky he saw a flock of wild geese, not flying in their usual formation but scattered any old how, as if something had frightened them. He was puzzled by the sight. Then he heard a clamour of applause from the troops ahead and sent someone to inquire the reason. What had happened was this: the Prodigy had been practising with a bow and arrows and had aimed at the geese flying overhead. Every

arrow had hit. In no time at all he shot a dozen or so birds, to the amazement of his companions. Song Jiang summoned the Prodigy to him. He arrived at the gallop with his bow bent and an arrow ready, and his horse's crupper loaded with dead geese. He vaulted from the saddle in front of Song Jiang and stood to attention.

"So you've been shooting geese, have you?" Song Jiang said.

"I was practising and I saw these geese flying past, so I had a shot at them and to my surprise every arrow hit."

"It is natural for a soldier to practise archery, and you have a talent for it," Song Jiang said. "But just think about these migrating geese, how to escape the cold they leave the northern mountains and cross over lakes and frontiers to seek the warm lands south of the River in search of grain and rice, and then at the start of spring fly all the way back again. This bird is an emblem of virtue. No matter if they're ten or fifty, the group is bound together by mutual courtesy, the seniors go first, the youngest follow behind, their flight is orderly, they abide by the rules of the flock. When they rest at night they set a watch. If one of a pair is lost the other grieves and will take no other mate all its life. It is a bird which has all the five virtues: humanity, righteousness, courtesy, wisdom and faith. If they fly past a dead goose they show all the signs of alarm: this is humanity. If a goose loses its mate it never takes another: this is righteousness. They fly in their proper order with no striving to be first: that is courtesy. To avoid the eagle they go via lakes and passes, that is wisdom. South in autumn, north in spring, never failing: this is faith. A creature so abounding in virtue, how can you harm it? As the flock wings through the sky they call out to each other. They are just like our company. Now you have shot these birds, it's like losing one of our number is for us. How would we all feel? From now on please do not harm this admirable bird."

The Prodigy was silent. He deeply regretted his actions. Song Jiang still mastered by his emotion improvised this poem:

Among rugged mountains a vast expanse of water;
Geese wing their way across the heavens;
Suddenly one of a flying pair is cancelled by an arrow;

Cold moon in the sky, clear breeze and heartbreak.

Song Jiang recited the poem. The words seemed to affect him deeply. That night they camped in the approaches to Autumn Woods Crossing. Song Jiang in his tent again remembered his sadness at the Prodigy's shooting the geese; he took out paper and brush and wrote the following:

Across the clear sky the flock is broken and the geese scatter in panic; their objective was simply to go down to the wintering grounds. For the grass is withered, the sand washed clean and the water spread out flat under a distant sky. It is hard to express all that one feels, at best one shares but a little of one's thoughts. At day's end the sky is veiled, evening mist rises from the ancient moat. Impossible to describe the sadness. Now that the reeds are gathered in, there is no more shelter. Alas, when will they return to visit the beauteous region? Birds call forlornly, the melancholy riverside is not a place where one would choose to linger. We await the return of spring days and the paired swallows atwitter in the eaves.

He gave this to the Professor and Taoist Gongsun to read. The sentiments expressed in the poem were gloomy and depressed in the extreme. Song Jiang was obviously plunged in gloom. That night the Professor and the others organized a party which only ended when they were all drunk. At dawn next day they mounted and rode south. It was near winter's end, but it was a wintry landscape they rode through, according well with Song Jiang's mood. They did not pause till they reached the capital and set up camp at Chenbridge, to await their orders.

Meanwhile Commissioner Chen and Marshal Hou had entered the city with the main army and had already told the Emperor of Song Jiang's achievements. They told him that General Song Jiang and his troops were on their way back to the capital and had already reached the frontier. The Emperor was full of praise when he heard from Commissioner Chen how hard Song Jiang and his troops had fought. The Commissioner and the Marshal were both honoured, as well as being rewarded with silver and silk. The palace chamberlain received orders to admit Song Jiang and his companions for an audience and to have them ride into the city in full armour.

In obedience to the imperial order, Song Jiang and the rest of the one hundred and eight put on their armour, dressed in embroidered robes, and with gold and silver banners rode through the Gate of Eastern Splendour to the Hall of Culture and Ethics for their audience with the Emperor. They kowtowed respectfully and gave him three cheers. It was a sight to gladden the Emperor's heart: all of them in brocade robes with gold belts, except the Professor, Taoist Gongsun, Lu Zhishen the Monk and Wu Song the Pilgrim, who wore their own appropriate dress. "We have heard much," he said, "of your bitter campaign and how hard you strove to suppress the bandits, how many of you suffered injury. Our heart goes out to you."

Song Jiang again prostrated himself and said: "Because Your Majesty enjoys such favour from heaven, we have come through, albeit with a few wounds. Now the traitors have surrendered, the West has been pacified. In serving Your Majesty's greatness how can we feel any burden?"

He prostrated himself again to show his gratitude, and then went on: "We beg now to present the captive Wang Qing to Your Majesty, in order that his case may be resolved."

The Emperor said: "I shall order the officials of the judicial committee to arrange for him to be punished with a lingering death."

Song Jiang told the story of how Bountiful masterminded the handing over of the city of Jingnan without harm to the people and modestly rejected any offer of advancement.

The Emperor said: "I am truly moved by such faithful service." He ordered the Military Council to try to bring Bountiful back to serve in the capital. Song Jiang and the others kowtowed again to show their gratitude. But what member of the Military Council was going to exert himself to acquire for the Emperor the services of an honest man? However, that is another story.

That same day the Emperor ordered the members of the Military Council to consider the conferring of rank and honours on

Song Jiang and his company. The Grand Preceptor and the President of the Council, Marshal Tong, discussed it and proposed the following: "Peace has still not been fully restored, so we cannot make these appointments yet. Let us give to Song Jiang the title of Guardian of Righteousness, licensed to bear arms for his sovereign as Emperor's Champion, and to his second-in-command the Unicorn the title of Warrior First Class, also licensed to bear arms for the Emperor, as a palace guard. The Professor and the other thirty-three will have the rank of full commanders in the armed forces; the Strategist and the other seventy-one will have the rank of vice-commander. Their army will be rewarded with gold and silver from government funds." The Emperor accepted this arrangement and ordered the Military Council to confer these titles forthwith and to pay the monies due to them in advance.

Song Jiang and company went to bow and express their thanks in the Hall of Culture and Ethics. The Emperor ordered the Secretariat to prepare a great banquet and presented Song Jiang with an embroidered robe, a suit of gilt armour and a fine horse. For the rest, from the Unicorn down, the reward was different: it was to be drawn from the treasury.

Song Jiang and his companions expressed their thanks and left the palace. Outside the Western Gate they mounted and returned to camp to rest and await their next assignment.

That day after the judicial committee had prepared a placard announcing his crime, the prison cart was opened and Wang Qing was taken out. The words "hack to death" were pronounced and he was hustled towards the market place. The onlookers were jostling and shoving to get a better view. Some were spitting and shouting abuse, others were moved to tears. Wang Qing's father, his former wife and in-laws, his whole family and household had been apprehended when he first declared his rebellion and suffered the extreme penalty.

Now only Wang Qing was left to face the executioner's sword. Two stuttering rolls of the drum and a cracked note on the gong, the sword drawn and glittering like fresh snow; black banners streaming above like a storm cloud! The executioner's awesome roar summoning the demons of hell! The time a little past noon.

Wang was dragged to the crossroads and the sentence was read out, ordering slow death by slicing. The onlookers might say to themselves:

The criminal always has something to teach us:
For dreams in the head the body must pay.
Surely the crime must have been heinous!
Why else should he suffer this way?

The chief executioner carried out the sentence and the felon's head was exhibited. Of this no more.

Having received their reward Song Jiang and his companions returned to the camp the following day. Now Taoist Gongsun strode into the command tent. He greeted them all with a very low bow and said: "Previously my teacher, the Blessed Sage, told me that after accompanying you back to the capital I was to return to him on the mountain. Now your achievement is complete and you have made your name, I must bid you farewell and take leave of the company, for I must return to study the Way with my teacher and look after my old mother for the remainder of her days."

Song Jiang had given his word and could not go back on it. But he was weeping inside as he said to Taoist Gongsun: "I remember the old days, when we first met, and it was like a flower opening. Now you must go and it is like the flower that fades and falls. I must be true to my word of course, but how will I be able to bear this parting?"

Taoist Gongsun said: "Had I abandoned you in the middle of something, then there would have been cause to reproach me. But now that you have fulfilled your task, you have to let me go."

Song Jiang tried hard to make him change his mind, but he would not. So as usual a feast was organized for all the company to bid him farewell. Cups were raised, with many a sigh. Everyone was sad and they all had gifts for him which he did his best to refuse. His friends however kept stuffing them in his pack. Next day, after a final farewell, Taoist Gongsun put on his hemp sandals, shouldered his pack, bowed low to the ground, and then set off northward. Song Jiang missed him sorely for many days and his heart was heavy.

In time it drew near to the first full moon of the new year, and government officials were all preparing to offer congratulations to the Emperor. The Grand Preceptor did not want Song Jiang and his companions to join this ceremony, because he feared that the Emperor would be obliged to give them all new official posts. He asked the Emperor to issue an order forbidding them to come to court for the ceremony, all except Song Jiang and the Unicorn who had official positions. The others, who had no rank, were to be excluded from the ceremony lest they offend the Emperor. At dawn on the day all the courtiers, including Song Jiang and the Unicorn in their uniforms, lined up in the court of the Water Clock to await the Emperor and to pay homage according to court etiquette. His Majesty held court that day in the Palace of Purple Dawn, where Song Jiang and the Unicorn after doing obeisance, waited in line below, not presuming to approach the throne. Gathered around the throne there were many notable beauties to be observed and much finery on display. Many a toast was drunk. After a whole morning of this the time came to express thanks and depart, and the Emperor was carried off in his palanquin. Song Jiang and the Unicorn changed their official robes and rode back to camp, flushed with drinking. When they arrived the others noticed Song Jiang's gloomy expression and seeing something was wrong came one by one to greet him, afterwards lining up on the side. Song Jiang merely hung his head and did not speak. "Why have you returned from court so sad, brother?" the Professor asked.

Song Jiang heaved a sigh: "Fortune it seems does not smile on me, my path is obstructed," he said. "We have smashed the Tartars and eliminated bandits, marched this way and that and suffered many hardships, and I have involved all of you in these things, yet without proper recompense. That is why I am sad."

"Just because things don't work out is not fit cause for grief," the Professor said. "Sorrow is to be shared and one should not take things too much to heart."

Iron Ox spoke up: "Don't you see, brother? When we were on

Mount Liang none bothered us. But you kept saying amnesty, amnesty, and now we've got the amnesty and it's nothing but trouble. If we could only get out of here and go back to Mount Liang it'd be great!"

Song Jiang blew up. "This black brute is at it again," he shouted. "We're servants of the crown now, loyal servants of the Emperor. Don't you understand anything? You still can't change!"

Iron Ox said: "You won't listen to me, but I tell you, you're going to regret it!"

Everyone laughed at him and then they all drank Song Jiang's health. They went on till late that night before parting. Next day they went with a few dozen cavalry into the city to give the compliments of the season to Marshal Su, Counsellor Zhao and the members of the Council and their coming and going was noted by many.

Someone reported it to the Grand Preceptor, who next day petitioned the Emperor to have a banning order posted at all the city gates to say: "All members of the expeditionary force are to remain in their camp outside the city and await orders. Without receiving an order from the highest authority they are on no account to venture into the city! Any violation of this order is to be punished by military law!" Someone saw this notice when it was put up outside the Chenbridge Gate and reported it to Song Jiang, whose gloom increased. When the others heard about it they were furious and would have rebelled, only Song Jiang prevented it.

The boat captains went to the Professor and told him they wanted to discuss something. The Professor went down to the boats, where the White-Water Dragon and the rest said to him: "The court has broken faith with us. Corrupt officials have usurped power and are standing in the way of honest men. The Leader has destroyed the Tartars, annihilated Tian Hu and now put down Wang Qing. All he's got for it is the title of Emperor's Champion, and we ordinary folk have not been promoted at all. Now there are notices everywhere prohibiting us from entering the city. Most likely those scoundrelly officials plan to break up our company and post us all to different places. We want to make a proposal to you, because we know that if we put it to the Leader he will reject it. Let us attack the capital and plunder it. Then we can go back to the Marshes of Mount Liang. The outlaw's life is the only one for us."

The Professor said: "The Leader will definitely not stand for that. You're wasting your breath. If the arrowhead's not good, do you break the shaft? Everyone knows a headless snake won't get anywhere. How do you expect me to propose this? Even if he agreed, there'd still have to be a way of putting it into action. If he doesn't accept it, you'll never get anywhere with this rebellion of yours!"

When they saw the Professor wasn't prepared to put forward the proposal, the boat leaders shut up. The Professor went back and while he was chatting with Song Jiang about the military situation, he said: "We always used to be completely independent, completely at ease. All of us had a good life. But since we received the amnesty, we have fought for our country and served our country, and not been under any constraint, but we have not been given responsibility, and our brothers are angry."

Song Jiang was shocked: "Has somebody been saying something to you?"

"It's a normal reaction, why should it need explaining? As they say, if you have riches and honour everyone wants you, if you're poor and a thief everyone shuns you. Look at the shape and the colour if you're judging the state of a beast or a situation."

Song Jiang said: "If the comrades are becoming disaffected, it would be better for me to die and go to the other world with my honour still intact!"

Early next morning he called a general meeting. When they were all assembled in front of the tent, Song Jiang began his speech: "I started off as just a local clerk in Yuncheng. Then I committed a serious crime. But thanks to the support of all of you, I became your leader. I have now risen to a government position. But you know the saying, 'Without pain no gain.' Success and trouble go together. We may not like this ban the authorities have imposed on us, but it is our duty to respect it. You must none of you enter the city unless you have a reason. We lived as outlaws in the mountains and forests and our manners are rough and ready. If we cause trouble, we will face the penalty of the law and also ruin our reputation. It is really all for the best that we are not allowed into the city. If you resent these restrictions and won't accept them, you had better cut off my head first, and then you can do what you like. For otherwise, if I am to live in the world without honour, I will have to kill myself and leave you free to do as you please."

This speech produced tears and protestations of loyalty from all of them. They dispersed and thereafter none of them went into the city without business there. But the fifteenth of the first month was approaching and it was the custom in the capital to have a display of lights to celebrate the first new moon of the year. All the streets would be festooned with lanterns and every government office would be lit up.

The Prodigy and Lungs were discussing the festival. "There's going to be this display of lights and fireworks in the capital to celebrate the new year, the Emperor and the people will all be having a good time. Why don't we two change our clothes and slip into the city to see it?"

As they spoke, someone else suddenly appeared and said: "If you're going to see the lights, please let me come with you." It was Iron Ox. He went on: "I know you didn't want me to know about it. But I heard everything."

The Prodigy said: "I'd have nothing against your coming with us if it wasn't for your temper. You're bound to cause a disturbance. You know this ban of the Military Council's forbids us to go into the city. If you go with us to see the lights and cause some sort of rumpus, we will have fallen right into their trap."

"I won't cause any trouble this time, I'll do exactly as you say!"

"All right, tomorrow we must all dress up as travellers," said the Prodigy. "You can come with us."

Iron Ox was delighted with this. Next day he dressed appropriately and waited for the Prodigy. Unfortunately Lungs was terrified of Iron Ox, and he went off earlier with the Flea. There was no escape for the Prodigy; he had to take Iron Ox with him to see the lights. He dared not enter the city directly through the

Chenbridge Gate, so they made a big detour and went in through the Gate of the Mounds.

Strolling along arm in arm they came to a house of entertainment called the Mulberry Club. They heard the sound of gongs coming from inside and nothing would suffice Iron Ox but that they should go in, so the Prodigy pulled him into the middle of a crowd. They could hear the voice of a storyteller upstairs. He was reciting from the *Romance of the Three Kingdoms* and had reached the point where Duke Guan has his bone scraped to remove the poison. The Duke has had this poisoned arrow in his shoulder, you see, and the poison has entered the bone. The doctor says: "In order to deal with the poison we must erect a brass post with an iron ring on top and put your arm through it and secure it with rope. Then I will have to cut the wound open and remove a proportion of the bone to get rid of the poison. I will stitch it up with oiled thread and apply an ointment externally and some special medicine internally. In two weeks it will be as good as new. The treatment for this kind of wound is very hard." The Duke gives a loud laugh and says: "A true man has no fear of death, so why should he be worried about an arm? I don't need your post and your ring. Why don't you just start cutting right away?" He calls for a chessboard and starts a game, offering his left arm to the doctor and telling him to scrape the bone and remove the poison. His colour does not change and he goes on talking and joking with the onlookers. When the storyteller reached this point there was a great roar of approval from Iron Ox: "That's what I call a real man!"

The rest of the audience turned and stared at Iron Ox and the Prodigy in amazement. The Prodigy hurriedly tried to shut him up: "What a country bumpkin you are, brother!"

Iron Ox protested: "You can't help applauding something like that!"

The Prodigy dragged him away from the Mulberry Club and they wandered down a narrow passage where they came upon a fellow intent on destroying a citizen's house: bricks and mortar were flying all over the place.

The citizen was saying: "These are times of peace, heaven and earth are supposed to be at rest! Just because I ask him to pay back some money he wants to tear my house down!"

When Iron Ox heard this he smelt an injustice and wanted to step right in and start a fight. The Prodigy was equally determined to prevent it. Iron Ox went on glaring at the man ferociously, itching for trouble. The man said: "I've got an account to settle with him. What business is it of yours? Any day now I've got to go with Marshal Zhang to fight south of the river, so you'd better not provoke me. If I go there I'm as good as dead anyway, I might as well fight you here, because if I get killed at least I'll get a decent coffin."

"What's all this about south of the river?" said Iron Ox. "I haven't heard anything about a mobilization order."

The fight having been averted, they went back down the passage and at the end of a side-street found a tiny teahouse. They went in and found a place to sit and have a cup of tea. Sitting opposite was an old fellow who invited them to join him. They chatted as they drank their tea, and the Prodigy asked: "Tell me, sir, at the end of this street we met a soldier involved in a brawl and he said he was going south of the river with Marshal Zhang and that there would be a mobilization. Is it true there's going to be a war?"

"You haven't heard then?" the old man said. "The bandit Fang La is in rebellion south of the river. He has occupied eight provinces and twenty-five districts, which he calls his country. Sometime soon he'll attack Yangzhou. The government have sent Marshal Zhang and General Liu to arrest him."

Iron Ox hurriedly paid for their tea and they raced back to the camp. They went straight to the Professor and told him about it. He thought it excellent news and went to tell Song Jiang about Fang La's rebellion and how the court had appointed Marshal Zhang to lead a campaign against him. Song Jiang said: "We are all of us wasting our time here, it's very bad for us. Don't you think we should send to Marshal Su and ask him to tell the Emperor we would like to offer our services in this war?" When they held a general meeting of the leaders everyone approved this plan. Next day Song Jiang changed his uniform and took the

Prodigy with him to the city to help explain things. They went straight to Marshal Su's. The Marshal was at home and as soon as they were announced he invited them in. Song Jiang stepped up to the dais and prostrated himself respectfully. The Marshal said: "What can I do for you, General? I see you come all dressed up."

Song Jiang said: "Because of the recent notices published by the Military Council, forbidding military personnel to enter the city unless summoned, I would not come without cause. I have ventured to come here because I wish to make a request. I have heard that Fang La has started a rebellion south of the river, that he has proclaimed a new dynasty and has overrun Runzhou and is likely to cross the river and attack Yangzhou. My army and I have long been idle, wasting our time in camp. We request permission to join the campaign and fight for our country. I would ask Your Excellency to forward our request to the Emperor."

The Marshal's reaction was most favourable: "Your words accord exactly with my thoughts, General. I shall support your request in every way. Please return to your camp and tomorrow morning I will present your proposal to the Emperor. I am sure His Majesty will give you employment."

Song Jiang returned to camp and told the others.

Next day Marshal Su attended the dawn court. While the Emperor was presiding over his officials, civil and military, in the Hall of Incense, he was told how Fang La was wreaking havoc south of the river where he had seized territory and proclaimed his own dynasty (a new year name) and was thus in rebellion and usurping the prerogatives of the Emperor and how an attack on Yangzhou was feared. The Emperor said: "But we have already appointed Marshal Zhang and General Liu to lead a campaign and we do not yet know the outcome."

At this Marshal Su stepped forward and said: "This outlaw poses a serious threat. Your Majesty has already appointed Marshal Zhang and General Liu, it is true, but we should send Song Jiang's two armies which have just returned victorious from the West to spearhead the attack. I am sure they will be successful."

The Emperor thought this was a good idea and immediately sent someone to the Military Council with orders. The members of the Military Council came to the palace to receive the edict, and Song Jiang and the Unicorn were ordered to attend for an audience with the Emperor in the Hall of Incense. When they had paid homage His Majesty gave Song Jiang the letter appointing him Commander of the Southern Pacification Expedition against Fang La, and appointing the Unicorn his second-in-command. Each was awarded a gold belt, a brocade robe, a suit of gold armour, a fine horse and twenty-five coloured silk coats with linings. The others were all given silk and silver with a promise of further honours if the expedition was successful.

After receiving their commissions Song Jiang and the Unicorn bade the Emperor farewell. The Emperor said: "Among your company there is one who is an expert carver of inscriptions, known as the Craftsman, and also one who knows how to cure sick horses known as Redbeard. Would you leave these two behind to serve me?"

They assented, thanked the Emperor again and returned to the camp.

The two leaders rode along contentedly, letting their horses follow their own pace. Outside the town they came to a marketplace where they saw a man who was playing with an object in his hand. It was contrived of two sticks with a string stretched between them which when manipulated by the hand caused an object to hum. It was unfamiliar to Song Jiang, so he had a soldier call the man over and asked: "What is that thing?"

The man replied: "It's a Tartar bell. You pull the string and it makes a noise." Song Jiang made a verse about this:

A low note and a high note,
Loud enough and clear enough to reach heaven;
But on its own a heroic spirit isn't much use;
Without a helping hand it won't produce!

Song Jiang said to the Unicorn with a laugh: "It's like you and me, you see. We might have huge talents, but without someone to help us along we won't produce a sound."

"Why do you say that?" said the Unicorn. "From what we know of the great leaders past or present, it's great personal ability they need and without it they won't do anything great however much they are promoted."

Song Jiang said: "I'm afraid I can't agree with you there. If it weren't for Marshal Su's generous support, we would never have been allowed to return to the Emperor's service. One should not forget what one owes to others."

The Unicorn knew that he was wrong and had nothing to say to that.

When they returned to the camp there was a meeting for all the leaders in the command tent. Except for the woman warrior Jade Arrowtip, who was pregnant and remained in the capital with the husband and wife team of the Butler to look after her and the doctor to attend her, they were all told to pack up and prepare their horses and armour and be ready to march, to join the campaign against Fang La. Later, when her time came, Jade Arrowtip was delivered of a fine boy with a square face and big ears. He was named Zhang Jie. Later, when she heard her husband had been killed by the rebel Li Tianrun on Lone Pine Heights she fainted from grief. Afterwards she went herself with the Butler and Mrs. Ye to Lone Pine Heights and they bore the coffin back to Hotshot's old home town of Zhangde for burial. Later still when the Butler became ill, she lived with old Mrs. Ye. She had a hard time of it bringing up the fatherless child. When Zhang Jie was grown he took part in the famous defeat of the Jin at Monk's Plain, where their general escaped detection by shaving off his beard. For this he was given high military honours, but later went home to look after his old mother until she died. Because she had remained constant to the memory of her husband, he obtained permission to erect a memorial arch in her honour. Thus ended the story of Jade Arrowtip and her filial and conjugal virtues.

But enough of this. We must return to Song Jiang who, the day after receiving his commission to march against Fang La obtained the gift of silk and silver from the government stores and divided it among the leaders for distribution to the army. He also sent Redbeard and the Craftsman to the court to attend the Emperor. He dealt first with the boats, ordering the captains to prepare poles, oars and sails and head for the main river, at the same time ordering the cavalry to prepare bows, arrows, spears and swords, uniforms and armour. It was to be a joint attack by land and water, and in order to keep up with the boats they must be ready to march immediately. At this point the Grand Preceptor sent one of his household to request the services of Magic Hand to do some writing for him. The next day some bigwig turned up in person to ask for Lungs because he had heard he had a wonderful voice and wanted to give him a position in his household. Song Jiang had to accede to all these requests. He had now lost five of his company and he was not at all happy about it. Finally, having made his plans with the Unicorn, he ordered all the leaders to prepare to leave the city.

Now, this Fang La had long been disaffected. His strength had grown gradually, and now turned into a serious threat. Originally he had been a woodcutter in the mountains of Shezhou. One day he had gone to the river to wash and in his reflection had seen himself wearing a crown and the dragon robes. Because of this he told people that he was destined to be emperor. At the time when granite was collected in the south, the people had become resentful and disaffected. Fang La took advantage of this to declare his rebellion, and built himself a grand citadel at Bangyuan Gap in the district of Clearwater, complete with gardens, halls and towers. He also had travelling palaces at Muzhou and Shezhou and equipped himself with a complete set of officials, civil and military, a military council, court servants and military commanders, the whole shooting-match. In all he seized eight towns — Shezhou, Muzhou, Hangzhou, Suzhou, Changzhou, Huxhou, Xuanzhou and Runzhou. Now he styled himself emperor and illicitly claimed authority over the whole region: it was a serious business.

The name Fang La originated from Taoist books. In one of them it says: "To thousands ten add a small stroke, in winter's depths give praise and honour. After crossing the river, he makes his appearance in the southern kingdom." For "thousands ten" it is more usual to say "ten thousand" which is written with the character *wan*. If you add a small stroke to *wan* you get *fang*. Winter's depths is the winter solstice in December and the festival which celebrates it is known as *la*. One to whom praise and honour are given is the ruler. So you have the two characters for Fang La, who declares himself ruler of eight towns south of the river, a region whose natural boundary is the Yangtze.

Meanwhile Song Jiang having selected his leaders and said goodbye to the worthy councillors, Marshal Su and Counsellor Zhao came to give him a send-off and reward the troops. The boat captains moved out into the Huai River and set sail for the naval base at Huai'an with instructions to assemble at Yangzhou. Song Jiang and the Unicorn thanked Su and Zhao, divided their army into five columns and headed for Yangzhou.

The journey was uneventful. The advance guard made camp at Huai'an, where a local official organized a banquet for them and invited Song Jiang into the city when he arrived. The official told Song Jiang: "Fang La's army is formidable, you must not underestimate them. Ahead of you is the Great River, that's the first hurdle you have to leap. On the other bank of the river is Runzhou, At present this stretch of the river bank is defended by Fang La's chief lieutenant and twelve others. Unless you can gain Runzhou as a base you'll find it difficult to defeat them."

Song Jiang therefore asked the Professor to devise a plan. Since the river lay in front of them blocking their path, it would be necessary to use the boats to lead the attack.

The Professor said: "There are two islands in the river opposite Runzhou. You can get some of our comrades to go there first to reconnoitre, to find out what is going on on the other bank and what sort of boats we need for the crossing."

Song Jiang summoned the boat captains to receive their orders. "Which of you are prepared to undertake a spying mission for me and find out what's going on across the river?"

Four of them volunteered. And if it had not been these four, things might have been different. We would not have seen the corpses piled high to rival North Peak or the waters of the Yangtze died red with blood.

If you want to know how Song Jiang's forces set about capturing Fang La, you must read the next chapter.

Chapter 111

White Eel swims to Temple Hill by night; Song Jiang succeeds in capturing Runzhou!

The three thousand one hundred mile long River Yangtze consists in fact of three rivers, the Hanyang River, the Xunyang River and the Yangtze River. From Sichuan to the sea it passes through many places. This is why it is known as the Great River. In the region of Wu and Chu two mountains divert the river's course. One is called Golden Island and the other Burnt Island. On Golden Island there is a temple. It covers the slopes of the mountain, and the place is known as Temple Hill. On Burnt Island there is a temple which is sheltered in a fold of the hill which hides its outline, so it is called the Hill Temple. The two mountains situated in the middle of the river lie exactly on the demarcation line between Wu and Chu. On one side is Yangzhou, east of the Huai, and on the other Runzhou in Zhejiang, today called Zhenjiang.

Now in Runzhou it is Fang La's right-hand man, Marshal Lü Shinang who defends the river bank. Originally a rich man of Shezhou, he contributed to Fang La's finances and was made chief of staff in consequence. His weapon is a long serpent lance and his military prowess is exceptional. He has twelve officers under his command who are known as the Southern Twelve. All are employed in the defence of the river bank in Runzhou. Under Marshal Lü's command is an army of fifty thousand soldiers from the south, spread out along the bank. Three thousand war vessels are moored under the Pavilion of Sweet Dew. On the north bank is Guazhou Crossing, and at this point the river bank is wide open, totally without cover.

Song Jiang's forces, complete with horses and boats, have proceeded by land and water as far as Huai'an, on their way to the assembly point at Yangzhou. Song Jiang is in his command tent, discussing the situation with the Professor: "We're not far from the Yangtze, here. The south bank is held by the rebels. Who is prepared to go on a spying mission for me, to find out what's going on across the river and see whether we can launch our attack?"

Four leaders volunteered. They were Mr. Chai the Little Whirlwind, White Eel, Madcap and Ruan the Seventh.

Song Jiang said: "Divide yourselves into two groups, White Eel go with Mr. Chai and Madcap with Ruan the Seventh. One lot get over to Golden Island and the other lot to Burnt Island. When you find anything out come back and tell us."

The four took their leave of Song Jiang, and each with a companion and dressed as merchants they took themselves off to Yangzhou. All along the way the people had heard that a big army was coming to suppress Fang La and had moved into the country to take refuge. The two groups separated in Yangzhou. Each man carried some provisions. Madcap and Ruan the Seventh and their companions set off for Burnt Island.

As for Mr. Chai, White Eel and companions, they arrived at Guazhou carrying their provisions and equipped with spears, sharp swords and halberds. It was early spring, the day warm and fragrant with blossom. On reaching the Yangtze they looked down from a vantage point and saw white horses on the stream and rolling misty waves. It was a fine sight! Looking across towards North Peak they saw a mass of green and white banners and an armada of war vessels lined up along the shore. On the northern bank, where they were, there was not a single tree.

Mr. Chai said: "We've seen houses along the way here but no people. There is no ferry to cross the river. How are we ever going to find out what is going on on the other side?"

White Eel said: "You find a house to rest in while I swim across to Golden Island and make inquiries."

"That sounds a good idea," said Mr. Chai.

When they reached the river bank, they found a row of huts, all with locked doors which they could not get to open. White Eel went round the side and climbed a low wall and slipped inside the area. A white-haired old woman popped out from behind a stove.

"Why did no one open the door?" he asked her.

"Well sir, since you ask," she said. "We heard tell as how the court be sending a big army to fight Fang La. We're right in the path of the storm here and they're all gone off to hide. They left me to look after the house, 'cos I'm just an old body."

"Where have all the men gone?" White Eel asked.

"Gone to hide in the country, all on 'em," she said.

"There's four of us and we want to cross the river," White Eel said. "Where can we find a boat?"

"You won't find no boats here. When Marshal Lü heard the army were coming to attack he requisitioned all the boats and took them over the river to Runzhou."

"We've got our own food," White Eel said. "We only ask you to give us shelter here for a couple of days. We'll pay you rent and we won't disturb you."

"You can stay here, no problem with that, but there aren't no beds."

"We'll make our own arrangements."

"But listen here, sir, I'm afeared the army be coming!"

"We can cope with that!" White Eel opened the door and let in the others. They leant their halberds against the wall and put down their packs, took out some dry food and pancakes and ate them. White Eel went back to the river bank. He could see Temple Hill in the middle of the stream:

> *The river arches like a turtle's back, the mountains stand tall as a dragon's crest. Twists of blue are glimpsed through floating wreaths of silver; white funeral scrolls unroll across volumes of liquid jade. Far off the golden halls, exposed to all the winds that blow; in the distance the bell loft rising on its many-storeyed stone base. The pagoda soars upward into the blue empyrean; the sermon hall ripples with the reflected light of green waves. The galleries open to a view of roving sails; the recreational hall is brisk all day with the sound of water. Over Temple Hill at night the will-o'-the-wisps play.*

After observing it for a while he said to himself: "Marshal Lü most probably goes there often. If I swim over to it tonight I'm bound to find something out."

He went back and conferred with Mr. Chai. "We're here now, and there isn't a single boat. It's difficult to know what's going on on the other side. Tonight I'll swim across to Temple Hill with my clothes and two big pieces of silver in a bundle on my head. I'll bribe the monks and find out how things stand. Then we'll go back and tell the Leader. You wait here for me."

"Don't be too long about it," Mr. Chai said.

It was a fairly bright night. The wind was soft and the river calm, water and sky were indistinguishable. White Eel stripped and tied his clothes in a bundle. He knotted a white silk sash about his waist and packed two silver ingots in a head band which he wrapped round his head and stuck a cutlass in his sash. He entered the water at Guazhou Crossing and headed out into the middle. The water only came up to his chest, so it was like walking on land. When he reached the island he found a small boat moored at the foot of a cliff. He crept up to it. He lowered the bundle of clothes from his head, took off his wet things, dried himself and put on dry clothes, and sat down in the boat. He heard the Runzhou drum beat for the third watch. As he looked out from his hiding-place he saw a boat approaching over the water. "That boat is moving very suspiciously," he thought to himself. "They must be spies!"

He was going to cast his boat off, but found it was moored with a thick rope and there were no oars. There was nothing for it but to strip off again, take his dagger and commit himself to the water and swim towards the other boat. The two men in the other boat were rowing hard, looking toward the northern shore, and clearly not expecting any danger from the south. White Eel surfaced and swam to the side of the boat. He pulled down on the gunwale and simultaneously made a broad sweep with his cutlass. The two rowers dropped their oars and dived into the river. White Eel immediately hauled himself on board. Two men emerged from the cabin. With one blow of his cutlass White Eel knocked one of them into the water while the other rushed back

inside in terror. White Eel shouted: "Who are you? Where is this boat from? If you tell me the truth I'll spare you!"

"If you please, sir," the man replied, "I'm steward to the Chen household in Dingpu village near Yangzhou. They sent me across to Runzhou to make terms with Marshal Lü and offer him provisions and he sent one of his officers back with me. He is asking for fifty thousand catties of rice and three hundred boats as a pledge."

"What is the captain's name and where is he?" White Eel asked.

"He's called Ye Gui and he's the one you just pushed in the river."

"What's your name, when did you take the offer of surrender across and what else have you got in this boat?"

"I'm Wu Cheng, I crossed on the seventh of January. Marshal Lü sent me to Suzhou to see the King's third brother, Fang Mao, and pick up three hundred banners and a letter of appointment for my master, Colonel Chen, making him governor of Yangzhou. His Royal Highness also conferred his own insignia and a thousand uniforms together with a warrant addressed to Marshal Lü."

"Who is this master of yours? How many troops and horses has he?" White Eel asked.

"Around a thousand men and several hundred horses," the other replied. "And he's got two very brave sons by his own wife. Chen Yi is the elder and Chen Tai the second. The Colonel is called Chen Guan."

Having obtained all the information he wanted, White Eel killed the man with one blow of his cutlass and threw the body in the water. Then he began to row and didn't stop till he reached Guazhou Crossing.

Mr. Chai heard the sound of oars and hurried out to see. It was White Eel rowing a boat towards him. He asked what was going on and White Eel gave him an account which pleased him greatly. White Eel disappeared into the cabin and brought out a bundle of papers, three hundred red silk banners and a thousand multicoloured uniforms, which he made into two piles for carrying. "I'm going back now to get more uniforms," he said. He rowed back to Golden Island and collected uniforms, headgear and some silver. By the time he got back to the Guazhou shore it was getting late and a heavy mist cloaked the earth. He made a hole in the bottom of the boat and pushed it out into the river to sink. When he reached the house he gave two or three taels of silver to the old woman and the two companions carried the rest of the stuff back to Yangzhou. At this time the army was encamped outside the city, and Song Jiang had been invited into the city where the officials had been feasting him all day.

Mr. Chai and White Eel waited until the party broke up and then spoke with Song Jiang in the rest house. They told him how Chen Guan and his sons had gone over to Fang La and planned sooner or later to help the army to cross the river and attack Yangzhou. They told him how a chance encounter on the river had served their turn. Song Jiang was delighted and asked the Professor to work out a plan of action.

"This is a great opportunity," the latter said. "Runzhou is at our mercy! We'll get Chen Guan first and the rest will follow. It just needs this and this. . . ."

A little while later the Prodigy had disguised himself as Captain Ye, while Snake and Scorpion as instructed had dressed as southern soldiers. After inquiring the way to Dingpu, Snake and Scorpion picked up the carrying poles and the Prodigy having received detailed instructions they left Yangzhou and headed for Dingpu. A dozen miles or so from the city they found themselves at the gate of Chen Guan's estate, which was manned by a score or more of smartly dressed retainers, all in the same uniform.

The Prodigy greeted these retainers, putting on a southern accent: "Be your master at home, friends?"

"Where are you from, sir?" they replied.

"I come from Runzhou," the Prodigy answered. "I got lost after crossing the river. I was wandering about all day till they told me to come here."

The retainers invited them inside and told them they could put down their loads. The Prodigy was taken to the back to see Colonel Chen. He prostrated himself and said: "Ye Gui, at your service sir!"

"Where have you come from?" the Marshal asked.

The Prodigy replied in a southern accent as before: "I'd make bold to tell you, Your Excellency, if we might speak alone."

"These men are all in my confidence, you may speak freely before them."

"Well, then, my name is Ye Gui, sir, like I said, and I am on the staff of Marshal Lü. On the seventh of January we received the confidential letter delivered by Wu Cheng. The Marshal was pleased with it and told me to escort Wu Cheng to Suzhou to tell the Third Prince of Your Excellency's proposal. The Third Prince sent word of it to His Majesty, who announced that he was appointing you governor of Yangzhou and that your esteemed sons would also receive honours when they met Marshal Lü. Wu Cheng was about to return when he suddenly caught a chill and became too unwell to travel. Fearing the plan could be compromised, the Marshal sent me to give you the royal letter of appointment, together with his own instructions, the official stamp and badge of office, three hundred banners and a thousand uniforms. He wants you to deliver your supply boats to Runzhou by a certain date." With this he took out the official order and handed it to Colonel Chen.

Colonel Chen was overjoyed. He immediately had an altar set up for burning incense and prostrated himself in thanks toward the south. Next he sent for his two sons. The Prodigy told Snake and Scorpion to fetch the uniforms and banners and bring them to the hall. Colonel Chen asked the Prodigy to be seated. The latter objected: "I am just an ordinary soldier. How can I be seated in the presence of Your Excellency?"

"You are the envoy of the authorities over there," the Colonel replied. "You have brought me the royal mandate. How can I not honour you? Of course you must sit down."

After repeated refusals the Prodigy was persuaded to sit down, which he did at a polite distance. The Colonel ordered wine but when he offered it to the Prodigy, the latter refused, saying: "I am a teetotaller." After two or three rounds, the Colonel's sons arrived to join the celebration. The Prodigy gave Snake and Scorpion a significant look to indicate that it was time to get going. Scorpion took out the drug provided by Doctor An and unseen by the enemy leaders dropped it in the wine jug. The Prodigy rose to his feet and said: "Although I have brought no wine of my own, allow me to participate in offering you congratulations." He filled a beaker with wine and offered it to the Colonel, inviting him to drink it off. Next he offered wine to the two sons, who also drained their cups. There were also some trusted retainers present, and each of them was served a cup of wine by the Prodigy.

At a sign from the Prodigy, Snake went outside, got his tinder-box and took out the signal rockets he was carrying. He let them off in front of the manor. The comrades lying in wait on either side heard the reports and came out to join them. The Prodigy waited till he saw they were coming and then drew his sword. He and Scorpion set to work on the drugged enemy. Soon they had cut them all down. The comrades were now kicking up a row outside the manor and burst in through the main gate. These ten were our friends Monk, Pilgrim, Tattooed Dragon, Morbid, Iron Ox, Eight-Armed Ogre, Winged Ghost, Pluto, Panther and Pill Monger. What hope had the retainers on the gate of keeping them out? Inside the Prodigy, Snake and Scorpion had seized the heads of the Chens, the father and two sons. Outside more troops were arriving, led by Whiskers and five others. They surrounded the compound with a thousand troops and whole of Colonel Chen's family was slaughtered. Some captured retainers took them to the river bank where they found three or four hundred boats tied up in the harbour and near the estate, loaded up with food supplies. A list was made and a report sent at once to Song Jiang.

On hearing that Colonel Chen had been killed, Song Jiang and the Professor decided to launch their attack. Everything was packed up. They bade farewell to Commissioner Zhang and headed for the Chen estate. The leading commanders were assigned to boats while messengers were sent to urge their own water-borne force to get a move on. The Professor said: "We must select three hundred fast boats and equip each with Fang La's banners. The first thousand troops will dress in their uniforms, the remainder will have to wear whatever is to hand."

Over two thousand troops were hidden in the three hundred transports. The Unstoppable pretending to be the elder Chen and White-Water Dragon as the second brother, were each to go in a big boat. The first squadron was led by Unstoppable and White-Water Dragon and with Unstoppable there were these ten leaders:

Eight-Armed Ogre, Winged Ghost, Pluto, Pill Monger, Panther, Skyscraper, Door-God, Forester, Rhinoceros, the Guv

With White-Water Dragon went these ten leaders:

Cave Dragon, River Rider, Comet, Red Star, Whitey, Executioner, Green-Eyes, the Young Master, the Daytime Rat, Nine-Tailed Turtle

The second squadron was commanded by the Pilot and White Eel. With the Pilot went these four leaders:

Knife, Uglymug, Stripes, Scarface

With White Eel were these four:

Flagpole, Ape, Spots, Nameless

With the third squadron went ten leaders divided between two boats:

Tattooed Dragon, Sergeant Lei, Morbid, Red-Haired Devil, Blossom, Hotshot, Iron Ox, Snake, Scorpion, Mr. Chai

Three hundred vessels, carrying a total of forty-two commanders, made the first crossing. Meanwhile Song Jiang and the others were taking the horses aboard war boats. A thousand boats including fast attack boats and others, all flying Song Jiang's flag and carrying a quantity of infantry and cavalry were prepared for the crossing. Two of the boat commanders, Ruan the Second and Ruan the Fifth were in charge of this operation.

We shall not go with Song Jiang's army to cross the river, but join the southern lookouts on North Peak at Runzhou when they spot the first three hundred boats setting out from the opposite shore. Each boat is flying the red flag signifying transports for clothing and supplies for the advance guard.

The southern soldiers hurriedly reported this to the authorities.

Marshal Lü summoned his twelve officers. They put on their armour, strung their bows, unsheathed their swords and went down to the river bank to see what was going on. They saw a line of a hundred boats in front approaching the bank. On the boats the two leaders were surrounded by a throng all wearing golden chain mail. All fine upstanding men. Marshal Lü dismounted and seated himself on a silver throne, while his twelve commanders lined up in two ranks along the river bank. When Mu the Unstoppable and the White-Water Dragon saw Marshal Lü sitting there on the bank they came to attention and saluted. One of the Marshal's aides shouted an order for the boats to heave to and the first hundred dropped anchor in a straight line. The two hundred behind them also came on, propelled by the wind, splitting into two groups, a hundred to one side, a hundred to the other, so they were stationed in three equal squadrons. A southern liaison officer went down to the boats and asked: "Where are you from?"

"My name is Chen Yi," the Unstoppable replied. "This is my brother Chen Tai. My father is Colonel Chen, Governor of Yangzhou, and he commands us to bring you fifty thousand catties of rice, three hundred boats and five thousand picked troops in return for the Marshal's favour."

The southern officer said: "The other day His Excellency sent Ye Gui to you. Where is he?"

"The Colonel and Wu Chang have both got flu and are being treated at the manor. They couldn't come," said the Unstoppable. "Allow me to give you this letter with the official stamp."

The major-domo took it and went to the river bank and reported to the Marshal: "The two sons of Governor Chen have brought supplies of rice for the troops. They have a letter."

The Marshal looked and saw it was the genuine article, so he ordered the two men to be brought ashore. The major-domo summoned them. As the Unstoppable and the White-Water Dragon went ashore, the other twenty followed. A corporal shouted out: "A minister of the Crown is present. Other persons may not approach." The others halted, while Unstoppable and White-Water Dragon stood some way off, inclining respectfully with crossed arms. After a suitable pause, the southern officer led them forward to make their obeisance, kneeling before the Marshal, who said: "Why hasn't your father come himself?"

"He has had intelligence that Song Jiang and his troops from Mount Liang are on the way," said the Unstoppable. "He fears there may be trouble in the district, so he is waiting at home. He does not dare absent himself."

"Which of you is the elder?" the Marshal asked.

"I am," said the Unstoppable.

"Has either of you had any military training?"

"If it please Your Excellency, we have had quite a bit," said the Unstoppable.

"This rice you are bringing, how is it disposed?"

"The bigger boats are carrying three hundred catties, the smaller ones a hundred."

"I suspect you may have some hidden purpose," the Marshal said.

"Our family are honest and trustworthy. How could we harbour any ill intent?"

"That's as may be, but all those soldiers on your boats look remarkably tough specimens. How can I not be suspicious? You two wait here, while I send four of my officers with a hundred troops to search the boats. If there's the slightest irregularity, you'll be for it!"

"We came here to serve you. Why should we not be trusted?"

Just at that moment, as the Marshal was giving the order for the search party to be sent, a scout reported that a royal messenger had arrived at the southern gate and wanted the Marshal to go and receive him at once. The Marshal quickly mounted and gave the order: "Guard the river bank for me and keep those two here till I return." The Unstoppable exchanged looks with the White-Water Dragon as the Marshal rode off. Then they summoned the others and started to enter the city gate. The guards on the gate shouted: "The Marshal only said those two were to enter. The rest are not allowed in!"

So the Unstoppable and the White-Water Dragon proceeded on in while the others waited at the gate.

When Marshal Lü received the envoy at the south gate he asked: "What is it that's so urgent?"

In hushed tones the envoy, who was one of Fang La's palace aides, told the Marshal: "According to the astronomer royal recent observations of the night sky have revealed numerous stars crossing into the territory of Wu, among them several which lack lustre, meaning that serious disasters impend. His Majesty has published a decree, ordering Marshal Lü to defend the river bank. If any strangers appear from the north they must be thoroughly investigated. If there is anything at all suspicious about them, let them be executed forthwith."

Marshal Lü had a shock. "I was just thinking that this lot look suspicious. Now I have confirmation. But please come into the city to read out the decree."

The envoy accompanied him to the government office and was just about to read out the edict when another messenger rushed in: "There's a messenger from Suzhou with an order from the Third Prince. He says: 'This offer of surrender from the Chens of Yangzhou is not to be trusted. We fear a trap. His Majesty has just informed us that the astronomer royal has observed baleful stars in the territory of Wu. The river bank must be fortified. I will be sending someone to inspect the work'"

Marshal Lü said: "This is just what the Prince is worried about. I must report it to him." He ordered them to lock up the commanders from the boats on the river and not let any of them return to the river bank. He also ordered a banquet to entertain the two envoys.

Meanwhile the men on the three hundred boats found that a long time had passed without any sign of activity, so the Pilot and White Eel with eight subordinates, all armed, disembarked from the boats on the left, as did the ten commanders from the boats on the right, spears and swords at the ready. The southern troops guarding the bank were powerless to stop them. Iron Ox, Snake and Scorpion sped on towards the city. The guards on the gate hurriedly barred their way. Iron Ox whirled his axes and with a cut and a thrust dispatched two of them. There was tumult in the city as Snake and Scorpion forced their way in brandishing their pitchforks. Under these simultaneous attacks the guards had no hope of closing the gate. Iron Ox continued to wreak havoc. The twenty Song leaders already there grabbed their weapons and joined the fray. By the time Marshal Lü's urgent order to fortify the river bank arrived, they had already entered the city. By the time the twelve rebel commanders heard the commotion and found their arms and horses, the Tattooed Dragon and Mr. Chai had already instructed the three hundred troops on the boats to remove their southern uniforms and disembark first, while the troops who had been hidden on the boats soon joined them.

The first two southern commanders arrived with reinforcements at the gate and were knocked off their horses and killed by the Tattooed Dragon and the Pilot. As the rest of the Song forces attacked, the other ten southern commanders fled into the city to protect their families. The Unstoppable and Iron Ox, already in the city, heard what was happening. They got a light from an inn and started setting fire to the place.

Marshal Lü hurriedly mounted and enlisted three commanders to help but by now the town was ablaze, the fire having arisen as if from nowhere. The Song forces over in Guazhou observed the signal and prepared reinforcements. After bitter fighting the four gates at last fell and Song Jiang's flag was hoisted on the walls. The carnage and confusion are difficult to describe … but you shall see.

Another hundred and fifty boats were assembled near the north bank and the horses loaded aboard. Ten commanders all in full armour, led by Scimitar, were to go with them.

When this force, including a thousand subalterns and two thousand troops, poured into the city, Marshal Lü was routed. He fled with his wounded to Dantu and the Song army occupied Runzhou. The fires were put out and a guard established on the four gates and then the commanders went to the river bank to welcome Song Jiang, who arrived in a paddle boat that came flying over the water towards them, with the wind behind it. They escorted Song Jiang into the city. Notices had already been posted to reassure the people. The commanders paraded to report their successes. The Tattooed Dragon, the Pilot and the Red-Haired Devil each presented the head of an enemy commander, Red

Star and Comet handed over a captured enemy commander, Eight-Armed Ogre and Winged Ghost another, and Hound exhibited the body of the rebel leader he had shot with an arrow. Runzhou had been taken, four of their commanders killed, two more captured, and a host of their junior officers had died.

When Song Jiang's troops were counted, it was found that they had lost three leaders, killed by arrows or trampled by horses during the battle: Door-God, Nameless and Nine-Tailed Turtle. Song Jiang's heart was heavy at this news and nothing could console him. "A man's life and death are fixed by fate," said the Professor. "True, we have lost three of our brothers, but there is the satisfaction of having removed the principle obstacle to our campaign south of the river. Why go on upsetting yourself? If we still aim to make a worthy contribution to our country, we should be discussing affairs of state."

Song Jiang said: "The names of the one hundred and eight are engraven upon the stone tablet, each representing a star. At the foundation of the company on Mount Liang, and again on Mount Wutai, we made a vow: that we would live and die together. The rot set in after we returned to the capital, when Taoist Gongsun left. Then His Majesty retained the Craftsman and Redbeard and the Grand Preceptor wanted Magic Hand. Someone else requisitioned Lungs. Now here in Zhejiang we have lost three more of our brothers. I know the Door-God did not have any outstanding achievement to his name, but I cannot forget the part he played in the establishment of Mount Liang. And to think that now he is a shade wandering in the underworld!"

Song Jiang ordered a sacrificial altar to be set up on the spot where the Door-God died and paper money to be offered up, together with a black pig and a white lamb. He poured the libation with his own hands. The two captive commanders were executed there and their blood sprinkled as an offering to the souls of the three dead heroes. Song Jiang then went back to the government office and distributed rewards. He wrote out a report and sent someone with it to Marshal Zhang, inviting him to come and see things for himself. Of this no more.

The dead bodies were removed from the streets and taken out

of the city to be burnt. The bones of the three slain warriors were buried outside the east gate.

Marshal Lü had lost the greater part of his force. With six of his commanders he had taken refuge in Dantu and had no intention of coming out to fight. He sent an urgent messenger to Suzhou asking the Third Prince for help. On receiving the message, Suzhou sent General Xing Zheng with reinforcements. Marshal Lü received the general, and after the usual polite inquiries about health, took him to the office and offered a full account of events: "By pretending to be Colonel Chen's surrendering troops, Song Jiang's forces managed to cross the river. Now you are here you must recapture Runzhou for us."

The general said: "The Third Prince had already heard that evil stars had entered Wu territory and sent me here with an army to guard the river. We did not know that you had suffered this reverse. Now, if I can have your support, we will work together to avenge it."

Next day the general led his army out to recapture Runzhou.

Meanwhile Song Jiang had conferred with the Professor in the Runzhou district office and decided to send the Tong brothers, Cave Dragon and River Rider, with a hundred men to search for Madcap and Ruan the Seventh, the two who had gone to Burnt Island, you remember. They also ordered troops out to attack Dantu. There were five thousand of these, under ten commanders headed by Scimitar. As they headed for Dantu they encountered General Xing Zheng's army. The battle commenced with an exchange of arrows as both forces manoeuvred into position. On the side of the southern troops General Xing rode out with levelled spear and six of his commanders in two groups. Scimitar responded by drawing his crescent blade and riding at the opposing general. After a dozen bouts or more, one of the two was knocked from his horse. It was a case of:

Close to the well's where the pitcher gets broken;
The general dies in front of his troops.

Which of the two it was that fell, and which was the victor, you must read the next chapter to find out.

Chapter 112

The Unicorn takes half the army to attack Xuanzhou; Song Jiang fights a great battle in Piling!

Now when General Xing and Scimitar fought, they had not completed fifteen bouts before the latter raised his weapon and with a great slash sent his opponent tumbling from his horse. Twin Rods immediately led a mighty charge and the six enemy commanders turned and fled southwards. When Marshal Lü saw his troops had been routed he retreated with his wounded to Changzhou. The ten Song commanders took over the town of Dantu and sent word to Song Jiang. The main army soon arrived and pitched camp outside the town. The army was rewarded and a message was sent to Marshal Zhang requesting him to assign troops to garrison Runzhou. Next day two staff officers arrived with a reward for the troops in Dantu, which Song Jiang accepted and distributed.

Song Jiang now called the Unicorn in to discuss plans for the campaign. "At present," he said, "Xuanzhou and Huzhou are both in the hands of the rebel Fang La. You and I will divide the army into two columns, and draw lots to decide who goes where." Song Jiang drew Changzhou and Suzhou, while the Unicorn drew Xuanzhou and Huzhou. Song Jiang called on Sterling to split the army into two equal divisions. Except for Blue-Faced Beast, who could not take part in the campaign because he was sick and was left behind at Dantu, all the leaders were allotted to one or the other column, forty-two of them with Song Jiang and forty-seven with the Unicorn.

Now keep this firmly in mind, everyone, that the Unicorn was to attack Xuanzhou and Huzhou with forty-seven commanders, while Song Jiang was to attack Changzhou and Suzhou with

盧俊義分兵宣州道

forty-two commanders. The boat commanders were a separate unit with their own plan of campaign, on account of Cave Dragon and River Rider having been sent to Burnt Mountain to find Madcap and Ruan the Seventh. They had come back and reported: "Madcap and Ruan the Seventh got to the river, killed a family there, stole a fast boat and went over to the Hill Temple on Burnt Island. When the abbot learnt they were from Mount Liang he invited them stay there and entertained them. After hearing about White Eel's exploits, they made further inquiries and found that Maogang would be a good base from which to attack down the coast. They send a report and are requesting boat commanders and boats prepared for battle." Song Jiang sent the White-Water Dragon and the other seven boat commanders with five thousand sailors to back up Madcap and Ruan the Seventh. There were thus ten leaders in this attack, with a hundred boats.

You understand, friends, that when Song Jiang divided up his army in Dantu he had only ninety-nine leaders, not even a full hundred.

The water-borne leaders had all the large boats for the assault on Jiangyin and Taicang along the coast, while the small boats gathered in the narrow waterways around Dantu ready to join the attack on Changzhou.

Now Marshal Lü and his six staff officers had fortified themselves at Piling in Changzhou. The governor of this place was Qian Zhenpeng and under him were two generals: one was Jin Jie, and the other Xu Ding, who was a close friend of the Governor. The Governor himself had originally been police chief of Clearwater, but after helping Fang La to gain control there he had received advancement. When he heard that Marshal Lü had been defeated and that Runzhou was lost and the army retreating on Changzhou, he told his generals to open the gates and let them in. He received them in the government office and entertained them, and then they discussed the question of defence. The Governor said: "Don't worry, Marshal. I know I am not especially talented, but I will work like a horse to bring about the downfall of Song Jiang and his villainous gang and send them scuttling back across the river. I will recapture Runzhou. They shall submit to my will!"

Marshal Lü's response was fulsome: "When you show such determination, how can order fail to be restored to the country? After your triumph, I will petition His Majesty for you myself and honours will be heaped upon you." A big banquet followed. Of this no more.

Meanwhile Song Jiang was leading out the troops allotted to him to attack Suzhou and Changzhou in a major offensive against Piling. His commander-in-chief was Scimitar, and under him were Thunderclap and nine others. This made eleven of them, who with three thousand troops halted before the walls of Changzhou amid a forest of banners and thundering drums to issue their challenge to battle. When he saw them, Marshal Lü said: "Who is going to drive them off for me?"

The Governor had his horse saddled and said: "I shall give it my all!"

The Marshal appointed six staff officers to go with him and five thousand troops. The gates were opened, the drawbridge lowered and the Governor sallied forth, brandishing a mighty blade and riding a chestnut stallion.

Scimitar responded by withdrawing his forces somewhat, until the enemy had taken up their battle positions, with the six commanders divided equally on either side of the Governor. Then Scimitar rode forward, resting his weapon, and bellowed: "Hear this, you rebels! You are fighting on the side of a traitor, whose actions offend against natural law and incur the wrath of gods and man! The forces of righteousness are at hand. Have you no fear of death that you dare oppose us? I swear to you that if we do not make you pay for it with your lives I shall never take up arms again!"

The Governor replied furiously: "You rabble are just robbers from Mount Liang! You have no understanding of heaven's will since you ignore the cause of a strong prince and choose to bow down before a foolish and unprincipled lord. You have the nerve to pick a fight with our great country. We shall give you such a beating that not even a scrap of your armour will be left whole!"

Enraged, Scimitar charged forward, his crescent blade flashing, while the Governor likewise drew his sword and charged to meet him. They fought over thirty bouts, till the Governor's strength began to fail him and he could scarcely hold out. Then from the ranks of the southerners two commanders, seeing his plight, levelled their spears and rode out side by side. These two came at Scimitar, one from either side. Two commanders from the Song ranks were provoked by this and charged, one wielding a deadly sword, the other a tiger's eye chain. They were the Tamer and Colonel Sun. The other southern commanders were waiting in two ranks in front of their lines. Marshal Lü hurriedly ordered two more of them to their general's assistance.

Now in fact one of these southern commanders, Jin Jie, had already formed the intention of surrendering to the Song and was really interested in creating disorder among his own side, so after only a few bouts he turned his horse and galloped back towards his own ranks. Victorious was not going to let this opportunity slip and gave chase. When the southern commander Gao Keli saw Victorious hard on his comrade's heels, he took up his decorated bow, fitted an arrow to the string, took careful aim and let fly. The arrow hit Victorious full in the face and he fell from his horse. Thunderclap hurriedly slapped his horse and whirling his wolf's-tooth mace charged to the rescue. But already another southerner, Zhang Jinren, had thrust his spear into Victorious and finished him off. Victorious and the Supremo were sworn brothers, and when the latter saw his friend die he was determined to avenge him. He shook off his opponent and charged back towards the main southern army to search out Gao Keli. The man he had been fighting gave chase but Thunderclap stood in his way. Gao Keli saw the Supremo coming and levelled his lance to receive him. Intent only on revenge, the Supremo failed to protect himself and received a thrust to the ribs from Zhang Jinren's spear, which spitted him and hurled him from his horse.

Seeing two of his commanders killed was intolerable to Scimitar and in a blazing fury he charged towards Changzhou. With a display of awesome might he dealt the enemy commander, Governor Qian, one blow which knocked him lifeless from his beautiful long-maned chestnut stallion. Scimitar was about to seize the horse when his own, hit in the leg by an arrow, stumbled and threw him. The southern commanders Gao Keli and Zhang Jinren galloped towards Scimitar, but he was rescued by Spearsman, the Ugly Son-in-Law and Hound who got him back to their own lines. Marshal Lü now led a ferocious sally from the city and Scimitar was forced to retreat northwards with heavy losses. The southerners pursued them for more than six miles.

After his losses that day, Scimitar decided to head back and report to Song Jiang. When he heard of the deaths of Victorious and the Supremo, Song Jiang wept. "I never thought when we crossed the river that we would lose five of our brothers!" he lamented. "It must be that heaven is angry with me and does not wish me to defeat Fang La, otherwise why should we suffer these reverses?"

The Professor said: "You're talking nonsense! Winning and losing, victory and defeat, these are normal events for a soldier, there's nothing unusual about them. Today was the day these two leaders were destined to die, that's all. Put aside your grief and let us discuss tactics."

At this moment Iron Ox rushed into the tent and said: "Let someone who knows the killers of those two lead me to the swine and let me kill them, to avenge my two brothers!"

Song Jiang ordered a white flag of mourning to be raised the following day and announced that he would personally lead the whole army against the city to do battle and achieve final victory. Next day he led a huge attack by land and water, setting out as soon as the boats had arrived. Iron Ox with Pluto, Eight-Armed Ogre and Winged Ghost and five hundred brave infantrymen went ahead to reconnoitre and arrived before the walls of Changzhou.

Marshal Lü having lost Governor Qian of Changzhou was greatly disturbed and had sent three urgent messages to Third Prince Fang Mao in Suzhou asking for help. He also sent a report to the court. Now he heard that five hundred infantry were at the city gates and that according to the banner their leader was the Black Whirlwind Li Kui, alias Iron Ox. "That blackguard is Mount Liang's most vicious bandit, a notorious killer," said the Marshal. "Who will go and capture him for me?"

Two distinguished generals presented themselves: Gao Keli and Zhang Jinren. The Marshal said to them privately: "If you capture the bandit for me, I shall use all my influence to secure your promotion." The pair of them grasped their lances and mounted and led out a thousand cavalry to do battle. When he sighted them, Iron Ox deployed his infantry in a straight line and grasping his two axes placed himself in front of them. Pluto was to one side of him, armed with a broad long-handled sword. On the other side were Eight-Armed Ogre and Winged Ghost with their spiked shields and steel javelins in their right hands.

So there they were, these four, wearing armour plating to protect chest and back and standing at the head of their men. The two southern leaders were like mountain cats that think they have got the better of a tiger, or magpies taunting an eagle. They had a thousand troops and had deployed them just outside the city.

There were several scouts among the Song army who recognized those two southern generals as the ones who had killed Victorious and the Supremo and pointed them out to Iron Ox. "See them two commanders? They're the ones as killed our two."

Iron Ox said not a word but took up his two axes and charged straight at the enemy ranks. Pluto, calling to Eight-Armed Ogre and Winged Ghost to follow with their whirling shields, rushed off to help him. All shouting in unison, the four of them fell on the enemy. Gao Keli and Zhang Jinren were shaken and turned their horses without even waiting to strike a blow. But the two shield-bearers were already under the horses' noses. When Gao and Zhang tried to strike downwards with their lances, Eight-Armed Ogre and Winged Ghost parried with their shields, and at the same moment Iron Ox swept Gao from his horse with a blow of his axe. Gao fell under the horse's feet and Eight-Armed Ogre shouted out: "Keep him alive!" But killing was in Iron Ox's nature and he could not restrain himself. One more blow and Gao's head was off. Pluto likewise had knocked Zhang from his horse and cut off his head with a single blow. All four now continued

宋公明大戰毘陵郡

to rampage through the enemy ranks. Iron Ox had tied Gao's head to his belt and whirling his two axes, plunged into the thick of it, giving no quarter.

A thousand southern troops died on the field of battle, and then as they fled into the city three or four hundred more, till Iron Ox and Pluto had reached the drawbridge. They wanted to fight on into the city, but Eight-Armed Ogre and Winged Ghost insisted they hold back. By now missiles were raining down from the city walls. The four warriors withdrew a little. They found their five hundred troops drawn up as before in a straight line. They had not dared to go into action. They had thought about joining the battle, but since Iron Ox was laying about him indiscriminately they feared he would not distinguish between friend and foe and preferred to keep their distance.

Now a cloud of dust announced the arrival of Song Jiang's army. Iron Ox and Pluto presented the heads, which were recognized as being those of Gao and Zhang. The others were critical: "Why did you take their heads?" they said.

"We killed a good many more. We intended to take these two alive, but our hands itched to do it and we couldn't resist," they replied.

"Since we've got the heads now, we'll put them under the white banner, to propitiate the spirits of Victorious and the Supremo," Song Jiang said. He wept a while as the heads were placed under the banner, and then rewarded Iron Ox and the other three. Then they all headed for Changzhou.

Back in that city Marshal Lü was exceedingly concerned. He discussed with Jin Jie, Xu Ding and the remaining four staff officers how to repel Song Jiang's force. All his generals had seen how Iron Ox fought and were quaking in their boots. None of them wanted to lead a counter-attack. The question was put to them several times, but they were as if struck dumb. No one spoke, no one dared offer a suggestion. With a heavy heart Marshal Lü ordered someone up onto the battlements to observe, as Song Jiang's army took up positions on three sides of the city and with drums and banners issued their challenge right under the city walls. Marshal Lü ordered all his commanders up onto the walls to organize the defence. They departed, leaving him alone in the inner chamber to contemplate his situation. He had no plan. He summoned some of the most trusted members of his entourage for further discussions. Their only suggestion was to abandon the city and run for it. Of this no more.

Meanwhile guard commander Jin Jie went home and said to his wife, Jade Orchid: "Song Jiang's army is camped on three sides of the city and we are short of provisions, we won't be able to hold out long. If the city falls, we are all destined for slaughter."

Jade Orchid said: "You are a loyal soul, I know you really want to return to your allegiance to the Emperor. There's the added motive that you used to hold an important post under the Song. The court never found fault with you. Wouldn't it be best to turn over a new leaf, capture Marshal Lü and hand him over to Song Jiang? I'm sure it's the most advantageous policy."

"But he's got four bodyguards, each with his own troops," her husband objected. "And that bastard Xu Ding, who is no friend to me, is very close to the Marshal. I fear the scheme could misfire and only invite disaster."

"You must act with secrecy," his wife said. "Wait till dark, attach a sealed letter to an arrow and fire it out of the city to inform Song Jiang that he can have the city with inside help. Go out to fight tomorrow and feign defeat. Then you can be credited with leading them into the city."

"That's a brilliant idea, my love," he said. "That's exactly what I'll do." The poem says:

Flee the dark and seek the light,
That's the way to put things right.
A woman with a loyal heart,
Helps a man to see his fault!

Next day Song Jiang launched a fierce assault on the city. Marshal Lü called a meeting. Jin Jie said: "Our defences are strong. We should concentrate on defence and not think of attacking. If we are firm in our defence we can wait till Suzhou sends reinforcements. Then we can join together to fight them."

"That makes good sense," the Marshal said. It was agreed that two of them should defend the east gate, two of them the north, Jin Jie would take the west and Xu Ding the south. They all went off to organize their guard. That evening Jin Jie wrote his confidential letter and tied it to an arrow. He waited till it was fully dark and all was quiet and then one of his scouts went up onto the battlements and fired it off towards the west. One of Song Jiang's men picked it up and hurriedly reported with it to the camp. The western camp was under the command of Monk and Pilgrim. When they saw the letter they hurriedly sent their subordinate Uglymug to report with it to the headquarters in the northeast camp. Song Jiang and the Professor were discussing matters and the tent was brightly lit when Uglymug presented Jin Jie's letter. Song Jiang was delighted and ordered all three camps to be informed.

Next day the leaders in all three camps attacked the city simultaneously. Marshal Lü was watching from a tower as Song Jiang's Thunderer prepared his guns and fired off an explosive shell which landed beside the tower and brought the corner of the tower crashing down. Marshal Lü fled from the walls in panic and ordered the commanders of the four gates to make a desperate sally. Three beats of the drum sounded and the city gates opened, the drawbridge was lowered. The two generals from the north gate advanced. Scimitar, mounted on the horse of the dead governor rode out from the Song ranks and took on one of them. As the two were going at it, Jin Jie led some bold troops out from the west gate. Colonel Sun engaged him. Before completing three bouts Jin Jie feigned defeat and galloped back. Colonel Sun, charged forward, with the Dandy and the Flautist close behind him, followed by Monk, Pilgrim, Red Star, Comet, the Young Master and Uglymug.

As Jin Jie retreated into the city Colonel Sun reached the west gate behind him and proceeded to seize it. Fighting broke out within the city and it became evident that the Song forces had got in by the west gate. At this point the people, who had been persecuted by Fang La beyond their enduring and had reached a point where their pent-up anger was ready to explode, hearing that Song forces had entered the city poured out to join in the fight. Song Jiang's flag was soon flying over the walls. Two of the southern commanders realized the city had changed hands and were rushing back to defend their families when Short-Arse and Steelbright cut them off from the left and caught one of them, while the Son-in-Law and Hound charging in from the right knocked the other from his horse and took him and his men prisoner. Song Jiang and the Professor led the main army into the city. On all sides southern soldiers were captured and promptly executed. Taking his friend Xu Ding with him, the Marshal left by the southern gate and fled for his life. Song Jiang's army could not catch up with him so they returned to the city to await orders and reward for their exploits. A third southern commander tried to hide in a commoner's house and was caught by the people and handed over. A fourth was killed by his own troops and his head taken. Song Jiang went to the government office and published a proclamation to calm the people, who flocked there, young and old alike, to give thanks. Song Jiang reassured them, saying that he recognized them as loyal citizens. The leaders were all invited to apply for their rewards.

When Jin Jie went to the government office to pay his respects to Song Jiang, the latter stepped down to receive him personally and invited him to take a seat. Jin Jie's relief was boundless, and he became again a loyal subject of the Song Emperor. This was all thanks to the good advice of his wife, as we already know. Song Jiang had the three captured commanders placed in prison carts and ordered Jin Jie to take them himself to Marshal Zhang's headquarters in Runzhou. Bearing the order and with the prisoners under close guard Jin went to Runzhou and handed them over. Before he left, Song Jiang sent Magic Messenger with an urgent letter recommending Jin to the army. Learning from this letter how highly Song Jiang rated Jin, the Marshal received him most hospitably and heaped upon him gifts of gold and silver, silk, a horse and wine. The Marshal's deputy, Liu Guangshi, retained Jin on his staff and gave him military rank to serve with the army. Later he was with Liu Guangshi at the defeat of the Jin and fought with distinction. Later still he was given his own command and died in the action at Zhongshan. That is the story of Jin Jie.

Marshal Zhang and his deputy rewarded Jin Jie that day and had the three prisoners hacked to pieces and their corpses exhibited as a ghastly example to all, following which someone was sent to Changzhou with the reward for Song Jiang's troops.

Meanwhile Song Jiang, after settling his troops in at Changzhou, had sent Magic Messenger to find out about the Unicorn's campaign against Xuanzhou and Huzhou. He had also received reports that Marshal Lü had taken refuge in Wuxi and had linked up with the reinforcements sent from Suzhou and was ready to attack again. To meet this threat he moved a force of cavalry and infantry south, consisting of Scimitar and nine others and ten thousand men. They set off at once.

The Magic Messenger now returned, together with Mr. Chai, to bring news of the Unicorn's campaign. He announced that Xuanzhou had been taken and that Mr. Chai was with him to report on the action. Song Jiang was delighted, and after Mr. Chai had paid his respects he got out the wine to celebrate and they went into an inner room, where Song Jiang asked for a detailed description. Mr. Chai produced the despatches and gave his own oral account.

Fang La's governor of Xuanzhou was Jia Yuqing. He had six lieutenants, whom he ordered to advance from the city in three columns. The Unicorn divided his forces into three columns to meet them. In the centre Twin Rods took on one of the enemy commanders and Twin Spears another. After ten bouts Twin Spears killed his opponent and the other enemy commander fled. Their forces were routed. On the left Leopard's Head and Hasty took on their opposite numbers. Leopard's Head's halberd dispatched his opponent and Hasty finished his with the axe. On the right Hotshot and the Unstoppable were fighting. The former knocked down his adversary with a stone and the Tiger-Killer hastened to finish him off. The Unstoppable's opponent fled. Four enemy leaders were killed that day and the rest of them took refuge in the city.

The Unicorn immediately ordered his commanders to take the city. They got to the gate but had no protection against the enemy soldiers on the walls. One of the leaders was struck and killed by a millstone that hurtled down. A hail of arrows also rained down on them, all with poisoned tips, hitting two more commanders, who both died when they got them back to the camp. After losing these three leaders, the Unicorn persisted all night in the attack. The guards on the east gate could not hold out and the city was taken. One enemy commander was killed in the fighting and the other escaped and led the shattered remnants of their troops towards Huzhou.

Monk had got into trouble during this battle and his whereabouts were unknown. The leader killed by the millstone was Whitey, and the two hit by poisoned arrows were Knife and Fleetfoot. The news that he had lost three more leaders grieved Song Jiang sorely. Whatever may have been the state of his five internal organs, his four limbs suddenly would not respond. One might indeed say that:

The flower scarce opens before the wind destroys it;
The moon so bright is quickly veiled by cloud.

Song Jiang fell senseless to the floor and if you want to hear how it stood with him you must read the next chapter.

Chapter 113

At Lake Tai a small gathering of heroes; In Suzhou with Song Jiang a major assembly!

The other leaders rushed to revive Song Jiang and after what seemed an age he came to and said to the Professor: "I fear that we are not going to prevail over Fang La. Ever since we crossed the river we have suffered misfortune. One after the other, we have lost eight of our brothers."

The Professor tried to rally him: "Do not speak like this or you will ruin our morale. Before, when we defeated the Tartars, we all returned safely and that was all according to heaven's plan. If this time some of our brothers have died, it simply means that they have completed their allotted span. You can't deny that since we crossed the river we have captured three important cities: Runzhou, Changzhou and Xuanzhou. Clearly this is due to the Emperor's standing with heaven and your reputation. Who says our cause does not prosper? You have no reason for this despondency."

Song Jiang said: "Of course it is heaven's will, yet still I think of the one hundred and eight, come together in correspondence with the heavenly stars and according to what was inscribed on the celestial tablet. We are close to one another as hand and foot. How can I not grieve when I hear such terrible news?"

The Professor insisted: "Stop worrying about it. You will only do yourself injury. Please think about how to send reinforcements to attack their Marshal Lü in Wuxi."

Song Jiang said: "Leave Mr. Chai to keep me company. Write out another order for Magic Messenger to take to the Unicorn asking him to attack Huzhou and then unite with us again as soon as possible in Hangzhou."

The Professor got Sterling to write out the order and sent Magic Messenger to Xuanzhou with it. Of this no more.

Meanwhile Fang La's Marshal Lü and Xu Ding had retreated to Wuxi where they met up with the reinforcements sent by Third Prince Fang Mao from Suzhou. These were under a senior general called Wei Zhong with ten lieutenants and a thousand men. They had been sent to relieve Changzhou but now joined in the defence of Wuxi. Marshal Lü explained how Jin Jie had delivered Changzhou to the enemy. Wei Zhong said: "You may rest easy, Marshal. I am going to get the city back for you."

At this very moment a scout reported: "The Song army is approaching. We need to prepare."

Wei Zhong rode out of the north gate at the head of his troops to encounter the enemy. They saw a huge Song force bearing down on them, led by Iron Ox, together with Pluto, Eight-Armed Ogre and Winged Ghost. Wei Zhong's spirits quailed and before they had even had time to form up his troops began to run. As they scurried back into Wuxi, the four foremost pursuers rushed into the town behind them. Marshal Lü fled through the south gate. Scimitar occupied the town. Wei Zhong and Xu Ding also made it out through the south gate and returned to Suzhou. Scimitar and his men now had Wuxi and sent a messenger to Song Jiang to report the fact. Song Jiang and the other leaders came to Wuxi and issued a proclamation reassuring the people and accepting them as loyal citizens. The army was stationed there and a message was sent requesting Marshal Zhang and his deputy to take over the defence of Changzhou.

Meanwhile Marshal Lü with Wei Zhong and Xu Ding had taken the remnants of their beaten army back to Suzhou to request help from the Third Prince, explaining that the Song forces were too strong for them and telling how his troops had been rolled back like a mat and the city lost. The Prince flew into a passion and ordered his military council to strip Lü of his command and execute him. But Wei Zhong and the others protested, saying: "Song Jiang's commanders are all battle-hardened, bold and skilful warriors. What's more, his soldiers are bandits from Mount Liang, well versed in fighting. It makes them extremely hard to defeat."

"I will suspend the sentence, then," said the Prince. "You can have five thousand men to spearhead an attack. I will command the main force myself and follow on behind you."

Lü prostrated himself in thanks. Then he put on full armour and grasping his long serpent lance rode out of the city.

The Third Prince mustered eight generals, all strong well-built men with plenty of battle experience. He put on his armour, grasped his square halberd, mounted his horse and after inspecting his troops advanced to do battle. With the eight generals riding in front, and twenty or thirty subalterns with fifty thousand southern troops drawn up in orderly ranks behind, he rode out through the palace gates to encounter Song Jiang.

By the time the vanguard under Marshal Lü, followed by Wei Zhong and Xu Ding, had passed the Temple on Cold Mountain and were approaching Wuxi, Song Jiang had received reports from his scouts and with some of his junior commanders had moved troops a few miles in front of the town. The two armies confronted each other, banners waving and drums sounding, drawn up in battle formation. Marshal Lü, boiling with anger, settled himself on his horse, took a firm grip on his lance and rode forward to challenge Song Jiang. Song Jiang in response turned and asked his commanders: "Which of you will capture that bandit for me?"

He had hardly finished when the Spearsman, firmly grasping his gold lance and settling himself on his horse, rode forward and engaged Marshal Lü. A shout went up on either side as the spears clashed. They fought more than twenty bouts. Then Marshal Lü parried and Spearsman's lance came in under his guard and knocked him from his horse. A roar went up from both armies. Iron Ox with his axes, Pluto with his javelins, Eight-Armed Ogre and Winged Ghost with their barbed shields rushed forward, throwing the southern contingent into utter confusion.

Song Jiang's army now met the Third Prince's troops head on. There was an exchange of arrows as both armies formed up for battle. On the southern side the eight commanders were drawn up in line. The Prince in the centre heard that Marshal Lü had been killed and was enraged. He rode out in front and abused

Song Jiang: "To me you are just a bunch of burners and looters, bandits from Mount Liang. The luckless court made you a general and told you to invade our land. Well, I'm going to teach you a lesson, when I've finished with you you'll know what fighting really is!"

Song Jiang pointed and said contemptuously: "And you're just a bunch of peasants! What makes you think you have a destiny? You a ruler? What a hope! Why not surrender right away and save your life? We are the imperial army! I'm going to finish you off, or I vow never to fight again."

The Prince roared: "I'm not going to waste my breath on you. I've got eight brave commanders here. Have you got eight you'd dare to pit against them?"

Song Jiang laughed scornfully: "I could certainly find two for each one of yours, but it wouldn't be honourable. Send out your eight and I'll send out eight of mine. We'll compare our fighting skills and see who comes off best. But let the rules be these: anyone who loses his mount shall be taken back to his own ranks, there are to be no snipers with arrows and no body snatching. If there is no clear victory, it must not degenerate into a brawl: the contest will be renewed tomorrow."

Fang Mao sent out his eight commanders, armed and mounted. Song Jiang said to his champions: "Hand over your commands before you go out to fight." Barely had he finished speaking when the eight rode forth. They were Scimitar, Colonel Hua, Spearsman, Thunderclap, Whiskers, Tamer, Colonel Sun and Hound. The pennants gates opened right and left to let them through. The drums set up a rapid rhythm on either side, while flags of many colours were waved and signal rockets sent up. With both armies shouting encouragement the sixteen met, each seeking out his own opponent and falling on him.

All the sixteen were brave men and they fought with great determination. After thirty bouts, one of them fell head over heels from his horse. Who was the unlucky one? It was the southerner Gou Zheng, whom Whiskers with a thrust of his spear had knocked from his horse. Gongs sounded on either side and the other seven pairs of contestants separated and returned to their own ranks.

When Fang Mao saw that he had lost one of his commanders, he felt things would go against him and withdrew with his army into Suzhou. Song Jiang urged his men forward and made camp close to the Temple on Cold Mountain. He rewarded Whiskers with promotion. Sterling wrote out a despatch which was sent to Marshal Zhang. Of this no more.

The Prince fortified himself in the city. He ordered his leaders to strengthen the defences on all the gates, setting out deer's antlers, positioning ballistas and crossbows on the walls, with a good supply of explosives and missiles, molten metal stored under an awning and bottles of acid on the battlements, in preparation for a dogged defence of the city.

When the southern army did not sally forth next day, Song Jiang took Colonel Hua, Spearsman, Tamer and Colonel Sun together with thirty horsemen to observe the city. He found that all round Suzhou on the outskirts was a mass of waterways and the walls of the city itself were solid. "This city won't fall to us in a hurry," he thought. He went back to the camp and discussed with the Professor a plan of attack. Some one came and reported: "The boat leader White-Water Dragon is here from Jiangyin to see you, sir."

Song Jiang had him brought in and asked what the news was from the coast. White-Water Dragon replied: "Since I was put in charge of the water-borne forces with Madcap, we have attacked the islands of Jiangyin and Taicang and other places down the coast. When their commander sailed out to oppose us, he was knocked into the sea by a spear thrust from Ruan the Seventh and his lieutenant died in a salvo of arrows. So we were able to take those two places. On the same day Madcap, the Pilot and White Eel took Jiading and the Ruan brothers took Changshu. This is what I came to tell you."

Song Jiang was excited by this news. He rewarded the White-Water Dragon and sent him off to report to Marshal Zhang and his second-in-command. White-Water Dragon went off to Changzhou and gave a detailed report on the taking of the two islands, and the killing of two enemy commanders. The Marshal rewarded him handsomely and sent him back to Song Jiang for further orders.

Since Suzhou was surrounded by wide expanses of water, Song Jiang realized he needed to launch a water-borne attack and retained White-Water Dragon for this purpose. He wanted boats to be prepared, ready for sailing. White-Water Dragon said: "Let me go and check the width of the channel and see how we can use our forces. When I come back we can make our plan." Song Jiang assented.

White-Water Dragon was gone two days. When he came back he said: "Just to the south of the city is Lake Tai. What we want is a small boat that can enter the Yixing channel and secretly pass into Lake Tai and thence to Wujiang to get intelligence of the southerners before we advance."

"Very well, only you need another leader to go with you," said Song Jiang. He ordered Skyhawk, together with Red Star, Comet, the Young Master and Uglymug to the coast to help the water-borne forces and replace the Tong brothers, Cave Dragon and River Rider, who were needed to assist White-Water Dragon. Skyhawk with these orders departed for the island of Jiangyin. Within two days the Tong brothers arrived and Song Jiang explained tactfully that they were needed to help White-Water Dragon carry out an important spying mission by boat.

So White-Water Dragon and the two Tongs set off in a light boat with two sailors to row. They rowed into the narrow channel at Yixing and after many twists and turns came out into Lake Tai. What met their eyes was a vast expanse of water, like a great sheet of jade:

> *Sky and water merge in the distance, the water seeming to rise into the sky; all around is water, not a speck of land to be seen, everywhere sky and water are of uniform brightness. The water's clear mirror is broken only by the reflections of egrets flying by in pairs; the perfection of the empyrean is shattered only by the gulls that soar heavenwards two by two. When the lake is a-glitter with spring, its wavelets shimmer like fish scales; swollen by summer's downpours, its billows challenge heaven; immaculate with autumn moonshine, it unfurls a golden path; dusted with winter snow, it fills the world with reflected light.*

When primeval chaos was first resolved, the water god appropriated this crystal mansion to himself.

As the poet says:

Over the vastness the seagulls float;
Green spring's the time to dye your clothes;
Going to and fro men wear themselves out;
At sundown it's time to head for home.

As they were rowing across the lake and drawing near to Wujiang they saw a flotilla of fishing boats, forty or fifty of them. "Let's pretend we want to buy fish," said the White-Water Dragon. "We can get some information out of them." They rowed closer, and he shouted out: "Have you got any big carp there?"

The fishermen answered: "If it's big carp you want, you'd better come home with us and we'll sell you some."

They followed the fishing boats and before long they came to a place all surrounded by twisted willow trees. Enclosed within a bamboo fence were some twenty or so houses. The fishermen first moored their boat, then helped the three leaders ashore and took them into a compound. The moment they stepped inside, seven or eight big fellows gave a loud shout and pinning them down with hooks dragged them into the house. Without a word of explanation they tied them to a wooden pillar.

They found themselves in a thatched hall where four bold buccaneers were seated. The chief of them had a reddish beard and whiskers and wore a robe with blue sleeves. The second was tall and thin, with a short beard and dressed in a dark green robe with a round collar; the third was dark with long whiskers and the fourth had a bony face with high cheekbones and a round beard. These last two were dressed alike in padded robes with blue sleeves. They all wore black felt hats and carried weapons. The leader shouted at White-Water Dragon: "Where are you lot from? What're you doing here on our lake?"

"We're from Yangzhou," he answered. "We came here to trade. We want to buy fish."

The one with the bony face said: "No point in asking 'em

questions, brother. They're obviously spies. Just whip their hearts and livers out; we'll have'em with our wine."

"After all those years as smuggler on the Xunyang River," White-Water Dragon was thinking to himself, "and a good while too as outlaw on Mount Liang, who would have thought I'd end my days here! Well, well, well!" He sighed and exchanged a look with the other two. "I'm to blame for getting you into this mess. I've turned you into ghosts!" he said. "There's only one way to go now."

"Don't talk like that, brother," they said. "We don't mind dying. It's only that dying like this is an insult to the Leader's name." Looking about them, they held their heads high and waited for death.

After hearing their talk, the four fishermen looked at each other and said: "This leader of theirs must be someone out of the ordinary!"

"What sort of people are you then?" the chief asked. "Can't you reveal your names to us? We'd really like to know."

"Go ahead and kill us, if you're going to," White-Water Dragon said. "We'll die sooner than tell our names. We don't want to be a laughing-stock!"

At this the chief of the fishermen jumped up and cut their bonds with a knife, releasing them all. He and the other three raised them up and invited them to sit in an inner room. Then he prostrated himself and said: "We're robbers and we've been around, but I've never seen men with such spirit as you! Please tell us where you are from. We really want to know your names!"

"You are obviously brave fellows," said White-Water Dragon. "So I'll tell you, and afterwards you can do what you like with us. We all serve under Song Jiang of Mount Liang. I am the White-Water Dragon and these two friends of mine are Cave Dragon and River Rider. We have been pardoned by the Emperor; recently we defeated the Liao Tartars, and after we returned to the capital we were given the task of capturing Fang La. If you serve Fang La, you'd better hand us over and get the reward. We won't put up any resistance."

When the fishermen heard this, they kowtowed again, and

still kneeling said in chorus: "We couldn't see what was in front of our noses. We treated you disgracefully! Forgive us, please forgive us! We certainly don't serve Fang La. We chose to seek our living in the greenwood long ago. Now we've ended up in this place, which is known as Willow Farm. There are hidden channels all around, but no boat can get in. We just use fishing as a cover, so we can make a living on the lake. This last winter we've learnt a bit about fighting on the water, that's why no one wants to meddle with us. We have long heard how Song Jiang of the Marshes of Mount Liang seeks out good men. We have also heard of you, and of a certain White Eel. We had no idea we were going to meet you here!"

"White Eel is my friend, and my comrade in the water-borne forces. At present he is in Jiangyin, arresting rebels. Another time I'll bring him here so you can make his acquaintance. May I ask your names?"

"Because we're of the greenwood, we all have nicknames. Please don't laugh! I am Red, this is Curly, that's Shark, and the last is Bony."

"There's nothing more to worry about then, gentlemen," said White-Water Dragon approvingly. "It's good to know we're all members of the same family! Our leader, Song Jiang has been made commander of the expeditionary force against Fang La. His present aim is to capture Suzhou and before deciding how to go about it he sent us three out on reconnaissance. Now we have met you, you can come with us to see the Leader. He's sure to take you on and after we capture Fang La the court will give you advancement."

"With all due respect," said Red, "if we were ambitious for office, we could have been generals under Fang La years ago. Fact is we don't want to serve. All we want is a merry life. If you need our help, we'll go through fire and water for you. But if you're offering us official posts, all I can say is we don't want 'em."

"In that case let us just declare ourselves blood brothers, how about that?"

The four fishermen were well pleased with this suggestion,

and had a pig and a goat slaughtered and wine brought for a celebration, as they and White-Water Dragon swore an oath of loyalty as brothers. Cave Dragon and River Rider followed suit.

The seven at Willow Farm discussed the problem of capturing Suzhou. They agreed that the Third Prince would not come out to fight. The city was surrounded on all sides by water and there was no way to attack it. The channel was so narrow it could hardly be attacked by boats. How would they ever take the city? Red said: "Stay here for a couple of days and rest. From time to time one of Fang La's people from Hangzhou comes to Suzhou on official business. That could be our chance to capture the city. I'll get up a group of fishermen and send them out to do some spying. When we hear that someone is coming we can make a plan."

"That's a great idea," said White-Water Dragon.

Red sent some of the fishermen off on their mission, while he entertained his guests with wine at the farm. After several days of this, the fishermen returned and said: "A dozen or so cargo boats have appeared at Pingwang all with yellow flags at the stern bearing the words 'Royal uniforms'. They've obviously been sent from Hangzhou. There's only half a dozen men on each."

"This is our chance," said White-Water Dragon. "I hope you're all going to help."

"We'll start right away," said Red.

"If just one of the boats gets away, the whole plan will be ruined," said White-Water Dragon.

"Don't you worry. I'll take care of it," said Red. He assembled sixty or seventy fishing boats. Each of the leaders was to go in one. Fishermen would be in the others, all with hidden weapons. They crept out of the small channels into the main river, spread themselves out and advanced.

That night the moon and stars were bright as the ten official transports anchored in the east river in front of the Temple of the Dragon Lord. Red's boat reached them first. A sharp whistle was the signal and sixty or seventy fishing boats approached and grappled the bigger vessels. On the transports men rushed up on deck and were pinned down with hooks and then tied together in bunches of five or six. Some jumped into the water and were hooked and dragged aboard again. The small boats now had control of the transports and sailed away with them to distant parts of the lake. In the fourth watch they all reached Willow Farm. Most of the enemy personnel, bound together with ropes, had big stones attached to them and were thrown into the lake to drown. The two commanders were retained for questioning. They turned out to be officers of Fang La's treasury in Hangzhou, bearing an official order and charged with delivering three thousand suits of new iron armour for the Third Prince in Suzhou. White-Water Dragon got their names and a set of official papers out of them and then they were killed. "I must go and discuss this with the Leader," he said. "And then we can finish the job."

Red said: "I will tell some of my people to take you. I think you had better go by the small channels." Two of the fishermen were ordered to row White-Water Dragon back in a light boat. White-Water Dragon told Cave Dragon, River Rider and the others the government transports must be hidden carefully in the small channels at the back of the farm and no one allowed to see them. "No problem," said Red. He went off himself to deal with the boats.

So White-Water Dragon with the two sailors travelling by small channels in their light boat arrived at the Temple on Cold Mountain and went ashore. He went to the camp and gave Song Jiang a detailed account of the preceding events. "Then Suzhou is ours!" said the Professor triumphantly. "You must give orders for Iron Ox, Pluto, Eight-Armed Ogre and Winged Ghost with two hundred shield-bearers to return with White-Water Dragon to the farm on Lake Tai, where they are to make joint plans with this fellow Red and his comrades and launch an attack a day later."

Equipped with these orders White-Water Dragon and his companions went back to Lake Tai. On the way they picked up Iron Ox and his group and escorted them to Willow Farm, where White-Water Dragon introduced them all to the fishermen. Red had quite a shock when he saw what Iron Ox looked like. Two hundred or more were treated to wine at the farm. On the third day, as they had planned, Red disguised himself as the treasury official in charge of the armour, with Curly as his lieutenant. They put on southern uniforms and took the official documents with them. The fishermen were disguised as sailors manning the transports and Iron Ox and his companions were hidden in the holds of the vessels. Shark and Bony were in charge of the last boats, which carried combustible materials. Just when they were about to start a fisherman came and reported: "There's a boat out on the lake that keeps going to and fro."

"That sounds very odd," said White-Water Dragon. He hurriedly went to see for himself. At the prow of the boat stood two men. They were Magic Messenger and Thundererer. White-Water Dragon let out a loud whistle and the boat shot towards them. "What are you doing here?" asked White-Water Dragon when they had come ashore and been introduced.

"The Leader sent Iron Ox off in a hurry," said Magic Messenger. "He forgot something important. We've been sent here with a hundred signal rockets. We missed him out on the lake and we were scared to come in close to shore. The rockets are to be set off tomorrow morning when you get inside the city."

"Good!" said White-Water Dragon, and had the rockets transferred to the boats with the armour and stowed away.

When Red heard this was Magic Messenger he called for more wine to entertain them.

Thunderer was hidden away inside the third boat with ten rockets. That night in the fourth watch they set sail from Willow Farm and steered for Suzhou. By the end of the fifth watch they were close to the city walls. When they saw the southern flag the guards on the walls hurriedly reported to the guard commander, Guo Shiguang, who came up onto the walls himself. He asked for a full report and had the documents sent up so he could examine them. He sent someone to report it all to the Third Prince's office. The documents were scrutinized and then someone was sent down to the boats to inspect them. Finally they were allowed into the city. Guo himself was sitting on a chair beside the water-gate and he ordered a further inspection. The boats were found to be stuffed with armour so one by one they were allowed to enter. When all ten had been allowed through, the water-gate was closed again. The Third Prince's inspector with five hundred men had now arrived on the bank. He ordered the boats to tie up. Iron Ox and his companions now made their appearance. The inspector was struck by the ugly look of these four and hurriedly asked who they were. But by this time Eight-Armed Ogre and Winged Ghost were already waving their barbed shields and firing off javelins. The inspector was knocked from his horse and when the five hundred troops tried to board the vessels Iron Ox leapt ashore with his two axes and cut down a dozen of them. The rest fled.

The others on the boats, including the two hundred shield-bearers, now came ashore and began starting fires. Thunderer set up his gun and started sending off signal rockets. He sent off ten in a row. The explosions shook the city towers. Fighting broke out everywhere. The Third Prince was holding a meeting in the government office when he heard the explosions and was so frightened his spirit nearly left his body. The guard commanders on all the gates, when they heard these incessant explosions, rushed back into the city centre. The rumour began to fly about that the army commander had been killed by a stray arrow and Song troops were already inside the city. Suzhou by now was in a ferment. No one could say how many Song troops had entered. Iron Ox and Pluto were charging all over the place with the two shield-bearers killing the southern troops. White-Water Dragon and Magic Messenger together with Red and company were guarding Thunderer as he busied himself with his rockets. Song Jiang had already detailed three army columns to take the city. As these rushed in the southern troops scattered before them and fled for their lives.

The Third Prince hurriedly put on armour and with a few hundred armoured troops was trying to force a way out through the south gate when he ran into Iron Ox and his gang, who set about the armoured troops and had them running in all directions. Monk also emerged from an alley, heaving his steel staff. The Third Prince could put up no resistance. He galloped back alone to the government office. From under the Magpie Bridge Pilgrim emerged and hacked at the horse's legs. One blow of his sword

宋公明蘇州大會垓

brought Third Prince crashing to the ground, and a second removed his head.

Pilgrim took the head back to the army to show Song Jiang and ask for his reward. Song Jiang was already in the city, sitting in the Prince's office. He ordered all the leaders to go round the town and search out and kill the southern troops. Almost all were taken. Only one of their commanders got away, together with a beaten remnant of the army, and went to Xiuzhou.

Heaven's mandate cannot be gainsaid.
Peace for usurpers is never within reach.
The Third Prince quickly loses his head.
Learn the lesson such examples teach!

Song Jiang went to sit in the Prince's office and issued orders that honest citizens and the ordinary people were not to be harmed and the fires everywhere were to be put out. He also issued a proclamation for military and civilians. He then summoned his commanders to the palace to receive their rewards. It became known that Pilgrim had killed the Prince, Whiskers had taken one commander alive and the Tattooed Dragon had captured another, Colonel Sun had killed a third with his rods, White-Water Dragon had killed a fourth with a spear thrust, Demon King had killed a fifth. The Ugly Son-in-Law had fought a ferocious duel with the garrison commander, Guo Shiguang, in which the two men mortally wounded each other and died under Horse-Watering Bridge. The rest had all captured junior officers and came to make their claims.

Song Jiang was sorely grieved by the loss of the Ugly Son-in-Law and sent someone to arrange the encoffining and burial at Tiger Mound Hill. The Third Prince's head and the two captives were sent to Marshal Zhang's headquarters in Changzhou to show justice having been done. Marshal Zhang had the prisoners hacked to pieces in the marketplace and sent the Third Prince's head to the capital. He sent a considerable supply of wealth to Suzhou to reward the army and issued an order requesting his deputy, Liu Guangshi, to fortify Suzhou and commanding Song Jiang to continue the campaign and capture all the rebels.

A mounted scout reported the arrival of General Liu and another officer to take over the government of Suzhou. All the leaders went with Song Jiang to welcome the General and his retinue to the city and take them to stay in the Prince's palace. After these ceremonies, Song Jiang and his leaders held a meeting. Scouts were sent to obtain news of the water-borne forces on the coast. It was reported that in all the places along the coast, when they heard Suzhou had fallen, the rebels had fled and that all the coastal districts were now peaceful. Song Jiang was delighted, and sent a report to headquarters, requesting Marshal Zhang to reappoint all the former officials and detail more troops to every district to protect the people so that all his water-borne forces could be withdrawn and brought back to Suzhou for further duties.

Within a few days all former officials had gone to their posts and the water-borne leaders were all back with the main force in Suzhou. They heard how the three Ruan brothers had lost the Young Master in the attack on Changshu and Red Star in the later attack on Kunshan. Madcap, Skyhawk and their group had all returned safely. The Young Master and Red Star did not know how to swim so when they fell in the water they drowned.

Song Jiang's heart was heavy when he learned that he had lost three more comrades. His sighs were endless. Pilgrim also wept when he thought of former times and the close ties between them all.

Red and his friends now wanted to return home and came to say goodbye. Song Jiang tried his hardest to make them stay, but to no avail. When they had been rewarded, White-Water Dragon was instructed to escort them back to Willow Farm. Cave Dragon and River Rider went with him, and on arrival the fishermen regaled them with wine. While they were drinking Red rose to his feet to toast White-Water Dragon, and made a short speech, which was to have no small effect: White-Water Dragon was to leave the Central Plain and set up a base overseas. Truly it is the case that

To save his life the toad will shed his skin;
For profit and fame the fish becomes a dragon.

If you want to hear what Red said to White-Water Dragon you must read the next chapter.

Chapter 114

In the battle for Hangzhou Song Jiang's plunged in mourning;
White Eel dies at Goldenflood Gate!

Now what Red told the White-Water Dragon was this: "I am not very clever, I'm just a country bumpkin in fact, but wise men say, so I hear: 'In this world there are both successes and defeats, men must rise and men must fall.' You, brother, have done honourable service on Mount Liang for a good many years. You have seen many battles and many victories. When you lot defeated the Liao Tartars, you didn't lose a single one of your comrades. But now you're up against Fang La, and evidently your confidence has received a blow. Maybe your luck has run out. You may ask why I don't want an official post. Because of the state world's in, that's why. When peace comes, there will be many who have it in for you. There's an old saying, 'It's the soldier who secures peace, but he never enjoys it himself.' How true that is! Since we are now blood brothers, why don't all of us, meaning you three too, while we've still got time, find us a quiet place to make a living — raise a little capital, get ourselves a big boat and some sailors to man it, and sail the rivers and seas till we reach the place to lay down our bones. Wouldn't that be a blessed state?"

White-Water Dragon heard him out. Then he threw himself down and said respectfully: "My dear friend, your words are truly enlightening and inspiring. The trouble is Fang La has not yet been defeated and I cannot abandon Song Jiang. It would be unforgivable. If I were to go with you now, I would be throwing away a lifetime of hard-earned honour. But if you can wait for me, until such time as Fang La has submitted, I and my two brothers will return. I really hope you will assist us and prepare the way. You have my word and if I don't keep this promise, you can say I'm no true man!"

The four said: "We'll get the boat ready, then, and we'll be looking forward to your coming. Please don't let us down!"

Both sides drank wine to conclude the pact and swore to keep their word.

Next day they bade farewell and returned to see Song Jiang. They explained to him how Red and his pals did not want to be given posts and only wanted to catch fish and live an easy life. Song Jiang sighed for a while, and then gave orders for the land and water-borne troops to prepare for sailing.

The province of Wujiang was now free of rebels. When they took Pingwang with a determined attack, Xiuzhou lay before them. This province's governor Duan Kai had heard about Third Prince Fang Mao's death in Suzhou and was busy packing up to leave when his scouts reported that a big army was not far off. Looking out over water and land he saw banners blotting out the sun from a combined force of boats and cavalry, and had the kind of shock that makes the spirit quail, the organs fail. The first detachment under Scimitar and Thunderclap was at the city walls; the boats moved up to surround the west gate. Duan Kai shouted down from the wall: "Don't attack! We surrender!" The city gates were opened and with incense and candles, with sheep and wine, Duan Kai welcomed Song Jiang into the city and had him taken to the governor's residence to rest. Since the Governor himself had been the first to welcome him, Song Jiang set him at ease, calling him a loyal official, issuing at the same time a proclamation to reassure the people. Duan Kai said: "We were indeed loyal to the Emperor, but we were under duress from Fang La and could not follow our own inclination. Now the imperial army is here, what else should we do but surrender?"

Song Jiang asked for some detailed information: "Who is in command of the defence of Hangzhou? How many troops and generals do they have?"

"Hangzhou covers a large area, thickly populated. It can be approached by land from the north. To the south is the river, to the west the lake. It is defended by Fang La's eldest son, Southern

Prince Fang Tianding. He has more than seventy thousand troops, twenty-four generals and four marshals, twenty-eight commanders in all. The two senior ones are very brave. One is a monk from Shezhou often called Tathagata, Precious Light, whose religious name is Original Enlightenment. His weapon is a big staff made of solid steel that must weigh over fifty catties. He is held to be a religious master. The other is Shi Bao whose chief weapon is a flying hammer that doesn't miss, though he also manages a sword known as the Wind-Slicer, which can cut copper or iron and slice through three layers of armour plate like thin air. There's also another twenty-six officers, all excellent soldiers and very brave. You must not underestimate them."

Song Jiang rewarded Duan Kai for this information and then sent him off to Marshal Zhang at headquarters to put him in the picture. Later this Duan Kai served under Marshal Zhang in the garrison at Suzhou, while Zhang's deputy, Liu Shiguang, took over the garrison at Xiuzhou, and Song Jiang moved his troops forward to Zuiliting and set up camp there.

When Song Jiang feasted his army and held a meeting to discuss the strategy for taking Hangzhou, Mr. Chai stood up and said: "Ever since you saved my life at Gaotang I have remained conscious of the debt I owe you and which I have not yet repaid. I now propose that I should infiltrate Fang La's lair to spy on him. If I am successful, it will be something to recompense the Emperor and also add to your renown. Have I your permission to do this?"

Song Jiang replied delightedly: "If you are prepared to go and beard the villain in his den and find out the lay of the land for us, it will enable us to launch an attack, capture Fang La and hand him over to the authorities. That will be no small service indeed and will bring honour and riches to us all. But I fear this mission may simply be too dangerous."

"I am not afraid of dying. Only it would be good to have the Prodigy as companion. He is someone who knows all the roads and can speak the local patois. In addition he knows how to adapt to circumstances."

Song Jiang said: "How could I refuse? The only problem is that the Prodigy has been posted to the Unicorn's command. We will have to send for him."

In the middle of this discussion, a sentry reported: "The Prodigy is here with a report from the Unicorn."

Song Jiang said excitedly: "This expedition of yours, brother, is bound to be a success! The fact that the Prodigy has just turned up here like this is an excellent omen!"

When the Prodigy had reported and been given food and drink, Song Jiang asked him: "Did you come by land or by water?"

"I came by boat," he answered.

"When the Magic Messenger came back he told us that the attack on Huzhou had started," Song Jiang went on. "How is it going?"

"When he marched from Xuanzhou, the Unicorn divided his army into two columns," the Prodigy replied. "He himself led a thousand cavalry against Huzhou, and killed the usurper's governor and five of his lieutenants. Huzhou capitulated and all the enemy troops were destroyed. A proclamation was issued to reassure the people, a request was sent to Marshal Zhang to secure the city, and I was sent here to report to you. The general's other column of troops was led by Leopard's Head with orders to capture Lone Pine Pass and meet up at Hangzhou. At the time when I left I heard that there had been heavy fighting every day on the road to Lone Pine Pass and they had not managed to take it. The Unicorn was planning to go there himself with the Strategist, leaving Twin Rods in command of the army, to guard Huzhou until someone was sent to take over there and with orders to strengthen the defences and pacify the people, and then proceed to take Deqing and rendezvous at Hangzhou."

"Can you tell me which commanders were detailed to guard Huzhou and take Deqing, and which were sent to attack Lone Pine Pass?" Song Jiang asked. "How many were sent off and how many remained with Twin Rods?"

"There are twenty-three for Lone Pine Pass and nineteen for Huzhou and Deqing. Here is the list," the Prodigy said. "At the time I left they had settled the arrangements and were planning to start the attack soon after."

"It's good that the attack will be on two fronts," Song Jiang said. "But Mr. Chai wants you to go with him on a spying mission to Fang La's den. Are you willing to go?"

"If those are your orders, of course I will go. I shall be delighted to accompany Mr. Chai."

Mr. Chai was well pleased: "I shall go as an unemployed scholar and you can dress as a servant. We'll travel as master and servant, and we'll take a lute, a sword and some books. No one will suspect us. We'll go to the coast and take a boat, travelling via Yuezhou. Then we'll take the small roads to Zhuji, cross the mountains and from there it's no distance to Muzhou."

A day later Mr. Chai and the Prodigy said farewell to Song Jiang, picked up their lute, sword and books and headed for the coast to find a boat. Of this no more.

Now the Professor said to Song Jiang: "On the south of Hangzhou is the Qiantang River, which connects it to the sea. If a number of people sail up from the coast via Redcliff Gorge, tie up on the river bank outside the southern gate and let off rockets and raise signal flags, it will cause panic. Which of you boat commanders would like to give it a try?"

Almost before he finished speaking, the Pilot and the Ruan brothers said: "We'll go!"

Song Jiang said: "On the west side Hangzhou adjoins the West Lake. We'll also want boat commanders for crossing that. You can't all go."

The Professor said: "Why not let the Pilot and Ruan the Seventh go to manage the boats, and the Ape and Yellow Dog go with them." So it was agreed that it should be these four with thirty sailors, taking with them a dozen or so flares and signal flags. They were to head for the coast and find a boat to take them up the Qiantang River.

You know, friends, telling this story is like flinging a handful of sand. When my predecessors recorded the events, they wanted to tell it all, every detail, but you simply can't tell everything at once. But gradually the plot will unfold and you shall know all. For the moment just try to remember the general direction. Later all that is most hidden will be revealed.

After designating his troops Song Jiang returned to Xiuzhou and planned the attack on Hangzhou. Suddenly he heard that an envoy from the capital had arrived with imperial wine to reward the troops. He went with all his officers to receive this gentleman and welcome him to the city. Thanks were expressed and there was a banquet in the envoy's honour to accompany the wine. During these celebrations the envoy mentioned that the Emperor was indisposed and the Medical Council had requested the services of Doctor An Daoquan. He was carrying an order to this effect and had instructions to take Doctor An back with him. Song Jiang dared not refuse. Next day when the celebrations ended arrangements were made to send Doctor An to the capital. Song Jiang and the rest went as far as the three-mile pavilion to see them off and drink a parting cup with them.

Meanwhile the bounty brought by the Emperor's envoy was divided among the leaders and after that they said their farewells, mounted and set off. As it was to be a joint attack by land and water, the boats sailed at the same time and they headed for Hangzhou. When the governor heard he fled to Hangzhou.

Now Fang La's son, Southern Prince Fang Tianding, was holding a meeting in the travelling palace — the site of this is the place we now call Flying Dragon Inn. Under his command he had four generals, all appointed by Fang La. He also had twenty-four senior commanders. That made twenty-eight in all in his garrison. They were all present to discuss the situation.

The Southern Prince said: "Since Song Jiang invaded across the river we have lost three cities to him. Now only Hangzhou remains as a shield for the south. If it meets with disaster, how will we defend Muzhou? Previously the royal astronomer declared that evil stars had invaded the territory of Wu, portending great disasters. It must have meant this bunch. Since they have violated our frontiers, you have a responsibility, all of you, to defend your country to the last drop of your blood. There must be no shirking!"

There was a chorus of reassurance: "Never fear, Sire. We have many excellent soldiers and commanders who have not yet had a proper go at them. Although we have lost a certain amount of territory, that is only because we did not have the right personnel in place. We have heard that Song Jiang and the Unicorn are advancing in three columns to attack Hangzhou. Your Highness and the Marshal should fortify the city, you can make it impregnable. We generals will each lead our troops into the field."

The Southern Prince was greatly encouraged by this and gave orders for the army to advance in three detachments and engage the enemy, leaving only the monk Precious Light to stay with him and guard the city.

Three generals divided the army, each taking one division. This done they were all rewarded and urged to start. Marshal Si Hengfang took one division of troops to relieve Deqing and set off towards Yuhang. We can forget the other two divisions, for we shall now join Song Jiang's army marching towards Linping Mountain, on whose summit they see a red banner flying. Song Jiang sent Colonel Hua and Thunderclap to investigate and at the same time urged the boats and carts to proceed with all haste to Chang'an Landing.

When Colonel Hua and Thunderclap with a thousand cavalry reached the mouth of the pass, they encountered the southern troops under Shi Bao. Two southern commanders riding in front, Wang Ren and Feng Yi, charged the enemy on sight. They thundered forward, lances at the ready. Colonel Hua and Thunderclap formed up their troops and then Thunderclap brandishing his great wolf-tooth's mace took on Feng Yi while Colonel Hua levelled his spear at Wang Ren. Four horses clashed and they fought ten bouts, but no one had the advantage. Colonel Hua and Thunderclap seeing the enemy commanders had reinforcements behind them, shouted out: "We'll take a rest!", turned their horses and returned to their own lines.

Colonel Hua said: "Do not renew this fight, brother. Let us go back to consult the Leader and consider what to do." The rearguard hurriedly turned back to report to the main army. Song Jiang now rode forward with four more leaders: Whiskers, Spearsman, Tamer and Colonel Sun. Feng Yi and Wang Ren again rode forward and shouted abuse: "Do the leaders we defeated not dare come back for more?"

Thunderclap, enraged by this, brandished his mace, gave free rein to his horse and charged Feng Yi. Wang Ren challenged Colonel Hua, but at this moment Spearsman rode forward with levelled spear. He and Colonel Hua made a perfect pair. one with a gold lance the other with a silver lance. Colonel Hua also urged his horse forward in the wake of Spearsman. He grasped his bow and fitted an arrow to it. Before Spearsman and Wang Ren could meet, he took careful aim and released an arrow. It toppled Wang Ren from his horse. At this the southerners lost heart. Feng Yi had a shock when he saw his comrade fall; before he had time to strike a blow he was hit on the head by Thunderclap and fell from his horse. The Song contingent charged and Marshal Shi Bao's forces were overwhelmed and retreated hastily to Look-out Hill, taking up a position near New East Bridge. By now it was getting late and no one had a clear plan, so the southern troops retreated into the city.

Next day Song Jiang passed Look-out Hill and took up a position where he could threaten New East Bridge. He ordered his army to be divided into three units for the attack on Hangzhou. The first of these consisted of infantry under Whiskers and five others, the boat crews under White-Water Dragon, and a contingent of cavalry and foot under Scimitar. The main force was led by Song Jiang and the Professor with seventeen others. The support group was under Skyhawk.

It's either too much or too little, that's the problem. I must now tell how Scimitar, leading the vanguard of the main army reconnoitred as far as New East Bridge, and saw no sign of the southern army. But he was suspicious and after withdrawing from the bridge sent a message back to Song Jiang. Song Jiang sent Magic Messenger with this warning: "We must not go in recklessly. Establish a roster for two of the commanders in turn to lead a patrol."

Colonel Hua and Thunderclap went the first day, Spearsman and Hound the second. This went on for several days — and still no sign of the enemy. One day, when it was again the turn of Spearsman and Hound, they took a dozen cavalrymen and rode as far as the North Gate of the city. They found it open. But when they went through to take a look at the drawbridge, there was a thunder of drums from within and a squadron of cavalry charged out. Spearsman and Hound turned their horses, but a cry went up on a road west of the city and over a hundred horsemen galloped forward. Spearsman fought for his life to break through the attacking cavalry. When he turned to look back he could not see Hound. Later he looked again just in time to see a group of southern officers taking Hound off a prisoner into the city. As he turned again to flee, an arrow struck him in the back of the neck. He galloped on with the arrow still stuck in him, six enemy commanders in pursuit. They came upon Scimitar who delivered him from his pursuers. When Spearsman got back he fainted from loss of blood.

After forcing back the southern commanders, Scimitar hurriedly reported to Song Jiang and told him what had happened. Song Jiang rushed off to look at Spearsman. He was bleeding at mouth, nose and ears and Song Jiang wept and then ordered the army doctor to try to save him. The arrow was pulled out and a special salve applied. Song Jiang ordered the wounded man to be carried down into one of the boats to rest and went to see him there himself. Spearsman lost consciousness four or five times that night, and they knew then that the arrow which had hit him was poisoned. Gazing heavenwards Song Jiang sighed and said: "Doctor An has been taken away from us by the authorities in the capital and now we have no doctor expert enough to save him. Therefore I must lose another of my limbs!" His grief knew no bounds.

The Professor came and implored Song Jiang to return to the camp and take charge of the military situation again and not to let personal grief ruin affairs of state. Song Jiang had Spearsman sent back to Xiuzhou for treatment but it seemed there was no antidote for the poison. He also sent someone off to get news of Hound.

Next day a soldier came and reported: "Hound's head has been stuck on a pole on the battlements at the North Gate of Hangzhou." Later it was learnt that he had been cut to pieces by the Southern Prince. Song Jiang was exceedingly pained by this news. In less than two weeks the news came that Spearsman had died. Overcome by the loss of two more leaders, Song Jiang gave no orders for his army to advance and they remained where they were, blocking the road.

Meanwhile White-Water Dragon and his party had advanced to New North Bridge and taken up a position there. After sending some scouts on to Gutang, deep in the mountains, to reconnoitre the route, he received the report of the two leaders' deaths. He discussed the situation with White Eel: "This road we're on, I reckon the important thing is that it controls the route between Lone Pine Pass, Huzhou and Deqing. If the enemy want to come and go along it and we stand in their way, they can fall on us from both sides. There's only a few of us, we won't be able to make a stand against them. Would it not be better to push on into the Western Mountains and take up a strong position there? The waters of the West Lake are the ideal battlefield for us. And behind the Western Mountains you come down to the West River, so there's a good escape route." He sent a soldier to inform Song Jiang and ask for his instructions. Later on they marched to Peach Garden Ridge, deep within the mountain range and made camp in what is now called Temple of the Holy Mystery. North of the mountains in the gorge of the West River they also set up a smaller camp, in what is now Gutang. A reconnaissance party was sent on to Tangjiawa. That day White Eel said to White-Water Dragon: "The southern army have all withdrawn into Hangzhou. For two weeks we have seen no enemy. How are we ever going to win fame stuck here in these mountains? I'd like to swim the lake and enter the city secretly through the water gate and start a fire as a signal. Then you can bring the army and seize their water gate and send word to the Leader and all three columns of the main army can attack the city together."

"It's a good idea, but I don't see how you will be able to carry it out on your own."

"If I had to give my life in order to repay the Leader for so many years of good treatment, it would not be a lot," said White Eel.

"Don't be in too much of a hurry then. Wait till I have informed the Leader, so he can arrange the back-up troops."

"I shall get going whilst you send the messenger. By the time I reach the city the Leader will know about it."

So that night White Eel took a dagger with a spade-shaped blade and concealed it on his person, and ate and drank his fill. When he reached the shore of the West Lake he looked about and saw blue hills on three sides, the green water of the lake and in the distance the city with its four main gate towers rising above the lake. Those four gates were Embankment Gate, Goldenflood Gate, Brightwave Gate and Lakeside Gate. You see, friends, this Hangzhou was once, before even the days of Song, called Clearwater City and it was under King Qian that it became Hangzhou, capital of the Ninghai commandery. Ten gates were built then: on the east Market Gate and Fodder Bridge Gate; on the south Tidal Gate and the Gate of Encounters; on the west Lakeside Gate, Brightwave Gate, Goldenflood Gate and Embankment Gate; on the north North Gate and Mount Gen Gate. After the Song court moved to the south, the city was further embellished: it became known as City of Flowers, or Peace Capital, and three more gates were added. But in those days, when it was occupied by Fang La, it was still the old city of King Qian. It had a circumference of thirty miles and though not as splendid as it was to become after the Emperor's move south it was exceedingly rich and orderly, the scenery of river and mountains was as beautiful as always and the people flourishing, whence the saying: "Above is Heaven but below we have Suzhou and Hangzhou."

The incomparable beauty of the West Lake in the days of Song is simply impossible to describe. White Eel stood on the shore and gazed for hours. It was a warm spring evening, the waters of the lake were suffused with purple and all around the mountains clustered in folds of kingfisher blue. "I was born on the banks of the Yangtze," White Eel said to himself. "Great winds, huge waves, I have seen all that a million times, but never did I see anything like the beauty of this lake. If I were to die right here, I would become a happy ghost!" So saying he took off his shirt and laid it out on the bridge. He wound a piece of red cloth about his head and wrapped his silk bathing costume around his waist. He donned a garment that left his torso bare and attached a knife. Barefooted he slipped into the water and began to swim along the bottom of the lake.

It was early evening and the moonlight was only faint as White Eel groped his way toward Goldenflood Gate. When he poked his head out of the water to listen, he heard the drum beat announce the hour: it was the last quarter of the first watch, half-past eight. All was quiet outside the walls, not a person to be seen. On the battlements close to the parapet there were four or five sentries. White Eel dived again and waited a while before poking his head out to have another look.

All was quiet on the battlements this time, no one stirring. White Eel made his way along towards the doors of the lock. They were protected by an iron grating. He felt along this and found it covered by a net to which a rope was attached. On the other end of the rope was a bell. The grating was strong and it was impossible to enter the city that way. When he touched the net it pulled the rope and the bell rang on the other end. Immediately there was a hubbub on the city walls. White Eel dived to the bottom and waited. He heard the soldiers come down to examine the net. When they found no one, he heard them say: "Must be a big fish disturbed the net. Must have bumped into it." They poked around for a while but they found nothing so they all went back to sleep.

A little while passed and White Eel heard the drum beat for the third watch, eleven o'clock. He waited till after half-past and then decided the soldiers must all be fast asleep. He swam close to the wall again. It was evidently impossible to enter the city from the water, so he climbed out onto the bank. There was no one to be seen up on the battlements and he decided to climb the wall. But if there was someone watching up there, he thought, he would lose his life. He had better make a test first. He found a clod of earth and threw it at the top of the wall. One of the sentries who was not sleeping gave the alarm and came to look at the water gate again. But he could see nothing moving so he went back up onto the wall and from the look-out scrutinized the surface of the lake. No sign of any boat. Of course all the boats on the West Lake by order of the Southern Prince had been

assembled in the Harbour of Compassion at Brightwave Gate, so there should not be any boats anywhere else.

"What are you making such a fuss about?" the other guards asked the man. "Must be a ghost," he muttered. "We'd better go back to sleep and not upset him!" This is what he said, but in fact he did not go to sleep but remained on watch concealing himself behind the battlements. White Eel waited till the next watch was sounded. All seemed quiet. He stole over to the wall to listen. The drum was silent now. He was still nervous about climbing, so he picked up another clod of earth and threw it. There was no response. He thought to himself: "It's already the fourth watch. If I don't climb this wall before dawn, I won't get another chance."

He was half-way up when he heard a challenge from above. All the guards were alerted. From half-way up the wall he plunged down into the water, hoping to conceal himself by diving. But bows and crossbows on the wall were pouring down a deadly hail of arrows and missiles. Thus did our unhappy hero die, right there in the water at the foot of Goldenflood Gate!

One expects a great fighter will die by the sword;
A watery death is the swimmer's reward.
It's close to the well that the pot gets broken,
Cut out the heroics, or you'll wish you'd not spoken!

Our story now divides. We will speak of Song Jiang who had received White-Water Dragon's report informing him that White Eel was going to enter the city from the water and send a fire signal and had informed the contingent at the east gate of this plan.

That evening Song Jiang was discussing things in his tent with the Professor. In the fourth watch a great tiredness came over him. He dismissed his aides and lay down on a bench to sleep. Suddenly he felt a cold wind. When he sat up to look, the lamp grew dim and he was assailed by an icy draught. As he strained his eyes to see, something appeared, not exactly a person and not exactly a ghost, in a miasma of cold air. This figure was covered in blood. It spoke softly: "I followed you for many years, brother. You treated me always with great generosity. Now my death repays you. I died at Goldenflood Gate, shot by an arrow. I have come to say farewell!"

Song Jiang said: "Can it be White Eel?" Turning to another side he saw three or four others, all covered in blood, though he could not make them out clearly. He cried out in pain, and suddenly awoke. It had all been a dream. Hearing him cry out the guards outside his tent rushed in. Song Jiang said: "Most strange!" He summoned the Professor to interpret his dream.

"You were just very tired, my friend," the Professor said. "What sort of strange dream did you have?"

"There was a current of cold air and I perceived the figure of White Eel covered in blood standing just here. He said 'I followed you for many years and you always treated me kindly. Now I have laid down my life for you. I died at Goldenflood Gate, shot by an arrow, and I have come to say farewell.' When I turned I saw three or four others also covered in blood, but I couldn't make out who they were. Then I woke up crying."

The Professor said: "Earlier the White-Water Dragon told you White Eel was going to cross the lake to enter the city and start a fire. That must have been on your mind, that's why you had this nightmare."

"I can't help thinking that White Eel is such a clever person, but yet there might be something quite beyond his control that has caused his death."

"To reach the city from the West Lake must be a most dangerous undertaking. I fear he could indeed have lost his life. It could be why his ghost came to visit your dream."

"Who are those others then?" said Song Jiang.

He and the Professor discussed it but came to no conclusions. They sat and waited for dawn. There was no sign of activity in the city and they began to get over their fears. At noon a messenger arrived from White-Water Dragon and told them: "White Eel tried to get into the city by Goldenflood Gate and was hit by an arrow. He died in the water and now his head is stuck on a pole over the West Lake as an example to the people."

Song Jiang was so overcome by grief at this news that he fainted. The Professor and the others were also extremely upset.

White Eel was such a good person and everyone loved him dearly.

Song Jiang said: "Had it been my father and mother the loss could not have been more painful. This news has pierced my heart."

The others tried to comfort him. "You must keep in mind our mission. You must not let your feelings get the better of you."

"I must go myself to the lakeside to mourn him."

The Professor warned: "You must not put yourself in danger. If the enemy hear of it they will attack."

Song Jiang said: "I know what to do."

He sent Iron Ox, Pluto, Eight-Armed Ogre and Winged Ghost with five hundred infantry to reconnoitre, while he himself followed with Madcap, Magic Messenger, Demon King and the Flautist and five hundred troops, travelling secretly to White-Water Dragon's camp by small paths through the Western Mountains. They welcomed him and took him to rest in the abbot's quarters of the Temple of the Holy Mystery. He cried a while longer, and then asked the monks to recite sutras and make offerings for the spirit of White Eel. The following evening he told the troops to set up a white funeral banner beside the lake bearing the words: "To commemorate the spirit of our brother, White Eel, bold and righteous commander." This was planted at the waterside while offerings were placed on the Bridge of the Western Mound and Iron Ox was given certain instructions. A watch was set up on the road north where it entered a defile into the mountains, with Demon King, the Flautist and Madcap concealed on either side; Magic Messenger remained with Song Jiang.

As soon as night began to fall, nearly the first watch, Song Jiang donned a white robe and a bronze helmet swathed in white silk for mourning, and made his way down from the mountain with Magic Messenger and half a dozen monks to the Bridge of the Western Mound. The orderlies had lined up offerings of black pig and white lamb and paper money. Lamps and candles were lit and incense was burning. Song Jiang wrote the name of the deceased on the tablet and cast his gaze downward from the bridge as he mourned. Magic Messenger stood a little to one

寧海軍宋江弔孝

side. The monks began to ring bells and chant, calling out the dead man's name and singing his praises and lowering the funeral banners. Then Magic Messenger read the eulogy and Song Jiang poured the libation with his own hands. He wept as he directed his eyes towards the eastern sky.

While Song Jiang was thus mourning, loud shouts were heard from either side and drums sounded simultaneously on the hills north and south. Two fierce forces were racing towards them intent on capturing Song Jiang.

If you want to know how Song Jiang and Magic Messenger dealt with this enemy, you must read the next chapter.

Chapter 115

The ghost of White Eel captures the Southern Prince; Song Jiang takes Ninghai Commandery with a trick!

Now when Song Jiang and Magic Messenger went to perform the ceremony for White Eel on the Bridge of the Western Mound, it was reported to the Southern Prince. He ordered out ten commanders to capture Song Jiang. Their forces were in two columns and each commander had three thousand troops. It was around midnight when the gates opened and the two columns swept out.

At just this moment Song Jiang and Magic Messenger were offering up the wine and burning the paper offerings. They heard a tremendous uproar below the bridge as Demon King and the Flautist on the left and Madcap on the right saw the lights and after lighting their own torches and dividing into two sections charged the enemy forces. When the southern troops saw that they had lost the element of surprise, they tried to turn back. Song Jiang's men harried both groups. One enemy column hurriedly crossed back over the river but were surprised beyond Baoshu Pagoda Mountain by Ruan the Second, Ruan the Fifth and Flagpole, who fell on them with a force of five thousand, cutting off their return route. One enemy commander was captured and another killed in the fighting. As for the other column, they were intercepted at Treaty Bridge by Iron Ox, Pluto, Eight-Armed Ogre and Winged Ghost with five hundred infantry. The two shield-bearers charged into the thick of the fighting, with dancing shields and javelins bared, and quickly accounted for one enemy leader, while Pluto and Iron Ox cut down two more. Most of the southerners died when they fell in the lake and were drowned.

By the time southern reinforcements were sent out from the city, Song Jiang and his army had withdrawn into the mountains. They gathered at the Temple of the Holy Mystery and each man claimed his reward. Between them, they had captured more than five hundred good horses. Song Jiang ordered Madcap, Demon King and the Flautist to join White-Water Dragon and his party in defending the West Lake camp and prepare to attack the city. Taking only Magic Messenger and Iron Ox with him he returned to the camp at Look-out Hill. The Professor welcomed them into the command tent and Song Jiang told him: "With this plan of mine we've killed four of them and captured another, whom we shall send back to Marshal Zhang to be executed."

Song Jiang had not received any news from Lone Pine Pass and Deqing, so he sent Magic Messenger, with instructions to report back as quickly as possible. Within a few days he returned and told Song Jiang that the Unicorn had already captured Lone Pine Pass and would soon have caught up with them. As he listened Song Jiang felt half pleased and half apprehensive. He wanted to know how the commanders had fared. Magic Messenger replied: "My job is just to report on the battle. They gave me a full account and here is the official report. Only please don't get upset."

Song Jiang said: "Are you saying that more of our comrades have been lost? Don't hide anything from me. Tell me the whole truth!"

Magic Messenger said: "When the Unicorn tried to attack Lone Pine Pass he found high mountains on either side with only a single narrow path running between. Their fortress was built right on top and had a group of very tall trees beside it, visible from all around. Below were dense thickets of pines. There were three enemy commanders in the fortress. At first they came down every day and fought with Leopard's Head, until one of them was wounded by Leopard's Head's spear. After that they wouldn't venture forth, but shut themselves up in the fortress. Later on Li Tianrun and four others arrived with reinforcements. They all came down to fight next day and after fifty or sixty bouts the Little Duke killed the leader of the enemy attack with a halberd thrust. After this the enemy retired to the fortress again and would not come out.

"Our troops down below waited for several days. Finally the Unicorn, seeing that the pass was steep and rugged, sent Golden Wings, Redeye, Tiger-Killer and Big Chief to pioneer a route. Li Tianrun, who wanted to avenge his comrade, surprised them, charging down the mountain and killing Big Chief. Tiger-Killer was wounded but got away. But if help had been any slower in coming they would all have been done for. The remaining three were rescued however and brought back to the camp.

"Next day Twin Spears, impatient for revenge, rode to the foot of the pass and hurled insults at the enemy commanders. He was careless: a shot from the mountain hit him in the left arm. When he returned to camp he was unable to hold a spear. A splint was made for the arm and he was determined to go out again next day and have his revenge, but the Unicorn would not allow it. After another day the arm was better and without telling the Unicorn Twin Spears got together with Hotshot and the two of them went off without horses to climb the mountain on foot. On top of the pass Li Tianrun and another challenged them. Twin Spears was determined to capture Li and went forward wielding his two spears. Li met him with a long lance and they fought ten bouts. Twin Spears was full of courage but his left hand could not hold the spear steady and he was forced to give ground. As Li chased after him down the mountain he was attacked by Hotshot with a spear. He dodged behind a pine tree and Hotshot's spear stuck in the tree. He tried to pull it out but it was stuck fast and wouldn't budge and Li's spear caught him and knocked him to the ground. Twin Spears saw him fall and rushed in with his two spears but another enemy commander came up from behind and cut Twin Spears in two with a sweep of his sword. The Unicorn heard what was going on and rushed to the rescue but by this time the enemy had retreated up the pass and there was nothing those below could do.

"Finally Blackface and Auntie Gu disguised themselves as refugees and travelled deep into the mountains. They discovered a small path and led the Executioner, Spots, the Flea and the

Daytime Rat up to the summit by this route. By midnight they had groped their way to the top and lit a beacon there. Realizing Song troops had infiltrated the pass the enemy abandoned their fortress and fled. When the Unicorn sent troops up the mountain, Blackface and Auntie Gu captured one of the original three commanders, the Executioner and Spots another and the Flea and the Daytime Rat the third. These three were all sent off later to Marshal Zhang at headquarters. The bodies of Twin Spears, Hotshot and Big Chief were recovered and buried there on the mountain. Some five miles beyond the pass the Unicorn caught up with the enemy and engaged them. He fought more than thirty bouts with Li and eventually killed him. The three remaining commanders fought on reluctantly and broke off as soon as they had a chance.

"The Unicorn will be here very soon," Magic Messenger ended by saying. "If you have doubts about any of this, General, you can read it all in the written report."

Song Jiang looked at the report but it did nothing to allay his grief. His tears fell abundantly.

The Professor said: "Since the Unicorn has won, we can now press home our attack. We will defeat the southern army here and then move to reinforce Twin Rods in Huzhou."

Song Jiang said: "You're right!" and ordered Iron Ox, Pluto, Eight-Armed Ogre and Winged Ghost to take three thousand infantry and approach by the mountain route. Iron Ox went off pleased as punch. Meanwhile Song Jiang's force attacked on the east. He ordered Whiskers and his original five thousand cavalry to advance from the village along the Tangzhen road to outside Market Gate and secure the eastern approach. In those days the road east along the river was a mass of houses and cottages and wayside inns and the area beyond the city a vast expanse of fields and plots of land. When they came within range of the city the forces deployed, with Monk out in front. Staff at the slope, he swaggered up to the walls and shouted: "You fucking bastards, come out and fight!"

When those in the city saw that it was a monk who was thus challenging them they reported it at once to the palace. Learning that it was a monk who wanted to fight Precious Light stood up and petitioned the Prince as follows: "I have heard that on Mount Liang they have this monk called Lu Zhishen who fights with a steel staff. I beg Your Majesty to come to the eastern wall and watch me trade a few blows with him!"

The Southern Prince was delighted and ordered eight bold commanders together with Marshal Shi Bao to go to the wall near Market Gate to watch the master fight. So there were the Prince and the Marshal sitting on the watchtower with the eight commanders on either side of them to see Precious Light show off his fighting skill. This was an accomplished fellow:

> *He is dressed in a cassock of fiery red, his waist bound with a black and gold sash, a chaplet all of precious stones hanging at his side; his shoes are deerskin slippers with nine eyelets, his breast is protected by a special corselet fashioned from animal skins and he wields a monk's staff of solid steel.*

The gates opened and the drawbridge was lowered and Precious Light rushed out with five hundred swordsmen on foot.

"So the southerners have got a bald fellow too!" said Monk. "I'll make the bastard taste a few hundred blows of my staff!" Wasting no time on words, he charged forward whirling his staff. Precious Light likewise advanced to meet him. As the two wielded their staves, what a contest!

> *Profound Wisdom is on the rampage, no room in that heart for benevolence; Precious Light is in a passion, no thought of mercy enters in there! Does the one respect the Buddha's law? Not likely! His thoughts are all of killing people at the dark of the moon. Does the other study the Scriptures? Not he! His entertainment is burning things down in a raging storm. The one, were he present at the meeting on the Holy Mount, would scorn the Buddha for twiddling his thumbs on the waterlily terrace; the other, were he standing before the Hall of the Law would snatch his magic weapon from the Guardian of Truth! One throughout his life has paid no heed to the doctrine of forgiveness; the other in all his days has found no time to acquaint himself with Holy Writ!*

They fought fifty bouts and neither had the advantage. Up in the watchtower the Southern Prince said to Marshal Shi Bao, commander of his army: "I've heard what they say about Mount Liang's Flowery Monk Lu Zhishen, but it didn't occur to me he could be as fantastic as this. His reputation does not lie. They've been fighting a long time, and he has given away nothing to our master, Precious Light!"

The Marshal said: "I'm absolutely amazed too. I've never seen fighting like this before!"

At this moment a messenger announced: "There's another enemy force at North Gate."

The Marshal hurried off to see. Meanwhile in the Song ranks Pilgrim had seen Monk could not get the better of his adversary and feared a mishap. Unable to restrain himself he rushed forward whirling his two swords and attacked Precious Light, who, seeing it was two against one, put up his staff and retreated to the city.

As Pilgrim impetuously rushed after Precious Light, another enemy leader appeared on a prancing charger and bore down on him with levelled lance. They met at the drawbridge, where Pilgrim dodged and, throwing away one of his swords, grasped the shaft of his opponent's lance, dragged both weapon and man to the ground and with a single sword blow split his skull. Monk rushed in to lend a hand and the Prince hurriedly ordered the drawbridge raised, after calling his troops back into the city. Whiskers likewise withdrew his army to the camp three miles out and sent a report to Song Jiang.

That same day Song Jiang marched to North Gate to issue a challenge. Marshal Shi Bao took up his mace and mounted. With his sword in hand he had the gates opened and rode out to meet his foe. On the Song side Scimitar responded. When they had fought more than twenty bouts, Shi Bao turned his horse and galloped off. Scimitar reined in his horse and returned to his own ranks.

"Why did you not pursue him?" Song Jiang asked.

Scimitar replied: "Shi Bao's skill is every bit as great as mine. If he broke off the fight, it must be some trick."

The Professor said: "It's like Duan Kai said. 'This fellow is expert with the flying hammer. He deliberately turns his horse and pretends to be defeated to lure you on into a remote spot."

Song Jiang said: "If you'd followed him you'd surely have met disaster. Let us call in our forces and return to camp." He also sent someone to reward Pilgrim.

Meanwhile Iron Ox and his comrades with their infantry had gone to reinforce the Unicorn and on a narrow mountain path ran into Zhang Jian and his defeated army. They made a vigorous attack. Yao Yi was killed in the fighting. The two Zhangs got away and fled up the mountain by the same narrow path. Here they met the Unicorn and fierce fighting ensued till they fled by a narrow path into the depths of the mountain range. They were hotly pursued and had to abandon their horses and flee downhill. Suddenly from a thicket of low bamboo two warriors emerged carrying steel tridents. Before the Zhangs could offer any resistance they were stabbed with the tridents and carried off captive down the mountain. Their captors were of course Snake and Scorpion.

This capture delighted the Unicorn. He now joined forces with Iron Ox and his party. A meeting of all the leaders was held and they went to the main camp on Look-out Hill to see Song Jiang. When the loss of Twin Spears, Hotshot and Big Chief was recounted, all were deeply affected.

When all the leaders had paid their respects to Song Jiang, the armies were combined and marched back to camp. Next day Zhang Jian was sent off to Marshal Zhang at headquarters where he was executed and his head displayed as an example. Zhang Tao was executed right there in the camp, his heart and liver cut out and offered to the spirits of Twin Spears, Hotshot and Big Chief, as was proper.

Song Jiang and the Professor decided as follows: to start with, the Unicorn would be asked to march his army to Deqing in support of Twin Rods and his group. When they had joined up they would make plans to capture the town.

With these orders, the Unicorn gave his army orders to march, heading for Fengkou. There they ran into Si Hengfang, sent by the Southern Prince to relieve Deqing and now in retreat. The Unicorn launched a murderous attack and Si Hengfang fell in the water and was drowned. The rest of his force scattered and ran.

After the Unicorn had met up with Twin Rods, they joined forces and repaired to the main camp at Pavilion Mountain, where they saw Song Jiang and a general meeting was held at which everyone gave their opinion. Now that both armies had reached Hangzhou, Song Jiang left it to Marshal Zhang and his appointees to take over the administration of Xuanzhou, Huzhou, Lone Pine Pass and so on and to post notices everywhere reassuring the people. Of this no more.

Song Jiang had noticed that Sergeant Lei and Stripes were absent from Twin Rods' force. Twin Rods told how Sergeant Lei had fought thirty bouts with Si Hengfang at the south gate of Deqing and been chopped from his horse, and how when Stripes was pursuing Huang Ai across the river, horse and man had fallen in and been stabbed to death by the southern troops. One enemy commander had been killed by a blow of Hasty's axe, and two more had been taken alive. Si Hengfang as we know had been driven into the river and drowned. Only one southern commander had managed to flee with his troops and his whereabouts were not known.

Song Jiang's tears flowed freely when he heard they had lost two more comrades. He said to the others: "When White Eel appeared to me in a dream the other day, I saw three or four on his right covered with blood and in torn clothing. Those who appeared to me must have been Twin Spears, Hotshot, Big Chief, Sergeant Lei and Stripes, who are now of the company of ghosts. If I take Hangzhou and conquer the Ninghai Commandery, I shall ask many monks to perform a ceremony."

The two latest prisoners were sent to Marshal Zhang for execution. Of this no more.

That day Song Jiang had oxen and horses killed to feast the armies.

Next day Song Jiang made his plans with the Professor and the forces were divided up as follows for the offensive on Hangzhou.

The Unicorn and twelve others to attack Tidal Gate.

Colonel Hua and fourteen others to attack Mount Gen Gate.

The Unstoppable and eleven others to proceed to the West Lake camp, and join White-Water Dragon and his men in the attack on Lakeside Gate.

Blackface and eight others to proceed to the camp on the east and assist Whiskers in attacking Market Gate and Fodder Bridge. Eight leaders from the eastern camp, including Skyhawk, to liaise with the other forces.

The commander-in-chief to take twenty-one leaders and attack down the road to North Gate.

This was Song Jiang's plan of action for putting all the gates under pressure at the same time.

Song Jiang led his large force down the highway to North Gate, halted under the walls and delivered his challenge. Drums and gongs sounded on the battlements, the gate opened, the drawbridge was lowered, and Marshal Shi Bao rode out to take up the challenge. On Song Jiang's side, Hasty, impetuous as ever, brandished his axe and without more ado flew at Shi Bao. The horses clashed, the warriors battled furiously, but before ten bouts were up Shi Bao dodged aside and galloped off. Hasty gave chase. Scimitar hurriedly shouted to him not to follow, but too late! Hasty received a blow to the head that knocked him from his horse. Redeye raced to the rescue but Shi Bao was there too and before Redeye could strike a blow Shi Bao's sword had cut him in two. The monk, Precious Light, charged out of the city with several bold commanders, and the Song force was routed and fled northwards.

At this point, however, Colonel Hua and Thunderclap charged from the flank and drove the southern troops back, enabling Song Jiang to retreat to his camp. Elated by his victory, Shi Bao returned in triumph to the city.

Song Jiang's army withdrew to the camp on Look-out Hill to recover. The loss of two more leaders, Hasty and Redeye, weighed heavily on Song Jiang's heart as he sat in his tent. "If they have such redoubtable commanders," the Professor said, "we can win only by guile, not in a direct confrontation."

"When we keep losing men and commanders like this," Song Jiang said, "what chance do we have of defeating them?"

The Professor said: "When we have regrouped, attack North Gate again. They are sure to come out to fight. We must feign defeat and lure them as far away as possible. Then we'll fire a signal and all the units outside the gates will attack together. As soon as our troops break through one of the gates they will start fires. This will cause confusion and panic and victory will be ours."

Song Jiang sent out Magic Messenger to inform everyone of this plan.

Next day Song Jiang sent Scimitar with some troops to North Gate to issue a challenge. Drums sounded on the battlements and Shi Bao rode out and engaged him. Before they completed ten bouts Scimitar hurriedly withdrew. Shi Bao's troops gave chase. Thunderer fired the signal. As it went off, every unit of the Song army gave a great shout and all charged forward together.

When the Unicorn with Leopard's Head and the others attacked Tidal Gate they found it open, with the drawbridge lowered. Eager to gain the first honours, the Red-Haired Devil urged on his horse and sword in hand charged into the city. Those on the battlements immediately cut the rope with an axe and the portcullis fell. That was the end of the unfortunate Red-Haired Devil! Both horse and man died there in the gateway. You see, when King Qian built Hangzhou as his capital he installed three kinds of gate: a portcullis on the outside, a heavy gate with two leaves of steel in the middle, and a wooden grill inside. When the Red-Haired Devil rushed into the gateway the portcullis above him was quickly dropped. As the enemy had troops concealed on either side, he didn't stand a chance!

When they saw what had happened, Leopard's Head and Twin Rods withdrew to the camp and reported to the Unicorn. The attacks on all the gates had failed — all had been repulsed. A messenger was sent to inform Song Jiang in the main camp. On hearing that the Red-Haired Devil had died, Song Jiang wept bitterly: "He should not have died, this comrade of ours. He was present at the very first gathering at Yuncheng, he followed Chao

Gai to Mount Liang; he lived through all those years of hardship and never had time to enjoy the fruits. He came safe through hundreds of battles, he never let his spirit be cowed. Whoever would have thought that he was going to die here today!"

The Professor said: "This plan was a failure, it was not the right way to go. It brought about the death of a comrade. Recall all units and let us make another plan."

Song Jiang was on fire, desperate to be revenged and appease his anger. His sighs were endless. Then Iron Ox, his lieutenant, said: "Rest easy, brother. Tomorrow I will go with Pluto, Eight-Armed Ogre and Winged Ghost and by hook or by crook we will grab that bastard Shi Bao!"

Song Jiang said: "He's a highly skilled fighter. How do you think you'll even get near him?"

Iron Ox said: "Don't you believe it. I'll capture him tomorrow, or I will never see you again."

"Just be careful then. Don't treat it lightly!"

Iron Ox went back to his tent. He poured himself a big bowl of wine, got a big plate of meat, and invited the other three in to drink with him. "The four of us always fight together. Today I boasted in front of the Leader that we will capture that bastard Shi Bao tomorrow. I hope you're game for it."

Pluto said: "The Leader is forever sending the cavalry in first, this time let us make sure that we go first and let us go forward with determination to capture Shi Bao. We four will win a share of glory for ourselves!"

Early next morning, after drinking themselves tipsy, they took up their arms and were ready to set out after asking the commander-in-chief to come and see them fight. Song Jiang saw they were half drunk and said: "This isn't a game. Don't play with your lives!"

"Do not patronize us, brother," said Iron Ox.

Song Jiang said: "I only hope your deeds live up to your words!"

Song Jiang mounted and rode with Scimitar, Golden Wings, Little Duke and the Halberdier to the city's North Gate. Drums rolled, flags waved as he issued the challenge. Iron Ox, desperately impatient, stood in front of his horse gripping his axes. Pluto was there with his sword, staring ahead with bulging eyes, eager for the fray. Eight-Armed Ogre and Winged Ghost, their round shields harbouring twenty-four javelins, stood on either side, spears at the ready.

Now drums and gongs sounded on the battlements and Marshal Shi Bao on a horse yellow as a melon, grasping Wind-Slicer, rode forth with two of his leaders to face them. The moment they appeared, Iron Ox, who feared nothing on heaven or earth, gave a terrible roar and with his companions rushed at Shi Bao's horse. Shi Bao raised Wind-Slicer to meet them and immediately they came to grips. Iron Ox swung his axes and cut the horse's legs from under him. Shi Bao leapt down and took refuge among a group of his own cavalry. Pluto had swept one of the lieutenants from his horse with a sword cut. The two shield-bearers let fly their darts, which filled the air like a shoal of leaping fishes, or a swarm of driven leaves.

When Song Jiang led his cavalry up to the walls, they were met with a shower of wooden blocks and ballista missiles from the walls. Fearing casualties he hurriedly ordered them to withdraw. Unfortunately Pluto had already rushed the gate. Song Jiang could only lament. Shi Bao, already safe inside the walls of his city, saw Pluto rush in and with a sideways swipe cut him in two. Eight-Armed Ogre and Winged Ghost gave Iron Ox cover as they hastily retreated. The loss of Pluto left Song Jiang even more heavy-hearted when they returned to camp. Iron Ox was also weeping when he got back.

The Professor said: "This plan was no good. Although we've killed one of theirs, we've also lost Iron Ox's second-in-command."

Whilst they were thus reflecting on their woes, Snake and Scorpion came in to report: "Scorpion and I reconnoitred to within six or seven miles of the South Gate," Snake said. "At a place called Grassy Village, we found a string of several dozen boats tied up on the river bank. We went and asked what they were. They turned out to be transports provided by Judge Yuan of Fuyang. I was about to kill the crew, but they began to plead with me. 'We are all loyal citizens of Song,' they said to me. 'We were drafted by Fang La. Anyone who resisted had all their family killed. Now the imperial army has come to deal with him, we have been hoping that we could live in peace again. We did not expect to run into more trouble!' After that I felt sorry for them and didn't want to kill him. 'What are you doing here?' I asked Judge Yuan. He said he had been told by the Southern Prince to go round every district and commandeer fifty thousand catties of rice. So far he'd managed to get hold of five thousand and was on his way to hand it in but when he got that far he heard the city was invested by a Song army and dared not proceed. So he'd tied up there. When I'd found all this out, I came to tell you."

The Professor was excited: "It's a heaven-sent opportunity. Those transports will be the making of us. The commander-in chief must write out the orders for you two brothers to lead the party and take along with you the artillery chief Thunderer, and fifteen others. Disguise yourselves as sailors and don't speak. Mix in with the boat crews and when you get inside the city you can let off signal rockets. We will arrange for the troops to back you up."

Snake and Scorpion called Judge Yuan ashore and told him what the Professor wanted. "If you are loyal citizens you will support this plan," they told him. "If the business succeeds you're sure to be well rewarded." The boat commander had to agree, of course, and the party of leaders went aboard. The crews were retained for general duties but their uniforms were taken from them and given to Short-Arse, Blackface and the Gardener so they could be disguised as sailors. Steelbright, Sister Sun and Auntie Gu dressed as boatwomen and the ordinary soldiers took on the role of rowers. They hid their weapons in the holds.

All the boats were now brought in close to the bank, while units of the besieging Song army remained in the offing. The boat commander went ashore and Snake, Scorpion and the other so-called sailors went up to the city gate and called out. The guards questioned them closely and then reported to the palace. On the orders of the Southern Prince, one of the commanders opened the city gate and went down to the river to inspect the boats. When he reported back, the Prince sent six commanders

宋江智取寧海軍

and ten thousand troops to keep guard on the northeast while the boats were unloaded and the grain transported into the city.

During this operation the Song leaders mixed with the sailors carrying grain and the women warriors followed them. In no time at all the five thousand catties of foodstuff had been moved inside. The six southern commanders marched their men back into the city. The Song army had renewed its siege and was positioned about a mile from the walls. That evening in the second watch Thunderer took out nine "mother" shells, went to the top of Mount Wu and let them off. All the leaders lit torches and began starting fires everywhere.

In a little while the city was seething with rumours: no one knew for sure how many of the enemy were inside the walls. When the news reached the Southern Prince in his palace he was in a panic. He put on armour hastily and mounted his horse. The guards on all the gates had fled. The Song forces were full of energy, every man eager to do his best to capture the city.

Meanwhile in the mountains west of the city White-Water Dragon and his group had got their orders and were advancing. They seized boats and attacked from the lake, coming ashore at Goldenflood Gate. The leaders each separately attacked the water gates.

Green-Eyes and Madcap were the first to climb the walls. All evening there was confused fighting in the city, only the southern gates were not surrounded and it was from here that the desperate rebel army fled. The Southern Prince had ridden out to find his troops but could find none, so with only a few infantry he too exited through the South Gate, scurrying off like a dog kicked out of the house, darting away like a fish escaped from the net.

The Southern Prince continued till he reached Five-Cloud Mountain, where a man emerged stark naked from the river with a sword between his teeth and bounded onto the bank. The Prince beat his horse wildly, desperate to get away from this terrifying sight. The horse, strange to relate, refused to move, beat it as he might. It was as if there were someone holding its bridle.

The strange apparition bore down on them and dragged the Prince from the horse's back. With one blow he cut off the Prince's head. Then he sprang onto the horse and head in one hand and sword in the other galloped off to Hangzhou.

Leopard's Head and Twin Rods, as they were marching their troops toward Six Harmonies Pagoda, happened to run into this man and thought they recognized him as the Pilot. It was a big surprise. "How did you get here, brother?" Twin Rods asked. The man gave no answer but galloped straight on into the city. Song Jiang with his army had already entered the city and he had taken over the Southern Prince's palace as his seat of government, so it was guarded by his men. They all had a shock when the Pilot galloped in. The horseman rode right up to Song Jiang, then slid from the saddle and threw the head and the sword on the floor. He kowtowed twice and began to weep. Song Jiang hastily embraced him and said: "How did you get here, brother? And where is Ruan the Seventh?"

"I am not the Pilot," the other answered.

"If you're not the Pilot who are you?"

"I am White Eel. Because I was killed by arrows outside Goldenflood Gate, my spirit is obliged to linger there in the water. By the grace of the West Lake's Dragon Lord of Rain and Thunder I have received the title of 'Lord of Splendour' and are permitted to reside in the Dragon Palace. Now that you have captured the city, I, as a spirit, have dealt with the Southern Prince. When I was following him out of the city last night, I saw my elder brother, the Pilot, in the river and borrowed from him his corporeal shell. I came out onto the bank and killed this villain at the foot of Five-Cloud Mountain. Then I came straight back to see you." The moment he finished speaking he collapsed on the ground. Song Jiang himself raised him up. When he slowly opened his eyes and saw Song Jiang and the others, the forest of weapons all around him, the thickets of soldiers, he said: "Am I really in the underworld with my brother White Eel?"

Song Jiang said, weeping: "Just now you lent your body to your brother and he killed the villain Prince Fang Tianding. You are not dead. We are all living men, you can touch us and feel us."

"Are you telling me that my brother is dead?"

"Your brother wanted to swim through the West Lake and enter the city by the water gate, to start a fire. Unfortunately he was spotted trying to climb the walls at Goldenflood Gate and he died there riddled with arrows."

With a wail of "My brother!" the Pilot fell to the ground unconscious. When they examined him, his limbs were lifeless, his eyes clouded, and his seven spirits and three souls had drifted far far away.

Indeed, as they say:

You won't escape the hand of Fate;
The Reaper's always on your trail!

If you want to hear how the Pilot fared after fainting from grief, you must read the next chapter.

Chapter 116

The route to Shezhou falls to the Unicorn; Song Jiang has a fight at Black Dragon Ridge!

When the Pilot heard that his younger brother, White Eel, was dead, he fainted from grief and remained unconscious for a long time. When he finally revived, Song Jiang said: "Take him to the tent to rest. We'll ask him later for his account of things on the coast."

Song Jiang got Sterling and the Magic Calculator to write out a list of everyone's achievements and a general assembly was called for nine o'clock. The White-Water Dragon and Madcap had taken one enemy commander prisoner, the three women warriors another, Leopard's Head's serpent lance had killed one, Snake and Scorpion had accounted for another, Marshal Shi Bao and four others got away. Song Jiang issued a proclamation to reassure the people, rewarded the army, and sent the two prisoners to Marshal Zhang at headquarters to be publicly beheaded. Judge Yuan, the bearer of tribute who had collaborated with them, was recommended for the post of magistrate at Fuyang and referred to Marshal Zhang for the appropriate letter of appointment. Of this no more.

While the leaders were resting in the city, an aide announced: "Ruan the Seventh has just arrived by river."

When Song Jiang summoned him to his tent and questioned him, he said: "I went down the coast with the Pilot, Ape, Yellow Dog and the sailors and we found a boat which took us beyond Haiyan. We were planning to make our way into the River Qiantang. Unluckily for us the wind and current were unfavourable and drove us out to sea. As we were trying to get back a storm wrecked our boat and we all had to swim for it. Since Ape and Yellow Dog didn't know how to swim, they drowned. With the sailors it was every man for himself, and they were dispersed in all directions. As for me, I swam towards the river mouth, but when I got to Redcliff Strait the current carried me towards Half-Tomb Hill. As I was trying to get back I saw the Pilot in the water near Five-Cloud Hill, but then I lost sight of him again. Yesterday evening I saw fires in the city and heard a string of explosions and I guessed you must be fighting in Hangzhou, so I came here along the river. Did the Pilot make it back?"

Song Jiang told him about the Pilot and then sent him to see his brothers. He put Ruan the Seventh in charge of the boats again and sent the water-borne forces back to the river to get their boats ready for an attack on Muzhou. Remembering how White Eel's spirit had appeared to him, he went to the bank of the West Lake outside Goldenflood Gate. There he had a temple built dedicated to the Lord of Splendour and made an offering there himself. Later, after Fang La was subdued and Song Jiang, who had earned much credit at court, reported these events on his return to the capital, the Emperor issued an edict conferring on White Eel the posthumous title of Commander of Splendour and sacrifices were made to him at the temple in Hangzhou.

But to return to Song Jiang in the palace: the thought of having lost so many leaders since crossing the river made him exceedingly gloomy. He went accordingly to the Temple of Mercy to arrange for the land and sea battle to be commemorated in a memorial service lasting seven days and nights, with a distribution of food for souls in the underworld and sacrifices offered up for their speedy release and the setting up of votive tablets. After the religious observances, the Southern Prince's palace was razed to the ground and all the valuables distributed among the leaders. Once calm had been restored in Hangzhou a celebratory banquet was held. After that Song Jiang had lengthy discussions with the Professor as to the best way to attack Muzhou.

Now, in the middle of the fourth month, they suddenly heard that General Liu Guangshi had arrived with an envoy from the capital. Song Jiang and his commanders went to meet them outside North Gate and welcome them into the city. They all went to the palace for the reading of an edict: "In view of the fact that Marshal Song Jiang, Commander-in-Chief of the expeditionary force, and his lieutenants have achieved outstanding successes against the rebel Fang La, we have awarded thirty-five bottles of imperial wine and thirty-five suits of cotton clothing to the senior commanders. The others will receive rolls of silk." The court of course only knew that Taoist Gongsun was absent from the force that crossed the river to fight Fang La, they did not know about the loss of the other leaders. When Song Jiang looked at those thirty-five robes and bottles he was deeply moved and could not hold back his tears. When the envoy questioned him about it, he explained about the losses and the envoy said: "The court of course knew nothing of all this. When I go back I shall have to submit a report."

A banquet was held for the envoy, hosted by General Liu, with the other commanders all seated according to their rank. The imperial wine was presented and all drank of it. The royal gifts intended for those leaders who had died were set aside and offered up to their spirits the next day. Song Jiang also set aside a bottle of wine and a suit of clothing for the spirit of White Eel. He went to the shrine to make the offering and dressed the clay effigy of the dead man in the gift robes. The envoy remained a few days longer and then returned to the capital.

Gradually the days slipped by and soon several weeks had passed. Marshal Zhang wrote urging the commander-in-chief to renew the campaign. Song Jiang and the Professor summoned the Unicorn for a meeting. "One lot has to go to Muzhou, advancing along the river to the viper's nest; another has to go to Shezhou by way of the trail over Sundance Pass. We now need to divide the forces between us for the attack. Which route would you like?"

The Unicorn said: "You are my superior and I am entirely at your orders. It is no business of mine to choose."

Song Jiang said: "All the same, we had better draw lots and see what is heaven's will." He had the two lists of leaders drawn up and then the place names were written on two papers. They burnt incense and prayed and then each drew one of the papers.

盧俊義分兵歙州道

Song Jiang drew Muzhou and the Unicorn drew Shezhou. Song Jiang said: "Fang La's headquarters is at Bangyuan Gap in Clearwater district. If you take Shezhou, you can make camp there and send word to let me know and then we will fix the day for a joint attack on the robber's den."

The Unicorn asked Song Jiang to apportion the troops. This done, the Unicorn, with a total of twenty-nine leaders and thirty thousand troops, took leave of General Liu, said goodbye to Song Jiang, and headed for the mountains beyond Hangzhou. The hard part of the journey began after Lin'an.

Meanwhile Song Jiang's army, after the boats had been made ready, the troops prepared and the leaders and men divided up, set out with waving banners on the allotted day for a joint attack by land and water, boats and cavalry giving each other mutual support.

At this time the plague struck in Hangzhou and several leaders were infected. These were the Pilot, Unstoppable, Comet, Crocodile, Panther and the Daytime Rat. Since they showed no sign of recovery, they could not join the attack, and the Irrepressible and Smiler were detailed to look after them. That meant eight leaders in all were left in Hangzhou. The rest accompanied Song Jiang on the campaign against Muzhou, thirty-seven of them, making their way along the river towards Fuyang.

We shall say no more of the advance of these two armies, but turn to Mr. Chai and the Prodigy, who after leaving them in Xiuzhou, had taken a boat in Haiyan, travelled via Yuezhou to Zhuji, crossed the river Yupu and arrived at the border of Muzhou.

When the border guards stopped them, Mr. Chai said: "I am a scholar from the central plains. I am conversant with heavenly geography and an expert in Yin and Yang. I know the six stations of wind and clouds and can analyse the heavenly bodies, I have a thorough knowledge of the nine schools and three religions, nothing is hidden from me. I saw from afar some form of heavenly emanation in the regions south of the river, that is why I come here. Why do you obstruct my path?"

Mr. Chai's speech seemed so extraordinary to them that the border guards asked him who he was. "My name is Ke Yin," he replied. "Master and servant we are and we come with none but friendly intentions."

The guard commander detained him and sent someone to inform the deputy chief minister, Zu Shiyuan. and three other important officials, namely Councillor Shen Shou, Secretary Huan Yi and Marshal Tan Gao. Someone was accordingly sent to take Mr. Chai to Muzhou. After the exchange of courtesies, Mr. Chai's eloquence, allied to his striking appearance, won them over completely. The minister was delighted with him and told Secretary Huan Yi to take him to Clearwater for an audience with the Prince. Fang La, you see, had established temporary offices in both Muzhou and Shezhou, but his central administration was at a place called Bangyuan Gap, in the district of Clearwater.

Mr. Chai and the Prodigy then accompanied Secretary Huan Yi to the Prince's citadel at Clearwater where they were first received by Chief Minister Lou, who was highly impressed by Mr. Chai's lofty language and powers of expression, and entertained him officially. The fact that the two men talked so well and were so educated and cultured, was already strongly in their favour. This Chief Minister Lou had once been a teacher, and though his knowledge was far from profound, Mr. Chai's eloquence impressed him enormously.

The following day at dawn the courtiers were drawn up waiting for Fang La to make his entrance, in the inner rank the wives, concubines and female attendants, in the outer rank four ministers and nine deputy ministers, as well as all the civil and military officials, followed by two ranks of officials, mace-bearers and courtiers. The Chief Minister now stepped forward and declared: "The Central Plain is the home of Confucius. Today we are honoured with the presence of a scholar named Ke Yin, who is conversant with both literature and warfare. He has abundant knowledge and is skilled in interpreting heaven and earth. He can identify six kinds of weather and explain heavenly portents, knows the three religions and nine schools, and of the one hundred schools of philosophy there is not one he is not familiar with. He has followed some heavenly sign here and is waiting outside. He offers himself to the service of our sovereign."

Fang La said: "Since this scholar has come to us, let him present himself at court in white robes."

The court usher relayed this order to Mr. Chai and escorted him into the court. Mr. Chai kowtowed and then stood up and saluted the Prince. He advanced to stand in front of the curtain.

Fang La recognized this man as someone outstanding, with his air of a true son and grandson of dragons, and was pretty well won over from the start. "You say you have followed a sign here," he said. "Explain yourself."

"My humble abode is in the Central Plain. I am an orphan. I studied by myself. I learnt the secret mysteries discovered by preceding scholars and the mysteries known to ancestral teachers. Recently I was making observations of the night sky and I saw a star of outstanding brilliance standing over the eastern regions of this land of Wu. I followed it here to its source, not shrinking from the trials of a long journey. When I arrived south of the river, I saw a trail of five-coloured imperial vapour emanating from Muzhou. Now it is given me to contemplate this august countenance, this truly lordly air, that shines more brightly than the sun and corresponds exactly to what the signs foretold. I can make no secret of my joy!" Having said this he kowtowed again.

Fang La said: "Although I rule over part of the southeast, at present Song Jiang has robbed me of some of my cities. He is advancing on us here. What should we do?"

Mr. Chai said: "In olden days they had a saying, 'Easily gained is easily lost, hard won means hard to lose.' This southeastern kingdom of Your Majesty's since its foundation has forged ahead like a mat unrolling, acquiring ever more districts. Although at present Song Jiang has seized some of these districts, fortune will soon turn again in your favour. One day not only the southeast but also the Central Plain will belong to Your Majesty."

This was all music to Fang La's ears. He offered Mr. Chai a brocade cushion to sit on, regaled him with a banquet and made him one of his ministers. From now on Mr. Chai was with the Prince every day and never failed to find flattering words for him. Within a couple of weeks he was everyone's friend, from the Prince down to his least officials. After this, having seen the justice of all his dealings, Fang La became truly fond of the man and asked the Chief Minister to open negotiations for Princess Golden Iris to be married to him. As royal son-in-law Ke Yin, alias Chai Jin, was given the rank of Master of the Rolls, while the Prodigy, who had changed his name to Yun Bi, became know to everyone as the Master's Man. After his marriage to the Princess, Mr. Chai came and went freely in the palace and knew all the goings-on, inside and out.

Whenever Fang La had some important military matter to decide, he invited Mr. Chai to the palace to advise him. Mr. Chai would repeat something like: "Your Majesty's emanations are correct, only there is a star with an adverse influence, it will take you six months to find peace. You must wait till Song Jiang has no more generals at his disposal. Then the malignant stars will withdraw and Your Majesty's enterprise will be back on track. You will make great advances and seize the whole Central Plain."

Fang La said: "But so many of my favourite generals have been killed by Song Jiang. What am I to do about that?"

Mr. Chai said: "I saw a sign last night. At present the indicators of Your Majesty's fortune are predominantly adverse but this will soon pass. Then the twenty-eight signs of the zodiac will favour you and your enterprise will be renewed. A dozen or so of Song Jiang's leaders will come over to you and they are the stars that will mark the start of a great expansion in your territory."

Fang La was well pleased with the answer.

We shall leave Mr. Chai to his role of royal son-in-law, and return to Song Jiang and the main army. They have left Hangzhou and proceeded to Fuyang. At the same time Precious Light and the other four southern commanders have marched the remnants of their defeated army to the pass guarding Fuyang and have sent to Muzhou for reinforcements.

Deputy Chief Minister Zu Shiyuan ordered two officers and ten thousand troops to reinforce the contingent guarding Fuyang. These two officers, Bai Qin and Jing De, who were both exceedingly brave men, joined forces with Precious Light and the others and occupied the mountains.

Song Jiang's army meanwhile arrived at Two Mile Bay. They

were advancing with the water-borne forces in the lead and the cavalry behind. When Marshal Shi Bao saw this he mounted and took up his shooting-star hammer and star-splitter sword and rode down the mountain to challenge Song Jiang.

Scimitar was about to take up the challenge when Little Duke shouted out: "Wait brother and watch me have a few bouts with the villain." Song Jiang watched from the pennants' gate as Little Duke with his halberd took on the Marshal, while the latter brandished Wind-Slicer. After fifty bouts, Little Duke began to flag. Then the Halberdier urged on his horse and charged into the attack. Even with his one sword against two halberds the Marshal gave nothing away to the other two. Then, when the combat was still at its height, Precious Light sounded the gong for the southerners to break off. What had happened was that he had seen how with a favourable wind the Song war boats had arrived close to shore and were lined up along the bank. Afraid of being caught between two fires, he ordered a withdrawal. Little Duke and the Halberdier however went on fighting and would not let their opponent get away. The Marshal fought on for another three or four bouts, and then Whiskers rode out with his spear and joined the fray. Three opponents at once was too much even for Marshal Shi Bao and he knocked their weapons aside and made off. Song Jiang pointed with the stock of his whip and they charged over Fuyang Ridge. The Marshal's troops did not stop to take up positions till they reached Tonglu.

Song Jiang continued his advance till nightfall and they camped the other side of White Hornet Ridge. That night he sent a party from the east under Snake and Scorpion, and another from the west under Iron Ox to attack the camp in Tonglu, and ordered the boat captains to attack along the river. When Snake's party arrived at the Tonglu camp it was around midnight. Precious Light was planning strategy with Marshal Shi Bao when they heard a sudden report. There was no time for most of them to mount their horses. They saw fires on three sides. Together with the Marshal they all fled and no one tried to make a stand. One of their commanders did not even manage to mount his horse and fled on foot along small paths. He ran into Short-Arse and

Steelbright, who fell on him and captured him alive. Iron Ox's party were busy killing and starting fires in the village.

When Song Jiang received the reports he ordered his army to strike camp and advance to Tonglu where they set up their position and stationed all the carts and horses. Short-Arse and Steelbright handed over their captive and claimed a reward. Song Jiang sent the captive southern commander off to Marshal Zhang at Hangzhou to be executed. That's the end of him.

Next day Song Jiang planned an attack by land and water. He assembled his troops below Black Dragon Ridge, which stood between him and Muzhou. Precious Light meanwhile led his troops up this mountain and occupied the pass. This pass over Black Dragon Ridge was close to the main river at a place where the cliffs were steep and the current swift. The enemy now held the top of the pass and the river below was guarded by their war fleet. Song Jiang's army camped not far off and built a stockade. Infantry commanders Iron Ox, Eight-Armed Ogre and Winged Ghost were sent with five hundred shield-bearers to reconnoitre. When they got within range of Black Dragon Ridge wooden and stone missiles rained down on them and they were unable to continue. All they could do was go back and report to Song Jiang.

Song Jiang next ordered Ruan the Second, Flagpole, Cave Dragon and River Rider and to take some boats up the river. Ruan the Second took a thousand sailors and a hundred boats and with fluttering banners and beating drums and singing war songs they rowed towards Black Dragon Ridge. But here, with the mountain at its back, was Fang La's whole fleet. Five hundred vessels were stationed here, with around five thousand sailors.

The first four of Fang La's boats were commanded by the Four Dragons of Zhejiang. These four had been boatmen on the river Qiantang. On joining up with Fang La they had been given high rank. When Ruan the Second and his party steered out of the mainstream towards the shore, the four southern commanders in the waterside camp already had wind of it and had prepared fifty fire boats. These were rafts of pinewood piled high with bundles of grass within which were concealed gunpowder and incendiary materials, tied with bamboo ropes and lined up along the shore. Whilst Ruan the Second and the others were busy rowing shorewards, the four southern commanders were watching them from upstream. Each of them now waved a pink signalling flag and their four fast boats shot downstream. Ruan the Second ordered his men to fire their arrows, and the four boats turned back. He ordered an all-out effort to catch them. The boats reached shore. The four commanders and a number of sailors leapt out and ran for it.

Seeing so many boats moored there, Ruan the Second did not dare land. As he was wondering what to do, he saw flags waving on Black Dragon Ridge; gongs and drums began to sound and all the fire rafts were lit simultaneously and began to bear down on them, driven by the wind. On the bigger boats at the back a cry went up. Bristling with spears and grappling hooks, these boats followed on behind the fire rafts. Since the opposing force was large and the shore was near, Cave Dragon and River Rider steered their boats ashore and then abandoned them and began to climb the cliffs. Once on top they made their way back to camp.

Ruan the Second and Flagpole tried to face the enemy. The fire boats came on blazing furiously. Ruan the Second dived in and tried to swim round to the stern of the boat. He was caught by a grappling hook. Terrified that he might face the shame of capture, he drew his sword and killed himself. Flagpole saw it was hopeless and tried to dive in, but at that moment a fire boat blew up and the explosion smashed his helmet and made mincemeat of him. The four southern commanders came charging along after the fire boats. The White-Water Dragon, Ruan the Fifth and Ruan the Seventh, who were at the back, saw the leading boats were in trouble and managed to turn their boat about and let the stream carry them down to Tonglu.

Let us return to Precious Light and Marshal Shi Bao on Black Dragon Ridge. When they saw their boat commanders had won, they led their troops in a furious charge down the mountain. Reckoning the odds were stacked against them, the Song army retreated to Tonglu and made camp. The southern forces withdrew to Black Dragon Ridge.

Song Jiang fortified himself at Tonglu. Miserable at the loss of Ruan the Second and Flagpole, he sat gloomily in his tent. He could get no rest; his dreams were disturbed. The Professor and the others could do nothing to animate him. When their mourning was over, Ruan the Seventh and Ruan the Fifth admonished him: "Our brother has given his life for the country. Had he died in the Marshes of Mount Liang, it would have been a death without honour. It is your duty to lead us and you should not be upset. You must consider the cause. We will take responsibility for avenging our brother."

Song Jiang cheered up a little at this. Next day he gave out new orders for a renewed attack. "Do not be too hasty," the Professor warned. "We must have a plan before trying to pass Black Dragon Ridge." At this point Snake and Scorpion spoke up: "We grew up as hunters, we know all about mountain passes. We will disguise ourselves as local hunters, climb the mountain and start a fire. It will give the bastards a shock and they'll abandon their position."

The Professor said: "It's a good idea but I'm afraid this mountain is very steep and you may not be able to find a way up. If you should lose your footing you'd most likely be dead men!"

Snake and Scorpion said: "When we two escaped from prison in Dengzhou we went to Mount Liang and in the shadow of your good fortune we served a good many years with you as leaders. Later we received the imperial amnesty and were permitted to wear official robes. To sacrifice our own comfort for the state and for the sake of avenging our brother can hardly be considered too much."

Song Jiang said: "There is no need for such wild language, friends. We must aim to complete this business successfully as soon as possible and return to the capital. The court cannot be ungrateful. Just do your best, and serve the country well."

They went off to prepare their packs. They dressed in tiger skins, stuck sharp knives in their belts and carried their tridents. They bade Song Jiang farewell and set off along small tracks toward Black Dragon Ridge. It was already the first watch. Along the way they ran into two sentries whom they killed. By the

宋公明大戰烏龍嶺

second watch they were just below the pass. They could clearly hear the drum beat in the enemy camp. They dared not take the main route, so they forced their way slowly upward through creepers and undergrowth. It was a bright moonlit night, almost like day. They rested and then climbed. They could see a light glimmering on top of the ridge. At the last stage they stopped to listen: the drum beat for the fourth watch! Snake whispered to his brother: "There's not much night left, it'll soon be light. We'd best get on."

They proceeded on up. So intent were they on climbing, their hands and feet fully occupied, that they allowed the tridents fastened to their shoulders and trailing behind them to scrape against the undergrowth. This made a noise and they were spotted by the enemy on top of the ridge. Snake was negotiating an overhang when he heard a shout from above, "Got 'im!" and a hook caught him by the topknot. As he reached for the sword at his belt a jerk from above hoisted him off his feet. In desperation he swung the sword above his head, cut the hook and instantaneously plummeted into the void. Thus did the unfortunate Snake, a hero of universal renown, meet his untimely end, falling from this thousand metre cliff. His body was torn to shreds on the rocks below, jagged and sharp as wolves' teeth.

When Scorpion saw his brother fall he tried to retreat down the cliff, but rocks were raining down from above and crossbow bolts, fired from cover of the undergrowth. The wretched Scorpion also, the famous hunter, died riddled with arrows on Black Dragon Ridge. The two bodies lay there in the undergrowth.

In the morning someone was sent down from the ridge to bring the bodies up and expose them. Information about all this was retrieved by Song scouts and it was reported to Song Jiang that Snake and Scorpion lay dead on Black Dragon Ridge. The news caused him enormous grief and several times he passed out. Then he ordered Scimitar and Colonel Hua to prepare the troops for an assault on the mountain, to avenge their four comrades. The Professor warned: "You must not be too hasty, brother. Those who died, it was their fate to die. If you want to capture the pass it is no good rushing things. We really must have a good plan and use cunning to gain control of the pass. After that we can launch an all-out attack."

But Song Jiang was very angry. "Who would have thought that we would lose a third of our companions," he said. "We cannot allow those villains to expose the bodies of our brothers on the mountainside. I must make a sortie tonight to bring the bodies back and give them a proper funeral."

The Professor said: "I am afraid that exposing the bodies is a trick. Do not act rashly."

But Song Jiang would not listen to him. He assembled three thousand picked troops, to be led by Scimitar, Colonel Hua, the Little Duke and the Halberdier. They attacked that night. When they reached Black Dragon Ridge it was the second watch. One of the soldiers reported: "There's two exposed bodies up ahead. I reckon it's Snake and Scorpion." Song Jiang galloped forward to see for himself. He saw two heads stuck on poles on two trees and on the trees a notice with two lines of characters. In the moonlight he could not make out clearly what they said. He ordered a flare to be lit and blowing on the flame saw by its light what was written: "Here too ere long will Song Jiang's head be exhibited."

Outraged, Song Jiang ordered them to climb the tree at once and get the corpses down. At that very moment torches sprang up on every side of them, drums and gongs began to beat. A huge enemy force was all around. Volleys of arrows fell on them from the mountain above, and from the river below the sailors from the boats began to pour up the slope. Song Jiang could only curse his luck. He had no idea what to do. If he tried to retreat, Marshal Shi Bao had him, the way was blocked. If he tried to go round, Precious Light appeared and attacked him. It was truly after the fashion of one of those tragic tales of history.

If you want to know how Song Jiang escaped from this predicament, you must read the next chapter.

Chapter 117

At Muzhou Precious Light is snuffed by an arrow; At Black Dragon Ridge Song Jiang is helped by magic!

In attempting to rescue the bodies of Snake and Scorpion on Black Dragon Ridge, Song Jiang has fallen into Marshal Shi Bao's trap. Enemy troops spring up on all sides, with Shi Bao in front and Precious Light blocking the way back.

"Dismount and surrender, Song Jiang, what are you waiting for?" Marshal Shi Bao bellowed.

Provoked by this, Scimitar slapped his horse, whirled about and charged. But before they crossed swords, a cry went up from the rear. The Four Dragons, commanders of the enemy fleet, had come ashore and joined the two commanders on top of the pass, Wang and Chao; they were now pouring down the mountainside together. Colonel Hua rode out to bolster the rear and engaged one of the leaders. They fought innumerable bouts and then Colonel Hua turned and retreated. Wang and Chao raced in pursuit. Colonel Hua fired two arrows in quick succession and they both fell. A cry of dismay went up from their troops who halted and began to retreat. The four boat commanders also came to a halt, after seeing the fate of their comrades. Colonel Hua had stemmed the tide.

But now another attack came in from the flank, led this time by Bai Qin and Jing De, the two officers sent with reinforcements by the Deputy Chief Minister in Muzhou. From Song Jiang's ranks two commanders rode out: the Little Duke, who took on Bai, and the Halberdier who opposed Jing. They were all locked in mortal combat and Song Jiang was urging his side on, when an uproar rose to the heavens in the enemy's rear and their army broke up. It was because Iron Ox and his two lieutenants, Eight-Armed

Ogre and Winged Ghost with their infantry had taken Marshal Shi Bao's cavalry from the rear. When Precious Light attempted to bring his troops up in support, he encountered Monk and Pilgrim, the one hacking with his two swords, the other heaving his steel staff. Each was followed by a thousand infantrymen as they charged into action. Behind them came Thunderclap, Skyhawk, Whiskers, the Dandy, the Flautist, Demon King, Steelbright and Short-Arse, with both cavalry and infantry, in a desperate charge. The Song troops scattered the forces of Marshal Shi Bao and Precious Light, rescued Song Jiang and the others, and brought them safely back to Tonglu. Shi Bao retreated up the pass.

Song Jiang thanked all the commanders. "If you hadn't come to the rescue my friends, I would now be a ghost wandering in the underworld like Snake and Scorpion."

The Professor said: "When you insisted on going and wouldn't listen to my humble advice, I was afraid something would go wrong, so I sent the others to back you up."

Song Jiang's gratitude knew no bounds.

Let us now turn to the discussion that was going on between Marshal Shi Bao and Precious Light on Black Dragon Ridge. "For the time being Song Jiang has retreated to Tonglu and is camped there," said the former. "If he goes secretly by hidden paths and crosses the mountain, Muzhou will be seriously threatened. Would it not be best for you to go yourself to the palace at Clearwater and request His Majesty to send reinforcements to secure the pass? Then we will be able to hold out indefinitely."

"What you say is quite right," Precious Light replied. "I'll go at once." He mounted and went first to Muzhou where he spoke to the Deputy Chief Minister: "Song Jiang's troops are formidable. We can't stop them and I fear we will be swept away. We are facing defeat. I have come to ask for reinforcements to help us hold the pass."

The Minister heard him out, and then together they rode over to Bangyuan Gap in Clearwater. They saw the Chief Minister first, and put in their request for reinforcements. Next day at the early morning audience, Fang La having ascended his throne and the ministers including Precious Light having made obeisance, the latter stepped forward, wished His Majesty long life and said: "Armed with Your Majesty's commission I went to help the Southern Prince defend Hangzhou. Unfortunately Song Jiang's troops turned out to be too powerful and we were unable to withstand their onslaught. Then Judge Yuan, who was in command of some transports, turned traitor and let them into Hangzhou so we lost the city. The Prince, eager for glory, went out to fight and was killed. Now Marshal Shi Bao and I have retreated to the pass on Black Dragon Ridge. Recently we killed four of Song Jiang's commanders, and our position is relatively strong. But Song Jiang at present is camped at Tonglu and I fear that sooner or later they will find hidden paths to infiltrate the pass; it is difficult for us to defend the whole mountain. I request Your Majesty to send us more commanders and picked troops as soon as possible to secure the pass at Black Dragon Ridge, repel the enemy and bring the whole region under control again."

Fang La said: "All our troops are already deployed. Recently the situation has been critical in Shezhou at Sundance Pass and we have had to send thousands of troops. There's only the imperial guard left, and I need them to defend the palace. I can't go scattering them all over the place!"

"If you won't send reinforcements, you leave me helpless. If the Song army gets through the mountains, how can Muzhou be defended?"

Chief Minister Lou stepped forward: "This pass at Black Dragon Ridge is really vital to us. I know there are still thirty thousand imperial guards. We could let Precious Light have ten thousand to defend the pass. I beg Your Majesty to consider it."

But Fang La would not listen to Lou's advice either. He insisted that the imperial guard could not be sent. The court was dismissed and everyone left the palace. Lou discussed the situation with his officials and it was decided that the Deputy Chief Minister should send a general and five thousand troops from Muzhou. Precious Light and the Minister went back to Muzhou and picked the troops, who were to be led by one Colonel Xiahou. When all this was explained to Marshal Shi Bao on Black Dragon Ridge, he said: "Since the court refuses to send the imperial guard, we will simply hold the pass, we will not go out and seek battle. Tell the four boat commanders to guard the river closely and fight off any boats that attack but not initiate any action."

We shall now leave them to their arrangements for the defence of Black Dragon Pass, and tell instead how Song Jiang, after the loss of his leaders, remained at Tonglu and made no move to attack. After twenty days or more of inactivity, a scout came and reported: "The Emperor is sending Marshal Tong with bounty. He has reached Hangzhou already. He heard that the army has been divided and has sent General Wang Bing to Sundance Pass with the portion for the Unicorn's army. He is bringing our gifts himself and will be here at any moment."

Song Jiang rode out some six miles with the Professor and his other commanders to meet Marshal Tong. Back in the government office, the imperial edict was read out and the bounty divided among Song Jiang's commanders. They prostrated themselves in thanks and then a banquet was arranged to welcome the Marshal.

Marshal Tong asked: "On the way here I heard that you have suffered losses."

Song Jiang said tearfully: "Previously, during the northern campaign against the Tartars, we were entirely successful and we did not lose a single commander. But this time before we even left the capital Taoist Gongsun had left us and we were deprived of several others before we set out. Since crossing the river we have lost a lot of leaders. And recently eight or nine fell sick in Hangzhou: their lives hang in the balance. We have made two assaults on the pass up there at Black Dragon Ridge and lost several leaders. Because the mountain is steep and the river swift-flowing, it is difficult to attack. We have not been able to break through. At this critical time your visit is most welcome."

Marshal Tong said: "The Emperor is fully aware of all you have achieved, General. He heard that you had lost some commanders, and told me to bring Wang Bing and Zhao Tan to help you out. I have sent Wang Bing to the other army to distribute their gifts." He then introduced Zhao Tan to Song Jiang and his companions and the feasting continued at the Tonglu camp.

When Marshal Tong mustered the army next day for an attack on Black Dragon Pass, the Professor warned: "Don't take it too lightly, Your Excellency. Why don't we send the Dandy and the Flautist to a quiet place along the river to ask the locals for directions and find a hidden route which will take us through the mountains? If we can get behind their lines and cut them off, we can take the pass with no effort at all."

Song Jiang said: "It's a good idea." He sent the Dandy and the Flautist off with a dozen men to search the countryside and ask the people about routes. A day later in the evening they returned with an old man. "Who is he?" Song Jiang asked.

"He's a local inhabitant who knows all the ways through the mountains and gorges hereabouts," said the Flautist.

Song Jiang said: "Old man, if you can show us a path that will take us beyond Black Dragon Ridge, I will reward you handsomely."

"I was born in these parts," said the old man. "Us ordinary folk've suffered something terrible at the hands of Fang La and we'd no way to escape. Heaven be praised that the imperial army is here now and us can have some peace again. I can show you a path as will get you beyond Black Dragon Pass. It comes out at Dongguan, that's pretty near Muzhou, to the north of it. Black Dragon Pass is round to the west."

Song Jiang, delighted, told them to give the old man silver and keep him in the camp. He had him provided with plenty to eat and drink. Next day he requested Marshal Tong to guard the camp while he took twelve commanders and advanced along the mountain track. They had around ten thousand men, cavalry and foot. With the old man as their guide they set off. The horses' hooves were muffled, the harness bells silenced and the men gagged to prevent talking as they marched. At Little Ox Mountain they found an enemy contingent blocking the way. Song Jiang sent Iron Ox, Eight-Armed Ogre and Winged Ghost forward. The enemy, numbering about four or five hundred, were wiped out by Iron Ox and his companions. They reached Dongguan around the fourth watch.

The local commander of the southern forces heard that the

Song army had got through to Dongguan. Since he had only two thousand troops at his disposal, he did not put up any serious resistance. At the first push he fled to Muzhou, where he told the authorities: "Song Jiang and his army have got past Black Dragon Ridge by taking hidden paths and are now at Dongguan." The Deputy Chief Minister in a panic summoned his commanders. Song Jiang had already ordered Thunderer to set off a string of explosions. Marshal Shi Bao and his force up on the pass heard them and were terrified. Marshal Shi Bao hurriedly sent out a reconnaissance party under Bai Qin. They found Song Jiang's banners everywhere, filling sky and earth, spread over the whole terrain. They hurriedly returned to the mountain and reported to the Marshal.

"Since the court has not sent us any reinforcements, we will just defend the pass, we will not try to relieve them," the Marshal said.

"That would be a mistake," said Precious Light. "If we don't send assistance to Muzhou, just think what will happen. If the palace is defeated, our own safety cannot be guaranteed. If you won't go, I will go to relieve Muzhou by myself."

The Marshal did his best to dissuade him, but Precious Light took five thousand troops and wielding his steel staff set off down the mountain with Colonel Xiahou.

Now Song Jiang on reaching Dongguan had not tried to attack Muzhou immediately. Instead he marched toward Black Dragon Pass, and so ran into Precious Light. The two armies gradually closed and battle commenced. Precious Light rode out in front and challenged. Colonel Hua whispered in Song Jiang's ear: "If we do this and this, we've got him!"

"Right!" said Song Jiang, nodding. He told Colonel Hua to work it out with Thunderclap.

Thunderclap rode out first and engaged Precious Light in combat. After half a dozen bouts he turned his horse and galloped off. The troops scattered in all directions. Thinking Thunderclap was beaten, Precious Light let him go and galloped towards Song Jiang to make him prisoner. But Colonel Hua of course was guarding Song Jiang and ready for this. He waited till the priest

睦州城箭射鄧元覺

was quite close, then bent his bow to the full and taking careful aim fired an arrow point blank. The bow was bent like a full moon, the arrow sped like a shooting star; it caught Precious Light full in the face. He crashed to the ground and the soldiers finished him off. Now they all advanced together and the southerners were routed. Colonel Xiahou could not fight on alone and fled to Muzhou. But when the Song troops reached the foot of the pass, blocks of wood and ballista missiles rained down on them and the advance was halted. Consequently they turned about and marched on Muzhou instead.

Colonel Xiahou rushed in to report to the Deputy Chief Minister: "The Song army has broken through to Dongguan. They killed Precious Light. Any day now they'll attack Muzhou."

The Deputy Chief Minister sent someone with Colonel Xiahou to the palace in Clearwater to ask Chief Minister Lou to tell His Majesty that the Song army had broken through by mountain tracks to Dongguan and would soon be attacking Muzhou, and to ask His Majesty to send reinforcements. Any delay would be disastrous.

Fang La got a shock. He hurriedly ordered Marshal Zheng, commander of the palace guard, to take fifteen thousand men and rush to relieve Muzhou.

Zheng said: "I will carry out your command, but I beg you to let me have the assistance of the imperial astronomer, to help me against Song Jiang."

Fang La granted this request and summoned his astronomer Bao Daoyi, known as the Sorcerer. When the latter was informed of the royal wish, he presented himself at the palace for an audience. He bowed very deeply. Fang La explained: "My lands have been invaded by Song Jiang's army. We have repeatedly lost cities and troops. Now his army has reached Muzhou. I hope you will be able to deploy your magic powers to save our land and people and preserve our patrimony."

The Sorcerer said: "Your most enlightened Majesty, I am just a poor Taoist, but in my humble opinion, Song Jiang's army will be swept away, by virtue of Your Majesty's divine favour."

Highly gratified by this answer, Fang La invited him to sit down and a banquet was arranged in his honour. When he had eaten and drunk he left the palace and joined Marshal Zheng and Colonel Xiahou to discuss the campaign.

The Sorcerer was in fact from the Mountains of Splendour. He had joined the monkhood in youth and had studied the black arts. Later he joined Fang La when the latter was plotting his insurrection. In battle he would use his black magic as a weapon. He also had a magnificent sword which was known as the Heaven Raker. It could fly through the air and kill a man at a hundred paces. On Fang La's behalf he had committed some horrifying acts which earned him his name of Sorcerer. Marshal Zheng had started off as a captain of infantry. From a lad he had practised with spear and staff. He had met up with Fang La by chance, and had risen to be commander of the palace guard. He loved Taoism and considered himself a disciple of the Sorcerer, from whom he had acquired knowledge of a number of magic tricks. In battle he could summon up clouds or mist and people called him the Devil's Marshal. As for Colonel Xiahou, he had originally been a hunter from a mountain district and could wield a trident. He had come to serve the Deputy Chief Minister in the Muzhou administration.

These three then were making their plans in the Marshal's palace when a doorman came and announced: "There's one of them sky watchers asking to see you, name of Pu Wenying."

When the Sorcerer asked what he wanted, Pu Wenying said: "I have heard that you, Your Excellency, with the Marshal and the General are planning a campaign against Song Jiang's forces. When I was observing the night sky, I noticed that the southern stars were all obscured, whereas the stars of Song Jiang and his commanders were mostly still bright. I am sure your plan is a good one, but I fear it may not have a good result. Would it not be better to go back to His Majesty and ask him to consider surrendering, in order to spare our country from misfortune?"

The Sorcerer flew into such a rage at this that he picked up the Heaven Raker and cut Pu Wenying in two. Then he announced what he had done in a memorial to Fang La, asking him to consider the matter closed. And that was that.

The historian has a poem:

In the southeast, the king's power fades,
Though wizards and sorcerers are his aids.
When one comes who knows heaven's will
Him the Sorcerer's sword must kill.

The Devil's Marshal was appointed commander of the vanguard, marching first out of the city to lead the attack. With the Sorcerer commanding the main army and Colonel Xiahou bringing up the rear they set off to relieve Muzhou.

Now as Song Jiang and his army were wondering how to go about storming Muzhou, a scout suddenly reported that southern reinforcements were on the way from Clearwater. Song Jiang sent Short-Arse and Steelbright out to reconnoitre. With three thousand cavalry they took the road to Clearwater. When the two forces met, the Devil's Marshal rode out to engage Short-Arse. Without a word the two leaders deployed their forces and set to. They fought eight or nine bouts and then the Devil's Marshal began to mutter a spell. A sudden shout of "Chrrr!" and from his helmet a cloud of black smoke poured out. In the middle of this black smoke stood a spirit warrior in golden armour with a mighty club, a proper demon-queller. He raised this weapon heavenward, and it came hurtling down. Short-Arse was paralysed with fear: his arm faltered and his legs grew clumsy, his skill with the spear deserted him and a single blow from the Devil's Marshal knocked him from his horse. Steelbright saw her husband fall and raced to the rescue, whirling her two swords. The Devil's Marshal turned on her, but after just one bout he galloped off. Steelbright, determined to avenge her husband, gave chase. Her adversary rested his spear and deftly reaching for a bag that hung by his side took out a square lump of brass, turned in the saddle, took aim and flung it in her face. She died before she hit the ground. Poor girl, beautiful and skilled at arms, it all ended here for her! The Devil's Marshal mustered his troops and the Song force was routed.

When the Song stragglers got back and told Song Jiang that the two leaders were dead and the greater part of the men, he was furious. He immediately stood his army to and ordered Iron Ox, Eight-Armed Ogre and Winged Ghost with five thousand cavalry to lead the attack.

The Devil's Marshal and his men were soon in sight. Song Jiang almost choking with anger rode out in front and shouted at them: "You rebel scum, how dare you kill two of our commanders!"

The Devil's Marshal responded by riding out, spear at the ready, to attack Song Jiang. But Iron Ox was not having it. He picked up his two axes and rushed forward, while Eight-Armed Ogre and Winged Ghost, weaving their shields, gave him cover. They charged ahead, trying to get to close quarters with the Devil's Marshal. But the latter turned his horse and galloped off, while his three antagonists charged on into the southerners' ranks. Song Jiang feared he might lose Iron Ox and quickly mustered five thousand cavalry and charged. The southerners fled in all directions. Song Jiang had the gong sounded to recall the troops. The two shield-bearers returned with Iron Ox.

At this moment a black cloud appeared all around them, masking the sun, a black mist which filled the sky, so thick you could not tell north from south or east from west and day was turned into night. There was no way forward for Song Jiang's army. The poem describes it:

> *Dark clouds every way you look, a black fog that fills the sky; wind and rain rage and spout. The heavens are angry, thunder roars. Mountain torrents shake the earth, all is confusion, as if the sky itself were falling. River gorges boil and churn as though the earth were opening up. Ghosts howl in sorrow, gods roar in sympathy. You can strain your eyes but you scarcely see a thing; your ears are filled with the sound of a thousand trees.*

When the Devil's Marshal had darkened the world with his magic spell, Song Jiang's army lost their way and stumbled into a place where the gloom was so deep that they could see nothing. All order was lost in the army. Song Jiang raised his eyes to heaven and sighed. "Can it be that I am destined to die here?" he thought. The darkness lasted from early morning to mid-afternoon. Finally it began to lift and a glimmer of light appeared: they saw the place was full of tall warriors in golden armour, who completely surrounded them. When Song Jiang saw this he fell to the ground in terror. He kept muttering: "Heaven grant me a quick death!" He dared not raise his eyes, and in his ears was the perpetual sound of wind and rain. All his men remained bowed to the ground, expecting death, waiting for the sword to fall. A little longer and the storm had passed. When Song Jiang looked up and saw the sword was not going to fall after all, someone came and raised him up, saying: "Stand up, please!" When Song Jiang raised his eyes and looked, he saw it was a scholar offering him this help.

Song Jiang's fear melted away. He stood up and exchanged courtesies. He asked the man's name.

"My name is Shao Jun," the other replied. "My home is here. I came today to let Your Honour know that Fang La's days are numbered. In ten days' time he will be finished. I have already helped you a lot. You have had a hard time of it, but relief is at hand, do you understand?"

Song Jiang asked again: "Master, when is it ordained that Fang La will fall?" But as he spoke the other gave him a push and he awoke. It was all a dream! He looked around and saw that the tall warriors surrounding him were in fact pine trees. He gave a shout and all his men jumped up and began looking for a way out. The clouds had receded, the mists withdrawn, the sky was bright, the air clean; beyond the ring of pine trees shouts could be heard.

Song Jiang led his men in a charge to break out, and they came upon Monk and Pilgrim fighting their way along the road and grappling with the Devil's Marshal. The Sorcerer on horseback saw Pilgrim on foot wielding his two swords and attacking his commander, so he drew his Heaven Raker. It flew through the air and embedded itself in Pilgrim's left shoulder. The blood spurted out. Monk rushed forward furiously with his steel staff and rescued Pilgrim. Pilgrim's left arm had been almost completely severed. Monk wrenched out the Heaven Raker. When Pilgrim came to, he saw that his arm had been cut through and was hanging by a thread, so he got his own sword and with a quick blow cut it right off. Song Jiang ordered some men to carry him back to the camp to rest.

Monk went charging off to do battle with Colonel Xiahou. After several bouts Colonel Xiahou gave up and fled. Monk went in with his staff and scattered the southerners while Colonel Xiahou escaped into the forest. Monk was not going to allow that and followed him deep into the woods.

Meanwhile the Devil's Marshal had brought up his troops, so Iron Ox, Eight-Armed Ogre and Winged Ghost charged him, brandishing shields, javelins, darts and axes. They were too much for the Devil's Marshal, who fled across the river gorge and made off. His three opponents did not know the way, but they were so avid for glory that they crossed too and raced after him. Three thousand troops appeared on the other bank of the river and cut them off. Eight-Armed Ogre hurriedly tried to turn back and was confronted on the river bank by two enemy commanders. He called out to Iron Ox and Winged Ghost, but already their pursuit of the Devil's Marshal had taken them far away. Further on the gorge unexpectedly became very deep and when Winged Ghost stumbled and lost his footing, he was finished off by the southerners' arrows. Eight-Armed Ogre slithered down the bank but was tripped by a rope and as he struggled to get up was cut to pieces in a flurry of blows. Poor Eight-Armed Ogre and Winged Ghost — what did it avail them now to be heroes?

Iron Ox was all alone as he plunged ever deeper into the mountains. The enemy troops on the river bank were gaining on him, and were only a few hundred yards away, when a thunderous roar arose behind. It was Colonel Hua, Thunderclap and Demon King coming to the rescue. They thrust the southern troops aside and continued on till they were able to reach Iron Ox and bring him back to safety. Monk however was still missing. When these leaders met Song Jiang they told him how the Devil's Marshal had been pursued across the river and how Eight-Armed Ogre and Winged Ghost had been lost and only Iron Ox saved. Song Jiang's grief was boundless. Of the troops engaged in the operation a third had been killed, Monk was missing and Pilgrim had lost his left arm.

Whilst Song Jiang was still mourning, a scout reported: "The Professor, Scimitar, Skyhawk, Whiskers, the Dandy and the Flautist have just arrived by water with ten thousand troops."

Song Jiang met them and asked the Professor about the situation. The Professor replied: "Marshal Tong has his own troops and Generals Wang Bing and Zhao Tan and General Liu all have forces of their own. They have reached Black Dragon Ridge. We left thirteen behind, but the others are all here with me to help you. Song Jiang told him: "We have lost some comrades, Pilgrim is crippled, Monk is missing. I can't help being sad."

The Professor urged him: "You must cast off your depression. Now is the time to capture Fang La. You must put the good of your country first and not allow grief to impair your own health."

Song Jiang pointed out the pine trees and told the Professor about his dream. The Professor said: "Since you have had this premonitory dream here, do you not think there must be a temple hereabouts, with a tutelary spirit whose aim is to protect you?"

Song Jiang said: "Your observation is a very good one. Let us search the mountain together." The two of them strolled off into the forest. They had not gone half a bowshot when they came upon a temple, with an inscription in gold characters which said: "Temple of the Black Dragon Lord". When they went in, Song Jiang had a surprise: on the altar was an image of the Black Dragon Lord, and it was exactly like the person he had seen in his dream. Song Jiang prostrated himself again and said: "Thank you for your great kindness in saving me, Dragon Lord. Although I have no way to repay you, I hope I may count on your help. If we can overcome Fang La, I will do everything in my power to persuade the court to build a temple to honour your name."

They prostrated themselves again, and went back down the steps. They read the inscription, and learnt that the god was a graduate of the second class in the Tang dynasty called Shao Jun, who on failing to pass the examination for the first class had thrown himself in the river and died. The Lord of Heaven in honour of his devotion to duty made him a Dragon Lord. This was a spot where whenever the people prayed for wind they got wind, whenever they prayed for rain they got rain, so the temple was built and they made offerings there in each of the four seasons. In view of all this Song Jiang ordered a black pig and a white sheep for sacrifice. After making their offering, they went out and had another good look around. All about them were the pine trees that had undergone the strange metamorphosis. To this day there is outside the northern gate of Yanzhou a temple dedicated to the Black Dragon Lord and the name of that place is Thousand Pine Woods. Ancient traces remain, as the poem tells:

The loyal heart is known to the spirit,
Who to the loyal gives secret help.
If you want to know who the Dragon Lord is,
At Thousand Pine Woods the tablet tells you.

After thanking the Dragon Lord for granting him his protection, Song Jiang left the temple and rode back to the main camp. There with the Professor he made plans for the attack on Muzhou. They went on till midnight, when Song Jiang suddenly felt exceedingly weary. He had just lain down on a bench when he heard someone say: "Graduate Shao would like to talk to you." Song Jiang hurriedly rose and went out to meet him. The Dragon Lord made him a deep bow and said: "But for my help you would have been captured yesterday by the Sorcerer, through those magic spells of his that can turn pine trees into men. But I am grateful for the respect you have just paid me and I want to tell you that in a few days from now Muzhou can be stormed and that in ten days' time Fang La can be captured."

Song Jiang was about to invite him into the tent to question him further, when a sudden gust of wind woke him and he found he had been dreaming.

He immediately summoned the Professor to discuss the dream. The Professor said: "If the Dragon Lord appears to you like this, I am sure it means we can soon attack and take Muzhou."

Song Jiang said: "It's just what we wanted!"

Next day at dawn he gave the orders. The main force was reserved for the attack on Muzhou, while the Dandy and the Flautist were sent to guard the main road from Black Dragon Ridge. Scimitar, Colonel Hua, Thunderclap and Whiskers were to lead the attack on Muzhou from the north. First Thunderer was ordered to fire nine explosive shells into the city. The shells fell with an earth-shattering din, a huge explosive force, and the troops in the city were frightened out of their wits and thrown into confusion without a blow struck.

After Monk scattered the enemy rearguard and pursued Colonel Xiahou none knew whither, the Devil's Marshal and the Sorcerer had taken refuge in the city and were discussing their plan of action with Deputy Chief Minister and other officials. Someone said: "The Song army is here, how can we save ourselves?"

The Minister said: "History tells us that when the enemy are at the walls, when they reach the moat, there is only one way to save yourself: face them and fight to the death! If the city falls we will all be captured. The situation is desperate. Our only hope is to attack!"

So the Devil's Marshal with a dozen or so commanders and ten thousand troops charged out through the city gates and faced Song Jiang. The latter ordered his troops to fall back half a bowshot to allow the enemy to take up a position outside the city. The Sorcerer had a chair brought out onto the battlements, while the Minister and his officials were all sitting in the watch tower as spectators.

The Devil's Marshal levelled his lance and galloped forward. On the other side Scimitar came out, wielding his blade. The horses met and they fought several bouts. The Devil's Marshal was no match for Scimitar. All he could do was parry and block, or dodge to left or right. So from his vantage point on the wall the Sorcerer made his magic, muttered a spell and shouted: "Chrrr!" As he pronounced the magic word and blew, from the Marshal's helmet there sprang a black cloud and in the midst of this cloud appeared a spirit warrior in golden armour, wielding a magnificent demon-quelling sword which he raised on high before letting it fall. Among the southern ranks a black cloud spiralled up.

Song Jiang summoned Demon King to see what was happening and ordered him to do some magic. He himself also

烏龍嶺神助宋公明

employed the secret formula he had learnt from the mystic books for turning the wind and dispelling darkness. Then from Scimitar's helmet a white cloud burst forth, in the midst of it a spirit warrior with flaming hair, a blue face, green eyes and flashing teeth, astride a black dragon and wielding an iron mace. He and the god in golden armour issuing from the Marshal's helmet did battle while the two armies cheered them on. They fought countless bouts until the warrior on the black dragon began to force the one in golden armour back. At this point Scimitar with one blow of his sword cut the Devil's Marshal from his horse. The Sorcerer had seen how the wind was rising and thunder crashing from the Song side and was just rising to his feet when one of Thunderer's explosive shells hit him. It smashed him to smithereens. The southern troops were routed and fled back into Muzhou as fast as their legs would carry them. Whiskers knocked one of their commanders from his horse with a spear thrust and Skyhawk killed another with a throwing knife.

When the soldiers inside the city saw the Sorcerer killed by a shell, they began pouring out over the walls. Song Jiang's men burst through the gates and pressed forward eagerly to seize the Minister and the rest. No one stopped to ask any names: they were all killed. The first thing Song Jiang did was to burn down Fang La's palace. The valuables in it were shared out among the army commanders. A proclamation was issued to reassure the populace.

But before they even had time to number their losses, a scout reported: "The Flautist has been knocked from his horse by a spear thrust on the road west to Black Dragon Ridge and cut in two by Marshal Shi Bao's sword. The Dandy tried to retaliate and Shi Bao, the bastard, killed him with his flying hammer. After his successes Shi Bao is sure to attack us."

On hearing of these two further losses, Song Jiang was sick at heart. He immediately sent Scimitar, Colonel Hua, Thunderclap and Whiskers to confront Marshal Shi Bao and try to capture Black Dragon Ridge.

Now had these four not attacked Black Dragon Ridge, things might have been different. For in Clearwater a rebel host is to be annihilated, at Bangyuan Gap the outlaw Prince taken alive, and in consequence the fame of Song Jiang and his company will live a thousand years, their deeds be proclaimed in a million chronicles.

If you want to know how Song Jiang prevailed over the enemy, you must read the next chapter.

Chapter 118

The Unicorn has a great battle at Sundance Pass; Song Jiang plans to capture the citadel at Bangyuan Gap!

Now as Scimitar and his three companions raced up Black Dragon Ridge they came face to face with Marshal Shi Bao and his men. "You bandits, how dare you kill our comrades!" Scimitar yelled at them.

When Marshal Shi Bao saw it was Scimitar he had no stomach for the fight. He retreated to the top of the pass and ordered his lieutenant Bai Qin to fight Scimitar. Two horses met, weapons were raised to strike, but before they had completed ten bouts, the gong was beaten urgently at the top of the pass to recall the troops. Scimitar did not pursue them.

Up on top of the pass there was a state of panic. Marshal Shi Bao had only been attending to the attack from the east. He had not been prepared for trouble from the west, where Marshal Tong now came storming up with a large squadron of cavalry. The chief Song general was Wang Bing and he took on the southerners' Jing De. After a dozen bouts Wang Bing knocked his opponent from his horse.

Little Duke and the Halberdier charged forward to capture the pass but before they got there a huge boulder came crashing down on the Halberdier killing both horse and man.

When Scimitar on the western slopes saw the tumult at the top of the mountain and learnt that there were Song troops on the west, he gave all his commanders the order to launch a concerted attack. There was fierce fighting on top of the pass, with the defenders pressed on both sides.

Little Duke met Bai Qin and they engaged in furious combat. After a couple of bouts Bai Qin thrust with his spear and Little

Duke dodged, allowing the weapon to pass harmlessly under his armpit, and then responded by slashing with his halberd. The two horsemen were so close they had no room to wield their weapons, so they cast them aside and wrestled with each other. They had come to a very precipitous part of the mountain where there was no firm foothold for the horses and the furious struggle of the riders suddenly caused both men and horses to plunge over the edge. Both men fell together to their deaths on the mountain!

By now Scimitar and his men were storming up the mountain on foot. With Song troops coming up on both sides, Shi Bao could see there was no escape either way and rather than face the ignominy of capture he killed himself with his own sword. The pass at Black Dragon Ridge was taken and Scimitar ordered Song Jiang to be informed immediately.

Down at the river base the four southern boat commanders, seeing Black Dragon Ridge was lost and Muzhou had fallen, abandoned their boats and fled across the river, where people living along the other bank captured two of them and brought them in to Muzhou. The other two got away and it is not known where they went.

The main Song army now headed back to Muzhou. When Song Jiang heard, he came out to meet them. Marshal Tong and General Liu entered the city and took up quarters there. After they had installed themselves, they issued a proclamation to calm the enemy troops and civilians, telling them to go about their ordinary business. Countless southern troops surrendered. Song Jiang distributed all the public stores of rice among the people, and the whole district was pacified and renewed its allegiance to the Emperor. The two captured boat commanders were cut to pieces and their hearts offered up to the spirits of Ruan the Second and Flagpole. Offerings were also made to the spirits of all the comrades who had died on Black Dragon Ridge. White-Water Dragon and the other boat commanders were enlisted again to prepare several boats and transport the captured officials of the bogus king to Marshal Zhang at headquarters. Song Jiang's grief at losing Little Duke and the Halberdier was boundless. He ordered no further advance. He was waiting till the Unicorn and his forces arrived so they could carry out a combined attack on Clearwater.

We shall leave Song Jiang in the camp at Muzhou and tell how, after the troops were divided at Hangzhou, the Unicorn, as second-in-command of Song Jiang's army with thirty thousand men and twenty commanders under him, took the mountain route to Shezhou. They passed King Qian's old capital of Lin'an and began to approach Sundance Pass. This was guarded by one of Fang La's generals called Pang Wanchun, known as the Master Bowman. He was the finest archer in all the regions south of the river held by Fang La. He had two lieutenants, Lei Jiong and Ji Ji, who could handle immensely strong crossbows and also fought with spiked maces. They each had five thousand men.

The pass, then, was defended by these three. When they heard that the Unicorn, second-in-command of the Song forces, was on his way, they readied their weapons and awaited the enemy's arrival. Now the Unicorn's army was very nearly at the foot of the pass and they sent out an advance guard of three thousand infantry under Tattooed Dragon, Madcap, River-Jumper, White-Spotted Snake, Tiger-Killer and the Pill Monger to reconnoitre. These six commanders were all mounted on war chargers, while the rest were on foot. They proceeded to the foot of the pass without encountering a single enemy soldier and Tattooed Dragon began to get suspicious and was about to call for a discussion. But before he could open his mouth they reached the foot of the pass and looking up saw a white embroidered banner with Bowman standing beneath it.

When Bowman saw Tattooed Dragon and his companions, he began to insult them: "You're a bunch of robbers, only fit for life on Mount Liang! You wangled yourselves an amnesty from the Song emperor. How dare you invade our territory, and pretend to be heroes. Have you heard that men call me the Master Bowman? I'm told that among your rabble there's someone they call Hua Rong the Archer. Send him out so I can give him a lesson in archery! You lot can have a little demonstration of my mastery right now!" Even before this tirade finished, an arrow was winging its way. It hit Tattooed Dragon fair and square, toppling him from his horse. The other five rushed forward to pick him up and get him back on his horse, intending to carry him to safety. But at that moment gongs rang out on top of the mountain and volleys of arrows were fired simultaneously from the pine trees on either side of them. They had to forget about Tattooed Dragon; it was every man for himself. When they reached the mouth of the gorge, Lei and Ji were positioned there on either side and the crossbow bolts rained down. Brave as lions they might be, but there was no escaping this barrage. There on the river bank the unfortunate six learnt all about the vanity of human aspirations! Tattooed Dragon, Madcap and the rest, not one of them escaped; they were just a pile of corpses on the mountainside!

Of three thousand infantry only about a hundred men survived and got back to tell the Unicorn what had happened. The Unicorn was thunderstruck. For a long time he stood there in a daze, like someone out of his wits or drunk.

The Strategist also grieved for his old comrades River-Jumper and White-Spotted Snake, but in the end he said: "Calm yourself, commander, or we will fail in the main task. We should devise a new tactic for taking the pass and killing their commanders, in order to avenge this horror."

The Unicorn said: "The Leader gave all these commanders and men into my charge and now before even winning one battle I have lost six of the leaders and three thousand men. Only a hundred have come back. If things go on like this, how will I ever be able to meet him in Shezhou?"

The Strategist said: "There's an old military saying: 'Topography counts for more than time, and good relations with the locals are the most important of all.' We are all men from the central plains, from Shandong and Hebei. We're not used to fighting along the rivers, so we don't have the territorial advantage here. We must get some of the local people to show us the way; we must learn from them all the twists and turns of the mountain trails."

The Unicorn said: "You are quite right. But who should we send to find out about this?"

The Strategist said: "I'd like to suggest the Flea. With his ability to walk on rooftops and scale walls he should be ideal for the mission."

The Unicorn accordingly summoned the Flea and the latter, after he'd had it explained to him, set off, equipped with some dry rations and a sharp dagger.

The Flea made his way deep into the mountains. He was so intent on finding his way the day passed quickly and it began to get dark. He came to a place where he could see a light glimmering in the distance. He said to himself: "If there's a light, there must be someone's house." Under cover of darkness he crept towards the light. What he found was a little thatched hut, with light filtering through the walls. He walked up to the front and peered in. An old monk was sitting on the floor reciting the scriptures. The Flea knocked on the door and the monk called to a young boy, who opened up. The Flea entered and prostrated himself before the monk. The latter said: "No need for ceremony, sir. How did you find your way here, in these times of strife?"

"I will not deceive you, Master," the Flea said. "I am one of Song Jiang's officers, from Mount Liang, they call me the Flea. We have been commissioned by the Emperor to capture Fang La. Unfortunately yesterday six of our commanders were shot dead by the enemy forces holding Sundance Pass. We don't know any way to get across and they have sent me to reconnoitre and find out what trails there are that cross the mountain. I have been wandering all day through some very wild places and now I've got here. I very much hope you will be able to instruct me, if there are some hidden ways to cross the mountain. I should be extremely grateful."

The old monk said: "The people here have all suffered persecution from Fang La, there is none who does not hate him. I live here through the charity of the people, whose offerings feed me. But lately the villagers have all been driven away and since I have nowhere else to go I just have to stay here and wait for death to come. It is a great cause for rejoicing that the Song army is here and everyone is pleased about it. If you capture the bandits you will be delivering the people from a great evil. I have been afraid to say too much lest they get to hear of it. But if you are a representative of the imperial army, then I can talk to you freely. Where I am here there is no way over the pass. But there is a path over to the west that will take you across. I fear though that the enemy may have blocked it and you won't be able to get through."

The Flea said: "If there is this path, Master, I would like to know if it connects with the enemy's camp."

The old monk said: "This hidden path comes out right behind the enemy camp. Downhill from there is the way across the mountain. Only I'm afraid they may have put big boulders across it and it will be hard to get through."

The Flea said: "Never mind about that. So long as there is a path, there's no problem about anything they may have done to block it; we can find a way to deal with that. After what you've told me, I'd better go back and report to the commander-in-chief. I'll be back to reward you later."

The old monk said: "If you see any strangers, please don't talk to them about me."

"I'm very discreet. I won't say a word about you."

The Flea bade the old monk farewell and went back to the camp. He told the Unicorn what he had heard. The latter was delighted and asked the Strategist to devise a plan for capturing the pass. The Strategist said: "If there's a path through the mountain, we've got them! You must send the Flea out again with someone else because there's an important job to do."

"What is the job?" the Flea asked.

The Strategist replied: "The important part is starting fires and letting off flares. The two of you must carry rockets and kindling materials with you. Go to the back of their camp and get the fires and the rockets going, that is going to be your job."

The Flea said: "If that's all it is, there's no need for anyone else to come with me. I can do it all myself. If you send anyone else along he won't be as good at climbing as me and it could mess things up. But if I go and carry out this assignment, how are the rest of you going to get up the mountain?"

The Strategist said: "That's easy. That ambush of theirs can only work once. I don't care about their ambushes. Whenever we find thick undergrowth along the way we shall set fire to it. Then it won't make any difference if they do have an ambush."

The Flea said: "Brilliant!" He collected the incendiary materials, tied the rockets in a pack and strapped it to his back, bade the Unicorn farewell and was ready to set off. The Unicorn gave him twenty taels of silver and a catty of rice to give to the old monk and ordered a soldier to carry it. In the afternoon he and the bearer took his former route to the thatched hut where he said to the old monk: "Our commander-in-chief sends his respects and offers you this small gift." He handed over the silver and the rice, which the monk took, and then sent the soldier back to the camp. Then he asked the monk if he would show him the way. The monk said: "Wait a little. You can go when it's really dark. If you go in daylight I'm afraid they may spot you." He prepared some supper for the Flea and when night came he told his acolyte to guide the Flea as far as a certain place and then return, taking care not to be seen. The boy led them deep into the mountains by hidden trails. Traversing the forest and skirting peaks, sometimes having to clamber on hands and knees, they covered several miles of trail through mountain fastnesses under a pale moon, till they reached a forbidding cliff, a jagged wall of rock. A single narrow opening was visible in the distance, but great boulders were piled up there creating a formidable barrier.

The boy said: "You can see the pass from here, commander. It's where that pile of rocks is. Beyond that there is a clear road."

"You go back now, lad," said the Flea. "I can find my way from here."

The boy left and the Flea brought his special skills to bear — walking on roof tops, remember, scaling walls, vaulting fences and doing dodgy deals — as he negotiated the piled-up rocks. Over in the east a red glow was filling the sky, arising among the trees. It was the Unicorn and the Strategist, who had struck camp and were advancing towards the pass, setting fire to the forest as they went. The four or five hundred men in the lead, were picking up their dead as they skirted the mountain and setting fire to the undergrowth, to rob the enemy troops in ambush of their cover.

Up on Sundance Pass Bowman heard that the Song troops were setting fire to the forest and said: "So that's their plan. They want to prevent our setting up ambushes. Well, we'll just concentrate on holding the pass. They'll never get through."

As the Song troops gradually drew closer, he and his lieutenants, Lei and Ji, took up their positions in the pass.

Meanwhile the Flea had made his way step by step up the mountain. He climbed into the crown of a tall tree and hid among the foliage. From this vantage point he was able to observe the three enemy commanders preparing their arrows and cocking their crossbows and settling down behind cover to wait. He could also see the Song troops starting up the fires as they advanced. Among them were Leopard's Head and Twin Rods, who reined in their horses below the pass and shouted: "You villains, how dare you offer resistance to the imperial army?" The southerners were just waiting for the chance to shoot; they had not seen the Flea, who was already behind their lines.

Cautiously the Flea climbed down from the tree and made his way to the back of the pass. There he found two piles of firewood. He took out his tinder box and kindled a flame. He set the rockets up on top of the firewood, laid a trail of gunpowder to ignite the further of the two piles, and then lit the fuse on the nearer one. As the fuses burnt he took more rockets and a light and climbed onto the roof of a building to set fire to it. The two piles of firewood ignited simultaneously and the rockets went off with a shattering bang. The effect on the troops guarding the pass was devastating. A great cry went up and they all tried to flee. No one thought any more about fighting. As Bowman and his two lieutenants rushed back to put out the fire, the Flea set off more rockets on the roof of the building. They went off with a roar that shook the whole building and the terrified enemy troops threw down their weapons, abandoned their armour and clothing and fled down the other side of the mountain. From his position on the roof the Flea was shouting: "There's ten thousand Song troops on the pass. You'd all better surrender if you want to save your lives!"

Bowman was frightened out of his wits, stumbling about in panic. Lei and Ji were scared rigid, too shocked even to move.

盧俊義大戰昱嶺關

Leopard's Head and Twin Rods led the charge up the mountain and dashed to the head of the pass. All the leaders were competing to be first and they chased the fleeing southerners more than ten miles beyond the pass. Colonel Sun captured Lei, the Fire General took Ji, Bowman was the only one who got away. Most of his troops were captured. The Song army made camp at the top of the pass.

With Sundance Pass now in his hands, the Unicorn rewarded the Flea. The hearts of Lei and Ji were cut out there on the mountain and offered to the spirits of Tattooed Dragon, Madcap and the other six, whose recovered bodies were buried there too. The rest of the dead were burnt.

Next day all the leaders armed and mounted. A report was sent to Marshal Zhang, informing him of the capture of Sundance Pass, and the troops moved on, making camp when they were close to Shezhou.

Now the governor of Shezhou was Fang La's uncle, Fang Hou. He had two assistants, civilian appointments, to help guard the town. One was Chancellor Wang, the other Secretary Gao. Under their orders were another dozen military officers and a garrison of twenty thousand men. Chancellor Wang had originally been a local stone mason. He wielded a bronze spear and had a fine horse, known as the Mountain Flyer, because it could traverse mountains and rivers as if they were level ground. Secretary Gao was also a local man, scion of an ancient family. His weapon was the rods. Because these two had considerable literary talents, Fang La had conferred high rank on them and given them temporary command of troops.

When the defeated Bowman returned he went straight to the palace and told the Royal Uncle: "The Song troops have overrun the pass because local people showed them the hidden trails to follow on the mountain. Our army has been routed and we cannot stop the enemy."

The Royal Uncle was outraged. He stormed at Bowman, saying: "Sundance Pass is our most important weapon against attack. If the Song army has broken through, it won't be long before they are at the gates of Shezhou. How are we going to keep them out?"

Chancellor Wang said: "Calm yourself, Your Highness. Remember the saying, 'Victory and defeat are a soldier's lot; you can't blame anything on a single battle.' Your Highness should postpone sentencing Bowman and let him lead the troops again with orders to win, to be first in the field and repulse the enemy. If he fails again you can double the sentence."

The Royal Uncle concurred and gave Bowman five thousand troops, with orders to go out and face the enemy and not come back till he had defeated them.

After Sundance Pass, the Unicorn pressed on to Shezhou and launched an attack with all his commanders. The gates opened and Bowman rode out to offer battle. The two armies took up their positions and Bowman rode out in front and issued his challenge. Golden Wings rode out from the Song ranks with his steel spear and engaged him. Before they had fought five bouts, Bowman fled. Golden Wings, eager to show his prowess, gave chase. Bowman twisted in the saddle and fired an arrow behind him. Golden Wings adroitly plucked the arrow from the air. Unfortunately it did not occur to him that Bowman could fire off two arrows in quick succession. Having caught one arrow he relaxed his vigilance and gave himself up to the chase. The bowstring twanged as Bowman fired a second arrow and Golden Wings fell. On the city walls Chancellor Wang and Secretary Gao saw the enemy commander fall and reckoning that Bowman had won the fight charged out with all the troops remaining in the city. The Song forces were defeated and retreated to a position ten miles away where they made camp. The leaders were counted and it was found that they had also lost the Gardener in the fighting. When she heard her husband was dead, Sister Sun the Ogress sent some of her troops out to bring the body back for cremation and she wept for a long time. The Unicorn's heart was heavy. His plan, he felt, had not been good, and he summoned the Strategist to develop a new one: "In today's attack we lost two more leaders. What are we going to do?"

The Strategist said: "Winning or losing, victory or defeat, it's all in the day's work for a soldier. Today the enemy saw us retreat and they'll want to make the most of it. They'll be thinking tonight is the time to take advantage and I'm sure they'll raid our camp. Let us redeploy all our troops and set up ambushes on all sides. Tie some sheep up here and then make certain arrangements. Twin Rods can set up an ambush on the left, Leopard's Head on the right, the Water General and the Fire General to the rear and the rest of you conceal yourselves all around along all the small paths. Tonight when they attack wait for the signal flare from the centre and then fall on them from every direction."

When the Unicorn had issued all the instructions, everyone went off to make their preparations.

Now Chancellor Wang and Secretary Gao were not without ideas. After discussing things with Bowman, they went to the Royal Uncle and put a proposal to him: "Today the Song army is defeated, They have retreated to a position about ten miles away. They are camped in the middle of nowhere and their army must be exhausted. Surely we should take this opportunity to go there and finish the business off?"

The Royal Uncle said: "Consider it carefully with all the commanders, and if it can be done, do it."

Secretary Gao said: "I propose with Bowman to carry out an attack on their camp. The Chancellor will stay here with Your Highness to guard the city."

That night the two commanders put on their armour and led out their forces, with harness bells muffled and the troops gagged to prevent talking. They reached the Song camp. The gates were closed and they were at first reluctant to go in. For a while they listened to the drum beat sounding the hours. At first it sounded clearly enough, but later it became confused. Secretary Gao reined in his horse and said: "We can't go on!"

Bowman said: "Why not, Your Excellency?"

"The sound of their drum is unclear. There's something up!"

"I don't think so, Your Excellency. They came back defeated today. They must be exhausted. They're half asleep, that's why the drumbeat is not clear. We're wasting time, Your Excellency. We ought to attack!"

"All right then!" with this Secretary Gao gave the word for an all-out attack on the camp. But when they got through the gate and headed for the enemy headquarters, there was not a single enemy soldier to be seen. All they found was a willow tree with a number of sheep tied to it. Attached to the sheep's legs were drumsticks, arranged to beat the drums. So that was why the drum beat had sounded so unclear! They had captured an empty camp. It was extremely ominous. The cry went up: "It's a trap!" As they turned to leave fire broke out in the enemy headquarters and explosions sounded on the surrounding hillside. On every side the troops in ambush sprang out and attacked. The southerners raced for the gate, but here they met Twin Rods, who roared: "Dismount and surrender, you bandits, if you want to save your lives!"

Secretary Gao's only thought was to run for it. He had no stomach for a fight. But Twin Rods was onto him, bringing his weapon down with a force that split his skull. Bowman fought desperately to escape from the encirclement and succeeded in getting away. But he was not watching out for Spots who was still concealed and with his hooked spear tripped Bowman's horse and captured him alive. The rest of the army pursued the southerners along the mountain trails until dawn and then returned to camp.

Back at headquarters the Unicorn ordered the leaders to be counted and it was reported that Scarface had been bitten in the foot by a poisonous snake on one of the mountain paths and the poison had risen to his stomach and killed him. They cut out Bowman's heart and offered it to the spirits of Golden Wings, Tattooed Dragon and the rest. The head was then sent back to Marshal Zhang.

Next day the Unicorn renewed the attack on Shezhou. They found the gates of the town open. No flag was flying on the walls and there were no sentries in the watchtower. The Fire General and the Water General eager for glory charged through the gate, the Unicorn following with the rest of the army. He had cause to lament. The other two had already gone through, but Chancellor Wang on learning that the force sent to attack the enemy camp had been destroyed had set up this pretence of an abandoned town and had dug a big pit just inside the gate. The two leaders bursting with heroism had taken no precautions as they entered and both men and horses had plunged into the pit. The spearsmen and archers concealed on either side stepped forward and slaughtered them. Unfortunate water and fire geniuses, their fame was buried with them in a hole in the ground!

The Unicorn grieved for the loss of two more leaders. He quickly gave the order that each man in the advance guard was to carry a sack of earth to throw in the pit and to go on in and massacre the southerners till the pit was filled with their bodies too. He led the charge into the city himself, on a prancing horse. He met the Royal Uncle, Fang Hou. They had fought just one bout before the Unicorn, driven by his burning rage, summoned up all his considerable powers and struck a blow with his halberd that swept his opponent clean off his horse. The troops in the city opened the west gate and fled. The leaders of the Song army fought their way forward to capture the southerners.

As Chancellor Wang was trying to escape he ran into Green-Eyes, who attacked with his spear. Wang counter-attacked, also with a spear. Since Green-Eyes was fighting on foot and Wang was mounted, Green-Eyes was soon trampled under the horse's hooves. The Guv saw him knocked down and rushed to the rescue. Wang was fiendishly skilful with the spear and the Guv had no chance against him. After several bouts Wang had a clear advantage and with a sudden spear thrust took the Guv's life. He died on the spot.

Colonel Sun, the Tamer, Forester and Rhinoceros now arrived on the scene and halted Wang's charge. He fought furiously against four adversaries at once and showed absolutely no fear. Then suddenly Leopard's Head joined the fray. This was another who could not be frightened and even if Wang had had three heads and six arms he wouldn't have been able to stand up against five. All of them now were stabbing and hacking away at Wang, and this time things were quite beyond the unfortunate Chancellor's control. The five Song commanders were soon galloping back with the head to show it to the Unicorn, who by now was resting in the Shezhou governor's residence. Order was restored, a proclamation was issued to reassure the citizens, the leaders were given quarters inside the town and a messenger was sent with a report to Marshal Zhang. At the same time the Unicorn informed Song Jiang that he was ready to attack.

Song Jiang and his comrades, remember, were at Muzhou, waiting for the armies to join up so they could attack the bandits' hideout together. He received the Unicorn's dispatch announcing that Shezhou had been reconquered and the commanders had occupied the city centre and were awaiting the command to move against the viper's nest. Song Jiang also learnt that they had lost Tattooed Dragon, Madcap, River-Jumper, White-Spotted Snake, Tiger-Killer, Pill Monger, Golden Wings, the Gardener, Scarface, the Fire General, the Water General, Green-Eyes and the Guv, thirteen leaders in all, as well as many junior officers. It was extremely painful and he grieved bitterly. The Professor did his best to animate him: "A man's living and dying are ordained by fate. This grieving is damaging to your health. Let us keep our eye on what is important, the national interest."

Song Jiang said: "You are right, but one cannot help grieving. I keep remembering how at the outset one hundred and eight names were recorded in mystic writing on the stone tablet. Who would have expected that now so many are fallen! One after another, so many of my limbs hacked off!"

The Professor tried to console Song Jiang and then wrote a reply to the Unicorn, fixing a date for the joint attack on Clearwater.

Now we shall leave Song Jiang and the Unicorn and turn to Fang La, sitting in council in his citadel at Bangyuan Gap in Clearwater, discussing with his officials, civil and military, how to deal with Song Jiang's offensive. When the remnants of the defeated army straggled back and told him Shezhou had fallen, and that his uncle, Fang Hou, the Chancellor and the Secretary were all dead, and the Song forces in two divisions were advancing to attack Clearwater, Fang La was horrified. To the ranks of his assembled courtiers he said: "All of you have received honours from me, you have your share of power in my government and enjoy great riches. How can you allow Song Jiang's forces to push you back like this and allow so many cities to fall, so that now Clearwater remains our only stronghold? I have just been told that the Song army is on its way here. How are we to confront them?"

Then Chief Minister Lou stepped forward and declared: "Now that the Song forces have reached Shezhou, it will be difficult to defend this palace. Since our numbers are small and our leaders few, I am afraid that unless Your Majesty leads the campaign himself our generals will not go forward with confidence."

Fang La said: "That is reasonable." He accordingly issued a proclamation in which he declared that every region and every district, every official and imperial servant, councillor or officer was to go forward under the sovereign's leadership to conclude the war.

Lou also asked: "What leader should we appoint to command the vanguard?"

Fang La replied: "I will appoint the commander of my own palace guard, the royal nephew Fang Jie, with Colonel Du Wei from my personal staff as his deputy. They can have thirteen thousand guards from the citadel and three thousand officers to lead the attack."

This Fang Jie was indeed Fang La's nephew, grandson of the Fang Hou who had commanded the garrison at Shezhou and had just been killed by the Unicorn, and he was eager to avenge his grandfather, so he really wanted this command. He was a scholar, but he had learned to manage the square halberd and was as brave as they come. As for Du Wei, he had been a Shezhou blacksmith skilled in the manufacture of weapons and was a close friend of Fang La's. He used six throwing knives and fought on foot.

Fang La also gave out another order sending Instructor Ho Conglong of the palace guard with ten thousand men against the Unicorn in Shezhou.

We will leave Fang La to his arrangements for countering the enemy on two fronts, and rejoin Song Jiang and his army as they set off by land and water, leaving Muzhou and heading for Clearwater. White-Water Dragon with his sailors and boats pushed off from the river bank while the Professor and Song Jiang rode with the land force. The Professor spoke as follows: "My one fear about this campaign is that Fang La may escape deep into the mountains where it will be difficult to catch him. If we are to take him alive so that he can be handed over and exhibited to the Emperor, we need cooperation from within. If we can make contact with one of his own people we will be able to get him. We need to know his whereabouts, so he can't get away."

Song Jiang said: "Right, in that case we must use the trick of pretending surrender, we must fight deception with deception, in order to set up a conspiracy within. We sent Mr. Chai and the Prodigy there as spies, but we have not heard anything from them. Who can we send now? It must be someone who can plausibly pretend to be surrendering."

The Professor said: "In my view the White-Water Dragon would be the best one to send. He can take some transports full of grain and pretend he is handing them over as a pledge of his good faith. Fang La is a peasant at heart and when he sees so much grain he won't be able to resist it."

Song Jiang said: "Good thinking!" He sent Magic Messenger by water to where White-Water Dragon was, to acquaint him with the plan and give him his instructions. As soon as White-Water Dragon had grasped what was wanted, Magic Messenger returned to the main army.

White-Water Dragon told Ruan the Fifth and Ruan the Seventh to disguise themselves as bo'suns with Cave Dragon and River Rider as ordinary seamen. With sixty transports, all flying newly altered flags signalling that the supplies they carried were intended as tribute, they sailed up the main river. When they approached Clearwater, southern war boats appeared up river and bore down on them, simultaneously firing arrows. White-Water Dragon shouted out: "Don't fire, I want to talk! We want to surrender and we are bringing these supplies as tribute to your prince, to feed his army. We hope you will accept us."

The commander of the other boats, seeing they were unarmed, held his fire and sent someone across to question them. He saw that the boats were indeed full of grain and a report was sent to Chief Minister Lou, saying that the White-Water Dragon had surrendered and was handing over grain supplies as tribute. The

Chief Minister ordered the men ashore. When White-Water Dragon had paid his respects, the Chief Minister asked him: "What exactly are you in Song Jiang's army? What is your position? And why do you want to surrender?"

"My name is Li Jun and I was born on the Yangtze. I saved Song Jiang's life when we raided the execution ground in Jiangzhou. Recently he received an amnesty from the Emperor. Since he was made general and commander of the government expeditionary force, he has forgotten what he owes to us. He has slighted me many times. Now with this invasion of your territory we keep losing more and more of our comrades and he himself cannot make up his mind whether to go forward or retreat, but he always forces us sailors into the front line. We are tired of being humiliated, and we have secretly diverted his grain supplies to hand over to you so we can surrender."

After all this the Chief Minister not only decided to trust him but also took him into the palace to tell Fang La about his surrender and the supplies. White-Water Dragon prostrated himself before Fang La and repeated his request. Fang La suspected nothing. He told the four boat captains to bring their boats into the government harbour and promised that when he had driven out Song Jiang's army he would reward them further. White-Water Dragon prostrated himself in thanks and went out to supervise the unloading of the supplies, for removal to the government granary. Of this no more.

We now return to Song Jiang and the Professor and their arrangements. Four commanders, Scimitar, Colonel Hua, Thunderclap and Whiskers were appointed to the vanguard and they led the army as far as the border of Clearwater, where they came into contact with Fang La's nephew, Fang Jie. The two armies took up their positions and then Fang Jie rode out with his halberd at the slope, while Du Wei on foot stood behind him. This Du Wei was in full armour with five throwing knives slung behind him and a seven-star sword in his hand. One behind the other they rode out in front of their army. Thunderclap was the first out on Song Jiang's side. Whirling his wolf's-tooth mace he charged Fang Jie. Now Fang Jie was a young man, but very determined and he handled the square halberd with great expertise. He fought more than thirty bouts with Thunderclap and neither had the advantage. Fang Jie could see that Thunderclap was extremely skilled, and was fighting with a lifetime's experience behind him; he gave his opponent no opening. The contest was at its height and Thunderclap continued to use all his skills, not offering his opponent the slightest chance. But he failed to observe the scoundrel Du Wei who had followed on behind Fang Jie's horse and who now darted out with one of his knives in his hand and flung it in Thunderclap's face. As he tried to dodge, Thunderclap was caught by a blow from Fang Jie's halberd and knocked from his horse. He was dead before he hit the ground. Poor Thunderclap, he was extinguished quite soundlessly! Fang Jie did not dare follow up this victory and the Song troops were able to drag the body away, using hooks. They were demoralized by the loss of Thunderclap and Song Jiang had to reorganize them to continue the battle as well as make arrangements for the burial.

Fang Jie was full of his victory. He stood in front of the ranks and yelled: "If there are any more of you Song warriors who fancy yourselves, come out and fight!"

Thereupon Song Jiang rode out in front. He could see that behind Fang Jie on horseback under a yellow silk umbrella was the rebel prince himself, Fang La.

Fang La now rode out in front and took control of the battle. When he saw Song Jiang there he sent Fang Jie off to fight and capture him. For their part, the Song troops were preparing to engage with the aim of capturing Fang La. As Fang Jie was about to do battle, a messenger arrived: "Instructor Ho of the royal guard and his men on their way to relieve Shezhou have been captured by Song troops under the Unicorn. Their forces have been destroyed and Song troops have reached the mountain behind us."

Horrified by the news, Fang La hurriedly ordered the army to fall back on the citadel. Fang Jie told Du Wei they must hold the front line to give the royal carriage time to get away. Having done this, they too withdrew.

宋公明智取清溪洞

As they reached the outskirts of Clearwater they heard a tremendous uproar rising heavenwards, and saw fires blazing everywhere, men and horses milling about. It was White-Water Dragon and the boat captains setting fire to Clearwater. When Fang La saw this he ordered the royal guard into the city to save it. They charged in and the situation became very confused.

Seeing that the enemy were in retreat, Song Jiang's forces gave chase. When they reached the city and saw the flames they knew that White-Water Dragon and his companions were at work. The troops were mustered and every commander ordered to attack on his own initiative. By now the Unicorn's men had also got beyond the pass and were coming up in support on either side, their arrival most timely. Song troops were attacking the Clearwater base from every side. Song Jiang and all his comrades were charging in from all directions, every one of them bent on capturing southern troops and razing Clearwater to the ground. Fang La now had only Fang Jie to lead the army and protect him and cover his withdrawal to the citadel at Bangyuan Gap. Song Jiang's main force now entered Clearwater. They burst into Fang La's palace, collected up all the illegal weapons, money and treasure, and after checking the palace stores set fire to it, burning down Fang La's whole establishment. The government warehouses were also ransacked. Song Jiang and the Unicorn's joined forces and made camp inside the city. The commanders all gathered to claim their rewards.

When the leaders of both armies were counted it was found that Perilous and the Ogress had both been killed by Du Wei's throwing knives, Rhinoceros and Skyscraper had been trampled to death in the mêlée by cavalry; the Executioner, Spots and Strongarm, who had received wounds so serious that the doctor was unable to save them, were dead too. Ruan the Fifth who had been first into Clearwater was killed by Chief Minister Lou. The Song leaders claimed the capture of ninety-two of the usurper's officers, and were duly rewarded. Only Chief Minister Lou and Du Wei were unaccounted for. A proclamation was issued to reassure the populace and the captured officers were sent off to Marshal Zhang at headquarters for beheading. Later a member of the public came and reported that the Chief Minister, having killed Ruan the Fifth and knowing that the city was lost, had hanged himself from a tree. As for the villainous Du Wei, he tried to hide in the house of his kept woman, Baby Wang, but had been handed over by her protector. Song Jiang rewarded the protector, and then sent people to fetch the body of the Chief Minister. He ordered Blossom to cut out Du Wei's heart and liver and the warm blood was spilt in offering to the spirits of Thunderclap, Ruan the Fifth, Perilous and the Ogress and all the rest who had given their lives in the battle for Clearwater. Song Jiang publicly offered incense with his own hands and then next day with the Unicorn marched to the citadel at Bangyuan Gap and invested it.

As for Fang La, with only his nephew Fang Jie to guard him he had withdrawn to his citadel. There his forces strengthened their defences and would not come out to fight. Song Jiang and the Unicorn laid siege to the place, but they had no means of getting inside.

For Fang La, however, it was like sitting on needles. When the siege had been continuing for a number of days and Fang La's spirits were at a very low ebb, a tall gentleman in court robes presented himself, bowing to the ground in front of the throne. "Your Majesty," he said, "I am nothing, but your munificence and grace are such that I must do my best to requite them by offering you my services, relying on the ancient knowledge of tactics I have acquired, the hidden secrets of warfare, all the lessons and experience derived from the manuals of military art. If Your Majesty will grant me the troops, I shall repel the Song invaders and restore national honour. Will Your Majesty accept my offer?"

Fang La was overjoyed and gave orders immediately for the palace guard to be put at the speaker's disposal to counter-attack and challenge Song Jiang, for whatever might result from it, this person was clearly someone outstanding.

Now if Fang La had not given command of his army to this person things would certainly have been different. For now there were to be heads rolling on the steps to the throne, hot blood gushing over palace walls. The viper's nest would be swept clean and Fang La taken, and Song Jiang would reach the pinnacle of his fame.

But if you want to know who this was who had volunteered to lead Fang La's army, you must read the next chapter.

Chapter 119

At Zhejiang by the riverside Monk passes away; Song Jiang returns to his birthplace in a silk robe!

Now the gentleman who had appeared on the steps to the throne and offered to lead Fang La's army out to fight was in fact the royal son-in-law and Master of the Rolls, Prince Ke Yin. After hearing what he had to say, Fang La could scarcely contain his joy. Prince Ke Yin was to be joint commander of the southern forces and with Yun Bi, known as the Master's Man, he put on his armour and rode out to take up his command. Fang La, after giving him his own gilt armour and royal robe and finding him a good mount, sent him forth. Together with Fang Jie, the royal nephew, Prince Ke Yin commanded ten thousand palace guards, with more than twenty subordinate officers. They rode out of the citadel and deployed in battle formation.

Song Jiang's army besieging the citadel had already allotted different sectors to the various commanders. Song Jiang was in the centre, and because he was troubled by the thought that two thirds of his comrades had been lost and they still had not captured Fang La and that the southerners would not come out to fight, his brows were knitted in a frown and his countenance expressed deep gloom, until, that is, a soldier came in and reported: "They are coming out of the citadel to fight!"

Song Jiang and the Unicorn immediately ordered everyone to mount and ride forward. As the armies took up their positions, Prince Ke Yin was the first to be seen riding out in front of the southern ranks to do battle. Was there anyone in Song Jiang's army who did not recognize him? For who else was it but Mr. Chai! Song Jiang ordered Colonel Hua out to take on the challenger. Colonel Hua galloped forward, his lance in the rest.

He stopped in front of the enemy and shouted: "What kind of villain are you, you traitor, daring to oppose our might? If I capture you, you will be hacked to pieces, your flesh and bones made into mincemeat! Your only chance is to dismount now and give yourself up."

Prince Ke Yin, Mr. Chai that is, replied very clearly: "I am Ke Yin of Shandong. Who does not know my name? You scum, you're just a bunch of outlaws from the Marshes of Mount Liang. Do you think I'm not a match for your tricks? I am resolved to exterminate you and deliver the city."

Song Jiang and the Unicorn had been listening to this. They thought carefully about Mr. Chai's words. There must be a hidden meaning. His name was Chai, and he had changed it to Ke. Well, *chai*, "firewood", and *ke*, "a wooden handle", were pretty similar. And his given name *jin*, "enter", had been changed to *yin*, "lead in", that was the same too. The Professor said: "Let's watch and see what happens when Colonel Hua fights him."

Colonel Hua, levelled his spear, made his horse prance and charged into battle. Two horses met, two kinds of weapons were raised and the two leaders became so closely embroiled that they blended into a single mass. Then Mr. Chai murmured to Colonel Hua: "Now please pretend to be defeated, brother." Colonel Hua heard. He went on fighting for another three bouts, then turned his horse and galloped off: "I disdain to chase you, you coward," Mr. Chai shouted. "If there's anyone else who thinks himself a fighter, let him come out and face me!'

Colonel Hua galloped back to his side and told Song Jiang and the Unicorn what had happened. The Professor said: "Send Scimitar out to fight him."

Scimitar raced out to fight, flourishing his bright crescent blade: "Do you dare take me on, you petty Shandong chieftain?" he shouted.

Mr. Chai levelled his spear and charged. Two weapons clashed and both men fought fearlessly. Before they completed five bouts, Scimitar also feigned defeat and galloped back to his ranks. Ke Yin did not pursue him, but shouted: "Is there anyone else among you who dares to face me?"

Song Jiang ordered Whiskers out. Whiskers charged, but he too was only pretending to fight and after five or six bouts he fled. When Mr. Chai pursued and threatened him with his spear, he abandoned his horse and scurried away on foot, while the southerners rushed out and seized his horse. Mr. Chai encouraged the southern troops to charge and Song Jiang ordered his troops to fall back about three miles and take up a position there. After pursuing them for a while, Mr. Chai withdrew to the citadel. Someone had already told Fang La: "Ke Yin is incredibly valiant! He's routed the Song army and beaten three of their commanders! Song Jiang has lost the battle and has retreated three miles."

Fang La was delighted and ordered a royal banquet. As soon as Mr. Chai had taken off his armour and changed his uniform, he was invited to sit in the inner palace. The King himself toasted him and praised him, saying: "I had no idea your fighting skills were so great! I only knew you, dear son-in-law, as a scholar. Had I known before you had such military prowess, we need never have lost so many cities. I hope you will use your talents to the full and teach these adventurers a lesson, restore our territory and allow us to enjoy peace and boundless prosperity."

"Have no fear, Your Majesty! You can rely on me to strive heart and soul for the nation's glory. I would suggest that tomorrow you go up onto the hill to see me do execution on Song Jiang and his ilk."

Fang La gave proof of his satisfaction by holding a banquet that went on long into the night before they all retired. In the morning he had oxen and horses slaughtered so the whole army could eat their fill, after which everyone armed and rode to the mouth of Bangyuan Gap to challenge the enemy, with banners waving, much cheering and a thunderous tattoo of drums. Fang La with his entourage went up onto the heights above the citadel to watch Ke Yin fight.

Song Jiang had given his men these orders: "Today's battle is not like before. It is needful for you to do your utmost. You leaders must make every effort to capture their chief, Fang La. But do not kill him. Every officer must observe them carefully and watch when Mr. Chai turns his horse and retreats. That is the moment to rush forward and capture Fang La. There must be no mistake!"

Everyone was gleefully preparing, unsheathing their weapons. All were eagerly anticipating the sacking of the citadel, all were ambitious to capture Fang La and achieve glory and rich rewards. Song Jiang now ordered his leaders to deploy their troops and take up their positions in front of Bangyuan Gap.

Just as Ke Yin was about to ride out from the ranks of the southerners, Fang La's nephew Fang Jie, mounted and carrying his halberd at the ready, said: "Stay your hand, Commander, and hold in your horse, until I have had a go at them. You can bring your troops in afterwards to mop up!"

Everyone on the Song side could see the Prodigy behind Mr. Chai, and they said excitedly: "Today all our planning is bound to pay off!" They were raring to go.

Now Fang Jie urged his horse on. From the opposing ranks Scimitar rode out to meet him, brandishing his famous blade. The horses clashed, and this way, that way, thrust and counter-thrust, they fought ten bouts. Then Song Jiang ordered Colonel Hua into the arena. Undismayed, Fang Jie fought bravely against two for a few more bouts. Though he could not win outright, he skilfully parried and dodged their blows. Song Jiang now sent out Skyhawk and Whiskers, who galloped into the attack. Pressed hard by four opponents, Fang Jie turned his horse and galloped back towards his own side. Mr. Chai, who was waiting for him in front of the southerners' position, waved his hand and the four Song leaders gave chase. Mr. Chai levelled his spear and charged Fang Jie. Taken aback by this turn of events, Fang Jie leapt from his horse and tried to flee. But before he could get anywhere Mr. Chai's spear had knocked him down. Following up behind, the Prodigy dispatched him with his sword.

The southern troops were totally bewildered. They ran for their lives. Mr. Chai shouted out: "I am not Ke Yin. I am Chai Jin, the Little Whirlwind, in the service of Song Jiang! And my follower here is Yan Qing, the Prodigy! We know all the secrets of the citadel! Anyone who captures Fang La will be rewarded with high office and fine horses. Troops who surrender will be spared, those who resist will be executed." Signalling to the four leaders and the rest of the Song army to follow, he turned and charged into the citadel. Fang La, who had been watching on the heights with his entourage and had seen Fang Jie killed and the army routed, realized the situation was desperate. Kicking over his gilt throne, he fled and headed into the mountains.

Song Jiang, with his army in five divisions, charged into the citadel, hoping to take Fang La alive. But Fang La was gone and they only got his followers. The Prodigy called to some trusted companions and burst into the treasury. They grabbed two loads of gold and valuables and then started a fire in the inner court of the main building. When Mr. Chai broke into the eastern palace, Princess Golden Iris had already hanged herself. He set fire to every building. The servant girls he spared, allowing them to run off. But when the army invaded the main palace, they slaughtered all the concubines, royal guards and members of the royal family, and plundered all the valuables. Song Jiang and the rest continued to search the palace for Fang La.

Ruan the Seventh penetrated into the innermost regions of the palace and came across a trunk containing the usurper's regalia: the royal cap, the dragon robes, the jade belt, the white jade tablet and the shoes. Seeing all this finery, he thought to himself: "These are Fang La's clothes. Why shouldn't I try them on, just for a laugh?" He put on the dragon robe, fastened the jade belt, slipped into the shoes and set the cap on his head and stuck the white jade tablet in his belt. He leapt onto his horse and whip in hand galloped out of the palace. It caused a tremendous commotion, as the soldiers thought it was Fang La. But when they rushed forward for a closer look they saw it was only Ruan the Seventh and everyone burst out laughing. To prolong the joke he rode up and down watching the looting that was under way.

In the midst of these goings-on, Generals Wang Bing and Zhao Tan, the two who had come from the court with Marshal Tong, arrived on the scene. They had heard the noise and heard rumours that Fang La had been taken and they were hoping to share in the glory. When they saw it was only Ruan the Seventh fooling around, dressed in the royal regalia, complete with royal cap, the generals berated him: "What, are you planning to follow in Fang La's footsteps, dressed up like that?"

Ruan the Seventh took it badly. Pointing at the generals he said: "Who the fuck are you? If it wasn't for our leader, Song Jiang, you two asses would have got your heads cut off by Fang La. Now that we've done all the hard work, you two think you'll come along and pretend to the Emperor, who doesn't know any better, that you had a hand in the victory."

The two generals were outraged by this and would have assaulted Ruan the Seventh. But Ruan grabbed a soldier's short spear and charged Wang Bing first. Twin Rods hurriedly rode between them. By now Song Jiang had been informed and he came racing up. When they saw Ruan dressed in the royal regalia, he and the Professor ordered him to dismount at once. The clothes were torn off him and thrown aside, while Song Jiang tried to make peace with the generals using conciliatory language. But although Song Jiang and the others did their best to calm them down, the two continued to harbour a grudge.

The ground was littered with corpses and the gutters ran with blood in the citadel that day. According to Song dynasty records, more than twenty thousand of Fang La's troops were killed. Song Jiang gave orders for fires to be started everywhere to make sure all the buildings were burnt to the ground. All the royal towers and terraces, palaces and courtyards, the delicate pavilions and gorgeous dwellings were consumed by the flames.

When Song Jiang and his companions were satisfied that the burning was complete, the troops were quartered at the entrance to Bangyuan Gap and a palisade was erected. The prisoners were listed and only the chief, Fang La, was missing. A thorough search of the mountainside was ordered and it was announced that anyone bringing Fang La in would be recommended to the Emperor for promotion; anyone providing information leading to his capture would be duly rewarded.

Now Fang La had in fact escaped from the heights above the citadel by means of hidden paths and headed for the wild country deep inside the mountains, traversing high ridges and impenetrable forests. Having shed his imperial robes, cast off his golden crown and exchanged his court boots for hemp sandals, he fled for his life, scrambling over the mountainsides. All night he was on the run. After crossing five peaks he came to a hollow in the hill where there was a thatched hut built in the lee of the slope. He was starving and he was just about to enter the hut to look for something to eat when from behind a group of pines a great fat monk sprang out, knocked him down with his staff and tied him up with a length of rope. This was none other than Lu Zhishen, the Flowery Monk. He took Fang La into the hut and gave him some food, then dragged him down the mountain till they met up with one of the army's search parties. Together they took the prisoner to Song Jiang.

Song Jiang was delighted to learn that they had captured Fang La. "How did you happen to be waiting there for him, Father?" he asked.

"After the battle at Thousand Pines on Black Dragon Ridge," Monk replied, "I chased Colonel Xia deep into the mountains, killing any enemy troops who put up a fight. I went so far that I lost my way. As I was trying to find the way back I came to a very wild patch of forest, where I met this old monk, who guided me to a little thatched hut and said: 'There's plenty of firewood and food. Just stay here and wait. When you see a big chap coming out of the forest, grab him.' That night I saw fires down the mountain. I watched them all night, but I didn't know where the paths were to get down. This morning I saw this bugger scrambling across the mountain so I knocked him down with my staff and tied him up. I had no idea it was Fang La!"

Song Jiang again asked: "Where is the old monk now?"

"I haven't the faintest idea. He disappeared after taking me to the hut and telling me about the firewood and food.

"That monk was obviously a *luohan* or bodhisattva," Song Jiang said. "This apparition led you to accomplish a famous deed. The Emperor must be told of it when we return to the capital. You can leave the monkhood and become a great official with a comfortable position in the capital and marry someone from a good family, conferring honour on your descendants and repaying your parents for all they have done."

Monk said: "My heart is ashes, I have no ambition for high office. My only desire is to find a quiet, pure place to go where I may rest my body and prepare my soul."

Song Jiang said: "If you really do not want to leave the monkhood, why not go to the capital and become abbot of some famous monastery? That too would be a way to pass on glory to your posterity and to honour your parents."

Monk shook his head and cried out: "I want none of that! To desire much is no use. If one can die with a complete body, that is more than enough."

Song Jiang was filled with sadness by what he heard, as were the others.

As soon as a role had been called of their commanders, Fang La was placed in a prison cart and sent to the capital to be shown to the Emperor. Song Jiang now ordered the army and all the leaders to depart from Bangyuan Gap and Clearwater and return to Muzhou.

Marshal Zhang now met with General Liu, Marshal Tong and two other members of the Military Council in Muzhou where all the armies were united in one camp. When they heard that Song Jiang had succeeded in capturing Fang La and was bringing him to Muzhou, they all joined in congratulations. When Song Jiang and his companions finished paying their respects, the Commissioner said: "I already know how hard you have striven on the frontier and how many of your comrades you have lost. Now your efforts have been crowned with success. Allow me to congratulate you!"

Song Jiang again prostrated himself and, weeping, said: "At the start we were one hundred and eight. When we dealt with the Tartars we had absolutely no losses. Then we unexpectedly lost the services of Taoist Gongsun, and later the Grand Preceptor retained some of our company. Since we put down the insurrection in Yangzhou and crossed the river, I regret to say we have lost seven out of ten. Although I myself have come out of it alive, what of my honour? What can I say when I return to family and home in Shandong?"

The Marshal said: "Don't speak like that. Remember the old

saying: 'Rich or poor, noble or base, our lot is given us; a short life or a long one, it's fixed by fate.' What does the proverb say? 'It's an ill wind that blows nobody any good.' What's the point in grieving over the leaders you have lost? You have distinguished yourself and achieved much and when the court hears of it you will be rewarded with high office. You will have position and honour and a fine house. You will return to your birthplace in sumptuous robes. Who can quarrel with that? Don't waste your time on other things. Just get on with organizing the army for the return."

Song Jiang prostrated himself in thanks and then went to summon his commanders. The Marshal had already given orders for all the captured insurgents and usurping officials, with the exception of Fang La, who was to be sent under guard to the capital, to be executed in the market place. In a few villages that had not yet been recaptured the rebels and corrupt officials, on learning of Fang La's capture, had either fled or given themselves up. They were spared and returned to being loyal citizens. A notice was circulated to calm fears and reassure the people. The rest, who had followed the insurrection but not done anyone any harm, were allowed to surrender and go back to their villages and were directed to return to their normal trades or plots of land. Once order had been restored to the whole district, guards were appointed to defend the borders and make the people secure. Of this no more.

The Marshal's officials now organized a banquet to celebrate the peace, honour the generals and officials and reward the army for its efforts. All commanders were told to conclude any unfinished business. Orders came from the court that they were all to pack up and set out in due course.

But Song Jiang continued to weep copiously whenever he thought of his dead comrades. The Pilot and five more of those who had suddenly fallen ill in Hangzhou together with Smiler and the Irrepressible, who had stayed to look after them, had died from the disease. Only Panther and the Irrepressible had returned to join the army attack. Remembering the hardships they had all undergone, he felt it only right and proper now peace had returned to organize prayers for the release of their souls. A tall banner was raised in Muzhou and a service for the release of souls, their deliverance from the nine infernal regions, and the remission of their sins was organized in one of the temples. Libations were made to the three hundred and sixty points of the compass.

Next day oxen and horses were slaughtered for the sacrifice and they all gathered in the Temple of the Black Dragon Lord to make the offering in thanksgiving for his protection. On their return to the camp, the bodies of all who had died in action were collected and prepared for burial. After the interment, Song Jiang and the Unicorn ordered their armies to rejoin Commissioner Zhang in Hangzhou, until the Emperor authorized their withdrawal to the capital. First everyone's achievements were recorded in a report which was forwarded to the Emperor.

There were now only thirty-six of the original company surviving, to wit: Song Jiang, the Unicorn, the Professor, Scimitar, Leopard's Head, Twin Rods, Colonel Hua, Mr. Chai, Skyhawk, Whiskers, Monk, Pilgrim, Magic Messenger, Iron Ox, Morbid, White-Water Dragon, Ruan the Seventh, the Prodigy, the Strategist, Tamer, Colonel Sun, Demon King, Thunderer, Sterling, Calculator, Uglymug, Iron Fan, Rhinoceros, Blossom, Panther, Irrepressible, Cave Dragon, River Rider, the Flea, Blackface and Auntie Gu.

So Song Jiang and his leaders and troops left Muzhou and set off for Hangzhou. Then indeed the mountains resounded with the sound of gongs summoning the troops, the countryside was filled with a red tide of victory banners!

The journey was uneventful. Marshal Zhang's troops were in the city, so Song Jiang was quartered outside at the Pagoda of the Six Harmonies, where they all rested for a while until Song Jiang and the Unicorn went into the city to receive their orders.

Meanwhile Monk and Pilgrim, who were also quartered at the temple, had been admiring the scenery around the city, which was quite beautiful, with magnificent views. One night when the moon was bright and a soft breeze blowing, water and sky uniformly translucent, the two went to sleep in the monastery. Around midnight the roar of the tide on the river was suddenly heard.

Monk was from Guanxi, west of the mountains, and had never encountered something like the Zhejiang tide, known as "Old Faithful". He thought it was war drums beating and imagined bandits were attacking. He leapt out of bed, groped around for his staff and with a loud shout rushed outside. The monks were amazed and came to ask: "What's come over you? Where are you off to?"

Monk replied: "I thought I heard war drums. I was going out to fight."

They all roared with laughter. "You're mistaken," they said. "That's not war drums. That's just Old Faithful on the river Qiantang."

It was Monk's turn to be shocked. "Why is it called Old Faithful?" he asked.

The monks flung open the windows and pointed out the tide to him. "It comes twice a day, regular as clockwork. Today is the fifteenth of the eighth month, the tide is due precisely at midnight. Because it never fails it's known as Old Faithful."

When Monk looked at that tide, it was as if his eyes were opened. He clapped his hands and laughed. "My teacher, Abbot True Knowledge, presented me with a mantra which says 'Meet Xia and take a prisoner' and during the battle in Thousand Pine Woods I did indeed encounter one Colonel Xiahou; then it's 'Find La and make an arrest', and in fact I captured Fang La also. Now it must be 'Hear the tide and awake from darkness, recognize Old Faithful and learn stillness.' Well, I've just encountered Old Faithful, so what comes next ought to be 'learning stillness'. The question is, can any of you lot tell me what 'learning stillness' might mean?"

"You a monk," they chorused, "and you haven't yet learnt that in Buddhism learning stillness means death?"

Monk grinned and said: "If that's what they call learning stillness, it's going to happen to me today. Would you please warm some water for me, I'm going to take a bath."

They all thought he was joking, but they knew what he was like and dared not disobey. An acolyte was ordered to prepare hot water for him to bathe himself. When he had changed into

魯智深浙江坐化

new monk's clothing, from the imperial gift, he told the soldiers under his command to fetch Song Jiang and asked the monks to bring him paper and brush. With these he wrote out an elegy and then went to the meditation hall, where he appropriated a meditation couch and sat down in the middle. He lit some fine incense and placed the paper beside him. He sat cross-legged, left leg resting on right, and his soul flew easily up to heaven. When Song Jiang received the message and rushed there with the others to see him, he was no longer stirring. The elegy said:

All my life long I never sought to gain merit;
My interest was only in killing and burning.
Now of a sudden the golden cord is cut,
The jade lock shattered;
Now Old Faithful rides on Qiantang's stream,
And I know at last who I really am.

When Song Jiang and the Unicorn read this their sadness knew no bounds. The other leaders also came to burn incense and pay their last respects. Marshal Zhang and Marshal Tong came and offered incense and paid their respects. Song Jiang distributed alms among the monks and arranged for a three-day service. He had the body enclosed in a red sarcophagus and asked Abbot Benevolence of the famous Mount Jing temple to officiate at the cremation. Monks from the Ten Houses of the Five Sacred Peaks also came to participate. The sarcophagus was borne in procession to the cremation ground in the inner court of the Pagoda of the Six Harmonies. Father Benevolence holding a torch stood before the sarcophagus. He gestured towards Monk Lu Zhishen and delivered this short address:

O Lu Zhishen, O Brother Profound Knowledge, you come out of the greenwood with your eyes of an arsonist, your mind full of killing, and all of a sudden you return with the tide: we shall find you no more among the living. O the sky's vault is filled with jade, the earth transmuted into pure gold!

Father Benevolence lit the pyre and all the monks began to recite sutras. When the flames had consumed the sarcophagus the bones were collected and buried right there in the courtyard of the Pagoda of the Six Harmonies. All the deceased's possessions, his monk's robes, his begging bowl, the wealth which had been his part of the Emperor's reward, were handed over to the pagoda for the benefit of the community. His monk's staff and cassock of black cloth were also donated.

Song Jiang inquired about the health of Pilgrim Wu Song. Though he had survived his wound, he was permanently disabled. He said to Song Jiang: "I am a cripple now. I don't want to go back to the court. I shall donate all my wealth and possessions to the community of this temple and become a free monk, or pilgrim, that's what I shall do. When you draw up the list of those who are returning, please leave my name out."

Song Jiang said: "I shall respect your wishes."

Pilgrim remained at the temple and died peacefully, aged eighty. But that was later.

Song Jiang attended in the city each day to await orders, until Marshal Zhang arrived with the main army. Two weeks after the Marshal took over in the city, the Emperor's envoy arrived with orders for Song Jiang and the rest of the company to return to the capital. Marshal Zhang and the other top-ranking officers left first. Song Jiang and the others took a little longer to pack up. Before they left, Leopard's Head suddenly became paralysed, Morbid died of a tumour on his spine and the Flea succumbed to cholera. These deaths were a heavy blow to Song Jiang. News came from Dantu that the Blue-Faced Beast was also dead and had been buried in the cemetery there. Leopard's Head's paralysis was found to be incurable so he was left at the temple in the care of Pilgrim. Six months later he too was dead.

As Song Jiang and the others were leaving Hangzhou to return to the capital, the Prodigy came in private to the Unicorn and said: "I have served you since childhood. I owe everything to you, master. Now that our task is completed, I would like to suggest that we resign the positions we were granted and go away quietly to hide our footsteps and bury our names, find some place where we can live out our days in peace. What do you think about this?"

The Unicorn said: "Since the time we were pardoned, we have gone through a hundred battles, laboured ceaselessly, suffered many a hardship. Many of our comrades have died but we two have been fortunate enough to survive. Now is the time to return home in glory, start a home, with a wife of good family and privileged sons. Why do you want to embark on a project that has no future?"

"You are mistaken, master," said the Prodigy with a wry smile. "My plan is the one which has a future. I'm afraid it's what you propose that has no future!"

This Prodigy one can say truly was one who knew when to advance and when to retire, or to put it another way, knew how to read the signs:

The battle's fought, the day is won,
A quiet retreat's his only thought.
Let worldly men for fame strive on;
Ambition's measure's always short.

The Unicorn said: "I've never for a moment wavered, lad, so how could the Court hold anything against me?"

The Prodigy said: "Have you never heard of all those faithful ministers and generals of antiquity whose services to the crown were rewarded with disgrace and death?

The Unicorn said: "What I heard was that they brought trouble on themselves through excessive ambition. Whereas I don't aspire to such heights, so I can't provoke such accusations."

The Prodigy said: "Well, if you won't listen to me, I fear you will come to regret it. If I go to tell Song Jiang I'm leaving, he is an inflexible man and I'm afraid he won't release me, so I shall say farewell only to you, master."

"Where will you go if you leave me?" the Unicorn asked.

"I shall not be far away from you," he replied.

"So be it," said the Unicorn. "But I'd still like to know where you're thinking of going!"

The Prodigy prostrated himself eight times and on the same day tied some valuables in a bundle and set off for who knows where. Next morning a soldier found a paper addressed to Song Jiang. This is what Song Jiang read:

Your servant Yan Qing, the Prodigy, humbly greets you and declares: Since you received me into the company I have received such favours from you as even with my death I could not fully repay. Now in view of my weakness and inadequacy I feel myself unfit for public service and beg permission to retire to the countryside and live as a private citizen. I wanted to bid you farewell, but I feared that your sense of responsibility would make it difficult for you to release me, so I shall depart quietly tonight. I leave you with these short verses and hope that you will find it in you to forgive me:

For the goose to go solo may be a surprise.
I resign my appointment, all honours despise.
With the pardon in hand I shall now prepare
To live far removed from the world's idle care.

After reading the Prodigy's letter and poem, Song Jiang felt truly saddened.

Song Jiang had the tablets awarded by the Emperor to leaders who had since died collected up and returned to the appropriate authorities in the capital.

Song Jiang's army set off, and when they reached Suzhou the White-Water Dragon, pretending to have caught a cold took to his bed. His men informed Song Jiang. Song Jiang himself went with the doctor to see him. White-Water Dragon said: "Brother, do not delay your journey or the Emperor will blame you. I am afraid Marshal Zhang will have been there a long time already. If you want to do me a favour, you might leave Cave Dragon and River Rider to look after me. When I am better we can come after you to see the Emperor. Please go on ahead with the army."

Although he had misgivings, Song Jiang could not waste any more time. He had to start. There was even a dispatch from Marshal Zhang demanding haste so he left the three boat commanders behind and set off with all the others for the capital.

As for White-Water Dragon and his friends, the three of them in accordance with their previous agreement went off to find the four fishermen. They spent all their capital building themselves a boat at Elmhurst, after which they sailed from Taicang Harbour for foreign lands. Later White-Water Dragon became lord of Siam. Cave Dragon, River Rider and the rest filled positions overseas and prospered, holding sway in other coastal regions. But that is part of another story, the story about White-Water Dragon.

After an uneventful journey Song Jiang and his men reached Changzhou and Runzhou, two towns they had previously fought for. Song Jiang could not help feeling the pain of it: only twenty or thirty percent of the leaders who had crossed the river still survived. After Yangzhou, when they reached Huai'an and knew the capital was not far off, Song Jiang ordered all his commanders to prepare themselves for their audience with the Emperor. On the twentieth of the ninth month they reached the Eastern Capital. Marshal Zhang and the main army were already in the city, so Song Jiang had to be stationed outside and they set up camp as before at Chenbridge to await the Emperor's orders.

At this point some soldiers from the company that had remained behind with White-Water Dragon in Suzhou arrived and announced that he had not been ill at all but simply unwilling to join government service in the capital, and that he had now gone off somewhere with Cave Dragon and River Rider. This gave Song Jiang further cause for sadness. When he told Sterling to draw up the list of leaders present in the capital, there were only twenty-seven of them on it, besides those who had died in the Emperor's service. A letter of thanks was written to all those listed and they were ordered to remain at hand in readiness for their audience. Three days later at the dawn court, when all the courtiers assembled to greet the Emperor, the Emperor ordered Song Jiang and his company to be summoned.

As the light slowly spread in the east, Song Jiang, the Unicorn and the others rode into the city. The people turned out to see them. This was their third audience with the Emperor. The first time, after the amnesty, they had paraded in the red and green silk robes that were the Emperor's gift to them, displaying the gold and silver tablets they had been awarded. After defeating the Tartars, at the Emperor's command they had ridden in fully armed. This time, since peace had been restored, the Emperor ordered civilian dress, so they were in the ceremonial attire of the court as they rode into the city. When the people saw how few of them remained, a great sigh went up. They reached the Meridian Gate and smartly dismounted and went in. A chamberlain led them to the foot of the palace steps. With Song Jiang and the Unicorn in front, they advanced and prostrated themselves eight times, then retreated and prostrated themselves another eight times. Finally they positioned themselves halfway between the two extremes and prostrated themselves eight times again — making twenty-four times in all, producing an effect of lively movement and ending in rousing shouts of "Long live the Emperor!"

The Emperor responded by expressing his sadness on seeing they were so few. He ordered them all to be admitted to the imperial presence and Song Jiang and the Unicorn led them up the steps. They knelt at the top before the pearl screen. His Majesty graciously invited them to rise and his attendants raised the screen. "I know that you have suffered many hardships in subduing the disturbances in the South and that you have lost most of your comrades. It causes me enormous grief," he said.

Song Jiang, his face streaming with tears, prostrated himself all over again and gave the following account. There were fifty-nine leaders, he said, who died in His Majesty's service, to wit:

Fourteen senior commanders: *Thunderclap Qin Ming, Spearsman Xu Ning, Twin Spears Dong Ping, Hotshot Zhang Qing, Red-Haired Devil Liu Tang, Tattooed Dragon Shi Jin, Hasty Suo Chao, White Eel Zhang Shun, Ruan the Second, Ruan the Fifth, Sergeant Lei, Madcap Shi Xiu, Snake Xie Zhen, Scorpion Xie Bao*

And forty-five junior commanders: *Door-God Song Wan, Nameless Jiao Ting, Turtle Tao Zongwang, Victorious Han Tao, Supremo Peng Qi, Whitey Zheng Tianshou, Knife Cao Zheng, Fleetfoot Wang Dingliu, Ugly Son-in-Law Xuan Zan, Star Kong Liang, Young Master Shi En, Hound Hao Siwen, Redeye Deng Fei, Big Chief Zhou Tong, Stripes Gong Wang, Pluto Bao Xu, Yellow Dog Duan Jingzhu, Ape Hou Jian, Flagpole Meng Kang, Short-Arse Wang Ying, Steelbright Hu Sanniang, Eight-Armed*

Ogre Xiang Chong, Winged Ghost Li Gun, Dandy Yan Shun, Magic Flautist Ma Lin, Water General Shan Tinggui, Fire General Wei Dingguo, Little Duke Lu Fang, Halberdier Guo Sheng, Golden Wings Ou Peng, River-Jumper Chen Da, White-Spotted Snake Yang Chun, Perilous Yu Baosi, Tiger-Killer Li Zhong, Pill Monger Xue Yong, Green-Eyes Li Yun, Guv Shi Yong, Skyscraper Du Qian, Scarface Ding Desun, Forester Zou Yuan, Executioner Li Li, Spots Tang Long, Strongarm Cai Fu, Gardener Zhang Qing, Ogress Sun Erniang

There were ten leaders who died of illness, namely:

Five senior commanders: *Leopard's Head Lin Chong, Blue-Faced Beast Yang Zhi, Pilot Zhang Heng, Unstoppable Mu Hong, Morbid Yang Xiong*

And five junior commanders: *Comet Kong Ming, Crocodile Zhu Gui, Smiler Zhu Fu, Daytime Rat Bai Sheng, Flea Shi Qian*

One senior commander achieved enlightenment and passed away at the Temple of the Six Harmonies: *Monk Lu Zhishen*

One senior commander who lost an arm had refused all honours and chosen a life of contemplation: *Pilgrim Wu Song*

One senior commander previously in the capital had returned to a life of contemplation in the provinces: *Taoist Gongsun Sheng*

Four had refused all honours and departed along the way: *Prodigy Yan Qing, White-Water Dragon Li Jun, Cave Dragon Tong Wei, River Rider Tong Meng*

Five were previously retained in the capital, including the doctor who was sent for by the court: *Doctor An Daoquan, Redbeard Huangfu Duan, Craftsman Jin Dajian, Magic Hand Xiao Rang, Lungs Yue Ho*

Thus twenty-seven leaders only were present that day at court.

The Emperor continued to express his grief: "Originally there were one hundred and eight of you, all corresponding to stars," he said. "Now there are only twenty-seven — and the four who have departed already. It is quite true that you have lost four-fifths of your company." He ordered that all the leaders who had died in the service of the Emperor should receive titles of nobility. The leaders who were present at this audience were given official posts, of which the secretariat was informed, with the exception of Auntie Gu, who was however given a title of nobility.

Song Jiang was to be imperial commissioner in Chuzhou and commander-in-chief of the garrison. The Unicorn was to be imperial commissioner in Luzhou and deputy commander of the troops. The Professor was to be chief of communications in one of the guards regiments. Scimitar was to be military governor in the district of the Northern Capital. Twin Rods was to be chief instructor with the Imperial guard. Other posts went to Colonel Hua, Mr. Chai, Skyhawk, Whiskers, Magic Messenger, Iron Ox and Ruan the Seventh.

All went to give thanks for the titles and offices they had received and each received in addition a generous financial reward.

Song Jiang told His Majesty how the Black Dragon Lord had appeared to him twice and protected both the country and the army, helping them to victory. The Emperor accordingly conferred on the Dragon Lord the title of "Dragon Lord, patron of loyalty and of virtue, provider of protection and purveyor of comfort". He also changed the names of Muzhou and Shezhou to Yanzhou and Huizhou, to efface the memory of the part they played in Fang La's uprising. Clearwater was renamed Peacehaven and Bangyuan Gap was opened up and converted into an island. The local authorities were ordered to build a temple to the Black Dragon Lord on Black Dragon Mountain, for which the Emperor provided an inscription in his own hand. Traces of this temple remain to this day. In recognition of what the people in many towns south of the river had suffered under Fang La, they were excused from taxes for three years.

When Song Jiang and the others had expressed their gratitude, The Emperor ordered a peace banquet to honour their achievements. All the officials civil and military were present, all the ministers and secretaries. When the leaders went to thank the

Emperor, Song Jiang took the opportunity to make a request: "Since we received the amnesty many of our troops have died. If there are some who would like now to return home, I beg Your Majesty to look kindly on them."

The Emperor assented and gave the order: "Any soldier who wishes to serve in the imperial army shall be given a hundred strings of cash and ten rolls of material and enlisted in a regiment of the royal guards, either the Dragons or the Tigers. Those who do not wish to serve, let them be given two hundred strings of cash and ten rolls of material and sent home to their villages to work as ordinary citizens."

Song Jiang had another request: "I was born and grew up in the village of Yuncheng. Since the time I fell from grace I have never dared return. Would Your Majesty graciously grant me some leave, so that I may go back and attend to the tomb of my ancestors and visit my family, before taking up my post in Chuzhou? Of course I would not go without Your Majesty's consent."

The Emperor was pleased with the respectful tone and granted Song Jiang an additional hundred thousand strings of cash to facilitate his return home. Song Jiang took leave of the court. Next day the Privy Council gave a banquet to celebrate the peace and the day after the Military Council gave their banquet. Marshal Zhang and all the other senior officers had already received important honours but that does not concern our story. Fang La, on the other hand, was taken on the Emperor's order to the market-place and cut to pieces there. His death lasted three days.

Honour and rank the one secures,
While the other a cruel death endures.
Men get their just reward at last,
Which for some comes slow, for others fast.

Song Jiang was given the leave he had requested. Those of his troops who wanted to continue serving in the army were rewarded and appointed to two of the imperial guards regiments as grooms. Those who wanted to leave the army were also rewarded and sent back home to serve the people there. The junior commanders all received rewards and were given military

宋公明衣錦還鄉

or civil appointments or sent off to serve on the frontier. With their official letters of appointment they went off to their posts where they helped preserve the peace.

When all this was settled, Song Jiang said farewell to them for the time being, and with his brother Iron Fan and a few hundred troops, carrying the Emperor's gifts, his luggage, uniform and campaign booty, left the capital and headed for Shandong. They were returning home in fine silk robes. The journey was uneventful. Formerly when he reached the neighbourhood his father and family would come out to meet him. Now when he got to the manor he learnt that the old squire was already dead, though the burial of the coffin had yet to take place. The two brothers could not restrain their grief. Their relatives and the retainers all came to pay their respects. Before he died, squire Song had left the fields and the household in very good order, all just as it had always been. Song Jiang organized a service at the manor and invited Buddhist and Taoist priests in to pray for his deceased parents. A constant stream of local officials visited. When the day and time had been chosen, the two brothers themselves carried their father's coffin to a place on the hill for burial. Many people came for the funeral that day, local dignitaries, family and neighbours, old and young, connections of all kinds. But enough of this.

Mindful of his as yet unfulfilled promise to the Mystic Lady, Song Jiang used fifty thousand strings of cash to pay stonemasons and others to restore the temple of the Mystic Lady of the Ninth Heaven and had new images installed in the two side galleries and new decorations, all of which was carried out with great care.

But time was passing and Song Jiang was afraid of incurring the Emperor's displeasure, so he appointed a day to end his mourning. After a few more days of Taoist ceremonies, he organized a big banquet to which he invited all the village worthies.

The next day his relatives gave him a banquet. No more need be said of this.

He transferred ownership of the estate to his brother, Iron Fan who, although he had received honours, preferred to remain in the country where he could attend to the farm and tend the ancestral shrine. All the wealth Song Jiang had earned he distributed among the poor.

Having spent several months in his native place, Song Jiang bade farewell to home and old friends and returned to the capital to be reunited with his comrades. Some of them by now had moved their families to the capital to live, and others had left for their posts elsewhere. The close relatives of those who had died in the Emperor's service had received a handsome reward and been told to return home and compensate the families. By the time Song Jiang returned to the capital, these had all returned home well satisfied.

In obedience to the court's order, Song Jiang had bade farewell to the members of the Military Council, packed his things and was ready to go to his post, when the Magic Messenger appeared with something to tell him. Magic Messenger sat down and said a great deal that was to have important consequences: Song Jiang while living was to become known as the Hero from Yuncheng and after death Lord of Duckweed Marsh. It will be true to say:

How noble and pure the breeze that is born in the temple!
How imposing the portraits in the mausoleum!

If you want to hear what Magic Messenger told Song Jiang, you must read the next chapter.

Chapter 120

Song Jiang after death goes to Duckweed Marsh; The Emperor dreams of a visit to Mount Liang!

When Song Jiang returned to the capital after his triumphant visit to his native village, he summoned his comrades and ordered them all to pack their bags and proceed to their posts. At this time the Magic Messenger came to see Song Jiang. They chatted for a while and then Magic Messenger stood up and said: "Don't think I am not grateful for my post, but I propose to resign it. I want to go to the Temple of the Eastern Peak in Tai'an and become a lay-brother and serve the temple. My greatest wish is to be granted an easy end to my life."

Song Jiang said: "Whatever gave you such an idea, brother?"

"I dreamt last night that the Lord of the Underworld had sent for me," he answered. "That is why I have made this resolution."

"Dear brother, you have always been the Magic Messenger in this world. No doubt you are destined to be the messenger of the gods in the next."

Magic Messenger said goodbye and after handing in his resignation went to the temple in Tai'an, where he joined the community as a lay-brother and diligently attended the gods each day, praying and burning incense with unfailing piety and devotion. One evening a few months later, without having been ill at all, he bade farewell to all the monks and passed away with a smile on his face. Later his spirit manifested itself many times at the temple of the Eastern Peak, and local people who prayed in the temple had an image placed there which was a perfect representation of his features.

Ruan the Seventh also received a title and said farewell to

Song Jiang and went to Gaitian as military governor. Not long after he was in trouble because Generals Wang Bing and Zhao Tan, moved by their old grudge from the time when they lost face because he shouted at them in Fang La's citadel, went on repeating to Marshal Tong the story of his misdemeanour when he dressed up in Fang La's royal regalia. Although it might appear just an impromptu joke, they said, in reality it was evidence of a dangerous tendency and in a backward place like Gaitian he was bound to stir up rebellion. Marshal Tong informed the Grand Preceptor who spoke to the Emperor and got him to publish an order and send it down there stripping Ruan the Seventh of his title and making him a commoner again. When this happened, Ruan the Seventh at heart was not sorry. Taking his mother with him he returned to Stonetable in the Marshes of Mount Liang and resumed his old trade as fisherman, caring for his mother till the end of her days. He lived till sixty.

As for Mr. Chai, the Little Whirlwind, when he saw the Magic Messenger give up his post and go into retirement, and when he heard how the court had removed Ruan the Seventh from his post and stripped him of his title because his prank with Fang La's clothes was interpreted as a sign that he wanted to imitate that rebellion, he was reminded how he himself had acted as a son-in-law to Fang La. He thought that if at some future date evil ministers discovered this and wanted to make trouble for him with the Emperor, he too would be dismissed from his post and how would he bear the shame? Surely it was better to recognize the problem now and take action to avoid it. On the pretext of suffering from an intermittent fever of unpredictable occurrence, which made it difficult for him to carry out his duties, he asked permission to retire to his estate. He said goodbye to the others and returned home to live an independent life there, dying suddenly one day without an illness.

Skyhawk was made governor of Zhongshan, which office he filled for six months, until he heard that Mr. Chai had retired and decided himself to claim that mental illness prevented him from carrying out his duties. He asked the Military Council for permission to surrender his post and return to his estate on Lone Dragon

Heights. Later with Uglymug he acquired wealth and had an easy death.

Scimitar commanded the garrison of the Northern Capital and was such a brave heart that everyone respected him. One day coming back very drunk after some military exercises he lost his seat and fell from his horse. He never regained consciousness.

Twin Rods received a command in the imperial barracks and every day drilled the Emperor's guard of honour. Later he took part in the campaign against the Fourth Prince of Jin and died in action west of the River Huai.

Whiskers achieved success in the Baoding garrison and later went with General Liu Guangshi to fight the Jin. He achieved high military rank.

Colonel Hua took his wife and family and his younger sister with him to his post in Yingtian. The Professor, who had never had a family, went by himself, with just a boy to serve him, to his post in Wusheng.

Iron Ox went off with two servants to his post in Runzhou.

Now you may ask why I have only told you where these last three went to, and not what happened to them later. That's because the previous seven you will not meet again so I had to tell you how they finished up. But the last three, together with Song Jiang and the Unicorn, you will be meeting again and you will see what befell them in due course.

Song Jiang and the Unicorn remained in the capital while they said goodbye to the others and saw them all off to their posts. Some had no official duties and went off to their families, well provided with gifts of silk, gold and silver from the Emperor. Back in their native places they pursued their own interests. The fifteen lesser leaders who had survived had been in the capital, except for Song Jiang's younger brother, Iron Fan, who had gone back to their estate. Uglymug accompanied Skyhawk back to the country. The Tamer was reassigned to his old post in Qingzhou. Colonel Sun went back with his younger brother Blackface and Auntie Gu to serve as before in Dengzhou. The Rhinoceros did not want to be a government official and went back to the mountains. Blossom returned to the Northern Capital with Scimitar and remained a commoner. Sterling had come to an agreement with Panther and after receiving their titles they were given leave to return to Waterworld and the Magic Calculator missed his old home and returned there as a commoner. The Strategist had become interested in Demon King's Taoist magic and the two of them became priests wandering among the rivers and lakes, winding up in Taoist Gongsun's establishment where they ended their days. Mu the Irrepressible went back to Jieyang and became a model citizen. Thunderer, with his exceptional skills with gunpowder, was reassigned to his old post as chief of ordinance in the Imperial guard. Five others remained in the capital, as before: Doctor An, who had been summoned there previously, became a bigwig in the Medical College; Redbeard, the vet, became chief overseer of the Emperor's stable; Craftsman had a post in the palace; Master Hand, the calligrapher, got a job in Marshal Su's household as private tutor and Lungs, the singer, remained a member of Prince Wang's household, living in clover till the end of his days. No more of them.

Now it was time for Song Jiang and the Unicorn to part, each going off to his own post. The Unicorn had no family, so with just some servants he took himself off to Luzhou. Song Jiang, after thanking the Emperor and taking his leave of the Military Council, headed for his post in Chuzhou, accompanied by some old family servants. We need say no more of all these partings.

Ever since the pledge made when Taizong succeeded Taizu, the Song dynasty's founder, that crimes under the preceding administration would not be prosecuted, the regime had been blighted by corruption. And the present emperor, who was both pious and intelligent, was impeded by evil counsellors who had wormed their way into his confidence and were enemies to all virtue, more's the pity. At this time it was those four notorious villains Grand Preceptor Cai, Marshal Tong, Gao the Ball and Marshal Yang who were turning the world upside down and constituted a blight on country, family and people. This time the two Grand Marshals, Gao and Yang, seeing how the Emperor honoured and rewarded Song Jiang and his lot, were exceedingly displeased. When they discussed matters they decided: "Song

Jiang and the Unicorn are our enemies. Now we see them becoming honoured officials, receiving all these favours from the Emperor. In their military capacity they have command of troops, as civilians they have power among the people. We members of the Military Council, how can we not be the object of scorn and laughter? There's an old saying: 'Without hatred you cannot be a minister, without poison you cannot be considered a man!'"

Yang said: "I have been thinking about this. We must deal with the Unicorn first. We can finish off Song Jiang later. That Unicorn fellow is formidable and if we began with Song Jiang and he realized what was happening, the business could turn nasty and cause us a real problem."

"What's your idea, then?" said Gao the Ball.

"We get some Luzhou soldiers to come and complain to the Military Council about the Unicorn, saying he is recruiting troops, buying horses and getting in supplies because he plans a rebellion. Then we'll send over their accusation to the Grand Preceptor's office. We fool the Grand Preceptor and when he reports it to the Emperor he requests permission for us to deal with it. We have the Unicorn lured to the capital and when the Emperor gives him wine, we put some mercury in the drink which will destroy his kidneys. After that he'll not be much good for anything. Then we can send someone with imperial wine for Song Jiang. The wine will contain a slow poison, so that in a couple of weeks he'll be beyond saving."

Gao exclaimed: "An excellent plan!"

The two villains sent someone they trusted to find two Luzhou people to make out the accusation for them. They told them to go to the Council of Ministers and warn them that the Unicorn was recruiting troops and so on in Luzhou and planning a rebellion and that he had sent someone to Chuzhou to enlist Song Jiang in the enterprise. Now the head of the Council of Ministers was Marshal Tong, who had his own reasons for hating Song Jiang and company. As soon as he received the accusation, he went directly to the Grand Preceptor with it. The latter read it and called a ministerial meeting. Gao and Yang were present at this, and it was agreed that the accusers should be taken to see the Emperor. His Majesty said: "To my knowledge, Song Jiang and the Unicorn have been engaged in suppressing bandits on all sides. They had thousands of soldiers under their command, yet they showed no sign of evil intentions. They have abandoned their old ways and reformed, how can they now be rebellious? We have done nothing to upset them, how can they plan to go counter to our will? This smells of a plot. Until there is further evidence I shall find it hard to believe."

Then Gao and Yang, who were there of course, said: "Your Majesty, whatever reason may teach, the human heart is impossible to fathom. The Unicorn must harbour resentment because he thinks his post is beneath him. Festering dissatisfaction has turned to thoughts of rebellion. Unluckily for him he has been found out."

The Emperor said: "Bring him here for me to question him and ascertain the truth for myself."

The Grand Preceptor and Marshal Tong remonstrated: "This Unicorn is a wild beast. His behaviour is unpredictable. If he is alarmed, he may take flight, which would prove most awkward. It could be very difficult to catch him afterwards. No, the best policy is lure him to the capital and then Your Majesty should give a banquet for him and speak to him graciously whilst we observe his behaviour and see if the story is true or not. If there is nothing in it there will be no need for any interrogation. It will just have served to show how Your Majesty values loyal service."

The Emperor agreed to this and a royal edict was composed and sent by special envoy to Luzhou, asking the Unicorn to return to the court because the Emperor had something to say to him. When the envoy reached Luzhou all the government officials went to meet him outside the town. He was taken to the government offices where the edict was opened and read. To put it briefly, the Unicorn went back with the envoy to the capital, both riding post horses. The journey was uneventful. They stopped at the court reception hall, and in the morning went to the gate of Eastern Splendour to wait for the dawn court. As usual, the Grand Preceptor and Marshals Tong, Gao and Yang were present and they took him to a side chamber to see the Emperor. When he had made obeisance, the Emperor said to him: "I wanted to see you personally." He went on to ask: "Is everything satisfactory at Luzhou?"

The Unicorn prostrated himself again and said: "Thanks to Your Majesty's munificence, the army and the people there are peaceful and prosperous."

The Emperor asked a few more questions and the audience dragged on until noon, when the major-domo came and announced: "The repast Your Majesty ordered is ready, will it please Your Majesty to give the order to start?"

By this time Marshals Gao and Yang had already secretly had the mercury added to the food that was on the royal table. The Emperor most graciously offered the Unicorn food from his own kitchen. The Unicorn thanked him humbly. The Emperor flattered him, saying: "Return to Luzhou and be diligent, take care of your military and civil officials, let nothing untoward occur."

With many protestations of gratitude the Unicorn left and returned to Luzhou. He suspected nothing of the four villains' plot. Gao and Yang said to themselves: "We've done it!"

When the Unicorn reached Yingzhou that night he felt a terrible pain in his kidneys. He could not stand up and he certainly couldn't ride a horse, so he had to travel on by boat. When he reached Sizhou on the river Huai he had arrived at the end of his allotted span of years and something was bound to happen. That night he got drunk and went to stand on the prow of the boat to pass the time. Just at that moment the mercury slid down into his guts and entered the very marrow of his bones. Through the effect of this and also because he was drunk, his legs went weak, he lost his footing and fell. The Unicorn drowned in the depths of the river Huai. Poor Unicorn, Wonder of the North! He was obliged to become a wronged ghost in the water. His servants fished out the body and buried it at a suitable spot outside Sizhou. The authorities sent in a report to the Military Council. Of this no more.

Now the first part of their plot was complete, the four conspirators presented the Sizhou report to the Emperor, saying: "The Sizhou authorities report that when the Unicorn reached the Huai he got drunk and fell in the river and drowned. We members of the Military Council consider it our duty to report this. Owing to the Unicorn's death we are apprehensive that Song Jiang may become suspicious and want to make trouble. We beg Your Majesty to send an envoy to Chuzhou with some imperial wine for Song Jiang, to keep him happy."

The Emperor agonized over this proposal. If he turned it down, it was impossible to say what else might follow; if he let it go ahead, he feared ill would come of it. But the result was inevitable. In the end with their lying tongues and subtle deceitful words the villains talked the Emperor into it and he reluctantly gave his permission, he had no means of refusing them. Instructions were given for an envoy to carry two jars of imperial wine to Chuzhou, with immediate effect. Naturally this envoy was a crony of Gao and Yang. Well, fate had only allotted Song Jiang a certain number of days. It was fated that this wine with the poison added to it by those evil officials should be brought to Chuzhou by the imperial envoy.

Now, since the day Song Jiang arrived in Chuzhou as commissioner, he had also doubled as commander of the army. When he took up his duties he was popular with both military and civilians; the people saw him as a father to them, while the soldiers looked up to him, the laws were respected, public affairs were in good order and since he had won the hearts of the people he was honoured by all. When he had leisure, he liked to walk outside the town. There was a certain place beyond the south gate called Duckweed Marsh. Here there was a hill surrounded by ponds. This hill was most beautiful, with abundant stands of pine and cypress, an exceedingly scenic spot. Although not great in area, the mountains clustered round it making a protected place in the hill's embrace, full of crooked crags and gentle slopes, surrounded by creeks and ponds in front and behind. It was just like the waterside camp at Mount Liang. The moment Song Jiang saw it his heart rejoiced and he said to himself: "If I were to die here, this is where I would like to be buried. But when I have the chance I will come here often to walk. It is a place to arouse joy and banish care."

To cut a long story short, about six months after Song Jiang arrived at his post, he heard the news that some imperial wine had arrived, and went out with the crowd to meet it. Back in the courtroom he opened and read the imperial edict, and the envoy presented the wine and made him drink some. In return Song Jiang invited the envoy to drink, but the latter excused himself, saying that he could not take wine. Song Jiang had some gifts to present to the envoy, who refused them and departed.

After drinking the wine Song Jiang felt a terrible pain. He began to suspect the wine had been poisoned. He ordered his people to find out about the envoy. It turned out he had drunk wine at the rest house on the journey. Song Jiang knew now that it was a plot and the evil ministers must have poisoned the wine. He said with a sigh: "I studied the Confucian teaching when I was a child; when I grew up I became a government official, and later unfortunately fell into a criminal way of life, but never once did I harbour a disloyal thought. Now the Emperor has been too easily persuaded by slander and has sent me poisoned wine. Though innocent of any crime I stand convicted. My death is not important, but there's Iron Ox as military governor in Runzhou and if he hears that the authorities have played this dirty trick on me, he will revert to the greenwood and raise another band, and then the honourable reputation we have striven to achieve will be ruined. There's only one thing to do." That very night he sent someone to Runzhou to ask Iron Ox to come at once, because he had something to discuss with him.

To tell the truth, Iron Ox had been very bored since he was made governor of Runzhou. He spent his time drinking with his officers, wine was his only solace. When he heard that Song Jiang had sent for him, he said: "If the Leader wants me, it must be something important." He went back with the messenger by boat. He entered the government office and prostrated himself. Song Jiang said: "Since the company split up I have missed my comrades night and day. The Professor is too far away, and I have had no news at all of Colonel Hua. You're the only one who is relatively close, at Runzhou. I sent for you because I have something important to discuss with you."

"What is it?" Iron Ox asked.

"Have some wine first," Song Jiang replied. He invited him to an inner chamber where food and wine had been prepared and made him eat and drink. He waited till he was tipsy, then said: "Dear brother, I have heard that the Emperor is sending me poisoned wine. If I am meant to die, what do you think we should do?"

"Start a rebellion!" Iron Ox roared.

"But we've no troops left, our comrades are all scattered, how could you start a rebellion?"

"I've got three thousand troops in Runzhou. You've got some troops here, we can count them in. The people will rise up. We'll recruit energetically and buy horses, and then we'll go for it! It'll be back to Mount Liang, it'll be great! Far better than having to put up with sneering officials!"

"Softly, brother," Song Jiang said. "There's another way." For in fact into the wine he offered in welcome he had put a slow poison. Iron Ox had drunk, and next morning a boat was ready to take him back. "Whenever you're ready to march," he said to Song Jiang, "I will muster my forces and come to support you."

Song Jiang said: "Brother, forgive me. The Emperor's envoy has already been here and given me the wine. Sooner or later I will die. All my life I have cared for just one thing: honour and loyalty. I would never allow anything to sully my reputation. Now I am condemned to die, though innocent, by the Emperor. The Emperor may let me down but I shall not let the Emperor down. I was afraid that after my death you would start a rebellion and ruin the reputation we had in the Marshes of Mount Liang for loyalty and for doing heaven's will. That's why I asked you here, I wanted to see you. Yesterday I put a slow poison in your wine. When you get back to Runzhou you will die. After your death they can bring you here. There is a place here outside the south gate called Duckweed Marsh where the scenery is just like the Marshes of Mount Liang. Let our ghosts be together! When I die I will be buried in this place. I have arranged it already!" He had spoken, and the tears poured down his face.

Iron Ox was also weeping as he replied: "Well, well, well! I served you in life, let me be a little ghost under your orders after death!" Thus he concluded. Already he felt a sensation of heaviness. In this maudlin state he bade Song Jiang farewell and boarded the boat. Back in Runzhou the poison had its inevitable effect and he died. Just before his death he instructed his staff: "When I die, please do take my coffin to Duckweed Marsh outside the south gate of Chuzhou, to be buried with my brother, Song Jiang." Those were his last words. When his people had prepared the coffin, they set off in obedience to his wishes.

One thing especially troubled Song Jiang, after he had said goodbye to Iron Ox: he would not see the Professor and Colonel Hua again. That evening, as the poison was beginning to do its deadly work, he told his people: "Please follow my instructions: bury my coffin in the country outside the south gate, at Duckweed Marsh. I shall be most grateful for your kindness. Please don't forget!" Those were his last words.

His servants prepared the coffin and organized the funeral. In obedience to his words the local officials, together with his personal servants, clerks and members of the public bore his coffin to Duckweed Marsh for burial. A few days later Iron Ox's coffin was brought from Runzhou and laid to rest beside Song Jiang's tomb. Of this no more. As for Song Jiang's brother, Iron Fan, he had fallen ill at home and when some of the family servants returned and said his brother had died in Chuzhou, being ill he could not make the journey to pay his last respects. Later, on learning that his brother was buried at Duckweed Marsh he sent some family servants to make offerings and check that the grave was all right and properly supplied, before they returned. But enough of that.

As for the Professor, who had been appointed chief of communications in the Wusheng garrison, after travelling to his post he often found himself unhappy, and kept on missing the intimacy with his old friend Song Jiang. One day he suddenly felt particularly uneasy and was unable to sleep that night. Next night he dreamt of Song Jiang and Iron Ox, who were pulling him by the sleeve and said: "Professor, we always held loyalty to be the most important thing and to do heaven's will, and we never went

宋公明神聚蓼

against the Emperor. Now the court has requited us with poison and we are dead, though guilty of no crime. They have buried us in the countryside at Duckweed Marsh. Professor, if you still remember the old days, please come and visit our graves." The Professor wanted to question them further, but he awoke and found it was a dream. He sat there weeping copiously and waiting for dawn. After this dream he was unable to eat or sleep, so next day he packed his bags and headed for Chuzhou. He went alone, taking no servants. When he got there Song Jiang was dead of course, and all the local people were grieving. He arranged a service and went to Duckweed Marsh, where he found the graves and made offerings to their spirits. Then he beat the mound with his fist and weeping said: "My honourable brother's bold spirit will not be eclipsed, I pray that it may shine forth. I am just a village scholar. First I followed Chao Gai, then I was with my brother Song Jiang. Brother, you saved my life and enabled me to enjoy good fortune. I have been through a dozen wars and come out on top, thanks to you. Now you have died for your country, and appeared to me in a dream. Rather than seek vengeance, I prefer to prolong this good dream and join you in the world of the Nine Fountains." And with this he burst into tears again. He was just about to hang himself when Colonel Hua leapt off a boat and appeared in front of the grave. When he saw the Professor they both had a shock.

The Professor asked: "You are serving as an official in Yingtian. How did you know Song Jiang was dead?"

Colonel Hua said: "After I went to my post I was not at peace for a single day. I kept worrying about my brother. Last night I had a strange dream. I dreamt that Song Jiang and Iron Ox came to me and pulled me by the sleeve and said that the court had rewarded them with poison and I saw the grave at Duckweed Marsh in the countryside outside Chuzhou. Song Jiang said that if I hadn't forgotten the old days I might like to come and see the grave. So I left my family and sparing no effort came here as fast as I could."

The Professor said: "I had the same strange dream, exactly the same as yours. That is why I came. It is very good that you came today. I miss Song Jiang so much, his kindness, his righteousness, I feel so lonely without him, that I have resolved to hang myself in this place, so that my spirit can be with him. I leave all the funeral arrangements in your hands."

Colonel Hua said: "If that is your intention, Professor, I shall follow you, so I too can be with our brother."

Thus did they keep to their old principle of living and dying together!

But the Professor said: "I want you to bury me here after my death. How will you do it if you die too?"

"I have been thinking how sorely I miss our brother's humanity, how I shall never forget his kindness. When we were on Mount Liang we had committed a serious crime, we were lucky to escape death. Thanks to the Emperor's amnesty, we went north to fight, south to fight, we achieved honour. Our fame has travelled far and wide, everyone has heard of us. Something led the court to suspect us, and now the slightest rumour will be enough to condemn us. If the plots prevail and we suffer an unjust punishment it will be too late then to do anything about it. Better to follow our brother and meet at the Yellow Springs, so we leave an untarnished name in the world, and our bodies will have proper burial!"

The Professor said: "Dear brother, listen to me. I have no family, there's only me. There is nothing to prevent my dying. You have children and wife, how can you look after them?"

"That's no problem. My coffers are full, and there are many members of my wife's family who can take care of things."

They both wept for a while and then hanged themselves from the tree.

The servants on the boats waited a long time. When their masters still did not return, they went to the tomb to see and found they had both killed themselves. They hurriedly reported it to the authorities. Coffins were prepared and the Professor and Colonel Hua were buried at Duckweed Marsh alongside Song Jiang's tomb, so there were four similar mounds in a line from east to west. The people in grateful memory of Song Jiang's virtue and loyalty set up an altar there, where offerings were made in the four seasons; all who made the pilgrimage to that place had their prayers answered.

We shall pass over the frequent manifestations of Song Jiang's spirit, and tell how the Emperor at his court in the Eastern Capital after awarding the royal wine to Song Jiang was often troubled in his mind, and hearing no news of Song Jiang became extremely concerned about him. Gao the Ball and Marshal Yang continued their life of ostentatious display and wasteful luxury, always standing in the way of reform and plotting against honest men.

One day when the Emperor was relaxing in the inner palace he suddenly bethought himself of Lily, and with two attendants followed the passage to her back door and pulled the bell rope. Lily hastened to receive His Majesty and went to sit with him in the bedroom. He ordered the front and back doors to be locked. When Lily, in all her finery, had presented herself, the Emperor said: "I have not been feeling very well lately, I had to call in Doctor An to treat me. I have not been to see you for many days. But I have thought of you a lot. Seeing you now gives me huge pleasure!

Lily said: "Your Majesty is too kind to me, I feel quite embarrassed!"

Wine was served and His Majesty enjoyed himself drinking. After several cups he appeared to become tired. Lamps and candles were lit and then suddenly a draught of cold air was felt in the room. His Majesty saw a man in a yellow shirt in front of him. Startled, he asked the man: "Who are you and where are you from?"

"I am the Magic Messenger and I serve Song Jiang of Mount Liang," the other replied.

"Why have you come?"

"My brother Song Jiang is waiting," replied the Magic Messenger. "He entreats you, Your Majesty to get in your carriage and come to him."

"Where am I to tell the carriage to take me?"

"Song Jiang knows a very beautiful place and he invites Your Majesty to walk with him there."

The Emperor stood and followed Magic Messenger into the

garden. His carriage was waiting. Magic Messenger invited him to get in.

It is as if mist and cloud have descended and there is a sound of wind and rain. In the place they come to:

Misty waters are everywhere, clouds and mountains fill the view. There is no brightness of sun or moon, water and sky are all one colour. The duckweed grows profusely, reeds clothe the islets in dense green: two by two the wild geese on the sand spit sadly calling, in pairs the exhausted wagtails perching on the edge of the withered lotus. Gaunt maples stand about like grief-stricken wives weeping for the absent loved-one, solitary willows face the wind, their branches like the sad eyebrows of lonely women. The moon is watery, the stars cold, the night long; the time is autumn, season of cold winds and heavy dews.

The Emperor is enchanted by the scene that meets his eyes and he asks Magic Messenger: "What is this place? Is it where you wanted me to come?"

Magic Messenger points to a road winding up the hill and says: "Please go on, Your Majesty. When you get there you will understand."

The Emperor drives on up the mountain. He comes to three gates and at the third he sees a hundred men bowing down to the ground, all in war robes and breast plates, with leather belts and bronze helmets and armour. Amazed by what he sees he asks: "Who are you all, my friends?" Then their leader, wearing a bronze winged helmet, embroidered robe and gold armour, steps forward and says: "I am Song Jiang of Mount Liang."

"I sent you to be military governor of Chuzhou," says the Emperor. "What are you doing here?"

"We have invited Your Majesty to our Ceremonial Hall, to hear the story of our unjust death."

The Emperor gets down and takes his seat in the hall. Looking about him he sees as if in a mist many warriors standing in line. He feels uncertain. The leader, Song Jiang, mounts the dais and kneels before him. Weeping he asks leave to speak.

"Why do you weep?" the Emperor asks.

"Even though we once opposed the Emperor's forces, we always retained our loyalty and never for a moment entertained thoughts of rebellion. After we received the imperial amnesty we first expelled the Tartars and then pacified three bandits and later we lost the greater part of our brothers. Your Majesty graciously commanded me to govern Chuzhou. Let heaven and earth bear witness, after I took up my post I had no secret relations with the military or the people. Now you have paid me with poisoned wine, but I died guiltless. I was afraid Iron Ox would be angry and it might make him disloyal to his sovereign. So I sent to Runzhou for him and poisoned him myself. The Professor and Colonel Hua killed themselves out of loyalty at my tomb. All four of us are buried at Duckweed Marsh outside the south gate of Chuzhou. The people have built a memorial hall there to honour us. Our spirits are not yet dispersed. They are gathered here now to inform Your Majesty that throughout our lives we were loyal from beginning to end. We beseech Your Majesty to hear us!"

The Emperor is horrified by what he hears. "I sent my special envoy with yellow seal imperial wine. Who could have changed it for poisoned wine then?"

Song Jiang says: "You can ask your envoy. He will know how the trick was carried out."

The Emperor looks at the stalwarts on all the gates and says sadly: "Where is this place that you are all meeting?"

"This is Mount Liang, where we all came together in the old days."

"But if you're all dead now, you should have departed for a new life. Why are you still here?"

"The Lord of Heaven took pity on us for our loyalty. He issued an edict appointing us tutelary spirits of Mount Liang. We have come here because of the complaint that we have not yet had the chance to lodge. We sent Magic Messenger to beg Your Majesty to come to the Marshes so that we might declare how we have been constantly loyal."

"Why did you not come to me in my palace?"

"Spirits of the underworld, how could we enter your splendid

忠義堂

courts and halls? So in your graciousness you have consented to come to us."

"Is it possible for me to look around?"

They all prostrate themselves again to show their appreciation of the favour and His Majesty comes down from the dais and turns his gaze upon the tablet which bears in large characters the words: Great Hall of Loyalty and Righteousness. He nods to himself and proceeds down the steps. Suddenly Iron Ox steps out from behind Song Jiang. Holding his two axes he bellows: "Emperor, Emperor, why did you listen to those four scoundrels' criticism and defamation? Now that you're here, it's time to settle accounts!" So saying he whirls his axes and runs at the Emperor.

From the shock of this, the Emperor awoke and knew it had all been a dream. His body was bathed in a cold sweat. He opened both eyes, blinking, and saw the candles and lamps lit. Lily appeared not to have slept. He asked: "Have I been somewhere?"

"Your Majesty just laid his head on the pillow and went to sleep," she said.

The Emperor told her all about his mysterious dream. She said: "When people are truly good they die and become saints. Could it be that Song Jiang really is dead and that he manifested himself in Your Majesty's dream for some purpose?"

"I shall have to make some inquiries," the Emperor said. "If it turns out that he is dead, I must build a temple for him and officially declare him a hero."

"If you do this, it will show that Your Majesty does not neglect his loyal servants."

The Emperor heaved many a sigh that night.

Next day around dawn the order was given for the court to assemble in the side palace. But the Grand Preceptor, and Marshals Tong, Gao and Yang were all afraid that the Emperor might ask about Song Jiang, and left the palace. Only Marshal Su and a few other senior officials were waiting there. "Have you had any news of the military governor of Chuzhou, Song Jiang?" the Emperor asked Marshal Su.

"Although I have had no news, last night I had a strange dream. It was very odd."

"Tell me about this strange dream of yours," the Emperor said.

"I dreamt that Song Jiang came to my house dressed in uniform, helmet and armour, and claimed that Your Majesty had sent him poisoned wine. The local people, honouring his memory, had buried him outside the south gate at Duckweed Marsh and set up a shrine where offerings are made in every season."

When the Emperor heard this he nodded and said: "This strange business is just like in my dream." He told Marshal Su: "Send someone you can rely on to Chuzhou to investigate this affair and come back and report quickly."

"It shall be done," said the Marshal. He left with the Emperor's order, returned to his palace and sent a trusted servant to Chuzhou to find out about Song Jiang. Of this no more.

Next day when the Emperor drove to the Hall of Culture and Ethics, he saw Marshals Gao and Yang standing on one side and asked them: "Does the Military Council have news of the military governor of Chuzhou?"

Both were afraid to answer and neither could think of anything to say. The Emperor was filled with suspicion and his displeasure showed plainly on his face.

Marshal Su's man after making his inquiries in Chuzhou told the Marshal how Song Jiang had drunk poisoned wine and was dead, and how the local people out of respect for his loyalty had buried him on a hill at Duckweed Marsh. He also told how the Professor, Colonel Hua and Iron Ox were buried in the same place and the people had built a memorial hall to honour them and make offerings to them in spring and autumn.

Marshal Su hurriedly called the man inside to prepare a report for the Emperor. The Emperor could not conceal his feelings when he heard it. At next day's dawn court he expressed his anger, reprimanding Gao and Yang before all the courtiers: "You corrupt officials, betrayers of your country, you have ruined my people!"

They both grovelled, knocking their heads on the ground in acknowledgement of their guilt. The Grand Preceptor and Marshal Tong also came forward and said: "People's life and death are destined. The Military Council had received no report, we did not dare to repeat news that might be false. Last night the report from Chuzhou reached us. We were just about to inform Your Majesty. . . ."

Once again the Emperor had the wool pulled over his eyes by the faithless four and they were allowed to get away with it. He simply told Gao and Yang to withdraw and then ordered the original official who was sent with the wine to be apprehended. But it turned out that the envoy after leaving Chuzhou had died on the return journey.

Next day Marshal Su saw the Emperor in the side palace and told him again about the apparitions of Song Jiang's spirit. The Emperor wanted to transfer Song Jiang's title to his brother, Iron Fan. Iron Fan however was sick and could not serve as an official, so he politely declined, saying he only wanted to be a farmer in Yuncheng. In recognition of his filial piety the Emperor granted him a hundred thousand strings of cash and three hundred acres of land to support his family and promised that if he had offspring the court would advance them. Later Iron Fan had a son, Song Anping, who passed the official exams and served in the imperial library — but that is another story.

In response to Marshal Su's report, the Emperor indited in his own hand a document granting Song Jiang a posthumous title of nobility in recognition of his loyal and valiant service and ordering a temple to be built on Mount Liang with a grand hall and images of Song Jiang and the others. He also donated to this temple an inscription in his own hand naming it "Temple of Loyalty and Pacification".

There is a poem:

The heavenly stars are returned to the sky,
The earth stars gone back under the ground.
From earliest days they were revered as saints
By historians ever regarded as heroes.

In later times Song Jiang's spirit made many appearances and the people continued to make offerings to it in the four seasons. In the marshes of Mount Liang, when they prayed for wind they got wind, when they prayed for rain they had rain. At Duckweed

Marsh in Chuzhou, because Song Jiang's spirit kept appearing, the local people built another shrine, a hall with two galleries, and even requested an imperial tablet for it. Thirty-six statues were placed in the main hall and seventy-two in the galleries. Year after year offerings were made there and thousands went to worship. Traces of it exist to this day. The historians have two funeral scrolls in the Tang style:

Blame not heaven for what man gets;
Recall how sovereigns pay their debts!
For the country's good they gave their all,
Till the Tartars' expulsion and Fang La's fall.
Heaven and earth stars, all are gone,
But slander and calumny still reign on.
Would that the deadly cup they'd refused,
And gone where men are better used!

And the other:

They lived life to the full, in death earned rank;
Of all a man may know no page left blank:
The horses of war whose whinnying fills the night,
The moon over the mountain spilling its light,
The apes that sadden autumn with their cries,
The clouds which gather and thicken as daylight flies.
Why seek rare compositions unlike to please,
When you can read of heroes such as these?
In Duckweed Marsh now lie they all at rest,
For eternal peace a hidden place is best.
Flowers their petals shed, birds dirges sing,
Remembering these whom nothing back can bring.